The Secret Keeping

Francine Saint Marie

Spinsters Ink
2006

Spinsters Ink, Inc.
P.O. Box 242
Midway, Florida 32343

Printed in the United States of America on acid-free paper
First Edition

Editor: Anna Chinappi
Cover designer: KIARO Creative Ltd.

ISBN 1-883523-77-X

Acknowledgments

My thanks to Linda Hill and Anna Chinappi at Spinsters Ink. To Robert and Janet Rosenberg. To Aliza and Embarek Mesbahi. And a sweet patron, who shall remain anonymous.

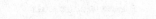

Part One
The Waiter

"It's sexual."

"Sensual, did she say?"

"No, I think she said sexual."

Spring was negligent this year and the irrational exuberance in Frank's Place was undoubtedly a product of its delay.

"I said *sexual*."

"We thought you said sensual, too."

Friday's happy hour had turned positively muggy.

"Sexual. Sensual. What's the difference, anyway?"

The popular corporate watering hole was swollen to capacity, hot with the heat of a synthetic spring and the dark suits usually found in there seemed finally to bloom, adorned at last in their blossoms of polyester, powdery pastels and paisleys and polka dots as bright and gay as poppies.

Off in the corner with the rubber tree plants, Lydia Beaumont sat, dressed entirely in black. Still wearing her overcoat, she gripped her half empty glass and skeptically viewed the display.

"I just had a dream about you," a seersuckered youth suggested in her ear.

"Oooh," she replied, dismissing him with a flick of the wrist, "nice line!"

She was waiting on spring for her second wind and nothing this year could force its entry. Winter, the identical twin to the dreary fall that had just preceded it, continued to grip the city and Lydia couldn't help feeling suspended in a permanent autumn. The balmy air of Frank's tonight, with its harsh perfumes and heavy colognes, only made it feel worse.

True spring. She had fruitlessly searched all week for signs of it, but even the cherry trees seemed to have given up hope.

"Liddy!"

Tonight Lydia's coat felt heavy and made of hair and she was certain she was being choked by the button of her shirt collar.

"You're looking like a tourist, Liddy."

Lydia turned in her chair, smiled obliquely. "Hey, Del," she asked, "what's the difference between misapprehension and mere apprehension?"

"*Ms.* Apprehension . . . life's not a spectator sport," Delilah chirped, walking away.

"Hey, what's a four-letter word for love?" someone from their table shouted.

"Laid!" another blurted and the group erupted with predictable guffaws.

It had been another rough week. Lydia was sick of the work crowd and she only felt a little guilty about it. She checked the time and faked a laugh. Her sentiments had somehow slipped beyond volatile this evening. She checked them, too, as she always did.

A four-letter word for love? Work. She had loved her work. But now the weight of it bore down harder and harder with every passing year and Lydia could no longer recall the reasons why she had pursued her profession. The ever increasingly younger throng she presided over were not like her when she was their age. They were difficult to manage and she hated to see them on her time off. All these revved up self-starters, fancying themselves galloping mavericks in the market place, all of them developing pronounced limps at the slightest hint of regulation. How she longed this year for a bonafide blast of warm spring air.

She glanced around, taking stock of who was there, who to avoid if she could help it. Friday the place was crawling with them. She was pleased to discover the blond reading contentedly at her window seat. Came in often. Obviously from a more civilized tribe, Lydia thought, as she studied the woman's cut of clothes to discern which one.

From? Unknown. Mostly rookies tonight, Lydia lamented, looking elsewhere. Lots of rookies from work infesting the place. Everywhere she went these days, every year more of them, each new onslaught more trying than the last. Busy, busy, busy. Shaking things up, knocking things down, fixing things, things that weren't broken. Her rookies, stacking risk upon risk like little toy blocks, scorning her advice as though they weren't obliged to take it, swaggering into happy hour like they owned the place.

Civilization. She sat back in her chair and drank deeply to the concept.

Lydia Beaumont was only thirty-six and still climbing, but she felt obsolete of late, frequently lonely in the new and improved world of international finance. The changes, too, did not impress her. Things were different, that's for sure, but they had gotten worse not better. A whole universe was being driven now on nothing but bald speculation and baby-faced chutzpah.

A breath of fresh air would be so nice. She'd love a breath of fresh air.

Love, loved, loving. She had, on an impulse just yesterday, looked it all up in an old college dictionary: to hold dear, to cherish, a lover's passion, devotion, tenderness, caress, to fondle amorously, like, desire, to thrive in. That one had appealed to her sensibilities the most, the reference to thriving, as in, "the rose loves sunlight." A very nice idea. She drank to that, too, framing the woman at the window seat in the wineglass, her blond head of hair an elegant flower stuck in Frank's bawdy bouquet. Thriving there alone, amidst the dandelions.

Love, loved, loving. All kinds of love in the world. That blond loves her solitude. She loves her book. Perhaps just as a rose does, she loves sunlight, too, sitting in a window on Fridays in the waning afternoon light. Loves. Who knows what else she loves? Is she somebody's long-stemmed rose placed in a vase on a sunny windowsill? If so, she's a white rose, all that blond, the creamy skin. What does mom say a white rose represents? Love and her mother and the mysteries of roses! Lydia laughed at herself and surveyed the working horde.

A barely-thirty crowd. She was more and more convinced that it may indeed be a world only for the very young. There seemed to be nowhere she could go to get away from them. They dominated her landscape now, light and shiny and strangely bold beyond their experience, disregarding reality and all its real consequences, skipping out, just at the right moment, before their wings melted off. She could trust them at least for that much.

Honor and chastity. A white rose represents the faithfulness of its giver, so her mother claimed. Lydia sipped the blond in her glass. Perhaps a yellow rose, then. What does yellow mean? She'd have to ask her mother. Why not just plain red? Oh no, she could guess at the significance of that color. No, not red, for God's sake!

Roses and sunlight. Scant little of either in Lydia's life these days. Seven p.m. She felt stiff in her chair, her neck and her shoulders hunched, sore from months of being cold. She eyed the window seat enviously, the blond still relaxing there with her mysterious book, posed like it was another day at the beach, casual, with just a splash of reservation, enough to ward off intruders.

Stop. Look both ways. Red. Don't go.

It was smart to be cautious, always wise to exercise care, especially when it concerned other people's money. Only punks weren't alarmed to lose people's money. Punks wouldn't mind misleading investors. Punks were unscathed by plummeting debt ratings, by markets fluctuating hundreds of points an hour, by shortfalls rippling across the globe and eventually hitting land with the destructive force of tidal waves. Superstorm economics, no big deal. They were so high above it all. Wouldn't it be nice to be able to read a book, Lydia Beaumont wondered, surrounded by a bunch of savages, to really soar above it all?

But it's the real world, Lydia reminded herself, a newly unsettled one, and savages and their mentors floated above it all. Uncorrected, never uncertain, they rose higher and higher, dirigibles on hydrogen and all those creative numbers. She knew them well. She knew they were addicted to the heights and hooking nearly everyone else they came in contact with; that they were dealers, dealing out highs with their quarterly projections of unsubstantiated growth and their wildly inflated earnings reports. She was always aware of them up there, brash new rulers of an endlessly expanding universe, to which they alone held the secret. Or so they implied in their glossy corporate brochures. They kept her on her toes.

A tangle of wannabe dancers was putting on the ritz and making a spectacle of themselves. She laughed out loud and then scoffed under her breath. There was no stopping them, no holds barred, she had learned, thinking suddenly of accountants. Good auditors, too, who once knew better worth—they autographed everything that fell from the sky, even if they couldn't read it.

The blond at the window seat was also watching the dance extravaganza, the corners of her mouth turning up as she saw the enthusiasts darting and jerking to a bossa nova they knew nothing about. It was a pretty half smile, the mouth poised as if there was something right on the tip of her tongue.

What would she have to say about all this? What do those lips talk about? Art? The book she read? What kind of a voice comes out of a mouth like that one? Something soft, Lydia bet. Soothing. Gentle. Tender. Sexy? Or was the right word sensual? Lydia caught the blond's glance and was startled to find herself staring at the woman. She shifted her attention outside.

On the other side of the glass was the street patio which had long been exorcised of its spirited revelers by the icy winds. It was nothing but a drab sidewalk in winter. They had all been dispossessed of it, forced to haunt the interior of Frank's Place where they restlessly waited for better weather and the good things that usually accompany heat. The music played . . . *the summer wind . . . came blowing in . . . from across the sea . . .*

It was more fun outside, Lydia mused, worrying her collar . . . *it lingered there . . . to touch your hair . . .* out there she could stand or pace, swing her arms, rise and look around her, and eventually, when the mood struck, as it often did, she could wander off unnoticed, leaving if she wanted to and conveniently forgetting to say good-bye. *In here, I can't move and if I get up to go, it's a big deal.* Her eyes came to rest on the table at the window . . . *the summer wind* . . . its occupant briefly looked up again from her reading and casually scanned the crowd before returning to it.

A cork popped. A new bottle. Red. That's an acquired look, Lydia concluded. Doesn't want to seem interested. I do that, too. More wine. Not interested? Maybe just a splash.

And yet she's always there, always deeply invested in a book, always with a glass of something barely touched, always alone and waiting, apparently for no one. She had become a familiar landmark at the window. At least to Lydia.

"Hey, what's a three-letter word for—"

Lydia huffed and cut the speaker off.

Calm was finally descending on the room, but then Sinatra threatened to spoil it all with an urgent song about Peru.

Now that she was thinking about it, there was only one night when Lydia hadn't seen the woman alone there. A couple had joined her one evening.

Couples . . . *come on fly with me . . . let's fly . . . let's fly away* . . . so then, perhaps she had a home nearby?

Lydia absently yanked at the thing annoying her throat and it was only when she felt her collar come loose, saw a button pinging free across the tabletop and ricocheting like a tiddlywink off a sea of abandoned glasses that she came out of her trance. She had been thinking of homesickness.

"You're scaring me, Liddy! What in the hell are you thinking?"

"You tell me, Del. I'm thinking I need to go to bed."

"Yeah! But there's not a decent one left," Delilah said, on another trip to the bar. "Joe's here," she added over her shoulder. "Be a big girl."

"Please," Lydia replied, holding up her hand, "or I'll leave."

Come on fly with me we'll float down to Peru . . . actually, it wasn't a bad idea . . . *in llama land there's a one-man band* . . . Peru . . . *and he'll toot his flute for you* . . . or anyplace warm and sunny, she mused, draining her wineglass . . . *come on fly with me let's fly let's fly* . . .

Her glass was empty. She attempted to land it on the cluttered tabletop.

God how she loved that man. Sinatra that is. Seemed like he had a song for every season, emptying a heart full of it, floating to Peru for the winter, moving the rubber tree plants, having a very good year, anywhere, anytime. She shook her head and smiled, drunk for a change, and from the table there came a warning tinkle, glasses clinking as she carelessly deposited her own beside them.

Let's take it nice and easy . . . more clinking . . . *it's gonna be so easy . . . for us to fall in . . .*

"It's not healthy, you know." Delilah was back.

Lydia watched the glass tip over on its side . . . *the problem now of course is* . . . her work . . . it was insane perhaps . . . *to simply hold our horses* . . . but she felt like jumping. Could it be, she half wondered, watching the glass head steadily for the edge of the table, but making no effort to save it, that she was hoping for something soft to land on. It rolled back slightly and she feared she might have to push it.

An elbow nudged her ribs. "It's not, you know," repeated its owner.

The goblet hesitated then smashed onto the floor.

Absurd, Lydia murmured, grabbing gently at the offending elbow. "What?"

"It's not healthy, I told you."

"Del . . . what isn't?"

"Oh, geesh, Liddy," Delilah said, taking in the catastrophe. "That's very, very unfortunate. And it saddens me. You shhhall have another."

"I shhhall," Lydia mimicked. She raised her arm and beckoned the waiter.

Table sixteen. The waiter nodded and made his way over. They were an attractive and lively group, regulars who like to sing and dance and never broke anything. Not usually, anyway. He could feel the crunch of glass beneath his shoe, the woman's fingers as she slipped a ten dollar bill in his pocket and whispered *I'm sorry*. He signaled the busboy with a circular motion of his hand.

"A glass of merlot," he then said, turning to Lydia with a smile. "Will that be all?" he asked, now addressing the table.

"We're hungry!" the group yelled. "Merlot? Merlot! I want some, too." "Can you bring us menus?" "I need a drink." "I have no idea what time it is." "Me, too." "Bring everyone some merlot." "I don't want merlot. I want a drink." "Do you know what time it is?" "I think you'd better bring us a bottle then." "It's early, I think." "I'm hungry. Can't we order something now, or do we need menus?" "He's bringing us menus." "What are you having?" "C'mon, it's early."

Food. She wasn't really hungry. She watched the blond toying with her dessert.

"It's curious don't you think, Liddy?" asked Delilah, her mouth and hands full, gesturing with a chicken bone in the direction of the window seat.

"She's a spy," interrupted someone from their party, "Is this spicy?" he asked, pointing at Delilah's platter. She ignored him. "C'mon, is this hot?" he demanded. She used a free elbow to push him away.

"She's not a spy, Liddy. She's a—"

"How's everything?" interrupted the waiter, suddenly appearing behind Lydia.

"She's a spy," repeated their persistent friend as he lunged past Delilah's jab.

"It's hot!" she threatened, as he made off with her platter. Those on the other end of the table cheered the chicken's arrival.

"Everything's fine," Lydia said, turning toward the waiter.

"Excellent," he answered and bending closer he whispered, "she's not a spy," and was gone.

Delilah glanced curiously at Lydia. "What?" she demanded.

"What *what*?" answered Lydia, dipping her finger into the wine.

"What did he say?"

Lydia rubbed the rim of her glass until it began humming. It tingled to the touch. Half past seven. She should just go home. "He said I'm the only civilized person at my table and that I should feel quite proud."

Delilah draped her arm on the back of her chair, crossed her legs, and dabbed at her mouth with a dirty napkin. "Bullshit," she replied, grinning.

* * *

"You're doing that thing again," asserted Delilah.

"What?"

"*That*, Liddy."

Nearby another friend had noticed it, too. "What . . . so . . . yeah . . . and . . . ," she imitated, sighing dramatically.

Lydia squirmed at the successful impersonation. "It must be time for me to go," she said, checking the clock once more. Eight p.m. "I'm speaking in monosyllables."

"Nah, it's early," said the other two in unison. They clustered their chairs around hers to began their weekly critique, starting first with the most-eligibles lined up haplessly at the bar.

On the opposite side of the room a woman sat reading in one of the window seats, her long blond hair done up in a loose knot pierced by a single hairpin to keep it from falling in her eyes. She had a fine shaped face, smart indications across the brow line, bright animated eyes that bore nearly all her expression. The nose and mouth, rendered in sure but delicate strokes, were countered by pronounced cheekbones and a firmly set jaw which dignified her looks and made her seem at once both pretty and handsome. So too, the frailty implied by a pale complexion was juxtaposed with wide disciplined shoulders and a strong, almost unbending quality about the neck. The slender rest of her lounged luxuriously in a chair, her creamy skin complemented by a rich, dark blue dress that began its long-sleeved tour scooped low at the collarbones and continued its travels closely tailored to the torso and hips. In the woman's lap and along the length of her outstretched legs the fabric collected into sensuous little ripples and its excesses surrounded her in flattering folds. They slipped over her hips and dripped down her sides, cascading to the floor in a waterfall of velvet.

Nine p.m. She really should go home, throw some weights around, dumbells.

"Liddy? Aren't you going to say anything?" Delilah asked.

"No."

"Don't you think you'd feel better if you did?"

"No."

"Wouldn't it at least be better to be on speaking terms?"

"No."

"But you see him everyday at work. Isn't it awkward for you?"

"No."

Ten p.m. There was no moon at all. A light drizzle was soaking the city which only served to underscore Lydia's ennui. No umbrella, she walked briskly to her apartment, stopping this evening at every crosswalk, finding herself waiting at them much longer than she actually needed.

She had spent a considerable amount of time in this city, living in it with her friends, those that she had met at university like Delilah and the others she had later met at work. In finance, they were all the same, none of them the type to sit in Frank's with only a book for a companion. She sought to remember the last book she had read. She couldn't. No books. No newspapers.

An aching sensation was beginning to creep in under her coat and clothes. An old feeling, she knew it had nothing to do with the cold, although the cold certainly didn't help. She shivered at the next intersection and set her briefcase down, pulling her gabardine tight to her chest and conferring with an amber light. Yellow means worthy, she suddenly remembered. Didn't it? Yellow roses. Worthy. Or yield. She grabbed the briefcase and ran to the other side.

The only thing Lydia did read was the financials. Nothing to brag on. The briefcase felt exceptionally heavy tonight. Her back hurt. She wished for a warm spring rain to make the city misty, to cloud it up. This one was as cold as snow.

Why hadn't she gone on vacation this year?

All-night deli coming up on her right. She had a sudden craving for sweets, she realized. All-night deli coming up on her right. Sweets or a cigarette? When was the last time she had a cigarette? She lingered undecided at the entrance. Or sweets for that matter? Her mouth had the aftertaste of wine in it, sour and woody. Bed was calling. No sugar tonight. She walked on.

* * *

Home. Inside her apartment it was warmer than usual. Downright balmy, like it had gotten at Frank's. She turned the heat off and scanned the bookshelf for something to read and, finding nothing of interest, sighed with disgust.

Why hadn't she gone on vacation this year?

The bookcase. Exactly like her father's with his tight rows of leather bound editions, none of which she had ever seen him read. She dragged her fingers over them. Dusty bindings. Like his, her books never came off the shelf either.

Financial papers on the coffee table. She cleared them with an impatient sweep of her hand and they landed in disarray on an otherwise spotless carpet. That accomplished nothing, she admitted. She stood over the debacle feeling foolish and wrestled down the overwhelming temptation to reorganize it.

Is there a problem she asked herself. Yes, but nothing she could put her finger on. She contemplated the possibility of a midlife crisis and did the easy math. Life expectancy, seventy-two. What a frightening sum. You do act like a tourist, she confessed. In any event, you certainly feel like one tonight. Or a spy, spying on whoever I am, on the name on the door. She glared at her belongings.

The stainless carpet, the curtained windows, the trophy books all seemed in tacit agreement. They didn't know her anymore either, or why she would be investigating them. She glared at them accusingly.

"She's not a spy," the waiter had said.

Lydia saw herself in the mirror and stopped short. Leaving for work in the dark, coming home in the dark, it was taking a toll on her, she suddenly thought, eyeing the impostor. She was shocked by the woman's disheveled appearance, the missing button on her shirt collar, the rain-soaked coat, the hair wet and dangling in her eyes. She went up to the mirror and inspected her eyes. More than just exhausted, there were shadows beneath them almost as blue as her irises. Her blue eyes. They had an unusual gleam in them. She was concerned about it. Not cool, she muttered, sitting down in the middle of the room as quiet as a sphinx.

"Excellent," she remembered the waiter saying. "Will that be all?"

* * *

Why did I bring this in here? Lydia wondered, accidentally kicking her briefcase as she crossed her legs under the table. Another Friday at Frank's Place and her friends were late.

The blond sat at the window seat, engrossed as ever in her reading. Now and again she seemed to stretch a little, a slight smile appearing and then disappearing from her lips. Lydia immediately thought of a cat reclining on a sunny sofa about to lick itself.

"May I get you something while you're waiting?"

She jumped in her skin.

The waiter smiled.

She blushed. "I'm sorry?"

"A glass of wine until your friends get here?" he asked.

She nodded and avoided looking at him. He had a funny expression.

"Red?" he suggested.

"What?"

"Red?" he repeated.

"Red?" (Red?) "Red! Yes, please, that will be fine."

Four thirty already. The girls were supposed to be there at four. With growing annoyance Lydia saw herself stuck alone in a bar looking available, something which she did not relish.

Regulars were steadily arriving for happy hour. As they checked their coats at the door they scanned the barroom hungrily. She visibly registered discomfort whenever one strutted by and said hello. They all reminded her of Joe.

Only ten more minutes, she promised herself. This is unbearable. She glanced over at the window seat. A book sure would come in handy right now. She raised her arm to signal the waiter and the blond looked over, smiled an acknowledgment and went back to her reading.

"May I see a menu?"

"Certainly," the waiter said. He returned with one a few minutes later.

Whenever she felt irritated she thought of Joe. An unrewarding habit she had just discovered. These past few days she found herself thinking of him a lot.

Joseph Rios. Everyone called him Rio Joe, but she doubted he knew that, not that it would bother him, not someone who spent as much time as Joe did making himself larger than life. He had cultivated that persona.

Rio Joe. The stuff of literature. "Good evening," came a come-on voice from her left. Oh, please, she screamed in her head. She put her face in the menu, pretended to read it. The technique proved surprisingly effective. Talking head gone.

Tall, dark and handsome Joe. Her junior by four years. She had met him at work and instinctively disliked him, detecting something a little too slick and rather illicit in his style. In a way she couldn't then explain, he'd given her the creeps. His interpretation that she was hard to get is what motivated him to pursue her so ardently. And it was nice to be ardently pursued. In the end . . . well . . . getting is the fun part for a Rio Joe. The romance left her with the same sick sensation she had after eating too much chocolate.

Love, sex, heartburn, nausea. This was as far as she could venture in her mind whenever she reviewed the matter. She could see far enough. She knew that he had broken her heart because it stopped in pain whenever she saw him or heard his name mentioned. She knew he was not one of her greatest accomplishments which is why she refused to discuss the mess with anyone.

Dear Joe. She had ended it months ago but still ran into him at work, still in Frank's Place, Fridays. Only recently had she stopped trembling at the sight of him. Only recently had she stopped wanting to lie down every time he was near. Only recently she discovered she wasn't thinking of him every moment of the day.

Lydia took a deep breath. Only recently, but thank God!

Another suit strolled by. She put her nose in the menu again—*lunch*? Wrong menu. Lydia blamed herself for not discovering it sooner. Everything's been out of whack this week, seven days like this, all gone awry in precisely this manner. She hailed the waiter one more time and attempted to disguise her frustration.

"Madam? Ready to order?"

"Yes, but I think you brought me the wrong menu," she said, handing it back to him.

"Oh," he said, taking it from her, "the right menu at the wrong time." He pulled another one out from under his arm and laid it on the table. "Or," he added with a wink, "the wrong menu at the right time."

She felt a tinge in her cheeks again and turned away without speaking. The clock over the bar read five. Swell, she thought. So where are my friends when I need them? Sinatra sang something about being irresponsible, being undependable. The blond at the window seat, reading. Reliable. That waiter was so strange. It's difficult to be alone, Lydia realized. She was sick of waiting. You can forget yourself, what you normally do or what you're supposed to be thinking. Isn't that old waiter kind of crazy? Sinatra sang about irresponsible madness. Lydia waited.

"I told you she'd still be here! Liddy, you're not mad, are you?"

"No, Del. I just love sitting by myself on a Friday afternoon, drinking by myself on a Friday afternoon, eating by myself on—"

"Oh, good. You ordered already?" Delilah slid Lydia's bread plate away from her and laughed at her friend's dour expression. "Oh, come on, Liddy" she said, pushing it back again. "I hate it when you pout. We were hoping you might mingle a little. We're not really all that late and you do look marvelous, dear. Arsenic obviously becomes you."

Half past five. The furniture around her scuffed loudly with a life of its own and Lydia was once more absorbed into the dull but comfortable roar of her table. She watched her friends coming and going, the girls falling one by one like flower petals into their chairs, each one exhaling on arrival about a week's worth of office air as they landed, the guys circling like hawks. Happy hour. Another respite. Exquisite nails tapped on the tabletop to the music. The ladies cooed about that one's sweater, this one's skirt, a new piece of jewelry, who they had recently run into. The guys heckled. It wasn't hard to be distracted—even the blond looked over—by the loud chatter, sordid details of cubicle life, funny stories, tales of intrigue. Gossip, gossip, gossip.

By six even the waiter was once again himself, once more the prerequisite aloof that one might reasonably expect a waiter to be.

Fine. Everything would return to normal, Lydia hoped as she glanced about the room and back to her own busy table. Normal, whatever that is. She turned in her seat to observe a few of her friends who had snatched up partners from the row of men at the bar. They were, as Del fondly called it, "doing their war dance." World War II. They were all faking it of course. Nobody knew these old steps except from imitating classic movies, but it looked right in the vintage atmosphere of Frank's Place and it belonged there with the old songs and posters and dim light. Warriors dancing.

Things felt right, at last, for the first time in a week. Lydia smiled back at the blond who then looked away. More right than wrong, she added, feeling like a pretty close facsimile of herself again. I am Lydia Beaumont, she said in her head, studying the profile of the reader, whoever she was. I am Lydia Beaumont. Whoever she was.

Maybe who you are depends largely on who you're with?

But back in her apartment she discovered, much to her dismay, that the air was still rarefied, as it had been since last Friday. She instantly fell into the strange mood again, the funk that was ruining her, and despaired to think that her evening at Frank's had been only a temporary success.

Standing at the foot of her bed, left unmade for the second time this week, she inspected the solitary impression that remained in the middle of it. It certainly showed how accustomed she was to sleeping alone. It looked odd. Maybe this was normal, the new normal of her life, regarding normal things as strange. She wasn't too comfortable with that. I'm not sleeping in this bed tonight, she told herself, and went to sit on the sofa in the dark instead, avoiding the bedroom mirror as she passed it.

All week Lydia had been distracted by Lydia. At Frank's she had tried to overcome herself by concentrating on the events going on at the table, the free-for-all she usually ignored. She was glad to be able to focus on something other than the hum in her head, on her aching back, but now sitting alone in her apartment like a house guest on the sofa, trying to reflect, she could scarcely remember a thing about the long evening. All she could recollect was her friends showing up late, the silly waiter with his menus, the blond in love with her solitude. In love. In love. In love. Or was it a self-imposed exile?

Reflect. It had to be at least six months ago. Maybe longer. But not a year. No, not quite that long, she doubted. Not more than nine? *Could it possibly have been more than nine months ago that I first noticed that woman sitting in there? Could be. Ah, I know why. Because before that, I was out on the patio. Right? I wouldn't even have seen her from out there. Right. For all I know she could've been coming in for years without my knowing, if she only sat inside. All that time on the patio and before then? Ah, well, before then there was that thing with Joe.*

She went into the bedroom to look at herself in the mirror. She could be coming down with something, going off into space like this, and her eyes looked funny. She'd see how she felt tomorrow and take it from there.

On the way back to the sofa she bumped into the papers she had piled on the floor in one of her new private compromises. She swore under her breath. *I don't have what it takes to be alone anymore. That's the thing.*

The thing. That thing with Joe. She stretched herself out.

Is this Joe's fault?

It felt good to get the weight off her shoulders.

Not having what it takes?

Off her back.

Being alone?

She let her eyes adjust to the darkness.

The longer it takes the farther you go—she had seen it scrawled across the ladies room wall in Frank's Place.

No. Not his fault, really.

She didn't know who was supposed to have said it.

The farther you go. She sat up uneasy.

He had never offered her anything.

There was a hopelessness at the thought of him. She felt it lodged deep in her womb. That was the ache, a killing consumption.

Ugh. She didn't know when her loneliness had stopped being Joe's fault. She pictured an empty glass falling over the edge of a table and forced herself to remember the last time he was in her apartment, showing up late for her birthday, and he had been with someone else, too. That was no secret, but it was her goddamned birthday she had shouted as he slammed the door behind him. She saw her glass of wine whizzing through the air at him, could hear it smashing against the wall. There was still a slight stain where it had trickled like blood to the floor.

Her blood, she learned too late. He had been after her blood, running her through every time he could. At parties. Behind her back. He even did her wrong in bed. On purpose. Many, many times leaving her there, for no reason, to be cruel, that's all.

The bright light of the kitchen made her eyes water.

It was overblown. A couple of months in bed. She had overrated him.

Lydia rose from the couch. *And you never even sent me flowers, you rat. Not one goddamned blessed rose.*

She turned on the living room light, feeling suddenly redeemed, and searched the room for her briefcase, then remembering where she had left it, and headed into the kitchen.

All week she had been popping in and out of bookstores, spending entire lunch hours peering at racks of paperbacks and on Friday afternoon, unable to determine any subject of interest, she had purchased a Sinatra CD from a street vendor on the way to Frank's Place. She took it out of the briefcase and put it in the player.

The clock on the wall showed midnight, but Lydia was wide awake, opening and closing the cupboards and refrigerator door. There was nothing to eat.

She had brought work home for the weekend with the idea of barricading herself in, but at this rate by Monday morning she knew she would starve to death. There wasn't even half-and-half for coffee.

The right menu at the wrong time, she suddenly recalled.

Or, the refrigerator door slammed shut one last time, an assortment of items clinking inside, *the wrong menu at the right time*.

"Excellent," she said in a voice like a waiter.

The music played.

Lydia worked feverishly all Saturday morning, as if she had an important appointment to keep and might not make it. She did without coffee or breakfast and by noon she was absolutely famished.

Lunchtime and not a crumb of food. She grabbed her coat and hurriedly left the apartment.

She entered Frank's Place alone at about half past noon. The waiter saw her before she noticed him. She hesitated at the door. He was waiting on the blond seated with her book at the sunny window.

Alone.

Lydia had never been to Frank's for lunch and it struck her as quite different from the raucous environment she was used to on Friday nights, a little more subdued than she had expected.

"Madam," said the waiter, "how nice to see you."

Lydia smiled cautiously. "Thank you," she replied, indicating by pointing that she desired a table at the back of the room.

He held her chair for her, placing the now familiar lunch menu on her plate.

"I don't think you'll be disappointed," he assured her.

She smiled the same, careful to remain composed. He had made her feel awkward the night before, almost like a child. She had not fully forgiven him for it. When he subsequently returned with a glass of merlot that she hadn't ordered she gave him an anxious look, which he utterly ignored. After that, through the rest of her meal, he acted virtually oblivious to her presence in the dining room for which she was exceptionally grateful.

That was more or less how he treated the patron at the window seat, Lydia observed, as well as the dozen or so other discreet diners seated in distant places throughout the room.

She liked how the place felt this afternoon, even though it was different than how she knew it. There was the low murmur of contented couples, the muted strands of the music in the background. The same songs, she recognized, but only softer, seeming instrumentally more civilized this afternoon. Same songs, same lyrics. Maybe a bit more daring.

Warm tones, charming light, peaceful time of the day.

There were others alone at their tables. Like her, they seemed satisfied. They talked, ate, *read*. But one didn't feel alone in this atmosphere. Not exactly. Except if one didn't want to be alone.

* * *

"Do you know what you're looking for?"

"No, not yet. I was hoping something would jump out at me."

Lydia's searches had led her to the conclusion that there were basically three topics of fiction: love, war and love *and* war. But nothing worth dying for is worth living for, she had determined early in life, so she came up empty-handed.

The nonfiction section held limited allure for her as well. Its shelves were dominated chiefly with how-to instruction manuals that explored the gamut of human interests from abdomens to the zodiac, self-help books that covered a myriad of ailments and complaints whether real or imagined. Self improvement, a big industry. These nearly always occupied an area of their own which was usually located in the front of the store right next to the checkout.

Bookstores overall had changed considerably from the last time Lydia had visited one. Now, with their wall-to-wall carpeting, their quiet reading areas, the out-of-the-way benches and comfy chairs littered with patrons absorbed in their seemingly sacred texts, the places more closely resembled libraries than anything else. Of course, unlike a library, you couldn't take your favorite book out. In the end you had to buy it.

Lydia spent the next week in much the same way as the last and failed to find anything to curl up with. She bought another CD.

Oh, yes, she hated her job. She hated her job. She hated her job. There were too many Joes writing Dear Johns. And too many like herself and her girlfriends reading them. Reading. The same letter, a chain letter, a pyramid scheme of lovers, loading the dice, moving from table to table, playing it like the numbers, exchanging commodities, leaving a collection of precious metals on the bedside. Junk bonds.

That's the marketplace, gambling over the limit, like Blackjack. Or Rio Joe.

These are dark thoughts again, Lydia reminded herself, still at her desk on Friday at four o'clock. One more time, the phone. Vice President Treadwell. Lydia groaned into her sleeve. It looked like she would be there a while.

"Hi, Paula. No, not bothering me at all. Oh, cocktails? You know

I forgot all about it. I'll put it on my calendar. Nah, I don't want a secretary, I like to be alone in here. A while, another hour or so. Okay, thanks, Paula."

Six(ish). Lydia arrived at Frank's just before six. The blond saw her first and smiled. The song on the juke was extra special loud, competing with her thoughts. She stood in the doorway, smiled back and then caught sight of Joe menacing the place with criminal looks, winking at her. She pretended not to see him and searched the room for her friends.

"Lydia!"

Her friends finally saw her and they hooted and howled out unseemly hellos. The seating arrangements had changed. She wondered how it had happened that they were now sitting closer to the center, in the blond's half of the room. Lydia glanced suspiciously toward the waiter, but he seemed to be unaware of her. She doubted the woman would be able to enjoy her book tonight and she grimaced as she made her way through the crowd to the noisiest table on the planet.

"Boo! Hiss!" came a rowdy greeting from her friends.

"Very nice."

"I am shocked, Liddy. Shocked I tell you. I think you did this to get even with us for last Friday. We've got a bottle . . . here . . . oh . . . ask the waiter for a glass . . . waiter! *Waiter!*"

Frank's was energized in a way that promised spring was near. Maybe that's why they were moving closer to the windows, anticipating summer on the patio again. For days now warm winds had been blowing in from across the sea. They lingered there, down by the waterfront, where Lydia could be found from time to time lost in her lunch hour searches for a good book. The heat came from down there. She was sure of it. Deep beneath the water it lurked, perhaps all winter, simply waiting for an opportunity. It was finally near.

"I don't know what you're suggesting, Del."

The waiter appeared with a glass and she thanked him.

"Liddy, sit down and drink."

She sat.

"Won't be long now," the waiter said cheerily.

"What won't?" she asked.

"Spring!" he declared, leaving the table with a broad grin.

From there he went directly to the window seat. Lydia observed the two of them lowering their heads together. Not about the menu, their conversation lasted only a few minutes before she saw him leaving again, the blond casting a furtive glance after him. What a busy man, Lydia thought. What's going on? Nothing, he seemed to be saying. She turned back toward the blond. Look up. Look up. Yes, smile. Yes! Green eyes. Smile back at her, fool. Show her you have all your teeth, as daddy would say. Daddy? What in the world am I doing? Is she naturally blond? Yes, naturally blond. Accessories? None. No jewelry at all, save a thin gold watch on the left wrist. Nothing on her fingers, either. No ring. It was warm in the center of the room, cooler by the wall, Lydia suddenly noticed. About my age. Beautiful hands. Writer's hands? Lydia studied them wrapped around the book. Can't tell. Or was she a musician? Artist? She squinted but couldn't make out the title. Green eyes, nice. A navy blue tailored pantsuit. Heels. No, definitely not an artist. Probably not a musician, either. Who in the world is this woman? What in the world is she doing here?

There was the waiter again, returning with a drink that had been sent by the guy at the bar pantomiming a toast to the blond. No time for a drink. She had a harried look tonight. Lydia analyzed her face as she paid her bill, collected her things. One last smile?

Yes. And then the blond with no ring was leaving, passing near Lydia's table, the right hip swaying upward, the left shoulder dipping gently down. She moved rather than walked. Or flowed—God the woman flowed just like water! Thirty fluid steps to the coat check. Lydia trailed her with her eyes until she was gone and then searched for the waiter. He was mixing drinks.

I'm out of my mind. Would it be improper to ask the waiter for the woman's name? Was there an emergency or something? Why was she leaving? I should ask him for that woman's name. She weighed it carefully, contemplating the vacant table with butterflies, trying to understand why the room seemed so empty. Was she planning to meet someone tonight? Ask the waiter for her name. *How would I explain it? I don't think I could! What am I thinking?*

All this time Delilah had been gabbing away. It was when she stopped that Lydia suddenly remembered her friend again. She saw her posed with her legs crossed, her hands clutched around her knees, wearing an insightful smile that Lydia wished to avoid. She smiled weakly back at her.

The music drifted over their heads and they sat eyeing each other, jostled in their chairs by people on missions to the dance floor or the bar. At their own table, their friends, oblivious, continued to shout and dare and cheer themselves on.

"You're being a Neanderthal, Liddy. I really mean it."

"I am?" A nervous laugh. "I don't know what you mean, Del."

"No?" Delilah leaned forward and Lydia felt compelled to do the same.

"Did you know, Dame Beaumont, that here on earth where most of us reside most of the time, that we are all perfectly safe from the destructive power of solar flares?"

"Del, I don—"

"That's because I'm not done. But that if you were actually to be near one, act-u-al-ly near one, Lydia . . . Neanderthal . . . Beaumont . . . you'd be dead in a matter of hours. Huh? I'll bet you didn't know that. I want you to think about it while we both get drunk here. I want you to roll it over in your mind," she said, raising her glass, "and I want you to respond in complete sentences."

Solar flares. Lydia sipped at her wine thoughtfully. The window seat was filled once more, this time with a loud and frolicking foursome. Neanderthal Beaumont, that's kind of funny. How should she respond? Probably best to say nothing, since something clever was out of the question. *I'm out of my mind. Is that a complete sentence?* She glanced at Delilah as she filled her glass again. Up at the bar she saw Joe trying to make her feel naked. It was easy to ignore him tonight for some reason. Peering back at her from behind the counter Marlene Dietrich looked as cool as a cucumber in a big, black-and-white poster that boldly declared

THE DEVIL IS A WOMAN. The devil a woman? Nah, Lydia doubted it. Pure nonsense. What could they possibly mean by that? She glanced at Delilah sipping her wine, waiting patiently. She'd know the answer. Lydia still had nothing to say. She gazed into Marlene's steely eyes. There was another poster beside that one portraying the actress as BLOND VENUS. Blond Venus. So what's so weird about that? Isn't Venus blond?

The women had met and become friends while finishing their MBAs. Delilah was the senior of the two. Now over forty and solidly single, she managed her personal affairs much as she handled matters at the bank she ran. Lydia, on the other hand, had never been committed to such a lifestyle. It had simply developed in that direction with the financial markets her primary focus in life.

It was in that capacity that she had met an underling named Joseph Rios, who quickly knocked her out of sorts, as Delilah liked to put it. Before then, no fraternizing. That had always been Lydia's policy in the past. She had made a fatal exception. Prior to that unhappy event, the two women had seemed like philosophical twins, stoics, taking comfort in each other's company whenever things got hairy, discussing and dismissing professional or personal difficulties as they occurred. A problem was a mere conundrum or a ridiculous quandary, never a quagmire like Rio Joe had become, faithless Rio Joe. The relationship had made Lydia different, changing her for the worse and even now it was impossible to be of any assistance to her because she refused Delilah's confidence. She could only guess that Joseph Rios had devastated her friend as months had passed since she had broken it off and she was still not fully recovered yet. And recovery seemed nowhere in sight.

There had never been any secrets between Lydia and Delilah, aside, perhaps, from the sticky details of that tortuous romance, which were easy to guess at anyway, judging from its long-lasting effects. On Delilah's part, she had shared everything. One-night stands, kinky interludes, pathetic lovers, even the unwanted pregnancy. The only thing that Lydia didn't know about Delilah was that she had to color her hair.

Delilah was now of the opinion that Lydia had not only become secretive, but morose and morbidly self reflective, dwelling, undoubtedly, on some supposed personal defects instead of admitting the obvious, that it had simply been an unlucky event, becoming involved with a man who was just a pathological misogynist. It could happen to anyone if you're not careful. Which Ms. Beaumont hadn't been.

The new Lydia Beaumont was troubling to Delilah. It was unhealthy to be so elusive and joyless. It was unhealthy not to date. And there were certain moments when Lydia even appeared tentative, undecided, dangerously suspended in a state of second guessing. This might happen even if she was only buying bread or ordering something in a restaurant. And now speaking in broken sentences. The voice trailing off effect was absolutely maddening. And that perpetually quizzical expression, as if all of life had instantly become curious and overwhelming. She pictured the sudden paralysis that overcame her friend whenever she happened to lay her eyes on that miserable, miserable man. Delilah wanted to see her cured of this and she constantly encouraged Lydia to at least say hi to him, in the hope that being able to do so would break the spell. But no.

Last week in Frank's. It was a spell her friend was under and Delilah was sure that she was falling deeper into it. To her way of thinking, Lydia just needed to get laid, that's all, and there were plenty of one-night-easy-overs standing at the bar. You don't throw yourself into the fire to escape a hot pan. Go for the easy conquests. That's how you get yourself back into the game. She'd work on this theme all through Wednesday if necessary. Both of them had taken the day off to go shopping together and to grab some nourishment along the way.

"I ask only that you be articulate and clever. I don't care if you talk with your mouth full, as long as you talk, Liddy." She glanced at her watch. "Go!"

"Okay, Del. Only four more years till I retire."

Delilah counted the words out on her fingers. "Give me at least ten more."

"I hate my fucking job. I hate my fucking job."

"That's lovely, dear, just lovely. Have some water. You must be exhausted."

Lydia grinned. "Del, have you ever . . . ?" her voice trailed off as she set the glass down without drinking anything.

"Try again, Liddy. I probably have."

Probably not, thought Lydia. Or she'd know about it.

"I'm going to be frank with you, Liddy. Ever since that creep dumped—"

"No, no! Please, Del. Not dumped. Come on, Del. Dumped?"

Delilah took a deep breath. "Walked all over you?"

Lydia sucked in her air, too. She stared out the window. "Walked is . . . well . . . a little harsh." She paused and looked away. "Okay, I'll admit to walked."

After awhile Delilah said, "Have I ever what?"

Lydia considered the question. She couldn't ask it now.

"Okay, whatever it is, if I haven't I would have. Especially if I were you, okay?"

Lydia laughed and feigned to be counting her words. "How am I doing?"

Delilah rolled her eyes, "I'd really like to know."

It wasn't a huge office, but it had a floor-to-ceiling window which looked down onto the street. If she stood at the far right end of it, she could peer out toward the harbor, midtown if she stood left of center, although there was another office building directly across the street. She liked to stand at the glass sometimes and watch the people below. They never noticed her.

It was a teaser. Sixty-five degrees by three o'clock. The end of the week and Lydia was daydreaming at her window. She was thinking of leaving when she heard the door open and close with a quick click. She turned and was not happy to see Joe standing there.

"Lydia," he crooned.

"I'm not going to endorse it," she said abruptly, "you know better." She grabbed her briefcase and began packing it up for the weekend. She had been surprised Thursday morning to find his paperwork waiting on her desk, complete with a cover letter that smelled like his cologne.

The odor had infiltrated her office and it served as a terrible distraction, which, she was sure, he had intended it to do. She made to leave and he grabbed her arm as she passed.

"Not once," he began. He liked her startled look.

She extricated herself and stepped around him. "No, so you know better, I said." She disliked his expression. "I'm leaving now," she added.

He blocked her exit. "Not even when I was screwing you."

He saw the blood rise to her cheeks.

"You approved of that, didn't you, your highness? Screwing your brains ou—"

"Your . . . these numbers don't add up . . . you . . ." she stopped and took a step backward.

He was pleased to see he could still wound her.

She grabbed the papers from the desk. "You can't make these projections," she said, throwing them at his feet. She watched silently as he picked them up, then sidestepped him and held open the door.

He was wearing his sneer. She had learned to hate it. "You have absolutely no right to speak to me that way," she whispered angrily.

He didn't reply.

"Get out," she finally said in a shaky voice.

He did.

C'mon to my house . . . my house-ah c'mon . . . happy hour . . . *I'm gonna give you candy . . . c'mon to my house . . .* ahhh . . . *my house-ah c'mon . . . I'm gonna give you . . . .* everything at Frank's seemed normal. That was reassuring. Lydia fumbled in the doorway with her jacket, decided at last to keep it on and then left the briefcase at the coat check instead. She then managed to collide with the rubber tree plants that lined the entranceway to the dining room and while her friends watched with bemused expressions she attempted to right them again. After this, she went back to the coat check and deposited her jacket.

Starting the journey all over and aware this time of the hazards, she proceeded stiffly through the aisle of plants to stand at last and rather stupidly at a now hushed table of raised brows. She glanced wordlessly from face to face, and then over to the window seat whose occupant also seemed somewhat stupefied by the performance. At least she had the wherewithal to nod with a smile and go back to her book. Whereas, at her own table, The Land Of Obvious, Lydia's colleagues sat with their jaws agog, gaping at her and expecting an explanation.

C'mon to my house . . . my house-ah c'mon . . . someone finally thought to give her a chair . . . *I'm gonna give you candy . . .* she winked at them and smiled sheepishly . . . *I'm gonna give you . . .* everything's fine.

"Death to the rubber trees!" declared Delilah.

Everyone clapped and resumed their conversations.

"What," she muttered to Lydia, "you don't get enough attention?"

"I guess not!"

"You're flushed. Is that from your stunning entrance or did something happen today?"

"It was stunning, wasn't it?"

"It was an abomination unto me and I forbid you to do it again."

"I can't make any promises, Del."

"Then we will have to get you a net." She handed her a glass.

A net? Lydia laughed, sipped her wine and picked at the appetizers. Yah! A net. Wouldn't that be nice? She realized they had all been seated one table closer to the window than they were last week and she searched the room for the usual suspect.

She found the waiter examining the row of plants in the walkway. Evidently he was satisfied that they were unharmed because he grinned when he discovered her watching him and made a rolling motion with his hands as he headed toward the bar. She stared at the row of glistening plants. They seemed to be trembling or laughing. She should ask him, ask him about the blond at the window.

"And now, if Dame Beaumont will kindly pay attention."

"Yes, Del, I am paying attention." She turned around, surprised to see the waiter already at her table.

"This comes to you anonymously," he announced with an empty face.

(Anonymous? Get out.) She took the small glass goblet from his tray and swirled its contents. Yellow—yield.

"Cognac," he said, still holding out his tray.

Cognac? Lydia glanced toward the bar. No one was claiming the gift. (Anonymous, c'mon?) The waiter's face was impregnable, the eyes suggesting only that it would be unthinkable for her to refuse the drink. Friends staring now. She felt conspicuous. She brought the cognac to her lips and swallowed it.

Fire. Fire in her mouth, on her tongue, smoldering in the back of her throat, down into her center. Fiery sweet. The blond was reading. What a delicious way to burn, Lydia was thinking. She smiled nervously and cleared her throat.

"A very good year," the waiter said. He leveled his tray and she placed the emptied glass on it. "Excellent," he whispered, leaving her aflame while anonymous looked on with hidden pleasure.

On a clear day . . . ten o'clock . . . *rise and look around you* . . . morning and *you'll see* whoa . . . *just who you are* . . . *on a clear* daylight . . . *how it will astound you* . . . *that the* phone *of your being* . . . *outshines every* wow . . . *you feel part of* . . . *every mountain, sea or* phone . . . *you can hear* . . . *from far and near* . . . the phone *you never ever heard before* . . . the phone was ringing . . . *and on that clear day* . . . *on that clear day* . . . ten in the morning . . . *you can see for* . . . *ever* . . . the phone . . . *and ever* . . . ringing . . . *and ever* . . . *and* ringing . . . *eh* . . . *ver* . . . *more* . . . click.

Lydia rolled over. The sun was streaming into the bedroom. It was ten o'clock and she had overslept. She shot out of bed remembering the work she had brought home for the weekend and with some trepidation searched the apartment for the briefcase which she had a sneaking suspicion she would not find. She was right.

Reflecting back at her in the bathroom mirror she found a sloppy version of herself and she lingered over it awhile finally deciding it was sexy. She went out to the kitchen and loaded up the coffeemaker. The briefcase was undoubtedly at the bar. She picked up the phone, thought better of it and reset the receiver. The gurgling sound and the smell of the coffee set her stomach rumbling and she played hide-and-seek with the refrigerator for a few minutes, then slammed the door in resignation.

Passing through the living room she followed the telltale path of drunkenly discarded clothes leading into the bedroom. She snatched them up along her way and quickly threw them into a hamper. It was getting to be a bad habit but it didn't look like she was going to make the bed today, either. She rummaged in the closet for something casual, glancing over her shoulder and out the window to guess at the temperature. Hot, hot, hot. She settled on a light gray angora V-neck and a pair of black slacks.

Good enough, she said, having arranged herself into some semblance of order. She looked at her watch. Eleven. The briefcase.

Probably happens all the time, Lydia thought, hastily gulping a cup of coffee. She got up from the counter and turned the coffee machine off. Her financials had been delivered; she tripped over them on the way out of the apartment. She held open the door and unceremoniously kicked them inside and then locked the door behind her. Waiting for the elevator she stole another look at the time. Half past eleven now. If she walked fast, she could get there before noon. It wasn't that far to go.

She ran, walked, ran the fifteen or so blocks to Frank's Place and when, breathlessly, she stepped inside, she congratulated herself.

The waiter smiled that smile of his and this morning she didn't mind it.

The blond smiled as well, nodding in recognition. Lydia hoped it was a good thing that she was memorable to her, wincing a little at the recollection of her pratfall, the death of a rubber tree ballet's premiere performance of the night before.

She inquired about the briefcase only to learn it had been given to one of her friends for safekeeping. It was no longer in the bar.

"A blond haired woman?" she pressed. She hopefully described Delilah.

"That's the one," said the waiter.

That's all right then, she thought, and when he asked her if she was planning on lunch, she affirmed, once again indicating that she would be most comfortable against the wall.

She found the dining room bathed in sunlight, the window seat aglow in it. Lydia sat shaded in the shelter of her own table for one and breathed a sigh of complete satisfaction. It had been such a long time ago, she couldn't even recall how long, since she had felt contentment. It was the wholesomeness of the noonday surroundings, she mused over dessert. It worked like Zen.

* * *

"There's someone waiting for you in the lobby," said the doorman.

"Oh? I bet I know who that is," Lydia replied. She found Delilah there, in good spirits, too.

"What'd you fall on your head last night?" she asked, holding up the briefcase with a wry grin.

"C'mon, Del. I'll make some coffee."

In the elevator Delilah asked, "who'd you leave with? I haven't seen you like this in awhile."

"God, I wish. I just ate. Are you hungry?"

"I brought biscotti. Mmmm—vanilla! Where did you eat?"

Lydia pushed open the apartment door and they both entered.

"Oh, just down the block," she lied. "Nothing fancy, you know."

Delilah dropped the briefcase in a chair by the door. "I tried to call you about that this morning." She eyed Lydia. "Jesus, this place is a mess," she said in horror.

Lydia got the coffee going and then stood in the living room next to Delilah.

"It is!" she agreed with a hint of delight. "I've been so busy."

Delilah's eyes narrowed. "Sit down, Liddy. We're gonna talk."

Lydia sat on the couch. She was not exactly opposed to it anymore.

Delilah set herself up with coffee and biscotti on the floor. "Okay. Talk."

"Del? Just like that? About what?"

"Talk."

Lydia went into the kitchen, returning a minute later with her own cup of coffee.

"Out with it, please."

"I'm thinking," she said, positioning herself on the couch. She took a few sips and looked thoughtfully out the window before speaking. "What do you make of someone going into a bar alone and just reading, reading all the time?" she asked without looking.

"Someone going alo—?" Delilah knew who. "I don't. I don't make anything about it at all. And you?"

"Tell me, Del. What's it mean to you? Objectively. Why would someone do that?"

Delilah whistled and they both laughed.

"Well, if I had to guess, and it's probably a pretty good guess, Liddy, I'd say it meant that *someone* was fleeing someone else. At least for a few hours, if you catch my drift."

She did. She stared out the window again. That's probably a good guess.

"I'm going to point out something else that's obvious here, Ms. Beaumont."

"What is it, Del?"

"She's a woman."

Lydia scrunched up her face and opened her eyes wide at her. (And?)

"Liddy . . . ?" Delilah got up off the floor and sat on the other end of the couch. She ran her hand through her hair in mild agitation. (Just wide eyes, no words?) Well, she thought, chuckling under her breath and leaning against the armrest.

"Well?" Lydia prompted.

"You did fall on your head," Delilah answered. She waved her empty coffee mug meaningfully and Lydia went out to the kitchen and refilled it.

"Why do you say that?" Lydia shouted from the kitchen. "Tell me why," she repeated, handing Delilah the mug and sitting beside her.

Delilah blew across it and stared at Lydia over its rim. Lydia smiled back.

"Liddy . . . she's a beautiful woman. But you can bet your life she has someone, a woman like that."

Lydia drummed the pillow with her fingers. "But, she doesn't wear a ring."

"Ugh! Wedding rings are not surgically attached, you know?"

Yes, she knew that. "But, Del, she never leaves with anyone. She's never *with* anyone." She avoided Delilah's eyes.

"Liddy?" came the vexed response. "How do you know all that?"

How did she know all that? She wasn't really sure.

"What are we talking about here, anyway?" Delilah demanded. "Do I understand what we're talking about?"

Lydia threw her arms up in the air. "I don't know."

The pouting lips. Hadn't she seen that look before? "There's easier pickings, Liddy."

Lydia sighed. "I'm not saying that. I simply find her interesting."

"Interesting? Let's try it this way. Have you ever even talked to her? You know. Hi, my name is Lydia Beaumont and I'm eager to ruin my life?"

"Ruin my life?"

"Or, hello my name is Lydia and I will not clean or bathe until you sleep with me." She swung her arm, implicating Lydia by her cluttered room.

Lydia clasped her hands together and took in her friend's amused face. "You think?" she asked. The place was a mess. She hadn't bathed today.

"That you want to sleep with her . . . am I getting this right? Yes, I think you want to sleep with her. Two straight women, for God's sake—you're after the mismatch of the century, Liddy."

Silence.

"Besides, that woman's trouble. I can feel it."

"What do you mean? How can a woman be trouble?"

"How? You're adorable. Trust me, kid, she's trouble."

"I do trust you—I find her attractive, that's all. That's as far as it goes."

"Attractive she is. But if it's a one-nighter you need, then order it from the bar. They'd be happy to oblige you, pardner, and you know it."

She groaned in response.

"That's my learned opinion, Liddy. Upon which, I urge you to rely."

Lydia sighed and went over to the window, her gaze wandering restlessly over the cityscape. Her drive was coming back. Out of commission for so long, she had hardly noticed it was missing till now. Now it was flooding through her veins again, with nowhere to direct it. Unlike Delilah, she had an aversion to picking up strangers, had no real knack for anonymous one-night stands. Even when she was younger she would always back out at the last heated minute. In fact, she was practically famous for that. Or infamous, who cares? Under her own pressure she had found herself reevaluating those apprehensions. She was at times researching the suits lined up eight to the bar. Her studies were, at best, inconclusive.

The sun was warm through the glass and she lifted her face up to it and shut her eyes, the heat of its rays on her lids, holding them down, heavy and almost contented. They glistened in the sun, lustrous. She loved sunshine.

"Del, I can't. I've tried."

It had finally reached that intolerable state where navigating herself through it was as treacherous as a minefield. The place looked like a college dorm instead of a grown woman's apartment and Lydia was too embarrassed to hire a maid.

She stood in the middle of it on a Saturday morning armed with an array of cleaning products and implements and wearing a mildly perplexed expression, blue jeans and an old sweatshirt with faded letters imprinted on the front that read, "I stink therefore I am." It was too late for wondering how it all had happened. She just had to clean it up.

She popped in a CD and began with the living room because it required the most attention, discovering in and around the couch a host of items one might find useful in the kitchen. Forks, knives, a service for twenty, if one didn't mind mismatched plates. She stacked everything that belonged to the kitchen in the sink and continued the treasure hunt, eventually coming across an unopened letter from her mother bearing a three-month-old postmark.

Lydia took off her rubber gloves and ripped it open guiltily. It was the same stuff, blah-blah-blah written in the flawless penmanship that all the women of that generation seem to have, talking in smooth flowing paragraphs about the sorts of things only those women have time to consider: her lawns, her gardens, the grandchildren she now accepted she would never have, as if it was possibly her own decision to make or accept. Lydia laughed out loud. The woman was relentless! She scanned the rest of it quickly. Not a mention of her dad. Well, he deserved that. She pinned the letter over her computer so she would remember to send the old gadfly an e-mail.

It was amazing how little progress she had made by noon. In some ways, what with the throwaways standing in teetering stacks and all, it actually looked worse.

It was just a temporary *phase* the room was going through, Lydia said, trying to bolster herself by using a favorite expression of her mother's. She stopped in her tracks when she heard it—having it come out of her own mouth was a bit alarming.

Poor mom.

It would be wrong to send her an e-mail, she decided then. She retrieved the letter from her office and taped it next to the living room phone instead. She'd try to give her a call this evening, she promised, as she tied her running shoes and grabbed a wool hat, heading off late for lunch.

Outside, the cold grabbed at her and, having forgotten a coat, she thought it best to jog the fifteen blocks to Frank's Place. She showed up hot and sweaty and loitered at the door until the waiter finally recognized her.

"And therefore you are," he said.

She gave him a puzzled look and started for her table.

"Madam?" He gestured meaningfully with his finger at the side of his face and when Lydia failed to comprehend he took her arm and discreetly led her to the mirror.

She laughed self-consciously at a silly reflection and wiped off an unflattering smudge of some unknown substance with the tissue he had offered.

"Do you need a comb?" he suggested benignly.

The hat. She pulled it off and smiled shyly as she took the comb from his hand.

"What's for lunch?" she whispered, excitedly fixing her hair.

"It's a surprise," he said, escorting her to her table. "Like your outfit," he teased.

"Oh my God," she said, suddenly remembering the sophomoric sweatshirt and spying the blond turning her head toward the window, her amusement palpable. "I was cleaning."

He held the chair for her and she sat down.

"We see that."

* * *

When you have nothing it's easier to see what you need.

In her cleanings on Sunday, Lydia Beaumont came across an abandoned pair of gold cuff links and a light blue dress shirt, both items belonging to a certain tall-dark-handsome named Rio Joe. She'd be damned before she would ever give them back to him and risk being reminded by one of those awful sneers that he had once been the master of *her* flame. She deposited them in the garbage chute and on Monday morning arranged to have the apartment completely emptied.

Weekdays. Fridays. Saturdays. In "a coupla weeks" the movers had come and emptied her apartment. Had she thought of the blond in Frank's Place in quite the vivid terms that Delilah had expressed? Is empty clean she wondered, bobbing through traffic like a robin in spring on her way to lunch. Maybe nobody noticed her funny walk. The spring in it. Just Delilah. Crunch. She felt a foot beneath her own and apologized to its owner. *When the red, red, robin goes bob, bob, bobbing.* Where was spring this year? Lydia thought of Delilah's warnings. Frying pans and fire. She was hungry. Starving. Lunch. Perfectly harmless.

To her credit she had built many a fortune, including her own, on being patient and methodical. She never panicked, she always rode it out. Those were fine attributes for a financial strategist and they served her well at Soloman-Schmitt, but they were not much of an asset in the case where she was dying to meet someone, dying to know their name. In this situation she was out of her field of expertise, in uncharted territory, and although the waiter seemed somewhat of an ally, Lydia was too cautious to enlist his aid in such an endeavor. It was prudent to be cautious, general principles of probability and statistics informed her that the chances of the blond reciprocating her affections were slim to none. At least, for the moment, she was in her world, albeit less than an acquaintance. At least, for the moment, the woman acknowledged her

existence there, smiling, sometimes even winking, other times mouthing
hello over the edge of her book.

Empty. Just a mattress, computer, telephone, answering machine,
coffeemaker . . . Lydia cradled her cup and contemplated her empty
rooms, her next move. Should probably tell Delilah about this, she
thought, smiling at the anticipated reaction. At least it's clean, she might
say in response. Is that all she should say?

Another cocktail party at the lavish suburban villa of Mr. and Mrs.
Paula Treadwell. Paula decided to play cupid with a forty-something
divorcee who had the paucity of mind to bring his children along. The
unhappy family of three *and* VP Treadwell hovered tactlessly at Lydia's
elbows all night, he with his my-children-need-a-mother eyes, the
children with their we-already-have-a-mother eyes, Paula with her he's-
so-wonderfully-stable eyes. Lydia found it necessary to excuse herself and
hid away for more than an hour in the upstairs library, drinking cognac
with a few associates and discussing ad nauseam the consumer pricing
index and prime lending rate. Later, when she got the nerve to go back
downstairs, Mr. Dad reappeared at her side. This time he told his kids
to scram, and she spent the rest of her sorry evening dodging his clumsy
innuendo and not so subtle proposals for "polite sex." Polite sex? No
thanks. Sly Rio Joe had spoiled her for that, she realized, in a cab at ten
o'clock, heading for home alone.

Chief financial strategist for Soloman-Schmitt, Lydia Beaumont kept
her eyes open at happy hours but nothing appealed to her. Nothing in a
three-piece suit, that is. She was up on a shelf somewhere waiting to be
brought down. She knew that, but so what? Get it up, Delilah urged her.
She laughed her off.

The grueling work week seemed somehow shorter now, less
demanding. Still the same nonsense, though. She stayed on the sidelines
of trouble, keeping VP Treadwell enlightened, monitoring, constantly

monitoring illicit things. It was bound to come to a head someday. When it does we'll pop it like a zit, Paula bragged. Fine.

She wasn't depressed about work anymore, didn't mind the empty rooms that greeted her when she came home. Fridays, Saturdays. She searched her catalogues for new furnishings, hoping to be moved by the offerings. Moved. She was moved. But not materially. Move. Moved. Moving.

She had been wrongly charmed. This, Lydia frequently suspected, was the case. This should greatly trouble her. It did not greatly trouble her. She was deliberately abandoning herself to a mistaken possibility. That was not good. It was a fantastic mistake. It felt good. It made her feel strangely connected to people. She was making a mistake. She was no different than anyone else. Did it hang off her sleeve? This should greatly trouble her. It was colossal, fantastic, maybe it even hung off her sleeve. She looked to the blond to stop it. It was her fault. No, she didn't stop it. Indeed, her eyes were always warm. Wasn't there a kiss in them? Kisses. Was it real or imagined? Weaker by the day. Unmistakable. Her head was dizzy. Her head swam. She kept all this secret. Jesus, how her head swam. Morning, noon and night. Is this platonic?

She did not know what was possible or impossible anymore. She could not conclusively discount that she may be in love with the occupant of the window seat. She had no idea what to do with her apartment. She couldn't find her CD player now. She must have sent it off with the movers. She could play CDs on her computer. Oh, that's right. That's all right then. She couldn't swear she wasn't in love. Thank God nobody noticed or asked her. She hadn't told Delilah yet about the furniture. That she had no furniture! God! Did she know anymore why she got rid of the furniture? She had no recollection of having possessed that urge. It had been an impulse. She had an impulse now. To scream with joy.

* * *

What had first attracted Lydia to her penthouse apartment were its large and airy rooms. She had liked, too, its lack of nooks and crannies, its white undecorated walls, the hard slate-gray flooring throughout it, how the click of her heels as she walked on that surface pierced the solemn air of the apartment and traveled into every room. The swift report issuing back, telling her of the vast emptiness that surrounded her was, at that time, pleasant and reassuring. It did not speak of isolation then, but rather of wide open spaces, room to live in, as opposed to the cramped and cluttered accommodations she had been used to.

It was the vast emptiness she wished to preserve, she had informed her decorator then. He had understood this, furnishing the penthouse with his sharply functional and utilitarian sensibilities, the kitchen completely in stainless steel. Over the large, otherwise sunny living room windows he had hung serious and industrial looking curtains. Devoid of pattern, their color was consistent with that of the floor and with the overall palette, the mostly cold grays of fabrics and metals that were sparsely arranged throughout her rooms.

That was years ago and Lydia had never disturbed it, except on one occasion, just a few months ago, when she had contacted the decorator again, for the purpose of selecting a rug or "something soft" to put on her hard living room floor. He had selected an industrial weave "inspired" (he said) by the "mood" of the place and the color of the furniture and floor. At least it was soft.

But her interiors had become architecturally undigestable and now Lydia found her penthouse cold and drab. Its repetitive emptiness and its nuanced reminders of emptiness were depressing and uninspiring and she felt on edge there, unable to relax. She had come to hate the uncomfortable couch, was repelled by the cold metals and rough fabrics of her chairs, despised the oversized paintings of polka dots that had been selected to liven the living room. That was all there was to it. The place, she had finally concluded, was simply a mockery of life. Emptiness was not a real life, not what she was after. At least not anymore. She began wondering about real people and how real people furnished real homes.

* * *

Her decision to redo the penthouse from the floor up caught Delilah off guard. She had been encouraged to believe by her friend's recent demeanor that the crisis had passed and that she was on the road to recovery from . . . well, from whatever it was that ailed her. Delilah gasped into the receiver. Lydia had emptied the posh apartment of all her furniture except a mattress.

"But, Liddy. Why?"

"I hated it, that's why."

"But you spent a fortune on it."

"I don't care about the money, Del."

"Just a mattress? Liddy! How will you live?"

"Plus I'm having parquet floors installed this week!"

"Floors—Liddy! You can't stay there then. When will they be done?"

"A week and a half they say. I'm going to do the rest after that."

The line was quiet. It was done. She knew Delilah was accepting it, probably smiling already at the entertaining picture she had created. Lydia Beaumont, interior renovator extraordinaire, covered with paint and—

"Liddy, you're nuts. Get some things together. You stay here till it's done."

"Okay. Tomorrow, though, Del. I'm leaving for lunch now."

"Where are you going? I'll meet you."

Lydia hesitated. "Nah, meet me at the paint store, Del. The one on the corner. Yeah, that's the one. Oh, it's no biggee, wait till you see. I'm picking them out by myself, Del. I'm thinking antiques. I don't know yet. One piece at a time. I don't care. Del . . . meet me at two. Yes, I have clothes. Two. See ya!"

Empty window seat at Frank's. Lydia stood at the door watching as the waiter sat an older couple there. It instantly put a damper on her spirits and she wondered elaborately over the reason why the woman couldn't lunch today. No clue from the waiter. He was his typical affable self as he escorted her to her regular table where she then lingered indecisively over the menu and unknowingly cast resentful glances over the edge of it and across the room.

Presently he returned and handed her a drink. She recognized it immediately.

"Cognac?"

"Yes, cognac."

"Anonymous?"

"But of course."

She grinned and took a small sip. "Mmmmm. And what do you think anonymous would want me to have for lunch today?"

"Well," said the waiter, "I can ask for you, if you give me a minute."

(Ask?) He didn't give her a chance to take it back. She watched in bewilderment as the waiter placed a phone call from behind the bar, watched his amiable facial expressions as he conspired with the unknown party on the other end of the line. Oh no, she worried. No time for this. Had she unwittingly made herself the object of romantic subterfuge? She downed the cognac and waited anxiously for him to get off the phone so she could call the whole thing off. He was in no hurry.

Fun with food. First cognac and now lunch. One missing blond. Lydia suspected a connection. There's a connection. It's obviously connected. She glanced at the waiter. Only he could say. He hung up and with an inscrutable expression went into the kitchen. She laughed to herself then. Forget asking him. What if there's no connection at all? Well. You can't be debauched by a lunch, she told herself, the cognac nestling warm in her empty stomach and slowly going to her head. She settled into her chair and surrendered.

It was not long after exiting for the kitchen that the waiter returned to her side delivering with a satisfied grin a chilled asparagus salad drenched in fresh raspberry vinaigrette. Finger food. Was she drunk or was there something suggestive about this? She blushed at its arrival. He set a fluted glass down beside it and made to leave again.

"What's that?" she asked.

"Champagne."

She smiled and shook her head. In deep. "Thank you," she said, taking a sip and waiting till he was out of sight before nibbling at the asparagus.

The lunch entree arrived and was not to be outdone by a salad. It sat flamboyantly before her; she gulped at the bubbly and tentatively inspected a French pancake overstuffed with creamed oysters, dripping with a butter sauce.

She sighed and whispered, "Impressive. And this is . . . ?"

"A crepe, madam."

Mmmmm.

"Enjoy."

She did.

The finale came as a bright, reddish liquid.

"Orange fruit soup."

Oh, sure. She brought a spoon of it to her lips and swallowed. Delicious.

"The check is taken care of," he said later, refusing her card.

"Oh my God," she said wistfully, "I could get used to this."

He smiled and without a slip said, "I'm sure your benefactor will be glad to know that."

She faltered at the door and he assisted her with her jacket. The question begged but she didn't dare ask it. Instead, she thanked him and stepped outside. It had become spring without her knowing it. She was hot under all her clothes.

"Something warm."

The clerk brought Lydia another batch of color chips and she oohed and aahed over olives and mustards for an hour while Delilah looked on skeptically.

She preferred white or off-white combinations and warned emphatically that the wrong paint will make the space seem too small.

Lydia wanted that.

"If you're not careful it'll end up looking like a Hungarian whorehouse."

"Hah! I've made worse mistakes!"

They spent the rest of the day walking the waterfront, scoping out the curios and antique shops. In one of them Lydia found a pair of black netted gloves still in their box.

"Now where would you wear these?" she asked Delilah. She was infatuated.

"Ooh. Slinky."

"Silk," uttered the blue-haired proprietor. "They are of silk."

Lydia couldn't place the woman's accent. She had a sly, sophisticated face covered with age spots and wrinkles, and the overall patina of wealthier days, albeit faded.

She slipped one of the gloves onto Lydia's hand.

"For the bedroom," the woman said in a sultry tone. "Special."

The universe contracted and then expanded again.

"A gift for the woman he wants in his bed," she added. "You don't wear them too long, I should think."

"I thought we we're looking for furniture, Liddy."

(Something for the bedroom . . .) "I'll take them."

The sun came out and Delilah went to greet it.

"Good luck," said the shopkeeper as Lydia was leaving.

The bell over the shop door tinkled as it closed behind her.

"I couldn't resist, Delilah."

"I see that. Now all you need is a dresser to put them in."

The Dow was barely 3000 when Lydia had started out, and even that, her father had assured her, was astonishing. In those days a four- or five-hundred point fall was considered a collapse and it still made her nervous when it happened.

Work was a rough ride from Monday through Wednesday and she spent most of that time fielding panic calls from jittery investors.

On Thursday afternoon, even though it was against policy, she turned her answering machine on and left work early.

She was staying with Delilah and hadn't been to the apartment since last Sunday. The contractors had begun the floor installation Monday morning as promised and she was as excited as a child for Christmas, even though it was nowhere near completion.

On arrival, she found only the parlor and part of the living room done, but she nevertheless beamed with joy when she saw how it brightened the place.

The foreman kept the men working, though it was clear they would rather have stood around bragging about their techniques. He took that pleasure for himself while he cast predictions about the time schedule and repetitively reminded her that even when they were done with the actual installation there would still remain an extensive cleaning and the expert application of three coats of finish.

"You shouldn't walk on it for a coupla' days," he said.

That was logical but disappointing.

" 'Specially not with them." He pointed at her heels and grinned.

She thanked him and headed back to Delilah's just a few blocks away.

"Hey! You're in a good mood."

"Del, wait until you see it."

"I can't wait. Come and tell me about it."

She was wearing a mud mask in preparation for a dinner date.

"It's gorgeous."

"The crew or the floor?"

"Oh, it's all beautiful, Del. What's on your face?"

"Nothing. I'm green with envy, Liddy."

"Each room is going to have a different pattern . . . but I can't walk on it for three days after it's done."

"Oh? Pass me that. Thanks. Can you crawl?"

"I'm just gonna roll on it when it's done."

"Yah! With no furniture to get in the way. That'll be easy."

"Got to paint the place first, Del. Get ready."

"What do you think I'm doing here? Isn't this about the same color?"

Delilah left around six thirty.

"If all goes according to my plan, Liddy, I'll see you tomorrow."

She gave one last look in the mirror.

"If not, I'll be home later to masturbate."

"Del!"

"Don't wait up!" she shouted gleefully.

The closing door and the now quiet apartment marked the first opportunity for Lydia to be alone in almost a week and she inhaled the moment like a breath of fresh air.

Supper time.

The unrewarding search in Delilah's refrigerator brought forth the image of her Saturday feast again and she worried anew about the empty window seat and what it all might mean. She opened and closed the cupboard doors searching in vain for something to eat. Nothing in the pantry, either. Delilah Domestic she is not. It was foolish, perhaps, to go too far with conclusions, she reminded herself about the lunch, as she looked for the freshness date on a box of crackers. Toss it, she said, looking for the garbage can. Hungry and nothing but fungus in the fridge. After all, she really didn't know anything. The benefactor, so identified by the waiter, need not be the blond, in which case it would be smart to stop playing with food and to exercise a bit more caution. Need not be. The blond.

But who else could it be? A man? What man? Ugh, a married man. She hadn't considered that possibility. Would a married man be that discreet? She pondered it, her head in the freezer. Nah, wouldn't a man be confident enough to publicly solicit her, married or not? Of course, she decided, rummaging through frozen lumps of aluminum foil. Whereas a woman . . . a woman trying to seduce another woman? She thought of the black silk gloves. She would never attempt it, not even with silk. That would take balls. Or tits, she laughed, still reluctant to rule it out. She discovered a triangular shaped wrapper in the back of the icebox and opened it out of curiosity. Pizza. Lydia cringed at the idea of it. Knowing Del, she thought, this could be ten years old. She stuck the slice into the microwave and peered at it through the glass with as much surety as a student performing a science project.

Ding!

The food held up under inspection and she sat down on the couch to eat it. Of course this meal didn't compare to creamed oysters, but that was no surprise.

Del was right, she thought, chewing gingerly and sliding an old movie into the VCR. She must have somebody. The reason why she wasn't there on Saturday could easily be that she was with someone else, somewhere else.

Lydia ruminated slowly.

It was a bit tough. And hard to swallow.

And the movie was stupid and the food sucked.

And the bed was uncomfortable and the sheets scratched.

And she hated not knowing what to think anymore.

* * *

The week closed high for Soloman-Schmitt. Hopes of a merger. Hopes, rumors, fears and speculation.

She missed her.

It was proving chancy lately, counting on Frank's for glimpses of the blond. She wasn't there Friday night nor the subsequent Saturday for lunch and Lydia found that the vacuum created by her absence could not be filled with anything else, no matter how exciting it was to see the progress in the apartment, with all the raw wood seeping through it, filling the place like the rising tide, no matter how busy she kept herself so that her mind wouldn't wander after the woman.

There was no substitute for her Saturday ritual and she could not go home yet. That's what she was inclined to do when she felt like this, lock herself in. Soon, she said, trying to reassure herself. Soon she could move back into her penthouse. Soon the woman would return and this time she would speak to her.

Reconstruction was taking longer than projected, however, and Lydia was advised by the foreman that the crew would require another week past the original deadline and that he was terribly sorry for the inconvenience.

This did not help matters any, but it didn't stress Delilah, either, who insisted that she was not put out by the delay and rather enjoyed having a roommate. It made her feel so young, she claimed.

That being the case, Lydia affected the most cheerful impersonation of herself as possible for Delilah, it being successful enough to prevent any skillful probing, but a far cry from an actual cure for what she was coming down with.

She made it to Friday, but the blond was still missing from Frank's Place. Saturday, the same. No more speculation now, she knew without a doubt that she was in love with her because without a doubt she was heartsick.

All throughout the following week a great black shadow hung over Lydia and by that Friday there remained no activity left which could promise any comfort or relief from it. The inexplicable disappearance was worse than anything Joe had put her through. It was almost impossible not to scream out loud. Moreover, she could tell that Delilah suspected her again and was once more growing concerned about her mood. There must be something I can do to get over this, she told herself. Something to alleviate the angst. But she couldn't even bring herself to imagine what it could be.

Twice she approached the waiter, tongue-tied but nevertheless prepared to ask about the woman. Both times she lost her confidence and bailed out without a word, cursing her cowardice all through the subsequent sleepless nights.

She—whoever she was—was gone. And Lydia Beaumont—whoever she was—had been all wrong in judging the matter. She was wrong to have underestimated her feelings, wrong to try to wait out the attraction like it was an affliction she expected to recover from, wrong to hope it would eventually disappear without leaving a mark. There was a disappearance all right. She just hadn't contemplated this kind of vanishing.

As it was impossible in such close quarters to escape from her friend's oversight, Lydia seriously considered going to a hotel, but in the end was paralyzed by the idea of offending Delilah. And although the work was finally coming to completion there, she additionally berated herself for having disrupted her life by throwing herself out of her own apartment.

This negativity was at last fully palpable. Lydia Beaumont was not herself again and Delilah knew why. She had seen the abandoned window seat the last few Fridays and the pall it had cast over Lydia. You didn't have to be a psychotherapist to decipher the meaning of that.

It was eccentric, not something Delilah would have thought she was capable of, but her tastes in lovers had always bordered on the exotic and she was not impetuous, certainly never fickle. There was, very likely, no way of undoing this.

She pondered the matter in silence as she observed the suffering.

* * *

So close on the heels of a broken heart, the last thing her friend needed was a full-blown case of love sickness, yet there it was, as plain as the olive in the martini she was having with Lydia at Frank's Place, Friday night. The woman at the window seat still unaccounted for and clearly not forgotten.

Delilah watched Lydia going through the motions and letting workplace neophytes rub at her elbows. She watched her harpooning the olive in her drink, playing catch and release with it until it was finally mutilated, and then ordering another one, abandoning the first, otherwise untouched. She saw her clamp her teeth when she smiled, talking through them as if they had been wired shut. After about an hour of this performance she grabbed her by the arm and led her outside.

"Let's go home, Dame Beaumont."

They walked a few blocks without speaking.

"I'm sure she's on vacation, that's all," Delilah stated.

Lydia disposed of it with a silent shrug and continued counting the cracks in the sidewalks, thinking of the spring and what on earth had taken it so long. It was nice to not have to walk home alone, she thought, and she shot Delilah a thankful glance, but declined to comment on her remark.

"When I was a little girl—"

"I am not a little girl, Del."

"I know you're not. Let's stop in here for some ice cream. You're a woman in love."

She was taken aback. "I don't want any—how do you know?"

"Because I'm not a little girl, either. Who doesn't want ice cream after a martini?" she asked, gently pushing Lydia inside the deli door.

Delilah decided the flavor and they went home to eat it.

"I can't eat. What did you mean, Del? Who goes on vacation now?"

"Yum—oh, you're depriving yourself. She's obviously on vacation."

"Go on, you have it." She watched Delilah wolf the ice cream.

"Vacation, Liddy. I'm sure of it."

Lydia weighed the possibility. It so didn't make sense to her.

"That never occurred to you, did it, Liddy?"

(NO.) "What am I going to do, Del?"

"Last bite?"

Lydia shook her head no.

"You need a plan."

"Plan? How do you plan for this?"

Delilah laughed. "Tell me all that you've done about it."

"Nothing," Lydia admitted.

Delilah threw the empty container and the spoon into her sink. "Oh, really? That much?"

At first, though she had no idea how she got there, it was quite pleasant. It was nice to be alone with just the gentle slapping of the waves against the little boat. Nice, the butterflies in her stomach as she lifted and fell with each wave, the fluttering sound of the solitary sail in the gentle sea breeze.

And it was so sunny.

But then the wind suddenly picked up and the ocean swelled around her. There were huge waves now rocking the boat, each time lifting it a little higher, each wave bringing her closer to the darkened sky and depositing her harder against the water.

The butterflies gave way to sea sickness. The boat jerked from side to side, rising and falling, groaning and listing. She saw the mast nearly touching the surface, felt the craft threatening to capsize. And from under the hull, there came a thud. Once. Twice. At the sides and then below her again. She could hear it through the wind and waves whipping at her, stinging her face and body. She flipped over. There it was behind her. Something was in the water, bashing against her boat, trying to see what the craft was made of, testing its worthiness.

Something big.

The waves crashed violently over the deck. She was tossed to the back and clung to the edge there, face up and drenched. The boat was filling. Over her head the wind tore at the remnants of her sail. She heard the crack of the mast and the rigging as it ripped free and the persistent thud, thud, thud of the thing, something that was circling her beneath the water.

Lydia was damp and inextricably bound up in her bed sheets when she awoke from her nightmare. It was still dark and she was not sure of the date or even what time it was.

But it was five o'clock on a Saturday morning.

And everything was fine.

Just a dream.

It was a morning opulent enough to rouse even the summer gods from hibernation and they woke on such a day no different than the mortals under their dominion, ambitious and edgy, eager to exercise their authority.

They stirred and stretched their powerful arms, reaching far into the brilliant sky around them. They squinted at their clocks, grinned and reset them, time arbitrarily altered just for fun.

Just for fun they tickled the universe in all its sensitive places and made it laugh again. Below them, they lengthened the day.

If humanity suddenly lurched at the whim of these capricious fingers, if its endeavors now moved only in fits and starts, if all its boats rocked free from their moorings, it was just business as usual returning, the industry of fair weather gods determined to rule their kingdom and to test their subjects' mettle. They were going to have fun this year.

The cherry trees were summoned by winged messengers and together they blasted a bright pink alert across the city. Indoors the wallflowers glowed and houseplants bloomed, bursting forth like popcorn. They stretched longingly toward their windows. The high and low places admitted the sun and displayed their finest linens. Decorated tables were sent outdoors and stood at attention on the sidewalks. Silver and gold settings relinquished their tarnish and gleamed on their own accord.

And at Frank's Place the waiter opened the patio.

Lydia Beaumont languished out there Saturday with zero expectations of the hot new spring. Still, she appreciated the sunshine. It was warm on her skin, stimulating to her blood, its heat long awaited. She basked in it, listening without too much resentment to the birds singing their I love yous. She even watched them up in their branches as they flirted and played tag.

Beside her table, on the sidewalk, flowed a multitude of fellow sun worshippers, bedecked, as she was, in their pre-summer best. She admired their flowers, their stripes, all the seersucker suits marching or meandering to similar churches like Frank's or wandering aimlessly, just to show off. She searched their ranks without meaning to, a habit by now. Searching for her favorite blond.

She found her, too, her body reacting first to her discovery, the heart leaping in her chest, the knees going weak with adrenaline, the arms wanting to lift up in the air, to hail the woman or hold her or both, the cords in the neck tense with a restrained yell, a whoop of joy trapped in there. She watched the woman nearing, those green eyes hidden behind sunglasses, her own eyes glistening, dewy with desire, the object of complete desire appearing in the flesh now, in full focus, her image once more in alignment with the one held so long in her mind's eye, emblazoned there. She processed the woman anew, her synapses fantastically tripping with information, her brain's search engine declaring a perfect match.

The blond left the parade and selected the table adjacent to hers.

The waiter came out to greet her and she smiled wearily as he held her chair. He lifted the umbrella and she removed her glasses, holding Lydia's gaze longer than usual.

Delilah was mistaken. The woman had not been on vacation, that was clear. She was not rested. Her eyes, typically bright and dancing, didn't have an ounce of joy in them today. Indeed, to Lydia, it looked as if she may have spent a good deal of the past month or so staying up late, crying. She waved with her book and whispered a soft hello. Lydia mouthed it back to her, her body leaning forward in a subconscious display of sympathy. The woman smiled then, laying her book on the table, her glasses on top of it. Something on the tip of her tongue, Lydia thought. Say it.

The waiter reappeared with his menus and he read off the luncheon specials while the woman listened distracted. He seemed uneasy today as did the blond, Lydia observed. She threw around some scenarios in her mind trying to determine which one she could use to get herself at that table.

Behind her a commotion sounded in the street, squealing tires and honking horns. She turned, as did the other patrons, to see what was going on.

A yellow sports car screeched up to the curb alongside the patio. It idled a minute in its own exhaust and then finally emitted a long-legged beauty from the passenger side who nonchalantly hung over the open car window as she laughed and chatted with the driver. After a few moments, she stepped away from it, turned and began cutting a path through the tables of curious spectators on the patio. The car exited the same way it arrived.

She didn't need such a grand entrance. She was tall and commanding with exotic good looks, the type of girl they wrote songs about, that got attention even in crowds. Used to being stared at, she was dressed perfectly for it, so that you knew in an instant that her body was as flawless as her twenty-something face.

She was quite the girl, walking in a gliding manner as if her feet didn't actually touch the ground, floating as if she had wings. As she neared her table, Lydia thought she could detect a slight snarl in the girl's smile. It was, she noted, possibly the only defect in all that astonishing perfection.

"Helaine."

Oh the shark has . . . pearly teeth dear . . .

Helaine? Out of the corner of her eye, Lydia saw the blond stiffen.

"Helaine," the girl cooed in a spoiled voice, stopping at the table next to Lydia's, bending to whisper in the tired blond's ear, her lips parting into a seductive smile for her audience . . . *and he shows them pearly white . . .* for "Helaine".

Daughter, Lydia hoped. Perhaps just her daughter?

The blond—Helaine—attempted a smile for the girl, failed.

Daughter, niece, sister, whatever, no. No resemblance. Girl too old. Blond too young, too nervous. Lover. Lydia leaned back in her chair and took them both in, sighing sadly at the picture they made. Lovers. Obviously lovers. She now knew too much about the pretty blond in Frank's Place. Helaine, she repeated inaudibly. It rolled beautifully off the tongue. Helaine, a woman named Helaine, not reading anymore but listening and looking for all the world as if she was being eaten alive. And not fleeing, as Delilah had suggested, but probably waiting the whole time. A beautiful lover, it all made sense. Alone and waiting for her lover, a pretty dangerous looking thing, but young and beautiful nonetheless. Well, why not?

Helaine, Helaine, Helaine. Helaine so-and-so. That rhymes with Joe, Lydia said, kicking herself. What a beautiful name. A beautiful name for a beautiful woman. And, if at all possible, the beautiful woman had become even paler than when she first arrived. She put her sunglasses on again, grabbed her purse and glanced briefly in Lydia's direction before allowing herself to be lifted from her chair and escorted to the sidewalk.

Let it be, Lydia told herself as she watched the girl claiming her prize, wrapping her arms around the pale woman's waist, guiding her onto the sidewalk, taking her away, the blond slowly fading from view, never looking to her left or right, not once looking back.

Lovers. The couple stood across the street now, looking like day and night.

Worth waiting for, Lydia forced herself to admit. A perfect ten.

They stood on the opposite side of the street, waiting. The girl raised a magnificent arm above her head, a cab pulled over, they were gone.

You know when the shark bites . . . with his teeth dear . . . gone, probably for good, Lydia realized . . . *so there's never . . . never a trace of red . . .* gone for good. For good, she murmured, wishing the song would end. What's good about it? She followed the cab with her eyes until it was swallowed by traffic.

The waiter. Where the hell was the waiter?

The waiter had been missing in action and suddenly appeared stone faced at the abandoned table. He dropped the umbrella and tucked a forsaken book and menu under his arm. Lydia lifted her hand to get his attention and, neglecting to smile, he acknowledged her, approaching her slowly, as if carrying ten trays.

She nodded quizzically at the book.

"Burns," he said in a flat tone.

"Burns?"

"The poet."

Burns. She smiled bitterly. Yeah, it sure did.

* * *

The week dragged her unwillingly along with it and Lydia was relieved Wednesday morning to get the good news that her parquet floors were finally done and ready to walk on. She had not shared her weekend revelations with Delilah and it suddenly seemed she could avoid it altogether, if she could just keep up appearances for a few more hours.

That same afternoon she got word from her antique dealer that the sofa she had been eagerly waiting for would be delivered this week.

The sweet old sofa. That was welcome news too. Now she could throw herself down in it and cry.

She had been charmed on the spot by it, lying in it while the dealer went on about value and importance. Value, fine. But she was more attracted to its worn finish, its threadbare arms and comfortably depressed pillows. There were ancient stains joyously scattered among its fauna and flora that whispered of good wine and fine food and it made the cheerful piece seem alive to her, that if she poked gently into its soft recesses she could get it to giggle and gossip.

She was in need of its good cheer; it would be there by Thursday afternoon.

For the rest of the day Lydia undertook to tie up the loose ends that had accumulated since winter. She came across Rio Joe's last cover letter, copied it and put the stinky original through the shredder.

He had switched strategies on her and all week she felt him circling again, all week casting her those long looks loaded with old suggestions. The renewed advance was filling her with an unwanted tension. She resented him for it and if he continued she feared an explosion, so she was constantly watching over her shoulder in an effort to evade him. She was not sure that she could make it to the weekend.

With that in mind, she closed her office door, working then without worry or interruption, and mulling things over until five. After that she hung around putting the office in order and at six, just before leaving, sent a brief memo to VP Treadwell. Satisfied, she locked her desk, her files and her office door and then left to have dinner with Delilah. Somewhere other than Frank's had been Lydia's only stipulation. She hadn't said why.

Armed with the diversion of the floors and couch, Lydia managed to escape her friend's careful analysis, as well as any inquiry concerning her plans for the upcoming Friday night. Even after dinner, as she packed her clothes at Delilah's and chatted, not a single word or emotion betrayed her.

By ten that evening, she was living in her own apartment again, admiring the beautiful floors, checking her answering machine, and filling a garbage bag with the outdated papers that had piled up in her hallway while she was gone.

At eleven thirty she placed a long distance call and had a friendly discussion with the person on the other end of the line.

At midnight she pulled her mattress out of the walk-in closet where it had been stashed by the workmen. She was going to replace that, too, eventually. She hauled it into the living room, threw some sheets, blankets and a pillow on it and went to bed where she lay wide awake into the wee small hours of the morning.

In the morning she stayed in her bathrobe with no plans to go to work. Instead, she waited until afternoon when the promised couch arrived. She had the deliverymen place it next to the mattress and they eyed her funny as they left the apartment. After that she showered, dressed and put on her makeup, placing one more call to a midtown address before making herself some toast out of the stale bread left in her refrigerator.

She had not unpacked her bag from the night before so there was no reason to fuss. She slung it over her shoulder, checked to see that the coffee was off and turned her answering machine back on before leaving the apartment and locking the door.

In the hallway she took a deep breath, clutched the map she had drawn and hoped it was accurate. Downstairs in the lobby, she advised her doorman of her plans and tipped him handsomely for his confidence. She then proceeded to walk to a nearby parking lot, stopping to chitchat with a talkative booth attendant who finally handed her the keys to a rental car.

It started fine, everything seemed to be in good working order, there was plenty of gas. She threw her luggage into the back, put the crude map on the passenger seat where she could refer to it when needed, pulled out of the parking lot and hurriedly left town.

She'd send Delilah a postcard when she got there so she wouldn't worry.

* * *

Happy hour and everyone wondered where Lydia was. They called her penthouse and left loud messages full of the jubilant sounds of the bar, singing poor versions of well-known songs, hoping that if she was there it might entice her to come out. It was odd for their friend to be absent, especially now that the patio had reopened.

The waiter thought so, too. He inquired twice about her.

The blond woman sat inside reading at the window seat, nursing a glass of wine. From time to time the spine of her book fell to the tabletop and roused her from her thoughts. She would then glance hopefully outside and over again toward the entrance, but whoever she was expecting never showed up. She left roughly at nine. Lydia's friends, sometime after midnight.

The waiter closed around two in the morning, turning the lights out after him and locking the door.

Done for the day. The chairs had been stacked on the tables. The shades had been drawn. The sign on the door read "closed" once more. In the darkness the rubber tree plants lining the walls trembled ever so slightly. They were glad to be alone there and proud of their flexibility.

Part Two
The Cab

" . . . everyone is searching for a tall, dark and handsome stranger . . . such persons are rare and there is simply not enough of them to go around . . . the real Mr. Right is very likely someone you already know."

Doctor Helaine Kristenson, *Keeping Mr. Right*

Helaine knew precisely the moment when she first laid eyes on her dark-haired stranger and it was not by happenstance in Frank's Place. The overnight success of her book the year earlier had proven to be a boon for her private practice and had enabled her to move out of her small downtown offices and to take the lease on the larger and more luxurious ones located midtown in the city's financial district.

She had always been attracted to the youthful vitality of this neighborhood and now enjoyed observing its weekday inhabitants from her twelfth floor window as they flowed in and out of the city's heart and rejuvenated its tired old veins. Weekdays the streets and buildings teemed with their optimistic activities. Even on the weekends when they had all gone home she could still feel their energy pulsing from the empty sidewalks and the high-rise windows.

Helaine had just finished her Friday with one last difficult session and was trying to unwind in a chair beside the window, drinking her tea and making final entries in her journal. The Friday ritual. She had been listening to music as she worked, Ravel launching *A Boat At Sea*, when she glimpsed the young woman standing and daydreaming in the full-length office window directly across the street from her. She put her pen down and counted up fifteen stories with her finger, guessing by the woman's elevation that she had probably earned the privilege of a few quiet moments there. The woman gazed out at the horizon, downtown, toward the waterfront.

The music played, tranquil in the background. Helaine stopped writing. The boat drifted further and further from the shore, dropping its oars and sails. She could hear the water as it lapped at its sides and feel the cool spray on her face as the craft bobbed gently in the waves. Behind it she saw a wake of brilliant sparkles. It spread like a blanket across the deep blue sea.

The figure on the fifteenth floor was so majestic on her cloud, so serene in her motionless state, so elegant in her black dress, that it struck Helaine that she might have invented her there. She sat stiff in her chair, afraid to look away lest the mirage should suddenly dissipate. The journal slipped from her lap to the floor with an important thud, but she didn't pick it up.

The woman in the clouds. A ghost ship perhaps. She wore a tight black dress, stood like a queen in her window surveying her defenses. Land and sea. Clear skies. The boat floated further. She was far more agreeable to contemplate than the list of irreconcilable differences scattered on the floor—Helaine kicked the journal aside and pushed her chair back so she wouldn't be discovered spying.

On the other side of the world, Dr. Kristenson's lover had disappeared on her again, initially to the catwalks in Paris and from there, according to the rags and dailies that covered such things, to Milan. She had received only one postcard from her, from neither of those locations, a hasty wish-you-were-here scrawled beneath faded red lip prints. Might not even be her own, Helaine reminded herself at the time, though she had saved it anyway, putting it in a secret drawer for safekeeping, safe next to the other similar mementos.

It was not unusual for Helaine to find herself abandoned, but this time Sharon had left her alone for a full six months. She saw the placid figure across the way finally make a move and watched as the woman began to preen herself, using her window as a mirror.

She had unreasonably high hopes that her lover would return soon since there was nothing preventing her from doing so, and she had been making periodic visits to the waterfront flat in search of her—it was not unlike Sharon to slip back without telling her and to lay around for days before calling.

The waterfront. Helaine used to like living there. The woman in the upper window raised her arms behind her head and tugged at her hair until it finally came loose. It fell carelessly into her face and onto her shoulders and she let it hang there for a few seconds before pushing it away with the back of her hand.

Helaine ached to find Sharon, but the quests to the flat produced nothing but disappointment and she had recently resolved to stop going there. She was waiting instead in a kind of self-imposed exile for the phone call that never came, checking her messages two, sometimes three times a day. Now and then she even perused the magazines that kept tabs on the supermodel and the other stellar creatures that Sharon Chambers circled the earth with. She was stung by those exposés, the lover beyond compare and her tawdry sexual escapades.

On that Friday afternoon Helaine had already thrown some magazines in the wastebasket when the woman on the fifteenth floor decided to comb out her hair, bending at the waist, tilting her head to the left and then to the right as she did it. It was similar to Sharon's, dark and silky, but Helaine didn't think she was quite as tall as she was. And she was slightly fuller in the hips, too, with supple, round breasts, which Sharon didn't have. Older, though by how much she couldn't determine. Helaine had begun to suspect that Sharon wasn't coming back. Worse even, that she might never have existed. The woman in black took her time appraising herself, turning herself around slowly as she examined her reflection. The dress had a cutaway back. She saw the woman lift it up, revealing her legs so she could adjust her stockings, doing each one carefully so as not to rip them. The legs were well toned all the way up the thigh, not like those of the willowy model, but more lithe and athletic, as were her arms and shoulders and that well-conditioned back.

Sharon was a bit of a phantom even when she was around, Helaine mused. That she could tell from her chair, the dark-haired woman had more color than Sharon, but then Sharon spent most of the daylight hours in bed and didn't get much sun, not unless she had to, say for a swimsuit edition. Even then she preferred lamps in booths over natural light—sunshine was bad for the skin. Helaine doubted that the sky woman had any real significant imperfections.

Behind these considerations, strands of music floated like clouds over a sparkling sea and Ravel's boat wandered aimlessly across its surface. Helaine leaned forward in her chair and felt the sun warm on her lap. In the clouds, the woman dreamily caressed herself. She was under mistaken assumptions. Wrong to suppose that the offices opposite hers had all been vacated for the weekend. Wrong to absently unfasten the side of her dress and reach into it.

There was, Helaine speculated, always the possibility that Sharon Chambers had flown the coop. This time for good. Would that be a nightmare, she found herself wondering, or a self-fulfilling prophesy?

The dark-haired woman studied her own reflection, using her free hand to perform an inspection of her outer garment, running it slowly down the length of her body and smoothing out along the way the small bunches of fabric as she came upon them. She patted them down over her rump and tucked gently around her breasts, her fingers lingering there unconsciously. The music faded softly in the background, deserting the boat and Helaine couldn't recognize what it had been replaced with. She had thought then, in a new light, of Sharon's bedtime stripteases, and as it usually did, a trill of excitement had gripped her inside. She felt the blood rush to her cheeks and got up from her chair. It was that old feeling. But it was not for Sharon.

If Sharon never came back . . . she was dissolving in the woman's hands . . . it would bring an end to the disappearances, to the forever waiting . . . the woman held up a compact and lifted her face toward the sky while she freshened her lipstick . . . it would complete the sorry searches on the waterfront . . . it would put an end to the secret keeping . . . Helaine sighed . . . she'd be gone, that's all.

She stood watching the upper window long after the woman had vanished from it. Gone. The idea tossed around in her head like a ship on a turbulent ocean. She smiled without knowing it. Lost at sea.

After a while the woman emerged from the building below and walked out onto the sidewalk. Helaine followed the black dress with her eyes for about a block, pleased to see it stop and enter Frank's Place. Ah, she said, finally dropping the blinds and taking in a deep breath. You must be the one they're all singing about.

* * *

When she was not in session counseling her patients, Dr. Kristenson indulged herself with opera and books and love poems and the perpetual springtimes of impressionist painters. She delighted in the likes of Bisét, Colette, Burns, the Brontés, Monêt, Manét and Sinatra. Sinatra, because he frequently sang about the weather and about flowers and the sky and the sea and his songs about women were generally so jubilant.

She was prone to idealism and to romantic notions that at inopportune moments would sweep her up and leave her weak inside. Almost forty, she was skeptical of ever conquering either of those tendencies.

She possessed a tolerant and generous disposition, was fascinated with people, wanted to see them happy with the world and personally satisfied. She rarely met a person she didn't like. People found her fascinating, too, with her casual elegance, the warmth in her voice when she spoke to them, her easy to traverse and sometimes porous boundaries. And her green eyes. People were always spoiling her about her green eyes.

She had charismatic features, especially the eyes and, as she discovered early in life, the kind of good looks that attract both sexes. That was fortunate, she quickly determined, since the feeling was nearly always mutual. In love, it was not a matter of preference to Helaine Kristenson. It was simply that all beautiful things were persuasive. That was the case whether they were men or women.

Not so long ago she had loved sex, loved everything about loving. She believed that she had been made for it, that she had been created for the purpose of intimacy, to love and be loved in return. She had not been designed a mere object to own and admire in secret, to fondle in a hidden pocket somewhere or to neglect after a time and forget someplace on a shelf. She was meant to be taken up, to be held frequently to the light and hung intimately around the neck. Her arms and legs were not there simply for begging. They were intended for grasping and wrapping tightly about the waist, to be worn around it like a satin ribbon. The soft thighs were to be slipped between, her sex coaxed and entered like a glove on a hand.

* * *

Suppertime. Time to sit at a table at Frank's. Helaine would eat dinner there once in a while, lunch every Saturday. It wasn't very far from where she worked and no one but the waiter ever recognized her.

The stranger was flawless, having her wine outside with her friends. Helaine watched her from inside in awe of the low-backed summertime dress. She had treated herself that Friday, followed the woman into Frank's. Why not, she had debated, take her mind off Sharon? It was a most successful distraction.

Nothing is more revealing than the arch of a woman's back, Helaine thought, tracing the woman's spine with her eyes to where it curved into the backside. This one was quite rare in that it didn't easily bend. But that's not what the young man circling her believed. Helaine watched as he invited himself into the woman's personal space. How he held her captive with his hand on her waist as she tried to step away from him. He touched her lightly on her cheek and relentlessly whispered suggestions in her ear. He was, as Helaine's friends might say, drop-trow gorgeous and good-for-the-go. He was, she could see, intent on wearing down the woman's resistance. She saw her smile weakly at him and accept the glass of wine he was soliciting.

Dr. Kristenson knew that the woman was in conflict over his attentions. The muscles in her shoulders flexed anxiously at his touch. She was visibly taken aback by his propositions yet she stood in place where he held her, lost in a state of uncertainty. An expert, he had dedicated himself to those ends, had gone to great lengths to create her current confusion. Helaine knew his type. The woman was a challenge for him and he was going to conquer her, to prove to himself that he could bend her. He was going to get that girl just for the fun of it.

The shoulders, the arms, the back. She looked strong enough to take it. It would be a shame if he broke her though, a shame to cast even one cloud over the life of a woman with stars like that for eyes. Such beautiful eyes.

Her eyes were . . . ? Blue.

"How's everything?" the waiter asked.

Helaine hadn't realized he was standing there. He smiled patiently. She picked up her book again. "Delicious. Could you wrap it for me?"

"I certainly can."

* * *

Eight months and only a postcard. Typical her friends told her. She is after your blue blood.

Her blue blood. How blue it was now. "I made my blood blue, Robert."

"True," he replied, "and Sharon makes it red."

They laughed together. A swell dinner.

"Be quiet," chided his wife. She was relieved to see Helaine smiling. "Why don't you sleep over tonight? You look like you could use a rubdown with velvet gloves."

Couldn't she? Helaine glanced from Robert to Kay and then at her plate. Out of the question. Such pretty people though, smooth as velvet. She studied their almond shaped eyes. Both hazel. They could be brother and sister. But blue eyes. Blue were the eyes of a perfect stranger. She looked at her watch. It was late and she simply smiled back at them.

Two months had passed since Helaine had been to Frank's Place for dinner. The dark-haired woman had made her ail. She didn't want to see her again. "Stop feeling sorry for me. I'm a big girl and I ought to know what I'm doing."

"We don't feel sorry for you. We're just worried—"

"Don't worry then. *Please.*"

"Don't worry?" Robert snorted. "Look at yourself. You're wasting away!" Kay put her hand on his arm to silence him.

It was the truth. Did they think that she was slipping? Wasn't she? Everyone exchanged glances. "So you think that I'm only half the woman that I used to be?" She offered a smile in case they took the question too seriously.

They were silent.

These three had known each other for more than twenty years. Something was different with Helaine and it certainly didn't seem to be age that was killing her.

"Of course not," Kay answered. "You're as beautiful as ever."

Robert agreed. "If not more."

Mmmmm. "Well that's good to hear!" She wanted to cry. A few years ago, as a friend, she had counseled them out of their crisis. Robert and

Kay falling out of bed, only that time it wasn't funny. She had saved them, they said, saved their marriage.

"But eight months?" Kay's face contorted with pain and Helaine looked away.

"Isn't there anyone? Someone you could at least, uh, you know?" Robert poured her another glass of wine as he spoke. "You know what I mean?"

A dark-haired stranger. Helaine stared into her wine. "You know," she began, "I like it better when we don't talk about this."

Naturally. They knew that.

"Might there be someone?" Kay asked, hopefully. "Is there, Helaine?"

"No."

"No?"

"Of course not."

They knew she wasn't lying.

"That's ridiculous, Doctor." Robert never liked Sharon.

"Robert—" But neither did Kay.

"Read the last chapter, Helaine. You wrote it."

"Robert . . . you're ruining the evening," Kay warned.

Helaine clenched her teeth biting the inside of her mouth and the tip of her tongue—ouch!—the glass fell from her hand. They watched as it came down awkwardly to the table, teetered on its base and then set itself right again without spilling a drop.

It was possibly a good sign Robert and Kay were thinking. Not a drop!

Not a drop, thought Helaine. What a bad sign.

"So then throw it," Robert said.

"Ooh, throw it, Helaine. You know you want to."

"Seriously?" An old college game. Lots of broken glass. They nodded enthusiastically. Why not? "Where do you want it?" She picked the goblet up by its stem and rose from the table, gripping the back of her chair.

"There," Robert pointed.

Kay cheered her decision. This was more like Helaine. "You're lying you know?" she said as she moved away from the table.

"There," Robert repeated.

Helaine eyed the spot and glanced at Kay. "About what?"

"Against the wall," Robert ordered excitedly. "Throw it, Helaine."

"That there's no one else," Kay pursued.

Helaine laughed, trying to dodge her. Well, there is no one else. "You're sure?" she asked, preparing to throw a curve.

Robert nodded, grinning in anticipation.

"I'm sure," Kay said.

Against the wall. "You'll have to clean up after me, Robert. I hate a mess."

"We'll clean up, Helaine. Throw it."

It was their glass. It was their wall. It smashed against the whitewashed brick, a shower of glass and burgundy red settling in little gleaming puddles on the hardwood floor. What do you see, she asked herself as she took in the red-spattered wall like an ink blot. Robert and Kay cheered themselves on like the old days. What did she see? The wine trickled along the edge of the bricks on its way down the wall. Something incriminating, she suddenly thought, stepping up to it. Something sinister. The bright shards of glass glittered forbiddingly at her feet, bloodied. She saw a menacing shape on the wall, a pile of bloody diamonds on the floor.

"Helaine?" Kay said, noticing her pallor. "You're so pale. Sit down."

She took a deep breath. "Too much excitement for this old gal," Helaine offered. "Will you call me a cab, Robert? I'd better go home or we'll be drinking from paper cups next time."

He left the room. Kay scrutinized her as she primped in the mirror.

"Maybe you're pushing yourself too hard. A little fun, you know?"

"I know," she answered. She did look pale. She turned and smiled one of her emptiest smiles. "There is no one, Kay. I'm sorry. There just isn't."

"How did you like it, Jon?" An evening with an old flame.

"It's really just a lot of screaming to me. All those conflicting emotions!" He smiled wryly, tapping his knife on the salad plate. He hated opera.

"It's like that sometimes. The microphones, I think. No star power."

"Star power. A must, heh?"

She avoided that. "It really doesn't hurt sometimes."

"I wouldn't know, Helaine. I'll wait till I hear it from you."

She fixed her gaze on his forehead. "Well, thanks for coming anyway."

"Would you have gone alone if I said no, Helaine?"

She thought to spare him but was too tired. "Yes, probably."

He leaned across the table. "Then thanks for asking me," he said. He reached with his leg under the tablecloth and she pulled hers away. "Come back to my place and seduce me, Helaine."

She gave a throaty laugh at his dare. "I wouldn't want to make a fool of myself."

"Okay." He resumed his tapping. "That bad?" Dr. Jon said. She regretted the direction of the conversation. It was too late to change it. "That bad, Helaine? Can't have a little fun with an old friend?"

He had gotten old. Around the eyes. She smiled. "Am I too oppressive, Jon?"

He plunged his fork into a tomato. "Hardly!"

"Okay." He was qualified to say so. She waited for the rest of his opinion.

"That's your problem, Helaine. You're willing to give too much space." He diverted his eyes when he said this.

"Oh?" She smiled weakly. "Is that what it is?"

He was sorry he mentioned it. "Yes," was all he managed then. He could feel her foot tapping against the table leg and he squirmed around in his chair to search for the waitress.

Too much space, wasn't that interesting? "But, Jon . . ." she completely despised the discussion, "you asked for more space." She had his attention once more. So now they were stuck with the subject.

More space. Yes, he had. "But I didn't expect you to give it to me, Helaine."

Mmmm. She saw him smile sheepishly at his confession. There was something charming about it, albeit sad. "You have such a strange way of complimenting me," she finally said. She would have liked to wring his neck and did her best to hide the notion from him.

He was relieved to have gotten away with it. "Some of us want our lovers to put up a fight, dear. I would have thought by now you would have tried that."

He was implicating her again. Love and war. She never believed in it and he knew that.

"I doubt it's what Sharon's asking for," she said at last. "I truly doubt it."

"You never know," he said, "seems pretty classic."

Gothic really, Helaine thought then. Bad opera. Maybe there's too much romance, too many little self-helpers, lonely hearts and talking heads. Dr. Jon and Dr. Helaine. We're all making a pretty good living at it with our hypocritical oaths and half-truths, our little confidences. Helping? Maybe. But was anyone being saved? She would have liked to know that for sure. Was it right to profit from this brand new religion? She eyed Dr. Jon. He seemed pretty content. Obviously he didn't feel it was a grim reaping.

"Then what would Dr. Jon advise a sorry ass like myself to do?" The food arrived as a form of salvation, but she was committed to an answer. "In your own words not mine," she added slyly.

They laughed, uncomfortable with their new positions.

"Well, you broke all the rules when you first asked out the 'tall, dark, handsome'," he said serving up her words anyway.

"Ugh. So I'm hopeless?"

He jabbed at his food absently. "No, I couldn't say that. But it may prove difficult to establish your boundaries now."

She smirked at that. "I have no boundaries. Remember?"

"That's right," he said, grinning and swallowing more than he could chew. "I'd get free of her then."

"Not 'work it out'?" she said, this time eating her own words.

He shrugged. "What's to work out, Helaine? Sharon wants everything and you give it to her. Does she even know what you want?"

She does. "Yes, she knows what I want."

He chewed pensively. "Well, has she ever promised to provide it for you?"

He was pretty good. Helaine looked out the window at nothing in particular. "All the time," she answered without turning her head.

Jon fell silent. He blew air through his nose. "Then you're a hopeless case."

They laughed at the diagnosis.

"Good enough. Let's change the subject, Jon."

"A fine idea. You want to talk about my love life instead?"

(No, not really.) "Okay. And how is your young wife?"

"*Ex*-wife, please." He smiled pleasantly at her, knowing he had it coming.

"Ex. That's what I meant," was all she said about it. She let him go on.

"*Ex*pensive." He sighed, laying his silverware on the plate and casting her his puppy dog eyes. "Very expensive."

"You should have taken my advice." She emitted a quick laugh, but he scarcely smiled in return. She regretted saying it, afraid of his expression.

"Really? But, my love, you never said a word about it. Not one word. In fact, you acted as if you didn't mind at all."

Is that right? It sounded sort of like her. She offered a thin smile back to him. It was over with, what difference does it make anyway? She pursed her lips, looking through him. Didn't mind? How could anyone have come to that conclusion? She raised her arm to signal the waitress, speaking in a constricted voice as she did.

"Well, Jon, you only told me you needed more space. You never said you intended to marry her." The waitress arrived. She faced her. "Water, please."

"That would have made a difference, Helaine?" He had revived, seemed to be enjoying this part of the discussion. "You would have fought then, Helaine?"

Fight, oh brother. Her lovers always seemed to be after more than love. The waitress came back with the water and she gulped it. She was thankful Jon was not her lover anymore and set her glass down with relief. "I only bring it up now because you asked." She smiled sweetly hoping to end it there.

"Flatter me, darling," Jon pressed, "tell me that you minded." His eyes twinkled at her discomfort.

She ignored him and pushed her food around awhile. A half an hour later he asked her again, the corners of his mouth turning up as he pursued her answer. Helaine chuckled nervously.

The waitress came back with the bill and they split it. She heard Helaine whisper through her teeth, "If you hadn't been lying, Jon, then you would have known the truth," but the girl wasn't quite sure what it meant. The man only grinned at the blond. He looked like a cat with a mouse.

After the waitress left the table Helaine extricated herself from the sticky conversation. "I don't mind anymore, Jon. Can you be satisfied with that?"

He drove her home and held her at the door. He had been an affectionate lover and had wasted himself on a gold digger. She wondered if she couldn't let him in.

"She is a disease," he whispered into her hair, "highly infectious." She let him caress her hips without commenting. He had hands as soft as a woman's. "You're safer in a leper colony." He kissed her neck. Lips as soft as a woman's.

"I don't want to discuss this," Helaine said. She toyed with the idea of letting him come in. "Seduce me, Jon."

Her perfume was intoxicating. "What are you wearing?"

She tried to remember. "Obsession, I think."

He laughed and held her at the waist, abandoning his plan. "I wouldn't want to embarrass you, Helaine."

Obsession. She saw the humor in it and though the idea had left her now she let him kiss her mouth, press into her body.

He was excited. "Ask me again." But she didn't. It was as hopeless as he had said. "I'll sing at your funeral," he taunted, leaving her at the unopened door.

"Hah!" She watched him drive away. Above her there was no moon at all.

None of her friends knew about the waterfront flat, only that she had once lived there, but not that she still kept the lease on it or that she had furnished it for Sharon, to Sharon's liking, to be used as a home for the wayward companion.

Helaine stood in the dark of it on a Saturday evening, once again breaking her promise to not go there. My friends might be right, she thought. I am terminal. She flicked on the lights.

It looked the same as the last time, Sharon's clothes strewn about it like flotsam after a shipwreck and as usual the girl had neglected to make arrangements for the place to be cleaned in her absence.

Helaine clung to the door and sighed. She had wanted to cry for days and now she did. It was nothing but a flophouse, the once beautiful waterfront flat with its spectacular views. She had redecorated it for Sharon, but this is how the creature really liked it. An absolute wasteland. She made her way to the couch. She didn't know why she bothered to keep the place. For a lover who was never there?

"I don't really live anywhere," Sharon had told her over dinner, when they first met. "I have lots of friends and I work for months at a time."

She modeled. That explained it.

"Then how can I get in touch with you again?"

"I'll call you," Sharon said coyly.

Helaine gave the girl her number. "When?"

"When would you like me to, Helaine?"

Helaine had hesitated. She didn't know why. "Anytime," she finally replied. It was her first mistake.

Sharon grinned fabulously, pleased with herself. "I have to go now. I'm late for an appointment."

"You work nights, too?"

Sharon slipped on her coat. "Sometimes." And then she was gone. Helaine paid the tab.

Sharon called late that very evening. "I was thinking of you," she purred.

She had roused the doctor from her sleep, out of her senses. "Ah. And what were you thinking about?" Helaine foolishly asked. She listened, moved and captivated by the speaker on the other end of her line, recklessly flirting with her, slipping under the spell of an obscene call and the power of all those suggestions. When the girl asked to come over Helaine drew in her air and said yes. Rules are made to be broken. Her second mistake.

Sharon came quickly, pleasured quickly, and left quickly. Record timing. "When will I see you again?" asked a tousled blond already in over her head.

"When do you want to see me?"

"Now. Stay for the night."

Sharon smiled provocatively. But it wasn't going to be that easy.

"I'm sorry," she purred again, "I can't, Helaine. I'll be back."

"When?"

"Soon," Sharon answered, pulling on her hose, buttoning her dress and admiring herself in the mirror as she put on her lipstick. She turned to face Helaine. "Soon," she repeated, stepping into her heels ready to start walking, wearing a satisfied expression.

"Tomorrow night?"

Sharon's eyes narrowed with calculation. She sat down beside her and stroked her breasts until the nipples went erect, holding them in her mouth, leaving them covered with her lipstick. "Pretty name. Helaine Kristenson."

"Thank you. Tomorrow?"

Tomorrow. Sharon leaned against the blond and closed her eyes, her hands teasing, traveling her creamy flesh, her tongue tempting the moist mouth, licking her lips. She felt long legs drawing her in. They might never refuse her, she suddenly realized, letting them enfold her, lying between them once more. The blond sighed and Sharon took a quick breath. She was quite a catch, she told herself. She heard the woman breathing excitedly, swaying gently beneath her and she wanted to make her come again. The mouth, the lips, the tongue requested it of her. She felt between her legs and was stricken by the sound of the woman's low cry, her urgent whispers. Her breath tickled her insides, moving them in ripples of excitement, with a bang bigger and better than cocaine. Oh, when she moaned like that—it felt just like falling! Falling? She pinned the blond to the bed and quickly entered her again. It was no big deal to tell the doctor she thought she might be in love with her. She could take it back tomorrow. She opened her mouth to speak but the clock beside the bed informed her she was late for her date and saved her from it. The blond would therefore never know this.

"No," Sharon stated when she had finished. "Not tomorrow." And then she left.

All Helaine ever knew after that was that her arms were always empty.

The beautiful waterfront flat, when it was her place, before Sharon moved in, when it was not yet haunted by anything. She wept recalling it and fell asleep.

The next morning she cleaned the hellhole, from time to time stopping in her labors to wonder over a miscellaneous tie or a checkered cotton button-down, a man's sock, tie clip, the like. No accounting for the hosiery. She threw them all in the trash where they belonged and tried not to bother herself about it. It was quite a way to stay on top, Sharon Chambers!

Now, alone in the newly clean space, Helaine weighed the possibility that she might be punishing herself. In the mirror she saw the puffy eyes, the creases which every year became more and more important to her features. They were unhappy lines. Picking up after a messy lover, accepting sloppy seconds, thirds, fourths. Who kept count? Feeling trashed all the time. Perhaps she was too old at last. Grays were hiding amongst the blond. She left them alone.

She had only vaguely considered it before. The age difference. Over a decade. All their differences. She picked up the phone and called a cab. It was not a relationship. It had not become one. It was a series of episodes, but not a relationship. Episodes. Some breathtaking, others, many others, just too shabby to dwell on. A relationship to some, but not the one Helaine had hoped for, not the one that had been promised, not the one which she felt entitled to have by now. It had all gone into free fall. She heard the cab honking below and locked the door behind her.

The "heart specialist." The "Love Doc." That's what the public called Doctor Kristenson. She didn't need her practice anymore. She could live off reprints and royalties and lecture fees if she wanted to. Or write another book. There were offers for that, as well.

But everything she practiced and preached had gone into *Keeping Mr. Right*. So far nothing new could be added. Besides, there might come the day when the book would fall from the best seller list. There would still be her private practice should that happen.

Rainy days. She was always prepared for them. She had worked hard and enjoyed doing it, but maybe Kay was right. Maybe she had pushed herself too hard. Six days a week since . . . oh . . . forever. She was tired.

And in a certain sense the book she authored made her feel like a hypocrite now. Now that she had reached the chasm of forty. Midlife, the hormonal peak and she hadn't had sex in months. Who knew when Sharon might get around to it? A great abyss spread before her and it grew wider by the day. The great abyss, at the bottom of it the bracken pool of her love life. She had written the bible on this. Take your time. Work it out. Fidelity. Mutual respect. What a hypocrite! And she was always eating her own words over it. That didn't help to restore her either.

How is it possible to be an expert and still end up with the same big nothing that drove others to seek her advice? Shouldn't she be prefacing everything she said these days with an I-dunno-but?

Or was it worse than that? After all, she did help her clients. At least fifty percent of them saved their relationships. Fifty percent wasn't bad. Could it be that she didn't practice what she preached? Was she in denial? Was she too laissez-faire about her own needs?

The final chapter, putting your lover on notice. Hadn't she done that the last time? Sharon had been gone then five months without a word and had slithered back to the waterfront without calling her. Helaine had discovered her there on one of her midnight searches.

"Why didn't you let me know?"

"I was going to. I just got here."

The flat was already in shambles and Helaine realized it had taken more than a few hours to accomplish that. But no, she had not pursued it with her. No, she remembered that she hadn't. Instead she had struggled not to cry in frustration.

"Five months, Sharon?" Her voice was squeezed tight. "Why? Why didn't you call? Or write?"

"Helaine . . . I was working." Sharon paced around her. "I have to work harder than the younger ones. My career is on borrowed time."

Oh, we're on that again, Helaine thought. Once more she had bit her lip. Wasn't it right at that point she had warned her, put her on notice? "But five months Sharon? Who would wait for you that long? Without a word?"

She would. Even longer.

They locked eyes.

"You would. Even longer."

She didn't respond. Helaine watched Sharon stripping off her clothes.

"How badly did you miss me, Dr. Kristenson?"

There was a bruise on the perfect skin, on the back of the arm. It worried Helaine and she forgot to be angry. She relinquished her position, let the naked woman lead her by the arm to the bedroom. "Are you all right?" she asked, fingering the bruise, her clothes coming undone, falling to the floor like autumn leaves.

"I fell, that's all. Some of these shoes." She licked at Helaine's throat. "If men had to wear them we'd all be running around in really sexy high-tops."

A joke? Sharon had made her laugh. She didn't believe her though. The model was too graceful to trip and it would have been newsworthy if she had. "That's a pretty nasty fall." She kissed it gingerly. "Does it hurt?"

Sharon flipped Helaine onto her stomach. "No," she whispered into the blond hair. "Where does it hurt you, doctor?"

Helaine spread her legs and Sharon quickly satisfied her from behind. Nothing of substance was discussed after that. Oh, that's right.

Dr. Kristenson sat in her office, the blinds drawn, thinking, thinking, thinking. It wouldn't be against the rules to grab a bite to eat on a Friday evening. It wouldn't be against the rules to have dinner at Frank's Place.

"She's back?" Robert asked as he set the table.

"No. Why would you think that?"

"I can usually tell, Helaine. You get that look."

He got the girl. The one at Frank's Place. Helaine knew it by the desperate look in her blue eyes. Desperate because he was already playing hard to keep. She smiled grimly. "Oh? What look is that?"

"You know. The one Caesar had." The silver clattered beside the plates. "When he said eh you brute."

"Hah!" She wished her well, hoped she'd survive her mistake.

"You know what happened to him, Helaine?"

"Please. You tell me, Robert."

"He died."

"Very funny," interrupted Kay. "You forgot the knives, Robert."

"What makes you think I forgot them?" he said with an affected voice.

They laughed as he headed for the kitchen.

"How is work?" Kay inquired as she counted the place settings. "Robert, you forgot a plate, too!"

"The same. Always the same. You wouldn't believe the *lies* that people lead, Kay." She circled the table, absently pulling at the backs of the chairs and pushing them in again.

"You're so lucky to hear them, though. It must be great fun keeping all those secrets."

Helaine agreed. "I love my work."

"Did I hear Sharon's back?"

"No."

"I invited Jon," Kay said. "I didn't think you'd mind."

The phone rang in the kitchen.

"He's been very depressed lately," she added. "She gets almost half of what he makes, you know."

Helaine nodded. She knew.

"And I think he's unhappy with his work, too."

Well, that's because he's a liar, Helaine thought. "I'll talk to him, Kay."

"I guess it's all the more reason not to get married," Kay said wistfully.

"Or to stay that way if you are," Helaine responded.

"I guess that's right, too. Robert! We need another plate!"

"Two more," he announced as he entered the dining room. He added the extra plates and silverware.

"Who else?" Kay asked.

"Anna called. She changed her mind when she heard you came alone, Helaine." He was amused by her expression.

"Anna?" Helaine repeated, raising her brows inquisitively.

"Yes. Anna."

"But Robert, that makes thirteen!" Kay complained. She didn't like him meddling and doubted his strategy.

Helaine took the news in stride and smiled graciously. "Well, that's nice. I haven't seen Anna in years."

"I know. That does make thirteen, doesn't it?"

"It's like the last supper, honey," Kay worried.

"Uh-oh." He wore an especially irreverent grin. "You know what happened to him, don't you?"

"You're going to hell, Bob," Kay reproached with a smirk.

The doorbell rang and he headed in that direction. "But you can call me, Robert," he said, over his shoulder.

They watched expectantly.

"It's God, Kay, and he's really hungry!"

"She!" the ladies corrected in unison.

"Ugh!" he replied, yanking at the door, "can you imagine?"

"Happy Birthday!" came voices from the hall.

"Welcome to the resurrection!" he shouted back. "Shall I hold your coats?"

"He loves these occasions," Kay said. "We're one knife short!"

"I'll get it," Helaine offered. She heard him introducing her as Dr. Kristenson and it was a good excuse to hide in the kitchen.

"This is Joan and Michael," he called out after her. "And that *was* Dr. Kristenson," he said turning to the young couple. They laughed identically, already.

"Please," Helaine said, returning, "call me Helaine." So they did. Kay called for her from the living room and she excused herself.

"That is Dr. Kristenson?"

"That's her!" replied Robert.

The door again.

Kay and Helaine had rounded up more chairs. "Get the door, Robert," said Kay between breaths.

"Okay. Get the wine, then."

A buzzer went off in the kitchen.

"I think the meat's done, Kay!"

"We've both read your book, Dr. Kristenson." Another couple, middle twenties, newlyweds. "Please call me, Helaine." There was Jon. He didn't seem too depressed. "Excuse me," she said with a pleasant smile which Jon thought was meant for him. "Kay," she said, "I think you should check the meat. The buzzer went off." The doorbell rang. "Kay," Robert called, "did you check the meat?" Kay was pouring the wine. "It's not done yet. Can you get the door?" "White or red, Helaine?" Robert went to the door. "There's dark beer in the kitchen, Jon." Jon headed for the kitchen. "Red," someone answered behind her. "White, Kay." A couple more couples. "Guess who's here," Kay quizzed as she poured a glass of red for Helaine. "Hello, Helaine . . ." The world's most impossibly sexy voice. Helaine knew it anywhere. The door again. She felt a hand touch her elbow. "Excuse me," she said to the newest couple. She couldn't remember their names. "Hello, Anna," she said, wishing this wasn't happening, "you're looking quite well," she added. Anna smiled, "you look wonderful, Helaine." "I can't find any beer," Jon complained. "Oh, wonderful," Kay replied, "ask Robert where he put it." "Wonderful?" Helaine repeated, "I haven't heard that in a long time." She reached out to stop Kay. "I think there's beer in the crisper, Kay." Kay nodded. "In the crisper, Jon," Robert shouted over his shoulder. "Happy Birthday!" "Gee, I didn't think to look there." Helaine laughed nervously and sidestepped Anna, off to the kitchen again. Kay cracked open the oven and the room filled with the smell of lamb. "Mmmmm," said Robert, "did you see Anna?" "Mmmmm," said Jon as he cracked open a beer. "Mmmmm. Yes, I saw Anna," Helaine answered. Jon shot her a glance and she ignored it. "God, you look wonderful," he said. She smiled gratefully. That's twice tonight. She should go while she's still ahead? "Thank you." "Helaine, can you help me with the oven?" She didn't want to get burned and hesitated. "I'll do it," Jon volunteered. "You know Stan, don't you Helaine?" Robert reintroduced the hush-it-up attorney. "Yes, of course, we've met." She held out her hand and he took it. "It's nice to see you again, Doctor." "Please, call me Helaine." He nodded politely. "I see you're doing very well with your book." She reclaimed her hand with a smile. "I've been very, very lucky," she replied. "Indeed," he said in return. "Excuse me," she heard herself saying again. It was too hot in the kitchen. "Beer or wine, Stan?" "There's dark beer in the crisper," said Jon. "Beer," she heard Stan decide as she left the kitchen. She passed through the crowded dining room into the empty living room and took a deep breath of the quiet. "You're back." She was not alone. "Anna?" She was tired and hungry, a little drunk. Not up to this right now. "Where's your cover girl?" Anna asked. Helaine sighed wearily. "I don't know. Have you seen her?" she replied. She really didn't know where the woman was. Anna laughed. "Actually, I did," she said, setting her glass down. "In a recent centerfold." Her hand rested on Helaine's shoulder. "Is that right?" Helaine answered. She wanted to beg out of this one. "How was she?" she retorted. Anna felt her slipping away and tugged at her sleeve. "I wouldn't know that." Helaine felt caught and blamed Robert for it. She attempted to laugh the woman off. Anna kissed her. "What are you after, Anna?" she asked, casting a glance toward the dining room. "Why don't you return my calls, Helaine?" Helaine exhaled. Impossibly sexy. Impossibly stupid question. "Because I wasn't sure what you wanted," she lied. Stupid answer. Anna grinned and leaned close to whisper what she wanted. Helaine cleared her throat and stepped back. "Is there anyone else?" Kay shouted to Robert. "No. Everyone's here, Kay. Put the food out." Helaine was starving and thankful for a reason to leave the room. "No, Anna, I can't." She made to leave. "Couldn't hurt," Anna teased. "Just for fun?" The food was being served. Fun. "I'm sorry, Anna. I couldn't." She left the living room and took her seat at the table, dismissing the proposition out of hand.

"Happy birthday, Robert. Thank you, Kay. I had a wonderful time."
"Goodnight, Helaine."
"Don't forget dinner, Friday."
"That's right, Kay."
"You pick the restaurant," Robert prompted. "Surprise us."
"Okay. Friday. Goodnight."

* * *

Only a woman knows what it takes to be a man.

There are a lot of theories about her client's type of problem. Complex ideas that she can't agree with. The question as to whether he has a physical condition has been disposed of. He does not. What he does have, Dr. Kristenson has determined, is a very bad attitude. He is a brute and his wife is beginning to understand that. The idea that he prematurely ejaculates to deprive a woman of satisfaction is absurd. It would imply a self discipline that he simply doesn't own. She privately believes he is an unsophisticated savage with no self control whatsoever, that he has always had sex like that and he always will because he is an inconsiderate misogynist with the mentality of a thirteen-year-old boy.

His various efforts to "rehabilitate" himself through extramarital affairs, with prostitutes, herbal remedies, ancient rituals, vitamins, cock rings, visualization . . . and now the exhaustive psychotherapy sessions, have produced no positive gains, either for him or, more importantly, for his wife.

He's had a blast. His wife is almost suicidal. They have been through five therapists including Dr. Kristenson. No more sessions for these two.

"But I'm going to continue sessions with your wife," she assured the man. That didn't trouble him. He smiled like a buffoon. The wife welcomed private counseling as the doctor had suspected she would and she recommended Dr. Jon to the husband. Jon had been an everlasting kind of man. Perhaps at the very least he could give the guy a couple of pointers. She didn't say any of that, of course. She simply handed him his card and concluded the tedious Friday session.

She sat for a moment after they had left. Beyond the closed blinds of the quiet office she knew a woman stared out at the horizon. She could practically feel her there. Sadder probably then she was ever meant to be. Helaine could not stop thinking about her. Even working with blindfolds hadn't helped.

She was alarmed by how much she looked forward to dinner with Robert and Kay at Frank's Place tonight. All just to peek at something she knew she couldn't have. She couldn't believe how jittery she felt inside! The gloom that had been left from the last appointment shed from her like an old skin and as she freshened her makeup in the waiting room mirror she thought she saw a familiar glint in her eye. Ah! She laughed at herself then. This was the harmless part of an infatuation. She promised, as she locked up the offices, to keep it that way. She rode the elevator down to the street and aimed herself for Frank's Place.

"I like it! Like Casablanca in here," Robert declared.

They had been waiting for her. "Sorry I'm so late."

"Roll out the barrel," he said, "great place. Does everyone have a gun?"

She laughed.

"No," said Kay, "they're just really happy to see you, Robert."

It was raucous tonight. "Overjoyed," Helaine added with a wink.

"Better keep an eye on those rubber tree plants, Robert," Kay teased. "They're moving."

"Rubber tree plants? You're kidding? Where?"

"Against the wall," Kay pointed with a chuckle.

They all shifted in their chairs.

"Oh yeah. Very nice," he said. "That one has eyes for you, Helaine."

"Which one?" Kay asked.

"There."

It was the blue-eyed woman.

"Which one?" Kay asked again. "I can't see without my glasses."

Helaine groaned as Robert pointed conspicuously.

"The pretty one with dark hair."

"Robert, please . . ."

"Classy. Do you know her, Helaine?"

Helaine hid in the menu. "Of course not. I don't know anybody here. That's why I like it. Please leave the poor woman be, Robert."

They laughed at themselves. They were still a bad influence on each other. The waiter brought a bottle of rosé and they ordered dinner.

"Why were you late, Helaine?"

"Oh, just a problem case."

"There's a lot of those," Kay said.

Robert nodded. "Yep. That's what the courts are for." He gulped his wine. "To get at the truth, if it can be got at. To throw justice at the infidels."

Helaine chuckled. "Like Christians to the lions, eh?" That woman was indeed watching them. How nice!

"Well, but only if they're lying!" He was pleased with that one.

"You two are so clever, a couple of cynics." Kay mocked. "You know her Helaine? She's lovely."

Helaine shook her head. "I thought you can't see?"

"I can see she's a professional of some kind. Smart."

"Who?"

"The dark-haired woman over there."

"Are you being obvious enough?" Helaine laughed. "I don't think you're being obvious enough."

"Nah," said Robert twisting his neck. "We're like you. Discreet."

"Yah!"

"You'll scare her away, Kay," he teased.

Kay had her reading glasses on. Helaine pretended to not be there with them. They were unpredictable goofs sometimes. She grinned at their reflection in the window. Their bobbing heads.

"No. That one doesn't scare easily. Look how she holds her head. A real queen," Kay declared. "She's definitely staring at you, Helaine."

Is that right? Helaine shot a glance toward her. Didn't scare easily? "Nonsense, Kay. Everybody looks at everybody here. If I had a dollar for every look I got at this table I'd be rich."

"You're already rich," piped in Robert. "So you've seen her before?"

The salads came to the rescue. "You can't be too rich, they say."

"Or too thin," he replied. "Eat. I'm wasting away."

"Me too," Helaine said, with a mouth full.

Plink. Plank. Plink.

Helaine fingered the keys of her baby grand, one hand wandering peripatetic across the black and white . . . *all . . . or noth . . . ing . . . at . . . all . . .* the other holding her head up . . . *half . . . a . . . love . . . never . . . appealed . . . to . . . me . . . if your heart . . . never . . . could . . . yield to . . .* as she sat slumped on the bench against the piano.

She rarely got the chance to play anymore. She knew the song though it didn't sound it. She was lost in her journey . . . *than I'd . . . rather . . . have*

. . . unaware that the tune was escaping from her . . . *nothing at all* . . . it had been in her head for weeks.

Must have heard it at Frank's Place.

After an eternity of foreplay Sharon still wouldn't penetrate her and Helaine's womb had begun to hurt from aching for it. The excitement in her chest had turned against her, too, and she felt a sadness there instead, a desire to weep. She sighed miserably into her lover's neck and upon hearing it Sharon stopped what she was doing, rested her weight on Helaine so she couldn't get up from the bed.

"Don't want to play, Doctor?"

"Sharon . . ." Helaine let go of her back and tried to slide out from underneath her, but Sharon went rigid and wouldn't permit it. "Sharon, please," she said in frustration. Her breasts were tender and the weight on them was unpleasant. She shifted her body to throw her off and Sharon grabbed her by the wrists and pinned her to the pillow. She tongued her stomach, pushing hard into the belly button and Helaine arched her back and sighed again.

"Make love to me, Sharon," she urged. She felt her biting at her nipples again and defensively jerked them away from her mouth. "Don't. Just make love to me."

"I hate that word," Sharon warned, biting at her neck.

"Don't do this. Why are you doing this?" Teasing, teasing. She groaned in exasperation. "Make love to me, Sharon."

Sharon laughed into the pillow. "That word. You know—"

That's right. Forgot. It had been so long. "Then fuck me—fuck me, if that's what you like."

Sharon let her wrists go. "Like? What I like?"

"Like. Want. I don't know," Helaine murmured, rolling onto her stomach. "Whatever."

Every part of her ached. She lay still, thoughts churning, searching for something better to say. Nothing came to mind. Between her legs she was quite swollen. She closed her eyes tight. The brilliant lights. She wanted them off now. Perhaps she could sleep, sleep away the fog that had settled on her soul tonight. Beside her Sharon had fallen ungodly quiet. She could feel the woman's malice and wasn't sure where it had come from. Tonight was bad. It was as if she had been watching herself all evening. Nothing seemed natural. She put her hand over her eyes. She hated being speechless.

"How long have I been gone, Helaine?"

"Sharon?"

It had been nine months. Helaine desperately needed sex. Playing games all night had made it an impossibility, too awkward. The woman beside her felt like a stranger, an immovable stranger in her bed, laying motionless and hostile. Why, she didn't know. "Sharon? What is wrong?"

No response. Perhaps because she hadn't gone to the flat to look for her? Sharon hated coming uptown. Not her set. Too quiet. "Sharon?" She listened to the sound of Sharon's body snaking across the sheets toward her. The touch of a stranger. She jumped at the feel of it and waited for her to speak, trying to interpret her silence.

"Masturbate for me," Sharon finally said, lying heavy on Helaine's back and probing along her sides.

Helaine tried to turn over. "Sharon . . . no." A police hold, or something like it. "Don't be rough with me. I don't like it."

"Don't? How long have I been gone, I asked."

"Shar—" Harsh hands. "Nine months."

"Like? Want?" She pushed Helaine's face into the pillow. "*Whatever?*"

"Sharon, you're hurting me. I can't breathe."

"*Love,*" Sharon teased as she leaned into her, "masturbate for me, I said."

"Sharon . . ."

"Or else."

"I don't like this. I really don't."

Sharon felt between Helaine's legs. "Liar."

Helaine brought her legs together. It was difficult to breathe.

"Call me darling. You haven't—open your legs—called me darling all night."

Darling? Was that true? All night? Helaine lay quiet and still.

"Against your will then, Doctor. What do you say to that?"

Darling all night. "I would never forgive you for it."

Sharon attempted to pry her legs apart. "Open, *darling*," she whispered, jabbing her chin into Helaine's shoulder blade.

"If you don't want to you don't have to. Leave me be, Sharon."

"That would be *darling*, Dr. Kristenson."

Helaine felt her legs giving. "Please . . . I said forget it."

"Spread your legs for me."

"Listen to—"

"Do it."

"Sharon, I don't—" her legs were open now.

The women lay locked in an ugly silence.

Helaine could hear her Sharon's rapid breathing. Hot breath on her back. "Sharon?" She strained to see her, but couldn't maneuver it. Sharon pressed down harder. "For God's sake, Sharon," she said through her teeth. "Let me go!"

Sharon released her arms. Helaine tried propping herself up on her elbows and was pushed down again. She listened behind her. "Darling . . . ?" There she said it. The sound of breathing, more weight on her back. "Talk to me, Sharon. Tell me what I've done."

"I don't want to talk. I'm concentrating."

"Concentrating? Please! On what?"

"Fucking you."

Helaine took a quick breath, exhaled. "Then at least let me turn over." More weight. She laid her face back into the pillow.

"You have such a perfect ass, Dr. Kristenson."

Sharon fondled her, running her hand up her sex. Helaine felt moist on her backside.

"The nicest I've had in months," Sharon drawled, feeling Helaine's body stiffen at the offense. She pushed against her anus.

"Sha—"

"You heard about all that, didn't you?"

Helaine tried once more to get up and failed.

"Easy," Sharon warned, tightening her grip.

Helaine froze.

"Perfect, Helaine Kristenson." She licked the small of her back and entered her in the rectum.

Helaine gasped and tried to fight her off.

Sharon withdrew and held her down again.

"Sharon, don't do this to me. *Please*."

"We'll just take a little ride, Helaine." She dragged the blond kicking across the bed and bent her over the edge of it.

They were both out of breath, the sheets massed around them.

"You're ruining me, you know? I can only do blonds now."

Ruined. Helaine was silent, her hair sticking to her neck and shoulders, stuck to her face. She tried to raise herself. Sharon leaned against her damp body and entered her once more. She stifled a scream.

"Where are you when I'm not fucking you, Dr. Kristenson?"

"I'm . . . this is . . . I'm—" Sharon had been hostile ever since she stepped through the door. Helaine tightened. "I'm not ready for th—"

"Because you're too tense. Relax, Doctor."

A flash of pain. Helaine groaned. "You're being too—" Sharon pushed deeper inside and Helaine moaned low in distress.

"When I'm not fucking your gorgeous ass, Helaine, where do you go?"

There was nothing to grab onto. It was pointless to answer. Sharon pushed into her and pulled out suddenly. In, then out again. Helaine put her hand over her eyes. They were wet.

"Relax your legs for me."

"Christ—" her feet barely touched the floor. She grabbed for the sides of the bed but couldn't reach them.

"Chill, I said."

Her arms were falling asleep. "Give me . . . a second. I'm—" her rectum felt full. She felt it begin to move in spasms. Pleasure for the first time in months. She hated herself for it. Sharon pressed against her stomach with her free hand and raised her up slightly from the bed. She clutched at the sheets around her in protest.

"Did I keep you waiting, Doctor?"

"Wait—"

"Did I?"

Helaine's insides rippled in waves, giving out without her consent. "What—what do you mean?"

"Waiting for me. I kept you waiting?"

"Waiting," she repeated. "I—" spasms. Pleasure and pain. "Yes." And hatred, coming in waves. Tidal. She couldn't prevent it. "*Jesus* . . ." Cries filled her throat, slipping off her tongue and falling from her lips into the bed sheets. She put her face into the pillow to smother them. Moans, sighs, cries, Sharon's favorite. She hadn't earned them tonight. "You're hur—"

"Then relax for me."

The pillow was wet. "I . . . slower . . . can't."

"Call me darling then."

"Slower. Slower then . . . *darling*."

Slower. Helaine relaxed her legs. Slow. She clamped her hand over her mouth. Slow, slow, slow, slow, slow, slow, slow, slow.

"*Love*," Sharon whispered. "God, I missed you."

Pleasure. Nine months. Helaine moaned.

"Ahh . . . you're a slut, Dr. Kristenson," Sharon murmured, kissing her shoulders and neck. "Do it for me. Masturbate."

Helaine shook her head.

"Pretend I'm someone else."

She would not. "Let go of me, Sharon."

"Never. Did you miss me?"

Her legs were closing once more. They were forced open again.

"Want to hear some highlights from my trip, Dr. Kristenson?"

Helaine winced.

No reply. Sharon pushed deeper inside her. "Lift," she demanded.

"I . . . my feet."

Sharon inched her further down. "Bend, Helaine."

"I can't."

"There," Sharon urged, placing a pillow under her stomach. "Now bend."

"You're going to hurt me . . . ?"

"No. Bend for me. Put your knee here."

Helaine lifted her knee. Sharon pushed. "You didn't answer me."

"You're—why are you—"

"Say more, like you missed me. *More, darling*."

(NO.)

"More, Helaine. Then I'll be gentle."

"I'm—I'm . . . more."

"More, darling."

"Shar—"

Sharon dropped her weight. Pressure. Too much pressure.

"More, darling," Helaine finally whispered, "gentle."

"Gentle what?" Sharon nudged.

"Darling . . . *gentle*."

Slow. Gentle. More.

"Say it, Helaine."

Her legs ached. "What—more?" She regretted letting Sharon in tonight.

"Fuck me, say it."

Helaine buried her face into the sheets. Pain more than pleasure now. Sharon's face was close to her own. She turned away from it. "Fuck me," she muttered, clenching her fists.

"Italy. Beautiful country, Helaine."

Helaine sucked in sharply.

"Italy, dear doctor."

Pressure. Helaine cried out.

"Such a beautiful count—"

"Shar—"

"Warm. Affectionate blonds," Sharon teased, now stroking Helaine's sex.

Helaine let out an anguished sigh, a series of muffled sobs. Then silence. Sharon held her closer. "So fucking beautiful. Such a beautiful little—" she backed her body into hers. "You're so w—"

"Sharon, Jesus . . . please . . . please, don't talk to me anymore." Her arms and legs felt broken. She let them fall slack.

"Dr. Kristenson?"

Helaine pressed her mouth into her arm and made a sound in her throat.

"Beautiful," Sharon murmured into the blond hair. "Beautiful," she said again, removing her hand from Helaine's stomach and stroking between her own legs. "*Helaine*," she called softly.

When Sharon finally rolled off of her Helaine lay for a moment where she was left, no sound, no movement, then, nauseous and shivering, she crawled back to the center of the bed and lay there on her stomach, the sheets bunched at her sides and in her face. On the floor she could see her rumpled clothes, left where Sharon had dropped them. In a minute she would be able to stand again, she hoped, and she seriously considered getting dressed and leaving. Behind her she could sense Sharon hovering, but she didn't have the energy to face her. She felt her hands closing her legs together. She shut her eyes, hid her face in a dampened pillow and listened to her heart beating in her eardrums. It sounded like the ocean. The deep blue sea. Maybe she could sleep. Her sentiments were irreparable though she may not have known it yet. She hoped that Sharon wouldn't dare make love to her now. She throbbed with discomfort. Her clitoris hurt, the desire to be satisfied there completely gone. Maybe Sharon would leave instead.

Sharon sat down next to her, waiting for her to say something. Helaine lifted herself silently from the bed and stood beside it in a torpor, her color washed out by the harsh light of the room. She squinted. The goddamned lights. They always had to be on for this, she thought, avoiding eye contact. Spotlights for these few-and-far-between's, these . . . whatever's. Sharon slid to the edge of the bed, studying her, and Helaine turned from her view although from the corner of her eye she could still see her, watching, grinning indecently, waiting, Helaine was sure, to make her next move.

All these miserable games, Helaine thought, measuring the distance to the bathroom. Ten feet. She steadied herself and started walking.

Sharon stood up, her interest renewed. She left the bed and followed in after Helaine, washing her hands at the sink and then blocking the doorway while Helaine quietly examined her own reflection and avoided her gaze.

The air was thick with bad energy and the sight of the toppled blond in the mirror made Helaine feel fainter. She shuddered. There was something sinister about the red traces of lipstick around the woman's nipples. Disassociated from her, there seemed to be three women in the small bathroom and Helaine suddenly felt trapped and claustrophobic in there, ashamed of her own silence, threatened by the figure looming in the doorway.

"That was awful, Sharon. What in the world is the matter with you?"

Sharon shifted in agitation. She looked poisonous but said nothing.

"Are you this rough with—"

"Oh, c'mon. Who the fuck is it, Helaine?"

"Who is—"

"Don't give me that shit. Who the fuck is it?"

Helaine was still dazed and it took her a moment to fully understand. She stood dumbfounded. How ridiculous she felt. An image darted into her mind and feeling scandalized by the suggestion she put it out hurriedly while the specter of a double standard glared at her from the doorway.

"Sharon," she said incredulously, "you must be joking."

Sharon scoffed. "No, I don't joke, Helaine. Is it a man or a woman?"

"A—Why would you think that?" Helaine was eager to get dressed again. She eyed Sharon anxiously. "You know me better than that."

"Two hours, Helaine? Two hours before asking me to fuck you?"

Helaine attempted to pass through the doorway without commenting, but Sharon stopped her with her arm. She distrusted her now, stepped backward. "Why should I have to ask you, Sharon? Why do I need to?"

Sharon smiled a ruthless grin. "Because I like it that way."

"You like it that way? Watching the clock for two hours and . . . ?" Helaine felt vulnerable in the doorway. Sharon grabbed her around the waist and she covered her breasts to protect them.

"*He*, Dr. Kristenson?" She pushed the hair from Helaine's eyes. "Or *she*?"

Helaine stared back in disbelief. She had no desire to pursue it. She extricated herself and slipped past Sharon, back into the bedroom for her clothes.

Sharon was not about to drop the subject. "Why didn't you come, Helaine?"

Why didn't she? Playing all evening, trying to counterfeit her orgasm, trying to get her to come without penetration, brutalizing her—"Why the hell are you here?"

"Why didn't you look for me at the flat?" Sharon demanded.

Helaine snatched a robe from the closet. "Why aren't you ever there when I need you?" She didn't like the sound of her own voice anymore.

Sharon looked triumphant. "I'm here now," she said defiantly.

Indeed. Helaine clutched the robe to her chest and sat down on the end of the bed, wrapping it around her shoulders. She studied Sharon Chambers, her magazine grin, her million dollar smile. It was a caricature of the intelligent one she used to have when they had first met. Sharon had changed it, enhancing her lips, improving her teeth, fixing everything she thought was wrong about her. In reality, she had no character left. It was gone. In its place was now a terrible perfection, the look of an exotic orchid cultivated indoors artificially, perishable out of its own glass house and incapable of thriving in a garden. The sly smile was now just a bit of a snarl. Her smart looks reduced to nothing more than raw animal cunning.

Character. It seemed Ms. Chambers couldn't even distinguish right from wrong anymore. Never apologized. Helaine stared at her, wondering if it might occur to her to do so but Sharon just smiled that crass magazine grin back at her. The most-beautiful-girl-in-the-world grin.

Tonight Sharon seemed to be wearing that title with a sort of tired pride. There was something dark lurking in those beautiful eyes, a look of chilling introspection. Helaine shivered. She could feel sorrow creeping up in her again. It came from a heavy womb and flowed into her heart.

"Sharon, I—"

The phone rang in the adjoining room. Sharon glanced over her shoulder and back and her eyes narrowed with suspicion. "Shame on you, Dr. Kristenson. You were expecting someone?"

"Of course not." Three rings. Helaine rose from the bed to answer it.

"Why isn't the machine on?" Sharon snapped.

"Because I'm here." Sharon blocked her exit. "I have to answer it."

Sharon beat her there. "Hello," she said brusquely, holding Helaine off with her hand.

"Sharon, give it to me."

"Helaine?"

"She's a little tied up right now. Who's calling?"

"Sharon, give me my phone!"

"Oh, really? Does she need me to call the police?"

"Who the hell is this?" Sharon demanded.

"Robert Keagan. That would be esquire to you. Put Helaine on, please."

Sharon handed over the phone. "Keagan Esquire," she muttered.

"Good evening?" Helaine answered, aware it came out strained.

"Helaine? Robert here. I see your prodigal brute has returned."

"Yes. How are you?" She kept one eye on Sharon.

"We wanted to invite you out for dinner. Kay loved Frank's. But I guess you'll be in hiding for awhile?"

She could not discuss this now. "You'll have to call me at the office Monday. I don't have my appointment book in front of me," she said in a hollow tone. She watched Sharon pacing like a warrior.

"Uh, I see. Okay. I should call on Monday?"

"Yes. That will be fine." She had lost sight of Sharon. "Yes, Monday then. Monday, Robert. I'll talk to you then."

"I hate that woman. You should see what she does to you."

She glanced into the mirror beside the desk. Yes, she saw it.

"We're in the middle of something here," Sharon interrupted.

"Thanks for calling, Robert. Say hi to Kay for me."

"Monday. I will. Talk to you then."

She put the phone down and turned on the answering machine.

"He hates me, Doctor. Why is that? Are you having an affair with him?"

Helaine sighed. "He's my lawyer, that's all. And an old friend. I have them, you know." Her taut voice. She pulled the robe on the rest of the way and tied it. "You cannot answer my phone. If it was a client—we agreed on that. I do not interfere in your life. Why are you bullying me tonight?"

Sharon smirked. "You do not have the right to fuck around while I'm away. I will interfere with that. You can count on it."

Helaine was taken aback. "I do not *fuck* around. What about you, Sharon?" She was not herself. "Weren't you going to brag to me about your Italian excursions?"

"I did Italy, Dr. Kristenson. How does that feel? You know about it, I hope?"

Yes, she had heard all about Italy. Yes, she had caught wind of it and even her friends were talking. She knew it all anyway, without having to be told or reminded, without having it thrown in her face. She folded her arms and stared at her feet.

"You better not be fucking around on me, Helaine Kristenson."

"Sharon? How is it that you can but I can't?"

Sharon shook her head and laughed.

"That is what you're telling me, right?" Helaine asked. "That I shouldn't even think of it?"

"I can because I am *the* Sharon Chambers. You can't because you are *the* Dr. Kristenson."

Helaine saw her grin again and looked away. It was a sad confrontation, a poor substitute for what she had been longing. *The* Sharon Chambers. She searched the woman's face for her lover, the one that had somehow gotten away, eluded the both of them. Could she still be in there, behind that animal grin? Did she love that animal? Did that animal love her or did it just like the taste of her? It smiled back inscrutably.

Demons and skeletons, Helaine was thinking. That's her real essence. And ghosts that haunted the creature by day and night. Here's a ghost: her father, leaving a wife and a little one to fend for themselves. Here's another one: a beautiful mother. And a beautiful daughter. The Chambers women. They were estranged. How long now, fifteen years? A mother banishing her daughter.

Two beauties in the same house, in an unholy battle for the illicit affections of the same man. It was not the oddest scenario the good doctor had ever heard about, but it was still quite tragic. Mother and daughter in a battle, youth gaining the upper hand, for a suitor who was taking his pleasure at the expense of both of them. That was Sharon's cross, an ugly secret that the press would never hear about. No, not that Sharon Chambers's first paramour belonged to her mother, but rather her broken heart over the resulting loss of her mother's affections. Probably the only thing her heart would break over. Ugly secrets, everybody had them, but here was a secret so secret that even Sharon Chambers didn't know about it.

A shudder again. Sharon grinned like a skull does. Involuntary. Of course she did, like a skull hidden by skin, she was hiding from herself and her secret, masked in a brand new smile, disguised in a stranger's face. A smile or a snarl or a sneer. Who cares as long as it's different than the real one, the one she was born with? Couldn't she be happy now, now that she no longer bore any resemblance to anyone, now that she wouldn't have to see her mother's face always glaring back at her in the mirror?

Sure she could, if happiness, like beauty, was only skin deep.

Sharon's expression had softened somewhat. Helaine tried to smile for her. "There is no one, darling. Believe me. I wouldn't do that to you," she assured. "Please," she said signaling for her to sit beside her. "Take this off for me."

Sharon slipped the robe off, pushed her backward into the sheets and pillows. Warily the legs opened again and Sharon lay between them. Weak from struggling, Helaine draped her arms around her lover's neck and, as was customary, whispered her name to her, sighing it gently into the silky dark hair, sighing with relief when, without hesitation, Sharon finally entered her.

It took over an hour for Helaine to orgasm. Her lover left shortly after that.

It was a terminally ill relationship. No saving it. The middle-aged couple seated before her quarreled as if Dr. Kristenson wasn't even there, each adamantly digging deeper into their positions. She gazed over their heads at the woman who had just appeared on the fifteenth floor. She was holding herself as she was prone to do this time of day, standing heroically and staring off toward the harbor. Helaine sighed with happiness at the sight of her up there and the sound of it contrasted so sharply with that of the grumbling couple that they ceased their discourse and looked at her quizzically. She smiled back as if she had been with them the whole while and they glanced accusingly at each other and then waited for the good doctor to speak.

She had written the book on all this, which they both claimed to have read. If so, then surely they knew they were in the final chapter. She instructed them to continue their conversation, avoiding, if they could, the use of the word "you" all the time. "Say 'I feel' or 'I think'. It's less accusing." They tried that for a few seconds.

Their issues were not too exceptional, the usual garden variety stuff. His wife was his infidel; her husband just needed to get over it. Both of them were heavily entrenched and in serious denial about the unfavorable future disposition of their marriage. In a way, Dr. Kristenson mused as they picked up their debate where they had left off, his wife was more right than he was. He probably should just get over it since she was unlikely to sacrifice her extramarital meanderings, counseling or not. She wondered how the woman would feel if he actually did, if he actually woke up one clear day and took a look around him and saw her at last, who she really was, and quietly walked away.

Dr. Kristenson kept one eye on the woman up in the window across the street. Her name she had learned last Friday night at Frank's Place was Lydia.

She overheard the couple attempting to discuss some of her theories about "working it out" but, in truth, it was rather too late for that. He had the right to quit on her anytime if he could find the strength to do it. She watched Lydia and listened to their pitched voices, nodding encouragingly at all the right times, urging them to continue whenever they halted their discussion and glanced in her direction.

Lydia.

It was the husband who persisted with these sessions. His perfidious mate only attended in order to placate him, to bury him alive in false hopes and deceive him into believing she was trying to reform. It was clear that this would never happen. She had already wasted a great deal of his time and good faith in this effort to suspend his disbelief. And his money. His money was probably the only thing about the man that his wife still found attractive.

Dr. Kristenson lamented her decision to follow Lydia to Frank's Place.

Not only because it was undisciplined and against the rules to do so, but because seeing the dark-haired woman up close had caused a kind of crisis in her which had yet to subside.

She rose up with the conclusion of the couples' session and booked them for another one the following week. In her journal beside the entry concerning them she wrote "impassioned" when what she really meant was "impasse."

Lydia. That was all she knew of her. She was Lydia, in the fifteenth floor window of the huge investment firm of Soloman-Schmitt. Lydia applying her lipstick. Lydia at happy hour. Lydia with blue eyes. Lydia at Frank's Place just down the block where Helaine liked to eat anyway.

Dr. Kristenson's day had ended and she was unsure of what to do next.

She was fabulous in bed. If she wanted to be. But even at the start it was in a distinctly mannered way, technical and adept, as if she didn't actually care to touch or be touched, except in appraisal. Foreplay, too, was a bit of a performance. She kissed very little, almost never held hands, and didn't have the patience for sweet nothings. At times she emoted so little warmth during the act that it seemed likely she had left her body completely, was floating somewhere above the two of them, hanging up there to get a better view of herself, to see how good she looked at it, or how good she was doing. It was, if Helaine thought about it too much, unnerving to have Sharon always watching like that. There was something strangely voyeuristic about it, a perfidy that went beyond her chronic unfaithfulness.

Still, there was nothing implicitly wrong with the lovemaking and Helaine was never left dissatisfied. It did not usually pay off well to criticize a lover so she never did. Besides every lover was different. It was wrong to compare them. She was optimistic that Sharon's quirks would eventually be cured, was willing to overlook the minor shortcomings.

But in her silent consent their love life developed into a practiced ritual with Sharon Chambers performing the rites, a consummate priestess in the bedroom. Lots of bedrooms, unfortunately. Sex, it's just sex, she insisted, a necessary evil, a tool for achievement. Helaine's objection to her persistent infidelities was always rebuked with that argument. He means nothing. She means nothing. Career, career, career. As if Sharon was the only woman who ever had to work. Helaine had grown tired of debating it. It was something she was expected to grin and bear.

Fate smiled on Sharon in much the same way, permitting her to succeed over it, as well. Her career skyrocketed. There was now, as far as Helaine could see, no reason for the promiscuous behavior to continue. Yet it did as if by a sick compulsion.

The legendary oversexed Sharon Chambers. Her new position: She was simply maintaining her mythical reputation.

Myth.

In their bedroom, however, Sharon no longer desired to be made love to. She only wanted to fuck Helaine. This version of lovemaking claimed the rest of their sex life and by the time that Helaine finally came to grips with what had happened to them it was impossible to change it. As impossible as getting Sharon to be faithful. Helaine saw herself immobilized, standing in a falling rock zone, her lover wandering recklessly on a path to disaster.

Sharon had had a fine day in the sun, better and longer than most people get out of living. All too soon, Helaine tried to counsel, it would be over and at the rate the model was going she would be destroyed by it in the end. She gently advised her to settle down. But Sharon Chambers did just as she pleased even when it was unpleasant and regarded every near miss as the proof of her indestructibility.

The fiasco in Italy had hit all the international papers even before Sharon had thought to return. Her off-color comments about the controversy as she was departing from Rome, suggesting derisively that her critics were guilty of being "too Catholic," had bristled a great many shoulders and, unfortunately for Sharon, many great shoulders as well. There were plenty in the industry who did not care for the supermodel as it was and she had already begun to stretch her friendships within it a bit too thin.

Sharon lay low for months before leaving town again. During that time Helaine watched as she further alienated herself from the people she needed with her angry, long distance diatribes and equally bizarre conspiratorial accusations. To make matters worse she impulsively fired her longtime agent and she did not know nor trust his replacement. Her extracurricular activities had earned her the added attention she coveted, but the press did not drool over her in quite the same way as they use to and she had frequent run-ins with the paparazzi that now and then trailed after her. She resented the declassé treatment, offended not so much by the ugly coverage but how it hindered her lifestyle.

That was a surprisingly good excuse for Helaine to keep a low profile, too. She refrained from visiting the waterfront flat since she did, after all, have her own reputation to consider. The handful of clandestine visits that Sharon made to her place did not accomplish much in alleviating the hostilities between them and by the time that Sharon had left for California, Helaine was so fatigued and unhappy that she really didn't miss her lover for weeks.

"I'll call you," Sharon had lied. "Don't go frigid on me, Dr. Kristenson."

"Don't worry, darling. It'll never happen."

With a prurient expression the good doctor watched Lydia through the blinds walking to Frank's Place. She was shocked to see herself doing this all the time, concerned by Sharon's insinuations and the methods she had employed against a mere suspicion. In the past few months she had gradually come to the alarming conclusion that, no matter what the circumstances were between them, Sharon would never permit herself to be replaced. There would never be a successor. This had been both implied and expressed in a number of horrifying ways. So it was with great apprehension that Helaine observed herself observing. And in her observations this Friday afternoon she had to finally accept that her heart was not her own anymore. That she did not recognize it as belonging to Sharon, either. That a foolish thing had happened to further complicate her life. Something she must run from or reckon with somehow.

She saw Lydia disappear into Frank's and her stomach growled. She laughed out loud at the sound of it. It actually growled! She was clinical. The hunger was obviously psychological. Great. And now she was even thirsty! She had to admit that her throat felt dry. She laughed at herself. It was almost funny, finding oneself at the mercy of an unheard bell, seeing herself like Pavlov's dogs, panting.

It wouldn't be funny if she fell in love with that stranger, she warned. Her heart leapt at the thought of it, stimulated by its own dilemma.

Another book signing, another lecture, another month. And then another. And another. There was every indication this was the rest of her life. That damn book! Someone wanted her to write a weekly column. She turned it down. She did not want to become a household word, her face in every kitchen like some popular detergent, making the whites whiter or the colors brighter, getting the spots out of all the glasses. She liked things as they were, somewhat confidential.

The rest of her life. It could be spent just like this. Waiting for Sharon Chambers, leering after Lydia so-and-so, whoever she was. That could go on forever, she worried. Or perhaps in a year it would be someone else. Worse, she could take up the offers of ex-lovers. Go back in time instead of forward. Or hang in the now, in emotional limbo, until her friends desert her.

The future. She wanted that to be a woman named Lydia, as unlikely as that seemed.

Lydia. It had yet to set in with her tall-dark-handsome that the blue-eyed woman had thrown him off. Helaine watched smugly as he relentlessly tugged at her chain. She still wore it, of course, but she didn't want to be taken prisoner by him anymore, watching as he flirted with her friends and took lesser women home, waiting until he got the idea to satisfy her. It was over before he knew it. He tugged at the chain in disbelief, pushed at all her buttons, but the woman no longer responded to him. He had lost her.

Good for you, Helaine thought, watching the woman struggle with her broken heart. It probably didn't feel like it to her, but that was the healthy thing to do. She shouldn't begrudge him for the heartbreak, though. A broken heart can make a woman out of you. If you're well meaning, it makes you a tender lover. If you're not, like poor Sharon Chambers, it makes you hard and cruel.

But it was a sorry thing to see nonetheless. It had taken some of the wind out of the queen's sails. She sat cheerless with her friends or sometimes stared off into the distance. Helaine felt her eyes on her sometimes when she sat reading in the window seat. Just as Kay had said, she was staring at her, with eyes of a sleepwalker, roaming eyes, something undefined beneath all that preoccupation.

Fleeting fantasies, Dr. Kristenson realized, humanity's cheapest narcotic. Everyone fell victim to them at some point. Romeo had put the woman up on shelf and in her current state of mind she felt most comfortable there. She was keeping herself from him and a world of similar suspects. That was understandable. She mistrusted her desires now and in repressing them they bubbled up in unexpected places. If she had too much to drink, she dropped her guard and there they were popping up in a fantasy. It was, after all, the safest place to keep them at the moment. Safe excursions, mental joyrides. Helaine had no objection to being her vehicle. She let her look as long as she liked.

Dr. Helaine Kristenson, not only watching but being watched, the sleepwalker from time to time searching her, undressing her with her eyes. Again and again she was stripped bare by her, until her conscience was hardwired for it, until she could feel it happening without even looking. She knew by the flustered expression that appeared on Lydia's face whenever she looked at her that she was shocked by what she saw herself thinking, so Helaine feigned to be unaware. Yes, it was opportunistic, but she was not going to discourage it. She wanted to be accessible, to pull the woman under a spell as deep as the ocean, to be as warm and comforting as a favorite blanket.

Witchcraft. Those fingers through the hair, subconscious come-hither stares. The young man had left a charm on Lydia. Dr. Kristenson bet the woman hadn't expected that to happen, that he would leave a spell on her, make her wander restless, leave her heart swollen and ripe for the taking. If she would ever let herself be taken again. IF. But not by him, though. That was obvious.

What an unlucky guy to be born such a fool! Helaine reveled in his misfortune.

"*Fatal exception*? What's that mean?"

(Computer problems.)

"That's the third time this week. We should update this, Dr. Kristenson."

Four o'clock. Her secretary was hoping to leave early this Friday. She glanced at her watch.

"Leave it until Monday, Jen." Helaine was hoping, too.

"It doesn't seem to be having any negative effect," Jenny offered as she put on her coat. "I'll look at it Monday." She was about to leave when the phone rang.

Exceptions? Yes, Helaine was thinking. They could be fatal sometimes.

"Good afternoon. Dr. Kristenson's." Jenny shot a look at the doctor. "One moment, please. I'm not sure if she's still here . . . a Sharon Eddlebaum?" she whispered.

Sharon? "I'll take it in the office. You can go, Jen." She waited for the sound of a closing door. "Sharon?"

"*Is the doctor in?*"

"Is everything all right?" Gone four months and a phone call? Helaine had heard scant little about Sharon's forays this time.

"*Calling to see if you miss me, Helaine. So there.*"

Missed her? A little. She swiveled the chair around and lifted the blinds. Lydia. She spun back, put her elbows on the desk. "Of course. Where are you?"

"*LA. On contract. Trying to behave myself. How's my favorite blond?*"

Helaine hesitated, fighting the urge to look over her shoulder.

"*That would be you, Helaine. I said how are you?*"

(How am I?) Helaine coughed. (Horny.) "What's your itinerary, Sharon? When do you return?" she asked, casting a guilty look over her shoulder.

"*Don't know yet. My agent and all. Busy. Busy.*"

Helaine overheard voices in the background. "Working?"

There was a brief pause. "*Yeah.*"

A painfully dissatisfying conversation. She wished she would come out with it. A phone call. Was she trying to prove something?

"*You going to be home tonight?*"

(NO.) "What time?"

"*Late.*"

Late? Of course, where else? "I'll be there."

"*I'll try to call then.*"

Try? How unnerving! Helaine's hands trembled in acute rage.

"*Helaine?*"

"Okay."

"*I've got to run, Dr. Kristenson.*"

"Where are you staying, Sharon? Don't you have a number?"

"*I'm leaving here tomorrow night. I've got to go. Be home tonight, Helaine.*"

Be home? "Okay." She loathed herself for agreeing to it. Where would she go anyway? She heard the click and a dial tone and slammed the receiver.

Lydia, up on her throne. Helaine dropped the blinds again. It was becoming a ridiculous battle. Up and then down. Up. Down.

She took a deep breath. Friday. Hungry. Thirsty. Etcetera.

If she had to guess she'd say it was her smell she had fallen in love with. The inebriating bittersweet of her. On her skin. In her hair. Like the flowering plum trees of her childhood. Childhood in her mother's garden. Before she was cast out of it.

And it was the sound of the beautiful blond. The reckless surrender in her voice, the bedroom voice, her pretty moans, the helpless orgasms, the drawn out dying when she was made love to. The resurrection. It was easy to love Helaine Kristenson. She was a goddess.

Snagging her was, as far as Sharon was concerned, her greatest conquest.

But Helaine was different last time. Cool. She suspected her, though she hadn't discovered a reason for it. She was not the type for affairs, Sharon knew, but still something had changed to make her doubt the woman. She couldn't quite put her finger on it. Perhaps she had left her too long? That had been a long time. And of course the coverage. Endless. The blond was very sensitive to that. Some people were about such things. She was glad she wasn't one of them.

It was two in the morning, Helaine's time. Sharon dialed her home. It rang once. Twice. Three times. Four? Five? Where was she? Six? Seven times?

"Hello?"

A sleepy sexy voice. Sharon's insides jumped. She listened quietly as Helaine repeated the greeting and then without speaking a word herself, hung up.

Good. Her lover was where she told her to be.

Saturday. Half a day at the office. The damn computer. Something wasn't working right. Helaine hoped that Jenny could fix it or the week ahead would be a mess. She attempted to shut it off. Another *fatal exception.* What is a fatal exception?

Maybe a fatal exception is what happened to spring this year, Helaine mused along the way to Frank's Place for lunch. It was certainly negligent. Rain. Snow. Cold. Not a bloody sign of it. She stepped into the foyer and took her coat off.

"Ah! Dr. Kristenson."

She smiled at the waiter, holding her finger to her lips.

He read lips she had learned from him. "Trust me," he said.

She did.

"This weather—I've left something warm at your table."

"A body?" she teased.

He laughed. "I'm sorry, no." He pulled out the chair for her. "We'll have to work on that."

She sipped the brandy he had set out for her and scanned the menu.

He was taking her order when Lydia walked in. "Ooh," he said to Helaine under his breath, "here's your warm body."

Lydia. "You're bad," she scolded into the menu.

"Let's make her ladyship feel welcome then." He tucked the menu under his arm and went to greet her.

Helaine grabbed her book and pretended to be engrossed with it, sending the woman her most casual smile as the waiter escorted her to a table on the other side of the room.

Oh, he was sharp. Son-of-a-gun, Helaine lipped in admiration. He grinned back, pleased with himself, his silver hair and spectacles gleaming with a fantastic light. She wondered how far he could go with this and sat back into her chair, watching from the corner of one eye as Lydia relaxed and sipped at a glass of red wine, compliments, no doubt, of the patient waiter.

Lydia on a Saturday, hiding all the way across the room, against the wall. Helaine cursed herself for the cable knit and baggy woolen trousers. It was so cold though and she hadn't expected her. She waited to see if it would make a difference.

It didn't.

Why was she hiding in the shadows then? Why not say something to me for God's sake? She sighed inaudibly and stared out the window without changing her pose. Was it too late to stop this?

Her food came, served with a wry smile which she ignored. A fabulous dish of seafood, she eyed it hungrily, but barely touched it. Her stomach was overstimulated and she felt strangely self-conscious bringing anything near her lips. She couldn't trust herself to that sensation. She felt compelled instead to lie down and Frank's was hardly the place for this. The waiter came back later and she asked him to wrap it up for her, putting her face into her book, back into chapter whatever. She must have read it fifteen times today, dumbly dragging her eyes over the words as if she were suddenly an idiot. What did she really know anyway? Stupid books. Case studies.

Sex, drugs and rock 'n' roll, and a few underaged prostitutes. Guess who's in the thick of it?

"Whoweee. Some people sure know how to live!"

Helaine eavesdropped, cringing as a blond-haired woman explained it all to Lydia. The story was on everyone's lips. Everywhere.

"The supermodel, Liddy. What planet are you from anyway?"

"I wouldn't know the woman if I fell over her, Del."

Helaine was glad to hear that. She sat back in her chair in relief. She was pressed for time tonight, a book signing and then later cocktails at the Keagans.

Lydia's table. They seemed to be moving in on Helaine lately. She bet that was no accident and searched the room for the waiter. He acknowledged her and started for her table.

Lydia. Helaine saw her smile and drop her head. She was glad the woman had never heard of *the* Sharon Chambers. It reflected well on her. She wished she had never heard of her, either. She smiled demurely and looked away.

Seven o'clock. Helaine paid the bill, collected her things, and made her way through the crowded bar. She was going to have to hear about Ms. Chambers all night, she was sure. The model and her colleagues had created quite a mess for themselves and, as for Sharon herself, she had outdone even her own reputation. It was time to make some long overdue decisions.

Beep. *"Helaine? Where are you? (impatient sigh) I'll try back later."* Beep. *"I'm coming back briefly. I've got to return in thirty days for—I'm sure you heard. Helaine? If you're there pick up. (pause) Shit. Where the hell are you?"* Beep. *"I'll be at the flat by Tuesday (noise in the background). Call me there."*

Worrisome messages from Sharon. Helaine erased them and threw herself down on the couch. Sharon, it's over. Sharon, I don't want to see you anymore. Sharon, we need to break it off. Sharon, I can't do this anymore. Sharon, I don't love you anymore. Sharon, you're on your own now. Sharon.

The sleepwalker in Frank's Place was emerging from her trance. Soon she would be wide awake. Helaine had worried that when Lydia did come to she might be horrified by how far she had strayed, but that did not seem to be the case. She blushed a lot about it, that's all. At this point Helaine knew it was simply inexperience holding the woman back. And the lack of encouragement.

Sharon Chambers loomed like a dark shadow over her happiness.

Helaine realized that she had mismanaged the entire situation. Had underestimated everyone and everything in it. Especially herself.

On the couch and off the couch again. Contemplating the future was proving to be a painful exercise. Helaine paced from room to room. There was a mountain of duties she had shirked or set aside. Doing so had led to a complicated turning point, a turn which she was in danger of missing if she didn't handle the moment right.

She could seduce Lydia, that seemed possible now, but she didn't want a backdoor affair with the woman. She very much doubted Lydia would tolerate being someone's other woman in any event. Especially another woman's other woman. No, not likely. Ugh! It was a complicated folly and Helaine didn't relish having to explain it to anyone. Oh, good faith—one of her own tenets—it was a lot easier said than done!

She lay on her bed in the darkened bedroom, listening to the horns and bells and yells of the world just outside her window. It was as if they had decided to throw a party and everyone was invited. She wanted to run outdoors and join them. Shout at the moon and count the stars in the sky. Fall down.

Falling, just like children in the damp night grass. Sixteen, she fell like this. Eighteen, she fell. Twenty. Thirty. Forty and falling. Falling in love to the ground, or in a back seat. She remembered the sensation, love with boys so young their bodies were still as smooth as girls. Girls. Pure love without hesitation, without a contract, rolling in love in the grass and all around her the starry skies of youth to hide and seek in. Joy without prescription, before her body hardened to the natural feel of it. Seventeen's joy. Lifting herself up in the brand new night and day. And twenty-one again. Wandering in yesterday's dawn, peering from it unafraid at green, cloudless horizons, the twists and folds of them looking just like unmade beds. Forty. A blue moon was recalling morning and playfully tugging at her night sheets. Forty. Her life lit up like a torch, burning the darkness away.

We all fall down. Helaine Kristenson knew she had fallen like that again. She could smell the grass around her, feel the dew on it where she lay staring up at the moon. Forty and the moon was blue. She couldn't change it back even if she wanted.

It was necessary to face Sharon. She had to confront them both with reality. She would, of course, omit any mention of Lydia. There was no point in it. Lydia was exactly the type that Sharon Chambers would want to eat alive. That had to be avoided at all costs. The tiger and the lady. Helaine smiled grimly at the prospect.

Tuesday. That would be the day. She was resolved to it. She would never again have to see herself searching the waterfront. Never.

She undressed and studied her body in the mirror. Not much had changed since she was last in love. She couldn't remember when that was. The gods had treated her well in the meantime, she acknowledged gratefully. Her face? Well, it seemed to have gone a bit sallow. Some wrinkles. Tired eyes. The skin was no longer perfect. Perhaps Lydia hadn't noticed these things. She stared apprehensively into the looking glass, straining to see what the blue eyes saw, no longer worrying about anything else.

"We have to talk."

"It's no big deal, Helaine. It's not true anyway. I don't do children."

"No, I really need to talk to you."

"Helaine, not now."

"When?"

"I just got a message—I wasn't supposed to leave jurisdiction. We can't talk about this now. I've got to go back to LA."

"LA? When, Sharon?"

"ASAP, they said. I've retained an attorney. Helaine . . . I don't know when I'll be back. My new agent quit."

"I'm too old for this."

"Helaine . . ."

"Do you understand what I'm saying?"

"Helaine, I know you're upset . . . it's a mess . . . I'll talk with you when I get back."

"Sharon, it's more than that. We need to talk now."

"More than what?"

"I can't do this anymore. I simply can't. Do you know how old I am?"

"How—No . . . actually I don't."

"I just turned forty. Forty, Sharon."

"Forty? Listen to me. I did not have sex with minors. I know how you are about that—"

"Listen to me. I don't care anymore and I don't want to hear about it. Not from you. Not from the press. Certainly not from my friends."

"I see . . . So you're having a midlife crisis on me. Is that it?"

"At least, Sharon."

"Let me come over. I'll make it better."

I don't think so, Sharon.

"Helaine?"

"It's too late for that now."

"You're seeing someone!"

"No."

"We'll work it out. Your words. When I come back."

"I want to see—If you can see people, I can."

"No, Helaine, you can't. I need to know you're waiting. You can't."

Silence.

"I'll be back in less than two months."

Two more months? "What do you want from me, Sharon?"

"That's simple. You."

(NO.) "This relationship is not acceptable to me."

"We'll work it out I said."

"I don't want to." Helaine's voice cracked. "It's too late."

"Helaine . . . let me come over."

"Seven years of this nonsense. I don't want to see you, Sharon." She sobbed it.

"Helaine . . . Hel-aine . . ."

"Don't! Don't do that to me."

"Helaine, I have to catch my plane soon. If I don't then they'll say I'm a flight risk. I'll be living in the LA county jail if that happens."

(Where you belong.)

"Helaine—Helaine, we'll talk about this when I get back."

Silence.

"Please . . . I can't do this now, Helaine. When I get back, we'll fix it."

"Sharon . . ."

"I've got to go. Everything will be fine. I'll call you from LA." (click)

"Sharon?"

There was no end in sight to the scandal. No word from Sharon in LA.

"She's a contagion. They should quarantine her."

Neither Helaine nor Kay disagreed. They glanced at each other and back to Robert.

"I still have the floor?" They usually stopped him from venturing too far with this subject. "You should give her the boot and send her walking down some other Joe's runway. They say she owns a place in LA County." He raised his eyebrows skeptically. "Did you know that, Helaine?"

No she did not. "Is that right?"

"Robert." Kay was ready to intercept but Helaine urged him to continue.

"Go on. Where else?"

"It's not clear. They'll find out though. It all comes out."

Helaine was visibly disturbed at the idea. "Let's hope not," she said.

Kay and Robert looked identically concerned.

"What's she worth?" Robert asked. "Do you know?"

Helaine shrugged. "She's a spendthrift and she's always got legal problems. I wouldn't know."

"And she's probably got a house and a lover in every port, like a good little sailor." He watched his friend's face but there was no reaction.

"A place in LA," Helaine murmured. "I should have guessed it. I really need my head examined, see if everything's working all right."

Robert was surprised by her declaration.

"Helaine, I swear you look radiant tonight. How can that be amidst all this nonsense?"

"She's in love," Kay blurted.

Helaine laughed.

"Don't laugh. I'd recognize that look anywhere. You're in love."

"No more Sharon?" Robert asked.

"Wait a minute. I think we're ahead of ourselves a bit. I merely suggested that I need my head examined. Now I'm in love?"

"You need a professional," Kay teased.

Mmmmm. She heard her pulse in her ears. "Who do you recommend?"

Robert was catching on. "Someone you don't know."

"A perfect stranger?" Helaine pressed.

"Know any?" asked Robert.

She did.

"Why not a perfect stranger?" Kay answered. "Everybody does it."

"Cheat, you mean?"

They fell quiet.

"Guys?"

"Well, how could it be cheating?" Robert asked. "Don't you read the papers? Could there be anyone who hasn't heard about this crap?"

"Robert's right. Who could blame you?"

"Sharon."

"You're kidding!"

"No, I'm not. She'll never let me go."

"Have you even asked?"

Helaine fidgeted in her chair. "Yes."

"Is that it? Is that why you're still with her?"

"She wants to work it out she says. You know, I'm uncomfortable with spilling my guts like this."

"Yeah, but Sharon's not. Your guts anyway," Robert added.

"What am I saying? I have no guts."

"Helaine! Don't say that."

"You've got guts all right, but they're filled with a worm. One that stretches from here to California."

"Okay, Robert. That's enough. Let 'em spill, Helaine."

"There's nothing to spill, believe me."

Robert snorted impatiently. Kay nudged his arm with her elbow.

"Then how's sex?"

"Rough, Kay, I hate it."

Robert fell silent.

"Helaine? You owe it to yourself then. There's nothing to work out."

"Kay . . . I know."

"And what about the other person? Do they know how you feel?"

"I never said there was another person."

"But there is, I can see it. They don't know?"

Helaine chuckled low. "Kay . . ." She couldn't finish it.

Robert grinned.

"Go on," Kay urged.

"They . . . umm . . . they don't know. No . . . I don't think so. I am in no position for them to know. How I feel, I mean. You know?"

They laughed out loud.

"Boy, I'd never want to see you on a witness stand. You'd ruin yourself," Robert said with relief. "You are in love, Helaine Kristenson? Yes or no, please."

"I don't know how it happened."

"There you go again. Your witness, Kay. She's in love. With whom, we don't know, except that it is no longer Sharon Chambers."

"That's all there is, I'm telling you. That's all," Helaine repeated.

"I'm assuming they feel the same way when I ask, do they know about Sharon?"

"You're good Kay. I can only guess that they feel the same way. We do not speak. No, they don't know about Sharon. She hasn't even heard of her." She regretted that last bit of information.

"Your witness, Robert."

"No, no. You're doing much better than you think."

"I don't know why you can't trust your old friends—"

"No, it's not that, Kay. I'm forty now. It's not the same. There's no guarantee the woman would . . . uhh . . . she's straight anyway."

"So you'll stay with Sharon instead of taking a chance. Besides, straight? I've never heard of such a thing."

"Dr. Kristenson is afraid of looking like a hypocrite I think," Robert offered.

"That is true, I admit it."

"So Sharon says she wants to work it out—which is absolute bullshit, you know—and you have no say? I don't understand that."

"It's complicated. I can't explain."

Robert didn't like the sounds of that.

Neither did his wife. "What are you afraid of?" Kay asked.

Afraid? Yes, afraid. Of everything. "I don't know. Maybe I don't want to be alone."

"Right," Robert muttered, "that would be so different than now."

"How long?" Kay asked.

"Sorry?"

"How long have you been in love with her?"

Helaine smiled. She was tired.

"Your witness, counselor."

Robert took over. "Let me get this right. You're in love with someone who doesn't talk—neither of you have spoken to each other . . . Sharon knows?"

"No."

"Hmmm." He shifted in his chair. "Would there be something if Sharon would relinquish the throne?"

"I think so, but she won't."

"Helaine, I can't stand it! Who is this person?" Kay was frantic.

Helaine held up her hand. "It's a mistake I made . . . with a little help. But it's impossible now. Sharon insists on working it out."

"You don't owe her that."

She sighed. "I can't do both."

"So you tried to tell her it was over. That's when she said all this?" Robert asked.

"Yes, before she returned to LA. My little flight risk."

"Look, I can tell you right now she's going to be tied up with that matter for quite some time. She could even get time. She's in no bargaining position, Helaine. Let her go, don't even discuss it. She's defending a criminal record now."

"What does it make me if I do that?"

"An honorable woman throwing in the towel. Give someone else a chance."

"But it won't look that way, Robert."

"Who cares?"

"She does," Kay interrupted. "Helaine, this woman . . . not like Ms. Chambers?"

"Not a bit."

"Tell me more."

"There is no more. It went too far as it is."

"How far?" Kay pressed.

"We're following each other like a couple of schoolchildren." Helaine was surprised she had said it like that. It felt good.

"Oh!" Kay gasped. "How fun!"

"It's not fun. It's exasperating. My gonads are swollen."

"Hers too I'll bet," Robert said. "Straight. Best kind, my dear."

Helaine groaned. "I wouldn't know."

"Maybe Sharon will go to jail," Kay said dreamily.

"Prison," Robert corrected.

"I don't want her to go to prison. I really just want her to go away."

"You've got to rethink this affair thing, Helaine."

"Tread lightly," Kay warned Robert, "and remember who you're talking to."

Helaine went to rescue him. "This woman . . . she's not . . . it couldn't be an affair. She isn't the type. If she found out about Sharon Chambers—"

"Well, we're not trying to be wily, but people do feel differently after they've been, you know, seduced. More amenable, if you catch my drift."

"That would not be the case here, I can assure you." She put her hands on her knees. "Sharon will not let me go, so that's the end of it."

"There's something you're not telling us, Helaine. You're being so secretive."

Not telling? That Sharon is hostile, aggressive and by now quite desperate? That she was afraid of how she would react? "Robert, the situation has become a complicated mess. I don't know how it got this way. The woman I've—her existence is making it worse. It's my fault and I'll have to fix it, but I'm not going to have an affair. I'm not going to let Sharon Chambers turn me into a liar and a cheat."

The lease on the waterfront flat. If it wasn't still in her name Helaine could be technically free of Sharon. But what was the right thing to do about it? It was not possible to transfer title, management had informed her, and they would not consider leasing to Sharon Chambers on her own application in light of her current circumstances.

The lease. It looked bad from a legal standpoint. She knew that much. That's why it was a secret. Robert would be furious. Saying it just evolved like that would not be an adequate explanation to an attorney unless you qualified it by saying that you were on drugs or you had a low IQ or you just had a frontal lobotomy.

The waterfront flat. A real nightmare. She brooded over it at Frank's on Saturday and—God—Lydia appeared in the entranceway.

They exchanged glances as the waiter seated her in the middle of the room.

Helaine felt a come-on expression taking over her smile and put her book up to her face to hide it. I'm in trouble here, she realized. LYDIA. And the goddamned waterfront flat. And a way too flamboyant albatross around her neck. She felt eyes all over her and gave in with an aching sigh. It was hers to lose now. A once-in-a-lifetime offer. With strings.

It was clear that Lydia had made up her mind, was anxiously waiting for a sign from Helaine. Someone had finally made a decision in the matter.

Helaine saw how it had transformed her from an otherwise cautious and reserved woman into a funny valentine, one that tripped over herself and wore dopey expressions and a chronic hapless grin. Neither woman knew what to make of this reaction. They exchanged looks of bewilderment over it, but neither said a word.

They sat on their fences senselessly as far as the waiter was concerned.

"You do that, Dr. Kristenson, and I'll ruin you." (Sharon's back and she's mad.)

"Sharon—"

"Ruin you! Do you understand me?"

She did. "You're threatening—"

"*Not threatening. Promising, Dr. Kristenson. I promise you I will make your life an absolute fucking nightmare.*"

This was worse than imagined. Helaine took the nearest chair and collapsed in it. "Sharon, my God, you can't keep me this way."

"*You don't think so? I'll bet I can!*"

Couldn't she? It probably happens to people like me all the time, she suddenly realized. Blackmail. She didn't know what to say.

"*Feeling enlightened, darling?*"

"Sharon . . . do you want . . . you need money?"

"*No, Helaine, that's not it.* (long pause) *I'm coming over and you're letting me in.*"

This was getting ugly. "I . . . even though . . . Sharon . . . what I said . . . ?"

"*That's your problem. I'll be there in twenty minutes. MY LOVE.*" (click)

"Harry, is anything wrong?" She had just spoken with the head waiter an hour ago.

"*No, Dr. Kristenson. Her ladyship is enjoying your cognac and wonders what she should have for lunch today.*"

"Oh, Harry." She put her head in her hands. "Harry, do I do evil?"

"*No evil can dwell in a temple as fair as your own, my dear.*"

No? She felt under a great weight of it though.

"*Aren't your intentions honorable?*"

They were. But what good was that?

"*Oh . . . see how she hungers. What should she eat?*"

She laughed into the receiver. "I feel certain you're going to suggest oysters. I just know it."

"*You're right. The works then?*"

"Harry, don't let me do wrong here. I'll hate myself forever."

"*You do wrong to leave her hanging. You'll anger the gods, Dr. Kristenson. Not to mention all the other obvious consequences.*"

"I've explained this as best as I can. Surely the gods see my plight and will show mercy."

"*Any sign of it yet?*"

"Of what?"
"Mercy?"
"No."
"Then what does that tell you?"

Ego is the harshest taskmaster.

Dr. Helaine Kristenson is a self-made woman. Technically that should mean that only she can destroy herself. She has just faked another orgasm to get her lover off her back and lies in the prison of her bed. Of her room. Her jailhouse. Her keeper is getting dressed, closing the door behind her with a loud satisfied click. There seems to be no escape from this and time, though appearing to stand still, is actually flying.

Helaine is letting it all slip through her hands and she knows it. The gods aren't angry yet, but they fast grow frustrated. The mirror on the wall looks back unhappily and is dissatisfied with her choices. Her values are appalling it says. A woman has been left hanging, suspended in limbo without a sign. Soon she will realize this.

A reputation is spared. A private life shattered. What does it add up to?

The sheets on the bed cling to her body like ropes and chains. They smell of misplaced passion, of defeat, even fear. And the mind is not at peace reclining there. It throws itself at the walls and wails like a caged beast.

Aw, there was someone else. Of course there was. What else could explain the difference in Helaine? When had she ever complained of being too sore to have sex? When had she ever lain limp in her arms, a dead fish in bed? When had she ever been unable to orgasm? When had she ever been anything but thrilled to see her?

"I can assure you there is no one."

"That's impossible."

"Ms. Chambers, I've been tailing your blond now for months and I've never seen her with anyone. She goes to work, goes home, now and then eats out. Even the theater—alone. I'm telling you, she's a real bore if you ask me. Works all the time."

"Don't you believe it. How about her patients? Could it be a patient?"

"What, in her office? I'd have to bug it. She doesn't seem the type anyway." The detective eyed Sharon curiously. "Classy broad, you know?"

She nodded. Probably not in the office. But where then?

"I have to tell ya I've never seen anyone cleaner. Usually, you know, it's right out there. Not too secret. Not as secret as people think, that is. A couple days and bang, you got 'em. Shoot some photos. Run to the bank." He fell silent while he pondered the supermodel's motives. "Or whatever," he finally added with a blank expression.

"Where does she eat?"

"Different places, but usually down the street from her offices. A place called Frank's."

"Usually? How usual?"

"Well, she hasn't been in awhile but it used to be Fridays and Saturdays. Dinner or lunch thing. Alone."

"Why did she stop going?"

He laughed. "What am I supposed to do, go up and ask her?"

Sharon was flustered. He had nothing. He was a jerk. "You're telling me that Dr. Kristenson has no life? You're saying that she works, eats and sleeps? That's it?"

"Alone," he emphasized.

"Well, that's just bullshit," Sharon blurted. "You keep your eye on her. There's something going on and I know it. You keep watching. You'll see." She rose from the chair and glared at the man behind his desk. The shabby digs he called an office. The cheap suit. She despised the operation, but she was certain that her blond had strayed. She threw him a wad of cash and headed for the door. "Call me when you find out. I want to know everything about him." She hesitated at the door. "Or her," she added with a snarl. "It could just as likely be a her."

The detective whistled under his breath as she slammed the door. "You're probably her only dirt," he said, once he was sure Sharon Chambers was out of earshot. He took out the file photo of a smiling

Helaine Kristenson and propped it up against a coffee mug. She was easy on the eye at least, if boring. RESPECTABLE. He didn't expect to find a thing. Actually, he privately hoped he wouldn't. He didn't like Sharon Chambers. She was much prettier in pictures. A little too lean and mean in person. And there was a predatory look in her eyes he didn't care for. He wondered about the blond as he looked over his notes and pored over the slim contents of her file. It struck him as odd, the supermodel's exploits on the front page news and yet her obsession over the private doings, if you could even call them that, of her upstanding lover.

Upstanding. Had he missed something? He truly doubted it. How could something be going on if you're always alone? He had gone into Frank's for a look-see and saw nothing amiss. The good doctor reading a book with her dinner, close by to work. A gal's gotta eat for Pete's sake. Only ever spoke with the waiter, a man about sixty with a wedding ring. Oh really, c'mon! Maybe she's having a platonic affair with the waiter! What kind of trouble could that get her in?

Trouble. That's what everyone who came into his office was making. What kind of trouble could this woman get into? How'd she get involved with the likes of Sharon Chambers anyway? That's a good question. He had not been able to figure her out. A bookworm? A prude? He leaned forward to study her photo. Was there something in the eyes? He rarely saw them, the woman always hiding her face in a book. He brought the photograph to his face. Is it in the eyes? Is that why she hides her face, less trouble that way? He made a mental note to take a closer look at Dr. Kristenson next time. Maybe even sit nearby.

Jealous Sharon Chambers. He grinned, squeezing her wad of money in his hands. Must be a good reason for it. We'll see, maybe it wouldn't be so dull after all, hunting the smiling blond in Frank's Place, just to see if she really does stray, hunting her like a dog for Sharon Chambers who was so sure she had or would. He took the photo from the file and threw the rest into a drawer.

Dr. Helaine Kristenson, if you're so hot to trot it ain't gonna do you any good to hide your face now. You're already in trouble. He stashed the money in his coat, took one last look at the smiling photo and tucked it into his breast pocket. Yeah, you're probably up to something. Don't let me catch you at it, though, or that Chambers dame'll eat you alive.

* * *

"Sharon Eddlebaum, Dr. Kristenson."

Helaine turned abruptly from the window. "Here?" she asked.

"No, on the phone. That's twice today. You didn't call her back?"

"Tell her I'm with a client."

Jenny started for the door.

"Jen?"

"Yes?"

"How does she sound?"

"Irritated, I'd say." She took in Helaine's worried expression. "Is there anything I can do, Dr. Kristenson?"

Helaine glanced toward the window. Lydia stood up in the clouds across the way, staring this time at the sky instead of the favored waterfront. She paced slowly, vexed it would seem. Helaine had an idea as to why. She hid behind the blinds and watched her on yet another hopeless Friday.

I was a machine once, she was thinking. Absolutely humming. A creature like that one I could have three, four, five times in a night and never be tired. Now I stand here sore and old. A rusty machine driven into the ground. Out of fuel. Steam. She saw the woman adjusting her hose. You beautiful thing. I wouldn't know what to do with you if I had a book showing me how.

"Dr. Kristenson?"

Helaine stepped back from the window, her hand over her heart. That was the truth of it. She was breaking down.

"Thank you, Jen, but I don't think so. It's nothing you should be bothered with." She sat at the desk wearily, Jenny still standing at the door with her puzzled face.

"You'd be surprised what I can get accomplished," Jenny offered again.

Helaine smiled. "Just tell her I'm too tied up right now."

She woke the next morning on her consultation couch, the white silk pantsuit an ocean of wrinkles. It was a clear day and she rose up and looked around her in dismay. The sun streamed into the office and she knew it was late morning. No Saturday appointments, she remembered that much.

In the waiting room mirror she got a good look at herself. She could see just who she was now, the pale imitation of what she used to be. She was a mere pelt thrown on a floor for someone to walk on, stretched across a bed, something luxurious for them to lay against. A floor length. She fixed her hair, wiped off yesterday's lipstick. A pelt like the one she had purchased seven years ago with the once and to be Sharon Chambers wrapped inside it, soliciting her from the catwalk with bedroom eyes, the girl in the fur, nude beneath it, asking her to dinner and leaving her with the bill. Wasn't that just like Sharon, leaving her hanging all the time until now when she knew it was over she couldn't keep her hands off? Wouldn't give her a moment's peace.

She hated the woman in the mirror. What had she done with that coat? She had put it in a closet, another secret keeping, because she was afraid to wear it in public. Didn't want to be spit on. She laughed an awful laugh. It had been perverse from the start. These past few months worse than anything. Afraid to be seen in public, to be spit on. She had allowed herself to be converted into a toy in order to preserve her reputation. Now she was being mauled to death by a shark! That's certainly what she felt like, a plaything for a dangerous animal. She would be ruined either way.

Sharon had been called back to LA. She was to leave this afternoon with her entourage of lawyers. Plea bargain if they could. Otherwise she was destined the status of a sex offender with all the limitations that came with such an undesirable title.

Another awful laugh. She was a sex offender as far as Helaine was concerned. How she came to be that way even Dr. Kristenson didn't know for sure. A lack of self-discipline perhaps. A spoiled lifestyle.

She was supposed to meet her before she left, but she had no plans to be her sendoff. She wanted to see Lydia instead. Just to look—she was in no condition to do more than that.

* * *

Helaine Kristenson and Sharon Chambers were rarely seen in public together, if at all. They sat quietly in a cab headed for the airport on Saturday afternoon. Helaine's lunch at Frank's had been interrupted. She hadn't expected Sharon to go there and wasn't even sure how she knew about the place. She silently reviewed the devastation.

Lydia had gone pale at the sight of Sharon Chambers. Obviously she hadn't contemplated that possibility, the possibility of a Sharon. That would most likely be the end of it, Helaine realized grimly. The finality of it was like a weight on her chest. In her mind she played out alternative interpretations, but they all ended with the same reasonable conclusion. It was pretty clear who Sharon Chambers was to her. Sharon had played it to the hilt for the onlookers and Helaine knew by Lydia's mortified expression that she understood what she was seeing.

Strangers, who cares, but Lydia? Helaine had to keep herself from screaming. It was a nightmare come true. What a miserable ending.

"Do you have any idea what kind of stress I'm under?" Sharon complained.

"I was working late. I fell asleep on the couch in my office. It happens sometimes, Sharon." She stared out the window.

"Why haven't you returned any of my calls?"

Why? "My work is backing up on me. Anyway . . . you know how I feel."

"I know how you feel and it doesn't matter to me."

Helaine shot a look at the cabbie. He didn't seem interested in their conversation.

"I can find you anywhere, Helaine. What are you up to?"

Helaine sighed. "Working, that's all. Where are your bags?"

"I've sent them ahead. Along with the attorneys."

"Can you drop me off at my place?" Helaine asked.

"No, ride with me there. Talk to me."

Talk? She couldn't think of a thing to say. She felt Sharon's eyes on her, on her face, her body. It was an unpleasant cruise. "When is your flight?" Small talk.

"Two."

Helaine glanced at her watch. A quarter past one. "I'm not going in with you."

Sharon laughed. "The esteemed Doctor Kristenson." She slid her hand between Helaine's legs. "Slumming?"

"Sharon . . . it was your idea to hide . . . this is not appropriate."

"No?" She pulled her hand back and grinned. "Was it ever?"

"I don't know."

They fell silent again. Helaine watched the cab pass her street. She threw her head back and closed her eyes.

"I don't know what to expect this time," Sharon said, out of the blue. "My lawyers are going to try to bargain community service. First time offense. We're hopeful. Lots of celebrities get off that way." She waited for a response but the blond just sat with her eyes shut. "I've . . . you know I've got a place out there. Did you hear about that?"

Helaine nodded.

"But I don't know what to expect."

Silence. Sharon sighed. "And I'm pregnant again."

Pregnant again. Helaine had nothing to say about any of it. Lydia had seen her with this woman. It was probably true that she wouldn't know her if she fell over her, but that was hardly the point. She had seen her with a lover, a beautiful young woman. It was over. She knew it.

"I'll never let you go," Sharon stated as if reading her mind. "Never."

Helaine sat up and folded her hands. "Am I suppose to be flattered by that?"

"I don't care if you are or aren't. I want you to know, that's all."

"You want—What do want from me, Sharon Chambers. *The* Sharon Chambers? Don't you get enough jollies without me?"

"I certainly try. How do you get your jollies without me?"

Helaine let out an impatient breath. *I long after strangers.*

"All of this is about my career. I've told you that before."

"All of this?" Helaine faced her now. "This is good for business, Sharon? All of this? I'll tell you what all of this is about. It's about my blood, which you have acquired an appetite for."

Sharon leaned into her face and kissed her hard on the mouth. Helaine pushed her away and wiped her lips off with the back of her hand. She saw the cabbie's eyes in the mirror and looked away without speaking.

"Appetite. I like that," Sharon said.

Helaine ignored her.

"You are fuckin' gorgeous, Doctor."

"There are other gorgeous women in the world, as you know."

"None like you."

"You know . . . I'm . . . I'm not your . . . you really need to grow up. That's your biggest problem. You're not twenty-three anymore, I'm not thirty-three. We're—"

"Who is it, Helaine? Who do you want to fuck so bad?"

Helaine glanced at the cabbie again, saw only the back of his head.

"Hmm? Who's after you? I'm not stupid you know."

Helaine wanted to stop the cab. "Nobody's after me," she replied weakly.

"You're lying. I know it. I wonder if they'd feel the same about you if they knew about me."

There was no reply.

"Hmm? Would they think you were so fucking sweet then?" She saw the blond tremble. Was it rage or was she going to cry? "I'll squash you both. I swear it, Dr. Kristenson."

Helaine banged at the glass divider. "Let me out," she ordered the cabbie and he pulled over to the curb. Sharon watched silently as Helaine handed the fare through the slot. "I'll walk," was all the blond said as she slammed the taxi door.

Sharon checked the time. "The airport. I can't miss my plane."

It was the sudden heat that had tipped him off to the potential of the day. The waiter had felt trouble blowing in the air all morning and had braced himself for it. The arrival of Dr. Kristenson after a long and notable absence, Lydia diligently waiting for her outside on the street patio. He was sure it would have something to do with them. He hesitated and stood poised inside the doorway, alerted by the sound of squealing tires and honking horns, and waited to see what trouble would look like.

He recognized the leggy woman right away. Magazines and billboards. And front page gossip. He had a bad feeling about that paper doll. He strained to read her lips as she spoke with the driver of the yellow sports car she had just emerged from, but he was only able to catch bits and scraps of her salacious remarks. She was putting on a show, building up the audience. The main attraction.

He was quite sure whose table she would be heading for. He studied the blond, waiting for her response. Out of the corner of his eye he observed Lydia. She looked on the unfolding event completely clueless, oblivious to what was just about to hit her. In fact, trouble slithered to within ten feet of her table before she actually saw it.

Fortunately it was all over before it began. Sharon Chambers simply threatened through her teeth to make a scene and the discreet Dr. Kristenson got up instantly and left with her, leaving everything behind but her purse.

Standing on the sidewalk, twenty blocks from home, Helaine stood trembling with rage and an indescribable pain filled her chest. She hoped it was a heart attack but didn't feel lucky enough for such a prognosis.

It was a warm day and she was dressed for it so she decided to walk back to her brownstone instead of being stuck in another cab. What she would do when she got there she didn't know.

She would return to Frank's next Friday and explain her situation. What's to explain? There was no explanation needed. It is what it appears to be. Even worse than that.

She thought of Sharon's threats. She thought of Harry's warning. She thought of a disappointed face.

The afternoon passed into night, the night into another day. Day after day the same agonizing, until it was yet another weekend. Friday, but the woman was not there. Not across the way, either. A week and then another week. No way to explain. No setting things right again. No return to status quo. No Lydia.

Harry spoke very little about it and it was better that way. Helaine knew she had screwed up. There was no remedy for the pain.

Lydia Beaumont had wandered off the beaten path into a lightly wooded area on the private side of the pond. She sat against a young birch, hidden from view in the ferns and cattails, and stared longingly at the water. She had no suit but it was eighty degrees and she was toying with the idea to skinny dip. Above her on the path she had just heard voices but they soon faded away. She was just about to strip when she suddenly heard the unmistakable sound of lovemaking coming from an area not far to the left of her. She froze against a tree, afraid to be discovered, and then slumped to the ground and lay there, hoping it would end quickly and quietly considering her options if it didn't.

After more than ten minutes of this, curiosity got the better of her and she raised her head and peered across a sea of ferns. Two women in the thick of it, not more than fifteen feet from her hiding place. If she got up to leave now they would know she had seen them. If she stayed any longer she was a Peeping Tom. She put her head down on her arms and closed her eyes. She would have to wait them out, it would be too difficult to explain otherwise.

Two hundred miles. Lydia had driven that far to get away from something like this, away from thinking of it all the time, but even here in the wilderness . . . she heard the frenzied sobs and gasps of orgasm and glanced at her watch. Fifteen minutes. She lifted her head and studied the woman's motions, resting her face on her arms again. It was genuine. She was close enough to them to see their glistening skin, the patches of sunlight that camouflaged their nakedness.

Three weeks in retreat and now this bringing it all back to her. Two women. The baths, the wraps, the massages, the peaceful walks. Lydia's troubles had seemed to peel away from her, one by one, like dead skin. The trouble with work, with—she had put it all out of her mind, she thought. Now here she was, lying face down in the woods, ambushed, the problem assaulting her, descending on her through the music of another woman's pleasure, the song of it rippling across her spine, the weight of it heavy on her shoulders, holding her in her place, bending her down beneath it, into the soft earth, ferns, moss. Into a bed of moss she went lonely, terribly lonely, only half of something she wanted to be, maybe because of it, only half of what she used to be. She felt the ground give gently under her and the scent of moss and of bittersweet filled her nostrils. She could hear the woman call out her lover's name, crying low when answered, could feel the tickle of her own hair against her cheek. It was an unbearable sensation. She pushed a lock of it away from her eyes and exhaled a long and unhappy breath.

Above them sounded the shrill protest of woodland tenants. Disturbed from their routine, they abandoned their perches and screamed warnings and epithets at the intruders. Unrequited! Unrequited! Unrequited! Lydia was convinced that's what they yelled. The lovers obviously heard nothing of the sort. She cursed them and checked the time—thirty minutes—debating whether or not she could crawl the twenty or so yards to the footpath without being noticed.

Ten, perhaps, but not twenty she realized. It was too far to go. She turned over on her back, inconsolable, and stared up at the sky through the canopy of birches.

It was a perfectly clear day. She still wanted her. A sigh of frustration slipped free from her and she put a hand to her mouth to prevent another.

"Yes, there," an excited lover instructed. The next words were choked.

Lydia heard a muffled response from the other woman.

"Mmmmm," came a quick approval.

She felt her heart jump and scolded herself for it.

The woman's voice raised up and then died down once more, settling into a seductive whisper of encouragement. It was followed by a low moan that drifted skyward to the treetops, which was soon chased by another. She could imagine Helaine here. Standing in the hot sun. Sitting in a window seat. Lying in the woods. Making love with her lover. It had not gone away at all. She shut her eyes and brought her hands to her ears, but it was too late for that.

She was a hopeless case. She saw this perfectly. That she was running, hiding, trying to block out anything that might remind her of Helaine. Moans and cries carried on the wind and taunted her. She wished to become numb again, impervious to the inspiration they sparked in her and castigated herself for wandering so far from the trail. Why the ladies had to pick this spot she hadn't a clue. She checked the time, sighed into her hands, closed her eyes.

She was at the beginning once more, the genesis, and once more trapped in the void, hopelessly lost now between an elusive heaven and an immovable earth. The depth of who she had been, Lydia Beaumont, was gone forever she realized, staring up at the sky. She admitted that something dark and formless had taken her place, as dark and formless as a body of water and on that water she could see the spirit of a goddess moving, her wake disturbing the surface, rippling on it, like goose bumps on skin. She could see the light, a reflection.

Shouldn't she just say it was good? Shouldn't she divide herself from this darkness? Call it a day? Call it a night? Yes, but then what of the morning? What of evening? She groaned low. Her heart was a firmament. She wanted to throw it across the water like a skipping stone, a shooting star, let her flame divide the water, gather it all in one place, that she might have dry land. Safe land, fertile and yielding.

Wouldn't that be good? And then the only darkness would be the sky above her at night, full of stars for wishing and for the signs of the zodiac, or to happily mark the seasons, the days, the years. Darkness then would be good, too, simply a place for the sun to sleep at night or for the creatures of the earth to rest in until morning. Creatures like her. And a goddess. A goddess must have sleep, too.

Another scream. Lydia felt she should applaud the lovers at this point. Wood nymphs. Lydia marveled at their stamina and listened for the climax.

Listening, she thought maybe it was just as well the blond was not available. How could she have made her happy like that? A minute or an hour, it's probably a question of experience. Perhaps she had been spared by the gods at the last minute. What did she know about such things anyway? There's no book on that, she bet. (Sobs and gasps through the ferns again.) Is there?

Ten minutes, maybe fifteen. One orgasm, that was all Lydia was used to getting, even from Joe. Clever Joe. She rolled over on her stomach and stared through the greenery at the two women, now kissing, now embracing, their stomachs touching. Breasts, lips, arms, palms, thighs. Cognac? Oysters? How exactly do you make love to a woman?

The lovers were trying to stand. Whoops. They were kneeling again. Lydia was finally able to see their faces. That one she had met last week. She had noticed that she wore a wedding band. The other one had just arrived. Both about forty-something, good shape. They had either known each other before or . . . ? Lydia scoffed ruefully. Nah, they had just met. She dropped her head down and undertook to memorize the patterns of moss as she rested on her elbows, contemplated her mistakes.

She who hesitates. It should be our tryst in the woods she thought grudgingly. Us scaring the birds off their nests. She had hesitated, that's for sure. More than hesitated, she had lollygagged as if she had all the time in the world. She could at last admit it, ridiculously stranded as she now found herself to be. Out of her league, an entirely new experience: incompetence. Why, she had never even spoken to Helaine, didn't even know her last name. Was there a whole universe of ready-wear women simply for the asking? Could she possibly be the only woman in the world who hesitated?

It seemed possible. She couldn't imagine Delilah being so inhibited. She should have confided in her sooner, told her what really she wanted. Why hadn't she? *Because I don't know what I'm doing—I've never pursued anyone, let alone a woman.* She took stock of the last six months. *Look how I screwed the whole thing up*, she lamented silently.

She pictured the twenty-something living doll that had materialized as Helaine's lover. That woman would never hesitate. *Which is why she has her and I don't. Which is why I'm stuck out here in the woods like a sex-starved maniac watching other women have a good time.* She thought about that, her thirty-six-year-old heart sinking like a wrecked ship to the bottom of an ocean. No, being bold wasn't the only reason. Helaine's lover was also young and beautiful, a perfect ten.

Then why do you make eyes at me? Why were you always alone? Why were you so miserable the last time I saw you, acting like you wanted to be near me?

Laughter in the woods.

The ladies were finally getting dressed, doing that clumsy dance that people do when putting their clothes on hastily. There was the sound of clinking belts and zipping zippers. The final touches. Licks and promises. Just for the record Lydia glanced at the time. They were heading her way. She lay low in the underbrush and made herself as small as possible as they cut across the ferns, passing within six feet of her on their way back to the path.

"I'm walking funny," the married one announced.

Lydia held her breath as they walked by giggling and whispering.

"That's because you're greedy."

"You're *sooo* right."

"I hope we weren't in any poison ivy."

"Wouldn't that be something to explain?"

"Imagine what Charles would say. Isn't that his name?"

"Charles!" They squealed at the mention of Charles.

"What are you doing for dinner?"

"You."

"And what's for dessert?"

"Me."

They reached the top of the knoll near the path, their voices trailing off at last. Lydia lay quietly for a few minutes before sitting up. Eventually even the birds were still once more.

Lydia stood up, brushed herself off and considered the water. It was hard to gauge the distance to the other side of the pond, but it was certainly quicker than the trail and it would rule out running into the ladies who were sure to be taking their time, strolling leisurely, being satisfied with each other. She tied her sneakers to her waist and waded in.

Back in her room Lydia changed for dinner and scheduled a facial. It was nice at the spa, but she should think about leaving soon. She regarded the rendezvous in the woods as a setback of sorts and it made it seem rather pointless to continue hiding out.

She sat in the dining hall trying to formulate a better plan and reddened when the wood nymphs appeared in the doorway, looking a lot less casual in their evening attire, yet nonetheless interested in each other. She would never have guessed just by looking at them, but then she was willing to admit that she was a neophyte at these things. She would never have guessed it of Helaine, either.

Helaine so and so. Yeah, it was time to go home. Lydia had a life to live.

* * *

"In love there is no east and west; no north and south. And there are no distinct borders or boundaries for dispute. Rather there are comfort zones and these must at all times be respected."
Doctor Helaine Kristenson, Keeping Mr. Right

Check this out, observed Dr. Kristenson. The way he's sitting, she could tell he was wearing one of his wife's things under his clothes. Look how stricken the woman seems today.

Dr. Kristenson selected a benign expression. Best to be diplomatic about it.

Dr. K: (clears her throat) How would you like to begin today's discussion?

S: Don't ask me. I am not the one having the problem.

Dr. K: O—kay?

M: (deep drawn out sigh) Dr. Kristenson, I just want a normal life. Like it was before. I want him to be (long pause—he is glaring at her, she is trying not to look at him) to be a normal husband. A normal man.

Dr. K: We seem to be backsliding on this. Can you each describe what has happened since we last met? (she looks from one to the other)

S: Nothing, Doctor. Nothing at all! She's got too many hang-ups. You know what you are, *M*? You're a rigid fundamentalist. And you're oppressing me with your hang-ups. (crosses, uncrosses his legs—he has recently taken to wearing her undergarments and wants her to have intercourse with him when he is in drag)

Dr. K: Let's bring it down a bit, *S*. Would you like to respond to that, *M*?

M: I'm sorry Dr. Kristenson, I've tried. (she is obviously depressed) I feel ridiculous. I can't help it. (she won't look at him at all now) I feel (long pregnant pause) ugly.

Dr. K: (passes on that one, waits for hubby's response)

S: If she loved me and respected my needs there wouldn't be a problem with it.

M: If you loved and respected me then you wouldn't need to wear my things!

S: See what I mean, Doctor? *My, my, my,* all the time *my!* You are so, so selfish *M.* You are ruining everything with this shit.

Dr. Kristenson held up her hands in the shape of a T and they quieted down. Eight sessions and the wife was still in extreme discomfort over this issue. She had tried it his new way and didn't like it. For her own reasons Dr. Kristenson was inclined to identify with the plight of the wife. The woman felt ridiculous in bed with him, enough so that she couldn't feel romantic anymore. He had pushed her too far with his fetish, a fetish she had never even known about until a few months ago, which is why they were in counseling to begin with. Now the woman was experiencing a kind of female impotence with her husband—she couldn't have sex with him at all. Their love life was simply not elastic enough to accommodate the kind of bedtime antics he had in mind and by forcing the issue on her, wearing her things and playing a blame game, he had crippled her feminine pride. The doctor sighed sympathetically without meaning to. She wondered why he hadn't at least had the courage to buy his own fancy underwear.

They waited gloomy-faced for her to speak, their bodies posed in the manner of those who are prepared to wait forever if need be for the right answer.

Dr. Kristenson wanted to say look mister, here's your wife's core issue: If you are not a real man then she must not be a real woman. But how could it help? She masked her annoyance and indicated with her pencil that they should continue their dialogue.

M: Dr. Kristenson, you're a woman. Can you understand how I feel?

Dr. K: (ummm)

S: She doesn't have the hang-ups you have! She knows it's perfectly natural.

Dr. K: (holds up her hand again; they are silent once more; she folds her hands around her knee and smiles bleakly) I am not here to take sides. I am here to help you work this out, if that's what you both want. An issue like this is only a problem if the marriage cannot withstand it. If that is the case, the behavior remains right for one partner, but wrong for the other and thereby wrong for the health of your relationship. (she paused to see if they comprehended her meaning) Do you feel that this might be the case?

M: Yes.

S: No.

"Del Lewiston," Delilah shouted, pointing at the empty chair. "May I?"

"Please do." Helaine was surprised she had come over. She shook the extended hand, "Helaine," was all she volunteered, "how do you do? Can I get you anything from the bar?"

"Oh no! I'm already three sheets—how's that go?"

Helaine smiled. "Three sheets to the wind—it's a sailing metaphor!"

"That's it!" She wasn't really drunk. "You look awfully familiar!"

It was a crowded, noisy night at Frank's. Helaine pretended not to understand her.

Delilah leaned forward and yelled above the room. "You know I've got a friend that's just gaga over you!"

Gaga? Helaine looked over her shoulder and back again. She nodded.

"Do you know which friend I mean?"

Helaine nodded again. "The feeling is—"

"What?"

Helaine grinned and leaned across the table. "I said the feeling is mutual!"

"Mutual? Oh, *mutual*! Good! Wonderful! Then what's the problem?"

Good question. "Where is she?" Helaine asked.

"Where?"

"Yes!"

"Moping somewhere."

"Oh? I'm very sorry to hear that. Do you know why?"

"Because—I'm not exactly sure how to put it! What's the problem, I asked?"

Helaine waited for the room to quiet down before answering. "There are complications."

Delilah indicated she understood. "Husband?"

Helaine laughed. "Uh . . . no. Just as bad, I'm afraid."

"Does my friend know this?"

Helaine coughed nervously. "She does now."

Delilah's eyes brightened with insight. "I see." She rolled the information over in her head. "You know ladies, it's a modern world out there. This would not be a 'complication' for the rest of us."

"But your friend?"

Delilah wanted to lie for Lydia but she was reluctant to misrepresent her. "Nah, she wouldn't go for it, I think. Not knowingly." She rose from the table seeing that the waiter was delivering Helaine's food.

Helaine liked her. "You're a good friend, Del."

"It was a pleasure to meet you, Helaine whoever you are, incognito. We've never had this conversation. S'aright?"

Helaine smiled confidentially. "Of course."

Delilah headed for the bar.

"News?" the waiter asked hopefully. He set a dessert down that Helaine hadn't ordered. "Eat," he prompted. "So where is she?"

She shrugged. "Didn't say."

He handed her a fork and knife. "Is she coming back?"

"She didn't say that either."

He grimaced. "What then?" His movements were drawn out, unnatural.

Helaine laughed at his expense and cut into the black forest. "She's gaga," she replied.

The waiter slowly loaded his tray, bending low as he did it. "Gaga?"

"Mmmm."

He hoisted up the tray and winked. "Gosh!"

She laughed. It was a relief to smile again even if she didn't know where Lydia was.

"Gaga," the waiter said, finally turning to leave, "isn't that French?"

The city was hotter than Lydia expected it to be. The trees along the avenues stood brooding and indignant, unhappy with the heat and their isolation. They seemed to resent the shaded walks beneath their limbs and the scorched humans who intermittently took refuge there. Here and there, at a taxi stand or bus stop, a blistering bench shone empty and forlorn in the full midday sun, the hardwood beside it deliberately refusing to provide any comfort.

She had a week left of her vacation. Summer in metropolis. Lydia had forgotten how sticky it could be. She plodded back from the car rental, the sidewalks burning through her sandals, and sighed with relief when she finally entered the air-conditioned lobby of her building. The doorman smiled his familiar greeting but even he looked hot and bothered. She should have stayed in the woods with the happy vegetation, she mused as she stepped into the elevator.

A pile of newspapers blocked the entrance to the penthouse. She climbed over them and unlocked the door, flicking the overheads on and tossing her bag in before her.

She smiled with delight at the blast of cool air that greeted her, the sight of the glorious wood floors. No more dingy welcome-homes. The place was inviting even without furniture. In the living room the old sofa stood as a lone sentinel and it beckoned her to come and tell her all about her trip. Beside it the answering machine blinked like a Christmas tree and she plopped into the waiting pillows and hit the play button with her thumb.

Ooh, what's that? A din from the club: the girls singing. Mom. Del. Mom. Hang up. Paint's here? The paint! Mom. Mom (oh brother). Dad? Del. Another hang up.

Lydia rewound it. Better call mom this week. And Del. Daddy can wait.

"Well, how are you?"
"A hundred percent and declining."
"Really?"
"Mmhmm, any day now I expect to start dying."
"Liddy! We start dying the day we're born."
"No, c'mon, Del. I don't see how that could be. When you're young you're growing and growing. That's the epitome of life."
"Dying and dying. I'm sure of it. It just looks like growth. I can see we're still morbidly preoccupied. So what's a vacation for anyway?"
"Painting, Del. Come see."

"Painting? Oh, that's right. Does it look like a whorehouse yet?"

"You won't believe!"

"You got anything to eat there?"

"Not really."

"Chinese?"

"Sounds good."

"It does?"

"Good enough, I meant."

"You did this? It's beautiful, Liddy. Look at those floors!"

"Sponge on the walls. Out of a book of course. I'm going to have wood trim installed. What do you think?"

"It looks like you know what you're doing. Ooh, Liddy, that table and chairs. Claw and ball. I like it. Ooh, what are those?" Delilah asked, pointing out two charcoal drawings hanging in the area Lydia now referred to as the sunroom.

"Master studies. Manet. Student's work from the forties. That's from *Luncheon in the Grass*."

"Yah! Some lunch. How come the men aren't nude?"

"You don't think it's funny? I thought of Frank's the minute I saw it."

"I think it's a riot! Who's that babe?"

"That's *Olympia*. A courtesan most likely, though. At least that's what the dealer says."

"Lydia Beaumont, she almost looks like you. Maybe you were a courtesan in your past life. That would explain why you're so cautious now." Delilah stepped back from the piece. "I swear she looks just like you."

Lydia laughed self-consciously. "You think so?" Perhaps that's why she had been attracted to it. Odd that the dealer hadn't mentioned the likeness, or maybe he thought it rude to point it out. Nice gentleman. Very polite. She'd ask his opinion about it next time. Curious she hadn't noticed it herself.

"And what does a courtesan sleep on these days?" Delilah inquired from the hallway.

"Getting there, getting there. Just an old mattress for now."

"Liddy, how you gonna get any action on that thing? It's shockingly Spartan of you, you know. Hey, but that dresser looks nice in here. Why didn't you polish it?"

A pair of black silk fishnet gloves hung from one of the drawers. Delilah recognized them. The women eyed each other in the mirror, Lydia frozen in the doorway.

"When are you going to ask her, my friend?"

"Del . . ." She wanted to put an end to it before they began. "I don't know."

"That is why you fled, am I right?" She placed the gloves where she had found them and turned to face her friend. "Ask the woman, Liddy. The very worse she can say is no."

"Ask her what, Del? Would she have an affair with me? I don't want an affair. Would she get rid of her perfect ten for me? Her beautiful, young girlfriend? Huh? What are the odds of that, Del? I wasn't born yesterday, you know." She headed for the living room, Delilah following after her.

"A perfect ten? Get real. There's no such thing."

"Oh yes there is, Delilah, and I've seen her." Lydia spun around and they stood face to face. "So what do you say to that?"

"What do I say? I say go look in the mirror, for God's sake. If that's not perfect then what is?"

Lydia was silenced by the compliment. She sat down on the couch, Delilah standing over her.

"It's just a little competition, Dame Beaumont, you can deal with that." She sat down beside her. "You deal with it every day. They're all the same punks. Spoiled. Arrogant. Stupid."

Stupid. Lydia doubted the shark was stupid. "I don't know. Besides I've never really asked someone out before. How do you go about it with a woman?"

"Well, how did Joe ask you out?"

Ugh, Joe. How did he? She thought back to it. It didn't seem that he actually had. No. He was just always circling her, his pretty manicured hands constantly reaching for her erogenous zones. She cringed at the thought of it. He had seduced her.

"All right," Delilah interrupted. "Forget it. How about before Joe?"

That was easier. "Flowers. Dinner. Love poems."

"And you can't afford flowers?"

Lydia chuckled. "I could buy her the Hanging Gardens of Babylon if she wanted them, but how would I get them to her? I don't even know her last name. And it doesn't matter anyhow. I don't like to share lovers, Del. You know that."

"So, obviously you think she'd say yes if you asked?"

Did she think that? "I don't want to share, that's all I meant."

"So you'll break your own heart? Like you did with Joe."

"He did me wrong, Del. Right from the start. I don't want that again. Why begin and then cry for something that might have been—you know that song?"

Yeah, but she didn't share the sentiment. It was fun to fall. "You are in love, Dame Beaumont?" It was a gimmee, a setup for an if-this-then-that. Hypothetical hyperbole. Delilah knew her friend would dodge it.

"I've made up my mind, Del."

"Oh c'mon. Love at first sight?" Delilah pressed. "*L—U—V?*"

Lydia smiled despite her unease. No, definitely not at first sight. It had been a slow awakening. Couldn't she gradually go back to sleep now? That's what she was hoping for. "I can't remember how it started. It just crept over me. Like a pox. LUV. Christ, Del, with a woman. I can't believe this has happened to me." She hesitated there waiting to be rescued, her head humming like a bee's nest.

Delilah offered nothing but an expectant expression.

"A womanizer like my father. Del, say something."

"Lydia Beaumont, have you ever slept with a woman?"

"No, of course not."

"Then you're hardly a womanizer. Besides, at this rate?"

"Have you?"

"Slept with your father?"

"Del! You know what I'm asking."

"Liddy, please stay focused here. You're going off on a tangent."

"Del?"

"I have never been in love with a woman. There, are you satisfied?"

"Is that a yes?"

(Oh, geesh.) "It was a long time ago. I was drunk. In all places,

Shanghai. Erotic and impractical. Mmmm. Quite impractical for a conservative investment banker like me."

"Solar flare?"

"That's right, a solar flare. Not quite the blond bomb as your Helaine is, but an entire month of electrical interference anyway."

Helaine? Lydia gulped. Delilah knew the blond's name? "How do you know—? Oh Del, tell me that you didn't talk to her. Tell me you didn't make me look like a child!" She moved closer to her on the couch; Delilah's lips moved like a fish gulping for air. "Delilah Lewiston, you didn't!"

"Liddy—"

"What did you tell her?"

"Liddy—"

"You didn't tell her anything! Oh, Del, what did you fucking say to her?"

Delilah sighed and stood up. "Liddy, I was only trying to get you laid. You are a child sometimes."

"What did she say? Tell me what she said to you."

Delilah walked toward the kitchen without answering. Lydia chased after her. She saw her going through the refrigerator.

"Del . . . please?"

"Why isn't there anything to drink in here?"

"Delilah Lewiston—"

"The feeling is mutual, Lydia Beaumont. Now get your act together."

"The feeling is mutual?"

Delilah was annoyed. "Your feelings. Hers. MUTUAL. You're making yourself look like a child. I'm at least trying to get you laid."

She went back to the couch empty-handed and threw herself in it with a loud sound of disgust, so loud it almost seemed to come from the furniture itself. Lydia stood over her speechless.

"Get some paper and a pen, Dame Beaumont."

"Paper and pen? What for?"

"A love poem."

"A poem? I don't know how to write a poem. What about—"

"Liddy, it is not a happy union, that's what I can tell. You've seen them together, not me. Get over how beautiful her girlfriend is. Do they look happy together?"

No.

"Paper and pen."

She vacillated over the request. "Is this what you would do, little Miss Shanghai?"

That prompted a throaty laugh from Delilah. "You wouldn't do what I would do."

There was paper in the briefcase. A pen. Lydia rummaged for the items, one eye studying Delilah as she sat with an arm over her eyes, her head nearly lost in the pillows. Her friend had slept with a woman. "Here."

"Not me. I'm not courting the woman, you are."

"Delilah, tell me. Describe what it's like. I've got fears about it."

There was no response from the pillows.

"You understand, Del?"

(Veni, vidi, vici, said the sofa.)

"Del, that's you, not me."

"You think too much, my friend. You're being impossible. And you're making it impossible." She rolled over on her side and stared at Lydia. "Liddy, don't make me pity you. Start writing, please."

"I can't do this. I'm not a poet."

"Then get a book. You don't think all the poems you got were written by the men who sent them, do you?"

"They weren't?"

"I doubt it very much. What, you think they grew the flowers, too?"

"What a bunch of frauds," Lydia exclaimed.

"Us too—what kind of poetry do you think she reads?"

Poetry? "Burns! She was reading Burns the last time I saw her."

"Robert Burns?"

"I guess so. You've heard of him?"

A helpless laugh emptied from Delilah. "This is going to be so much easier than you think, Liddy. Grab some Burns on one of your excursions. You'll see what I mean."

* * *

Sherlock Holmes had nothing substantial to report to Sharon Chambers about the Love Doc. He had begun to think that title a bit specious since the doctor apparently had no love life of her own, unless you factored in the insanely possessive supermodel who was paying a mint to have her followed while she plea bargained in LA.

Casing out Frank's was an act of futility, though she had resumed her original habit of Friday dinners and Saturday lunches. But she still ate there alone.

He had discovered that she looked very nice in navy blue, striped linens and flowing silks. Privately he would have liked to see her step out a bit, something more flashy now and then. She could pull it off, he thought. A bright red dress, mid-thigh, cut low in the front, way down in the back. Liven things up a bit. Course she might not look so much like a doctor then. Or a bookworm.

"Altho' my bed were in yon muir,
Amang the heather, in my plaidie;
Yet happy, happy would I be,
had I dear Montgomerie's Peggy.
When o'er the hill beat surly storms,
And winter nights were dark and rainy;
I'd seek some dell, and in my arms
I'd shelter dear Montgomerie's Peggy.
Were I a baron proud and high,
And horse and servants waiting ready;
Then a' 'twad gie o' joy to me—
The sharin't with Montgomerie's Peggy."

—Robert Burns

Except for the two of them seated at their separate tables, the dining room was finally empty, the bar vacated. Outside, only a few lunch stragglers still sat on the patio, apparently immune to the wilting heat.

The worst she could say is no.

Lydia watched Helaine take the slip of paper from the waiter's tray, the long fingers anxiously unfolding it. The blond had clearly not expected to see her again, let alone the love note. She cast curious sideways glances in Lydia's direction and then a long and pensive look out the window after she had read it.

The feeling is mutual, get over how beautiful her girlfriend is. Lydia was trying. The blond bomb. Electrical interference. Short circuits. Solar flares.

She was more rested than the last time Lydia had seen her, although at present the woman had lost some of her normal composure and appeared to be considering a hasty retreat in an effort to regain it again. Lydia watched her slip the note inside her blouse and gather her other things into a purse. Despite her obvious confusion, the blond looked quite well. Beautiful. It was too much to hope that the source of her recovery was due to that she had not been with her lover for awhile. She hoped for it anyway as Helaine filled out her bill, handed it to the waiter and without a word swished past her table in a whisper of fine fabrics, her soft silks billowing like the sails of a tall ship, the scent of sandalwood wafting on her breeze and descending like a cloud all around Lydia, in her hair, on her skin. Lydia lowered her eyes and drew the intoxicating air deep into her lungs.

Running away? Now, is that supposed to happen? Lydia rested her chin on her hand and watched out the window as the woman evaporated into traffic.

That was a waste of courage, she told herself, wishing she had never been born.

"Congratulations," whispered the waiter. He deposited a napkin beside her plate and disappeared without further ado. "Lydia", it said on the outside. Dear John, she bet, waiting till he was out of sight before reading it.

"Her flowing locks, the raven's wing,
adown her neck and bosom hing;
How sweet unto that breast to cling,
and round that neck entwine her!
Her lips are roses wat wi' dew,
O, what a feast her bonie mou'!

Her cheeks a mair celestial hue,
A crimson still diviner!"

Signed simply, "Helaine." The waiter returned with Lydia's bill.
"What is your name?" she asked.
"Harry."
Harry. A fine name. A wonderful, uncomplicated name. Easy to
remember. She smiled like a child. A perfect name in a perfect world.
Harry. Just as light as a kite in her cloudless sky. "I really don't know what
I'd do without you, Harry."
He grinned impishly. "You'd better figure it out soon."

The first week back and everything she touched turned to gold. No
conundrums, no hassles. Corporate governance at its best. Lydia could
almost stand leading the tribe again. Rumors abounded concerning an
inside trading scandal and all of Rio Joe's activities were suddenly under
scrutiny. It shouldn't surprise anyone, she wanted to say. He was likely
the mastermind.

He acted like a hunted animal these days, sending her beseeching
looks as if she was his only salvation. She ducked them, allowing them to
drift past her without interception. He had sought to become a lone wolf
in the firm, alone he really was.

At free moments she studied Helaine's handwriting. She wished
the blond had given her number, but then what? Forget her beautiful
girlfriend. Think of the sensuous Lin Lydia, the elegant scrawl. Maybe
the blond was a writer, that would explain her interest in books. Lydia
couldn't recall seeing her with one last Saturday. Had she written this
poem from memory?

Friday morning a dozen red roses arrived at her office. She feared them
at first, almost certain that Rio Joe was resorting to different tactics, but
when she saw and recognized the handwriting on the envelope her heart
jumped out of its normal place and hid all day in her throat, disguised
there as a suppressed scream of joy.

" . . . *by night, by day, a-field, at hame,*

The thoughts o' thee my breast inflame:
And aye I muse and sing thy name—
I only live to love thee.
Tho' I were doom'd to wander on,
Beyond the sea, beyond the sun,
Till my last weary sand was run;
Till then—and then—I'd love thee!"

She placed them, Robert Burns, on a stand in the window, speculating over them all day. That Helaine knew her name had not surprised Lydia. At Frank's her friends yelled it all night. It would be odd considering how loud they were not to have heard it at least once. But where she worked? Too titillating. It cast a bit of intrigue over the affair. She pondered it at the window standing beside her bouquet.

She had already made plans to meet her father at the club this afternoon or she would have sought the blond out at happy hour. Discreetly, of course, in case she wasn't alone. The red, red roses . . . *what the hell am I thinking?*

One more day, is what she was thinking, preparing herself for dinner with her father. She was just going to get her feet wet, test the waters as Delilah had suggested she should do. She would ask Helaine to join her for lunch tomorrow and take it from there. One more day.

She put her lipstick on and adjusted herself for her father's inspection, in a low grade dread over the inevitable inquisition which had become so routine in their relationship. She hoped this time he would not have the gall to set up a double date with her as he had done the last time. She had very nearly walked out on dinner that night, hooked up without advanced warning to the son of his most recent squeeze, the three of them waiting for her to arrive like cats would for a mouse. Poor mom. Why she wouldn't divorce him, Lydia didn't know. Maybe just not living with him anymore was enough. She often wished her father was as smooth and debonair as he actually looked.

Stepping out on the sidewalk fifteen flights below, the heat was high, burning away the last weeks of summer. Suffocating humidity. It sat heavy on her shoulders shocking her air conditioned body. She was not going to struggle with it today. She stood on the corner and hailed a cab.

Above her, across the street, Dr. Helaine Kristenson stood at the blinds again. She had been engaged in that activity all day, ever since the roses she had sent first appeared in Lydia's window. She had a great deal of apprehension now and it mingled with elation to create quite a potent poison to her nerves. For the moment, she was not going to struggle with it. She wouldn't have to. Lydia was not going to Frank's tonight.

A strange sense of relief claimed Dr. Kristenson once she realized this. She watched the taxi pull into the traffic and disappear around the corner without fear as to where it was going. It was not Lydia's whereabouts that worried her anymore. It was Sharon's.

It is Saturday. Two women stand in the entranceway of Frank's Place. They aren't aware of each other yet, or the similarity of their missions. A blond woman older than both of them, and the object of their desire, is seated at her usual table for lunch. She has noticed them up there. Her eyes flash red lights, green lights, even yellow, without her knowing it. Different signals to both of them which get crossed in the air. If the three ladies were dots on a piece of paper and you drew lines connecting them, you'd be drawing a triangle, the blond of course at the apex. Both women are equally beautiful in their own right and although the last thing the blond wants to see today is the two of them in the same place at the same time thinking the same thing, it provides for an unusually good opportunity to compare them with each other, which she is also doing without meaning to. Both are young, but one is older than the other. How much older? You can't tell. Both have dark hair, the older one's is more brown than black. The younger woman is taller than the other, perhaps by three or four inches. She is an exotic thing with an animal's grace and snarl. The defending champion, she wears a spoiled expression and is on a constant prowl, this very second admiring the strapless back and legs of her unknown rival. Her rival is a fine physical specimen with an elegance that borders on regal. She is armed in this contest with lofty ambitions and with unassuming good looks that come from deep beneath her skin.

And she has blue eyes, Helaine's favorite color. Her instincts are good. This second she senses someone behind her and is turning around to see who it is. At the same moment a hand expertly brushes against her bare back and a bedroom voice offers a disingenuous apology for the trespass as its owner passes too close to her on the way into the dining room. This woman seems oddly familiar and she follows her with her eye, glimpsing a cautionary glance from the blond as she does it. In her eyes she sees a yellow light flashing, then the light turns suddenly red and she balks. On the periphery the waiter finally appears heading for the entrance with a look of stupefaction. The seat Lydia wants, the one next to the blond, is now occupied and the sight of those two women together again instantly jogs her recollection. She turns pale, leaves. "Madam, wait," says the waiter.

"Harry?"

"Please. Let me seat you for lunch."

"Harry—"

"Please. This is just the tricky part, believe me."

Lydia gazed past him, sized up Helaine's tortured expression, her panicked body language. The dining room was less than half filled. She could be seated inconspicuously if she consented to it. "Three's a crowd," she whispered.

"Of course."

Lydia was silent, her face darkened with disappointment.

"She really wasn't expecting her," the waiter assured.

What does that mean? "I can't do this, Harry. I'm not the type."

It was pride talking. All that pride. "It's too late for a' that," he said.

She let go a bitter laugh. " 'For a' that, an' a' that, our toils obscure, an' a' that . . . '?"

"Yes, but 'the man o' independent mind, he looks and laughs at a' that'."

She considered those words. What was happening to her, quoting poets? Courting Venus? Letting herself be boondoggled again, this time by a woman?

" 'The course of true love never did run smooth,' " he began again.

"Okay, okay, okay." She could not outdo him, nor did she want to try. "Sit me there," she said, pointing at a location close to the unhappy couple. She saw a look of relief come over Helaine's face as the waiter led her to the table, but short of that the blond refused to acknowledge her.

The menu. Lydia put her face in it, listening for the voice she had hoped to hear today, but she heard only sliced and muffled responses, nothing to go on.

They had been together, she realized, staring over the top of her menu. She knew it by the younger woman's eyes, eyes fresh with a conquest, like a shark's. She knew it by the way Helaine tried to hide it, by the way she checked her movements so it wouldn't show. Yesterday or even today, Lydia thought, trying to discern the topic of their discussion. You are mine, the young woman seemed to be asserting to the beleaguered blond. Not a pleasant conversation. Under their table she could see the shark stretching her legs out to entwine Helaine's in them. She wanted to kick them herself and willed Helaine to do it for her, but the blond merely mumbled something and hid her face with her hand. It was the first time she had ever seen her flushed.

Oh God, Lydia thought, hailing the waiter, *what am I doing here?* He blocked her view as he took her order.

How good they looked together, she admitted, after he had gone, the sparks still flying between them, smoldering, though she could tell they were igniting something far more flammable than sexual passion, something quite a bit more adulterated than true love. Corrupted, but it was easy to envision how it must have been before that, before whatever it was had happened to ruin them. It was easy to see how darkness once complimented the light, posing no more harm to it than a cloud would by covering the summer sun in a breezy afternoon sky. Easy. Too easy.

There was a quick glance from Helaine. Bear with me, it said, I'm sorry. Lydia looked guiltily away. Wasn't she hoping to benefit by their catastrophe? Wasn't she guilty here of opportunism?

Lunch was ruined. Appetizers. Lydia pushed them around her plate, eyeing the blond fatale who just yesterday had sent her roses and today mere helpless glances. Strained, apologetic glances full of half-formed explanations and unspoken promises. Lies, probably. Lydia watched with dismay as the shark's hand disappeared under the tablecloth and

Helaine's face drained once more of its color. She saw the blond discreetly push her chair back from the table and send a warning look toward her lover, with lips blood red and hostile. The shark grinned insolently at her, removed her hand, and scoured the room instead.

As if things weren't complicated enough, Sharon Chambers was searching for the woman she had run into at the coat check. To her delight she found her conveniently seated only a few tables away. She liked the looks of the woman, her cut of clothes, the strong back and legs, and she was thinking that if she got the chance she'd proposition her, that she'd make a fine dessert. She sent those intentions her way, indifferent that Helaine was suddenly aware of them.

And now, thoroughly flustered, Lydia threw her fork down and headed for the ladies' lounge, a hapless move that both Helaine and the waiter simultaneously recognized for the huge mistake it was. Only Sharon Chambers mistook it for meaning something else. She waited an appropriate minute or two and nonchalantly followed after her, licking her chops all the way to the bathroom.

The waiter rolled his eyes heavenward and stepped behind the bar, scribbling on a piece of paper as he eyed Dr. Kristenson. She rubbed her forehead wearily and ran her hands through her hair, her agitated fingers displacing her hairpin and sending it flying across the tabletop. There was little he could do for her at this point. He watched a proverbial straw falling in slow motion from the sky and waited for the distinctive sound of a breaking back.

Ten minutes. Helaine shot a volley of anxious looks toward the ladies' lounge, reclaimed the hairpin and scooped her hair back before rising from her chair and aiming herself in that direction. The waiter intercepted her before she got that far, handing her a note with a piece of tape attached to it.

"Best I can do," he said, sheepishly. The note read "Out of Order."

"Indeed," she said, appreciating his tact. "Thank you." She taped it to the bathroom door and pushed herself inside, standing quietly in a dim hallway before deciding how to proceed.

She had never been in this room, was not familiar with the layout. She moved cautiously along the length of a long wooden partition until she glimpsed Sharon and then Lydia in the mirror around the bend. Their voices floated over the divide, taut and flat. Water was pouring from a faucet. Clearly they had not heard her enter.

"Decency?" That was Sharon. "Decency's not much of an asset in the bedroom, darling."

Darling. Helaine cringed.

"No? Well, maybe you ought to try it sometime."

Lydia's lipstick was smeared. So was Sharon's. You're a misery, Helaine thought, glaring at Sharon's reflection.

"Let's," Sharon pursued. "I'm an excellent student."

"Look . . . I don't need a student. Now give me my lipstick."

Helaine heard the sound of plastic hitting the floor, pieces of it scattering. What she couldn't see was Sharon grinding Lydia's lipstick into the floor with her sandal.

"Do you have any idea who you're talking to?" Sharon hissed, indignant.

She wouldn't know you if she fell over you, Helaine screamed in her head.

Lydia sighed impatiently and turned the water off. "Oh, please. You're not going to try to impress me, I hope, because you're already operating on a deficit."

Helaine smiled. She wasn't sure how Sharon Chambers was going to take that one. This was probably her very first NO. A deadly quiet filled the lounge and it hung heavy and toxic around the two women. Helaine could see Sharon's face in the mirror and didn't care for her expression. She thought fast and retraced her steps to the door, reaching behind her to open it and then closing it loudly again.

Sharon came sailing around the bend. "I'm out of here," she said hotly. "Meet me at the flat, Helaine."

"I—"

"At the flat, Dr. Kristenson!" She slammed the door behind her, oblivious to the consequences, or to the sign that was taped on the other side of it.

* * *

"Are you okay?"

"I'm fine," Lydia replied. She turned to the mirror, took out a tissue, wiped off her mouth.

Helaine observed her from behind.

"Doctor?" Lydia asked in the mirror.

"Yes. A doctor." She hesitated before confessing her name. "Dr. Helaine Kristenson." There was nothing in Lydia's face to indicate that she recognized it.

"Medical?" Lydia asked. She faced her again, leaning against the counter, grasping the edge of it in her hands. They were about the same height, her and the doctor. She smiled again. A doctor. In a gray tailored tunic with a heart shaped front, linen lined with satin, just a splash of lace, tapered in above the knees, gathered at the waist, hugging the hips, the sleeves nothing more than wide straps dangling over the tips of the shoulders as if they would fall down her arms if she wanted them to. Full breasts, wide shoulders, long neck, a blond halo of hair, eyes afire, more than a little something to get burned in . . .

"No," Helaine answered. "Just a psychotherapist."

"Oh." Lydia smiled self consciously. A pleasant voice, exactly what she had expected her to sound like. "Can you read minds then—I hope not?"

Helaine chuckled. "Sometimes."

Sometimes. Lydia nodded and averted her eyes. At her feet lay the remains of her lipstick dispenser, smeared and tracked across the floor. It made the bathroom look like the scene of an accident. Helaine saw it, too, and frowned.

"Please tell me she's just one of your patients," Lydia said, trying to effect a laugh.

Helaine grabbed some paper towels and bent to the floor. "She's not," she said without looking up. "I'm sorry to say."

Lydia watched her clean in silence. It was probably a ritual between them, she thought, noticing the gray dress slowly riding up Helaine's thighs, the tops of stockings, clips holding them in place. Down. She could see down the front of it now. She took a step forward and then stopped, embarrassed.

Helaine looked up then glanced at herself. "Lydia," she said, as she cleaned the mess. "Lydia *what*?" She had put a corset on this morning, mostly to remember what it was like to be Helaine Kristenson. She had instantly regretted it when she saw Sharon come in, but she was not in the least bit sorry now.

Lydia what? Lydia what? "Helaine—"

Helaine laughed low, stopped what she was doing. "No, dear. I'm Helaine. And you are . . . ?" She watched the blood rise to the woman's cheeks, smiled. "Lydia? What is your last name?"

"Beaumont . . . I'm Lydia Beaumont."

Beaumont? That's a familiar name. "Well," Helaine answered, shifting so the dress could slide higher up her thigh, "Ms. Beaumont, if you keep blushing like that, I'm just going to have to kiss you."

Lydia glanced in the mirror, laughed shyly. "You sent the cognac, I hope?"

"I did."

"And the oysters?"

Helaine knelt on one knee and set the paper towels down. "And the oysters. And the roses." She leaned forward, but didn't rise. "You like?" she asked.

One more step. Lydia put her hand on Helaine's shoulder. The dress strap fell down. "Like? Yes. Absolutely," she answered. "Love."

Helaine took a quick breath. "Good," she heard herself say, "I'm glad." Lydia's hands were at her neck. She let her lift her face, closed her eyes. She rested her cheek against a firm stomach. "Ms. Beaumont, how did you get a body like this?"

How? "I . . . work in finance." Lydia said, placing both her hands on Helaine's shoulders. "It's, uh, sort of an extreme sport." Down went the other strap.

"Extreme," Helaine repeated. "May I?" she asked, taking Lydia's right hand and bringing it to her lips. A sigh. "I'm extremely in love with Lydia Beaumont," she whispered, kissing the palm with her tongue. She felt Lydia jump. "What does Lydia Beaumont think I should do about it?"

"What . . . you should . . ." Behind them, to their sides was a bank of mirrors, a pretty portrait of two women in every one of them. One blond. One brunette. What she should do about it? They looked good together. She should—Lydia stroked the blond head below her, reached for the hairpin and removed it. A yellow wave cascaded onto her legs, a soft face pressed gently into her stomach. "Am I still blushing?"

Helaine opened her eyes, took in Lydia's face. "You are."

She was. She could feel it. "Then do what you have to," Lydia dared.

There was unfinished business at the flat. She had planned to buy her freedom today, say fare-thee-well to Sharon Chambers. Making out with Lydia Beaumont wasn't supposed to have happened yet. Making out!

Helaine walked slowly toward the harbor. Life has a force all its own, she mused, so we're never too early or too late. She could add that new observation to her book. What else, she wondered, could it do? Could it handle Sharon Chambers's wrath, provide the antidote for her poison, prevent whatever harm would come of today's confrontation? Wouldn't that be nice? She floated, propelled by an unseen force, the touch of a new lover still on her lips, her perfume lingering, without her knowing it, in her hair. Tomorrow or the next day, she promised herself, everything will be fine again. As for today . . . she floated away from her body, watched it with apprehension as it moved closer and closer toward Sharon.

"Ya know, Frank, you sure have some nice looking broads in here!" the man said, appraising a dark haired woman as she left the dining room, the last of the lunch customers to go. He swiveled his barstool around to beam at the waiter. Harry grimaced and placed the bill at the side of his glass.

Three times during the course of this guy's liquid lunch he had been required to inform him that his name was not Frank. He refused to correct him again. The checkered suits, the beady eyes, the stupid grin, the bald patch on the back of his fat speckled head. Harry had been wondering for months what a guy like that was doing hanging out in a place like Frank's, and the simple truth was that he didn't trust him.

Today "Checkers" (which is what he privately had nicknamed him) had abandoned his table and come up to the bar for his lunch, not long after Sharon Chambers had crashed the party. Harry wasn't sure, having been distracted, but it almost seemed the two of them knew each other, that they had acknowledged each other in a brief exchange. It was curious and Harry was troubled over it.

"See ya, Frank," Checkers drawled, nearly dragging the stool with him as he tottered away from the bar.

Harry smiled with disdain. Well, he thought, watching the big guy stagger through the patio doors and teetering on the sidewalk, if he's spying he won't remember what he saw today. He laughed as he wiped the bar down. Poor Checkers! He had served him drinks in triples. Four triples for lunch today!

She calls him Daddy. He calls her Queenie. It's an improvement over Princess, which is what he called her for the first two decades of her life. He calls her mother The Grim Weeper.

"Daddy, please. That's not nice."

"Then why do you laugh with me?" Edward Beaumont teased his daughter.

"I'm not laughing with you. I'm laughing at you."

Lydia was thinking of her last conversation with her father as she walked from Frank's to her apartment. She didn't know why, possibly because it took her mind off Helaine, heading right then to her lover's apartment, for a little heart to heart.

"Negotiation's the name of the game, Queenie. It's the only way to get what you want. Otherwise, you've just got to steal it."

Negotiating. Negotiating. Lydia had negotiated a soft option and a hairpin curve. It was now about twenty blocks away from her, engaged in thought, with its blond hair flowing on its very own breeze. That's too far away for Lydia to see the woman halt in her tracks, search her hair, and suddenly remember the missing hairpin lying on the floor of the ladies' lounge at Frank's. Also too far away for Helaine to go back and retrieve it. She was just a few blocks from the waterfront.

A missing hairpin, life under a magnifying glass, her hair flowing in a golden wave of liberation, incriminating her somehow. Helaine rarely wore it down. She stood at the corner by the basketball park, rummaging in her purse for something, anything to tie it back with.

The boom boxes blared, the basketballs thumped against their backboards, rubber squeaked against the court, glistening bodies danced and groaned with joy in the bristling heat, with a rhythmic *fwack, fwack, fwack* of an orange rubber ball and a blur of arms and legs, the jubilant *clink* of men throwing themselves into the chain linked fence, calling *yeah* and *yo* to the *boom, boom, boom* of a tireless bass. *Twoong!* Rim shot. *Swish!* Basket. There was music everywhere Helaine turned. The *tick, tack, tick* of speed chess with the subsequent murmurs of disappointed tourists finding themselves caught in split second checkmates. Honking horns and tweeting cell phones were the birds of this jungle. No one paid them any mind. They didn't trouble her today either. They blended nicely with the *sizzle* of the hot dog vendor, the *twang* of helium balloons that bounced over the heads of meandering pedestrians. She closed her purse . . . *click* . . . let the hair hang down on her shoulders . . . *whenever I'm near you . . . I hear a symphony* . . . she recognized strands of songs coming through the chain linked fence, and that one, too . . . *your body is a wonderland* . . . descending on her from one of those balconies; all the vaguely familiar tunes drifting happily toward her, delaying her, staying her, as they emanated from the sidewalk cafes, from the dark pubs with their rich blue notes . . . *I cover the waterfront* . . . she passed the T-shirt and tattoo parlors . . . *are you strong enough to be my man* . . . the sluggish crowd swallowing her up and keeping her presence there a secret. Helaine was lost in it . . . *zip, zip, zip* . . . the only one really moving, a brown beauty on roller skates with sleek muscular thighs, well toned biceps. She wove in and out of the street, onto the sidewalk, arms wide open, a strong back, like Lydia's. With arms wide open. *Zip, zip, zip* . . . arms wide open. At a standstill now, Helaine longed to be kept there, stuck with music and strangers until Sharon had no right to expect her anymore, till it was all over, till it was too late. Lydia's number. She had committed it to memory in the bathroom. She couldn't dare write it down . . . *swish* . . . *tick* . . . *fwack* . . . *fwack* . . . *clank* . . . *sssst* . . . Sharon had no right to expect her anymore . . . *twang* . . . *baby ,baby* . . . *boom* . . . *boom* . . . *boom* . . . *I hear a symphony* . . . *zip* . . . *zip* . . . *sssst* . . . *twooong* . . . Lydia's number . . . *yo* . . . *hey* . . . *rrrring* . . . *yeah* . . . *rrring* . . . Lydia . . . *tick,*

tick, tick . . . tack, tick . . . checkmate . . . she wanted to call her right now
*. . . fwack . . . fwack . . . fwack . . . swim in a big sea of blankets . . . twang
. . . boom . . . boom . . . sssst . . . your body is a wonderland . . . uunnh . . .
clang . . . rrring . . . fwack . . . thud . . . rrring . . . boom . . . boom . . . ssssst
. . . hey . . . zip . . . zip . . . swish!*

Lydia Beaumont walked slowly, feeling heavily compromised. ("The
name of the game, Queenie.") For the very first time she had solicited
her father's advice, albeit he didn't know it, nor how she intended to use
it. With his words in mind, she gave Helaine a week to tell her lover
good-bye, making an exception for her, for the tender mouth, the soft
lips swollen from all those kisses. She regretted parting with her and was
actively hoping beyond hope that something wonderful would happen
to prevent her from reaching her current destination, the flat where her
lover lived, whose name she had forbidden her to speak. No, she didn't
want to know a thing about the creature. She never wanted to see her
face again. And she didn't trust her alone with Helaine and prayed to the
powers that be for intervention.

The powers that be didn't think her request was unreasonable. In fact,
they wondered why it had taken her so long to make it. They had just
scheduled a month of Indian summer simply because enough people had
asked for it. After all, some people like it really hot. So hot, hot, hot it
would be, well into autumn. As to the Kristenson-Chambers-Beaumont
affair, they had already decided on a winner, so from here on in it was
the winner's to lose. Small favors for the contestants were definitely in the
offing, they agreed, after only five minutes of deliberations. It was nice
to be needed.

"Helaine!"

Who's that? She turned, her hand raised to block the sun from her
eyes.

"Helaine! *Helaine!*"

That sounded like Kay. Helaine squinted in the noonday sun. It was
Kay. It was Robert and Kay crossing the street toward her.

"I didn't recognize you with your hair down," Robert said.

"I told you it was Helaine. You look fabulous. Have you eaten yet?"

"Yes—I mean no! What brings you two down here?"

"Such a nice day, that's all."

Kay groaned. "He loves it hot like this. I wilt. Let's eat then, or are you heading somewhere?"

"No, no, just walking," she lied. "Let's," she urged. "There's a lovely place down by the water." She glanced at her watch. "We won't need reservations now. It's almost two o'clock."

"Seafood I hope? I'm in the mood for fish," Robert said. "I'm hungry enough to eat a shark."

Helaine laughed, glancing down Sharon's street as they passed it. It must be a good omen running into them when she did, she mused. Fate. Destiny.

Lydia was only a few blocks from home by now. She had meandered the whole way, stopping at the vegetable stands and chitchatting with the sidewalk vendors. She stopped at a brilliant flower stall, bought some red gladiolas. She didn't mind the heat—it seemed to bring the people out and she needed to see people right now. The idea of being alone made her feel sad and lonely and she knew once inside . . . she hesitated at her building. Oh, it would be cool inside. There was work to be done. That could take her mind off of things for awhile. The flowers were dripping wet leaving her skin and clothes misty where she held them. Her nerves tingled and she was convinced that somehow she would feel it if it happened—she would know the minute that someone else was making love to the woman.

The doorman pushed open the door and held it for her. "Ms. Beaumont," he said, steaming in his uniform.

A cold breeze rushed at her. Nah. She did not want to be alone.

"You have a visitor," he said, pointing toward the lobby.

She peered cautiously inside. "Del! Thank God."

"Look at you. Liddy, you look fabulous. Why thank God?"

"Just thank God. Boy am I glad to see you. Tell me, why did we never marry?"

"I was waiting for you to lose your cherry."

Lydia gasped and grinned. "Oh my gosh, you're fresh," she said, shoving the wet bouquet into her friend's arms. "There's probably a law against you."

"At least one! Have you eaten, yet?"

"No—yes—I mean no!"

"No. Yes. Here, let's try this again. Have you eaten yet—you've done something haven't you? And don't tell me no. I always know when you're fibbing."

"No. Eaten I mean." The elevator doors opened at the penthouse and she fumbled at her door. "I've done something? It shows?"

"Yah! Let me put these in water and we'll go eat then. Yes, something. Something blond methinks."

"Oh, Del. I am in love with that woman."

"Is that L—U—V?"

"Oh," she said, losing the smile. "At least that. Yes, I'd say so. At the very least."

In her dream, Helaine half lay, half sat on the couch in her consultation room. She was spilling her guts to Dr. Kristenson who sat poised and neutral in the red leather armchair, her penetrating eyes focused on something just behind Helaine's head, her lips fixed with a Mona Lisa smile. The inimitable Dr. Kristenson—herself.

"Oh, c'mon, Helaine," she said cheerfully, her lips never moving as she spoke, "you know what an archetype is."

In his dream, Joseph Rios leisurely ate breakfast on a sunny patio with Lydia Beaumont. They sat at a wrought iron table with matching chairs, between them a large vase of long stem roses, as red as her lips. She was pregnant. His wife.

* * *

In her dream, Sharon Chambers caught Helaine and the blue-eyed woman at Frank's making out in the ladies' lounge. There was something written on the bathroom mirror, but she couldn't read it. It was impossible to pull the two of them apart. She glimpsed herself in the mirror. Her eyes were red from crying.

In his dream, Harold D'Angelo, the maitre de at Frank's Place, made love to his wife, dead of cancer these long five years. With her red hair hanging on her naked shoulders, she was just as beautiful as ever.

In her dream, Lydia Beaumont wrote "I love Helaine Kristenson" in red lipstick on a bright blue sky, the letters floating dreamily over the city, looking just like an advertisement left by a skywriter.

In his dream, Lawrence Taft, the balding private eye, saw Helaine Kristenson wearing the tight red dress and stiletto heels he had apparently bought for her. He was afraid to lose sight of the blond so he held her about the waist as they crossed the street together. He tried to concentrate on the traffic, but he couldn't keep his eyes off those legs.

In her dream, Delilah Lewiston was in a sailboat with her best friend, Lydia, drinking red wine and breaking bread when she noticed a storm coming up fast on the horizon; the shore a mere pencil line, so far away from them that there simply wasn't enough time to get the vessel back to safety.

In his dream, Robert Keagan was on a sailboat with his best friend, Helaine, drinking red wine and breaking bread when he noticed a storm coming up fast on the horizon; the shore a mere pencil line, so far away from them that he wasn't certain there was enough time to get the vessel back to safety.

In her dream, Kay Keagan was on a sailboat with her best friend, Helaine, drinking red wine and breaking bread. A brief storm had just passed over them and it had forced the vessel somewhat further inland than they had wanted to be.

He was in love with Lydia Beaumont. But, unlike most people in love, he didn't know it. And, unlike most people in love, it was having a deleterious effect on his life, compounded by the fact that the woman abhorred him and refused to even look his way. He could put his head in her paper shredder and he doubted she would even call an ambulance.

Rio Joe sat downcast in the sauna of the men's club examining himself after an unsatisfactory game of squash. He was convinced that his penis was smaller, that the testicles, too, had mysteriously shrunken, were more flaccid than they ought to be, or than he remembered. The night before he had mistakenly called his date Lydia as he screwed her. Worse, she knew who Lydia was. His cheek was still stinging this morning when he woke up. And the bed, of course, was empty. For weeks now he had been wrestling a sickening sensation in his stomach. Nothing, not sex, not masturbation, not playing squash, not boiling the woman out of his system in a sauna, seemed to bring him any relief. He was so distracted by his condition that he had even fucked up at work. Papers were flying at him now like he was caught in a hurricane and the demands for his explanation were piled sky high on his desk. He was drowning in bullshit. And the bitch queen—still wearing his bracelet, the snake one, with its tail in its mouth—acting like it's no big deal, with her red roses from some dickhead. Some dickhead reaping all the benefits of *his* expertise. Shit! Now she won't even say hello. Aw, baby! If he could get his hands on her. If he could be inside her just one more time, hear her moaning, whispering his name to him, dying in his arms. If he could snatch just a few more I-love-yous from her fabulous mouth, her lips, her tongue. Smell her. Everything would be sweet again. Jesus, to hear those dying breaths! Mmm . . . mmm . . . mmm. How he missed them. Nobody, but nobody, fucked like Lydia Beaumont did. She was absolutely made for it.

He smiled without realizing, his penis standing at attention, waiting for an order, the tip of it glistening with futility. Another false alarm.

Her flight was at seven. Helaine was a no-show at the flat. Sharon felt more than a little jilted when she woke up from her nap at half past five. She had told the doctor over lunch that she had to fly back to LA and had looked forward to a little physical therapy before leaving. That bitch queen in the bathroom—had no fucking clue who she was talking to—kiss my ass!

The stress of all this crap was beginning to show in the mirror. She saw the cheerless face in the looking glass, the bleary eyes, bloodshot and veined with a bluish tint beneath them. So? It's the strung-out look all the young ones are wearing. She threw some things in a bag and called a cab, dialing Helaine's place after that to leave a message. It rang and rang and rang . . .

An archetype? Of course Dr. Kristenson knows what an archetype is. It was the statement that plagued her so much and the unanswerable question that remained upon waking: Who is the archetype in question? Lydia? Sharon?

What were her archetypes anyway? It would have to be father and mother. No brothers, no sisters. A few aunts and uncles she rarely saw. Neither grandparents were alive when she was born. It had always been the three of them: her elderly parents and she their little miracle.

She was an only child, born in the autumn of her parents' years, her happy people, happily married till death did they part . . . within six months of each other. Happy, but not rich, although surely not poor. At least not dirt poor. These original models, her prototypes, they never prepared her for anything but happiness. So why unhappy then? Why Sharon?

She had run free as a child. Nothing displeased her parents, nothing tarnished their parental pride in their blessed offspring and she never disappointed them. Not "Lana." Lana, the happy baby, the golden child, the homecoming queen, the college grad, the doctor, the author, the millionaire, the self-made woman going into the twenty-first century, her parents gone now, friendly apparitions housed in the landscape of her mind, housed in a home on that landscape without hidden rooms or locked doors or skeletons, a happy house filled with happy exchanges. Nothing had ever been left unsaid, no dark secrets kept from her parents. For that she was eternally grateful.

Lana. Lana had died with them. No one called her that anymore. She was Dr. K. or the Luv Doc. Who was Lana now?

Who's Lana, Dr. Kristenson asked herself, coming from the office of property management for the waterfront flat. There had been a year and a half left on her lease. She paid it out, including a rather hefty maintenance fee, all nonrefundable. Sharon could stay there then until the lease expired, provided that no activities of the sort they were reading about lately took place on the premises. If they did, she would be evicted. She would also face eviction if she was convicted of the current criminal charges against her, as several tenants had already expressed concerns about the supermodel's questionable reputation. Fine, that was their business, Helaine cordially advised, as she was no longer an interested party as far as Sharon Chambers was concerned. Considering the recent revelations about Sharon's real estate holdings, none of which she had known of before, she doubted that the model would ever find herself without a roof over her head.

Shouldn't there be a dark specter from her past, some long gone demon whose empty shoes a Sharon Chamber's had so nicely stepped into? But there isn't one, Helaine concluded at one o'clock in the office of the real estate broker who she planned would handle the sale of her townhouse.

"It would be quicker to rent it, Dr. Kristenson. Perhaps with an option to buy."

"You can manage that for me?"

"Of course."

"How long will it take you to find what I'm looking for?"

The agent glanced at the computer and across the desk at Helaine. "A week? Two?" She scrolled the screen. "Unless you want to rent. I've got a lovely place midtown. Isn't that near your offices?"

"I hate modern. It isn't one of those?"

"No. I know what you need. It's only seven stories. Penthouse." She tapped earnestly at the keyboard as she talked. "Six big rooms. Patio and garden. Private elevator. Parking. Central air. Skylights in bedroom, bath. Eat-in gourmet. No maintenance. Blah, blah, blah. Let's see. Yup. Available . . . now." She flipped the screen around, displaying a few interior photos provided by the owner. "Ready now," she repeated hopefully. "You want to see it?"

"Any ghosts?"

"No," the agent giggled. "None listed. Young executives relocating. San Francisco. Want to see it?"

Helaine didn't have time for that. Sharon had left last Saturday, the day she had stood her up. She would be back soon. Helaine was sure of it. And there was a phone number bouncing around her brain like a rubber ball. She hoped to dial that number by Friday. Or else. "No, it sounds perfect. I'll take it."

Helaine left, content with her selection. She felt she was operating at a hundred percent for a change. Tomorrow she'd call the movers and get her things out. Tonight perhaps she'd stay with friends, if that was all right with Robert and Kay. She went back to the office and called them without telling them too much. In fact, she lied altogether. The townhouse was being painted, was what she actually said. It was only a half-truth. She'd correct it next week.

Archetypes. Generally, we're looking for real people. Larger-than-life people. Sadly these are usually scary types, or extreme types, *Mommy Dearest* types, Mary Poppins types, Henry the Eighth types, Atilla the Hun types, memorable and influential people that loomed over us, most likely when we were no bigger than bread baskets. At their core—at our core—they are real people, completely indispensable to us. They die, or disappear, we replace them . . . with a close facsimile thereof.

She was so preoccupied with her inquiry that she sat dazed through her afternoon sessions and even felt obliged to apologize to one bemused couple.

Lana. She had liked the nickname, enjoyed being her, yet no one but her parents ever called her that. After they died four years ago, she never heard the name again.

The Kristensons' daughter Lana, for as long as she existed, was infallible, never made any goofs in her life, never failed at anything. When she disappeared, she was survived by Helaine who did make some mistakes. Sharon Chambers was certainly the proof of that. The years of misery . . . there was so much distance between who she was now and who she had been seven years ago that her former self seemed to have taken on a mythical shape of its own. Lana had become to her a *perfect* stranger. She could see that from the red leather chair, see the trap that she had set for herself as a result. Lana doesn't err, therefore, somehow, Helaine couldn't either.

Sharon Chambers? A mistake—but it couldn't be a mistake. Oh, but it was. She had spent years denying it, disguising it every day of her failed and sorry romance, converting Sharon's lies into promises she would wait for.

There was something scary about that, about being in denial. She stared through the couple on her couch as if they weren't there. For how long had she been in denial? Four years? That could be. The loss of her parents had thrown her. But hadn't it been bad before that? Wasn't it really more like seven years of misery? In fact, to be perfectly honest, hadn't she been dissatisfied with the relationship since the moment she first took the model to bed with her? She nodded to herself. The couple nodded back, encouraged to continue their conversation. Yes. She admitted it. But if that was the case, and of course she could see it was, then she was still Lana Kristenson when she had first met Sharon.

Lana, Lana, Lana. Dr. Kristenson weighed the implications, still nodding her head after her clients had left. Back at her desk she saw the light on her phone blinking as if concurring with her conclusion. Lana was an archetype.

"Yes, Jen?"

"There's an awfully pretty box here with your name on it. Looks like a love letter attached to the ribbon. Shall I tell the messenger to send it back?"

A box! "Jenny, don't you dare!"

"You'll have to come and sign for it then. Your signature is required."

Monday, eight in the morning.

"How long, if I can ask?"

The guard sized the woman up before answering. Her looks didn't trouble him. "I'd say she's had her offices in here about three years."

Three years, Lydia repeated in her head. She stared at the white lettering of the professional directory, a strange exhilaration coursing through her veins. There was a story here, an erotic bedtime tale she wished to be told. Right this minute!

Dr. Helaine Kristenson, twelfth floor, the plaque read. So the telephone operator had been correct about the address! It was no mistake. Helaine's offices were practically across from her own.

Lydia could think of nothing else. She stood back from her own window, all day trying to catch sight of the blond head on the twelfth floor without being seen, all day resisting the urge to phone her there. Across the street, you scoundrel! The discovery that Helaine was less than a stone's throw away from her, and had been all this time, aroused in Lydia an excitement that surpassed all others known to date and as she tried to work she grew more and more preoccupied with the dozen roses still in a vase by her window. There were as well other obvious and sensually distracting features about the situation to be considered. She did, until it was necessary for her to go home early.

Tuesday was a repeat of the day before and so on until, with the end of the week nearing and feeling professionally impaired by her sensations, she decided to work with her back to the window, stoically refusing to take any breaks. She was on a fixed timetable now. Helaine was to call by Friday to inform her that the mission had been accomplished. But since their Saturday meeting, Lydia had fallen into a state of readiness, heightened by Monday's revelation, and she had wished to hear from the blond much sooner than that.

As the days slipped by without word, she caught her attention entirely missing from her work, saw her imagination running amok with disturbing visions. Her emotional deluge had begun to drown her and she bobbed up and down in an endless stream of unhappy possibilities. Twice she battled her hand from the phone.

By three o'clock Thursday, no word, her spirits sinking, Lydia gloomily packed her briefcase and once more headed for the solitude and safety of her penthouse, this time overloaded with misgivings. They trailed behind her like tin cans after the wedding.

She could practically hear them clanking as she rode the elevator down, her state of mind in such commotion that by the time she noticed herself stuck alone in there with Rio Joe it was too late to do anything about it.

And before she could prevent it he had her cornered and was interrogating her about the roses. She dropped the briefcase and he kicked it aside.

"Who is he?" he whispered into her hair, his hand groping her.

She reached for the switchboard. He grabbed her arm.

"Joe. Let me go or I'll scream." His chest heaved against hers. She could taste and smell his thoughts. "Let me go or I'll scream."

He pressed his cheek against hers and pushed her into the corner. "Scream then, Lydia. You know I love it when you scream."

She felt her skirt hiking up. "Joseph . . ." The elevator stopped. *Ding!* The doors opened revealing them to a group of surprised executives.

"Oh! Sorry!" Lydia heard from the hallway. "We'll get the next one." The doors closed again. The bell tolled.

"Scream for me, your highness."

She was silent. Overhead the floor numbers glowed in a slow motion countdown as the elevator descended toward the lobby. By the tenth floor he had worked the skirt up past her thighs.

"Who sent you the flowers, Lydia?"

"Joe, for Christ's sake! Are you out of your mind?" She was wet— always wet now—and didn't want him to know it.

He knew it. The elevator stopped. *Ding!* She glimpsed people waiting and hid her face in his shirt.

"Use the other one," he snarled over his shoulder.

"Excuse *us*," someone quipped humorously. The doors closed. *Ding!*

She heard laughter through the floor and saw the elevator ascending this time. He reached into her blouse.

"Joe, let me out of here."

"Lydia," he murmured in an unusually tender tone. He was breathing heavily, his hand caressing her between her legs. "You want it."

"Shit . . ." she swore under her breath. "Oh, shit." She did. Her nipples were hard. "It's over Joe—" she gasped, as he slid his fingers inside her. Too late. She let him stroke her one . . . two . . . three . . . until she slumped back into the corner . . . four . . . five . . . six . . . seven . . . eight . . . nine . . . *ding* . . . the doors opened wide and she came to him, so fast he lifted his face to hers in surprise.

"Whoa, sorry!" someone shouted.

Joe regained himself and fumbled furiously with the front of his pants, pulling her close as he did.

She quickly pushed him back again. The elevator bucked before heading downward. "It's over Joe," she repeated, her eyes issuing a warning as she managed to free herself from him.

He took her by the wrists. "Then why are you wearing my bracelet?" he asked, lifting it to her face.

She looked from it to him, wide-eyed and dumbfounded. There was no explanation to offer the man. Just a foolhardy choice in accessories, she guessed. She had utterly forgotten he had given it to her. Over him she saw they were finally approaching the lobby. She could tell by his face that he was no longer mindful of the elevator. *Ding!* He turned, startled by the bell, and she fixed her rumpled skirt, grabbed her briefcase and breezed past him.

"Lydia?" he called, as she stepped out of the elevator.

Such a strange sound in his voice. It filled her suddenly with a sense of pathos. She glanced back at the elevator, past the crowd waiting to board it, and saw him as they might, a desperate man, his zipper down, his suit coat abandoned on the floor, his shirttails partially hanging out of his pants. She took the bracelet off her wrist and tossed it to him, a consolation prize perhaps. He made to catch it and missed, diving for it as it bounced off the wall behind him and fell unceremoniously at his feet.

The doors started to close again and someone moved forward

tentatively and stopped them, the others filed in after him like sheep. A woman ran by Lydia who had not yet seen the spectacle at the elevator.

"Hey! Hold that elevator!" she yelled.

Lydia walked away, her face blank, the tension in it gone for the moment.

"Ms. Beaumont?"

She turned to find a young security guard wearing a concerned expression and somewhat out of breath. She didn't know he had witnessed the scene on a video monitor, that he had recognized the female VIP being molested in the elevator, and that he had run from floor to floor in an effort to rescue her from her assailant.

"Yes?"

"Are you all right?" he asked breathlessly, "I've got her," he reported into his wireless.

She listened to the static filled response and gave him a puzzled look.

He pointed at the cameras hanging from the ceiling. "Security," he stated, "in the elevators, too. I saw—do you want to file a complaint?"

She hesitated. Joe was getting in deep with the firm. She couldn't bring herself to sic security on him as well. "Thank you," she said at length, "but I don't think it will happen again."

He looked bashfully at his shoes. "I'll make a record of it just in case."

"I appreciate that. Thank you. I mean it." She left him standing there with his radio buzzing, a pencil poised for taking notes.

"Wait!" she overheard as she was exiting the revolving doors. "Hold that—" *Ding!*

Lawrence Taft woke with a splitting headache and no memory of how he had earned it. He had had a couple of drinks at Frank's after Sharon Chambers made her surprise appearance there but the events that followed were shrouded in a haze.

But the bottom line was NOTHING. There was nothing going down at all, not at all. He popped some aspirin. This is it, he decided. Friday would be the last stakeout. He was becoming too attached to his pigeon. He could feel it under his skin. The way she wore her hair, the way she sipped her tea. And his memory? Not remembering an entire day. Friday was it, and then he was out of there.

Helaine held the small box to her nose and sniffed it.

"What are you doing, Dr. Kristenson?"

The envelope attached to it smelled like Lydia Beaumont's perfume.

"Savoring, Jen." She took it back to her office over the objections of her curious secretary.

"As fair art thou, my bonie lass, so deep in love am I; And I will luve thee still, my dear, till a' the seas gang dry . . ."

Helaine set the envelope next to her phone and ripped open the box. Fishnet. Was it lingerie, her favorite? She preciously removed a pair of evening gloves from the blue tissue paper. Black silk. *Mmmmmmmmmmmmmmm.* She slipped them on and went to the window to raise the blinds, glancing at the time. Four o'clock.

Lydia wasn't there.

Lydia got out of the shower around four thirty. She dawdled at the bedroom mirror for awhile, then lay on her brand new mattress, her wet hair done up in a towel wrapped like a turban around her head. She had settled for something new to sleep on, was the proud new owner of an extra plush queen size mattress and box spring, a brand new solid brass headboard and frame. She liked the golden shine of it. It matched Helaine's hair. And the floors, of course.

She took a power nap to rid herself completely of the thoughts regarding Rio Joe and twenty minutes later rose up refreshed and hungry, her thoughts returning instead to the question of dinner which she decided she would eat by the window in the sunroom, once she figured out what she was going to have. She threw on a silk kimono and went back into the bathroom to do her hair, considering food stuffs as she put on a little makeup. It was her intent to be positive until Friday. Then, if the call didn't come, she would take it from there.

She saw the answering machine winking at her on the way to the kitchen. She hit play and kept walking.

"Darling . . . ?"

Lydia froze, balanced tenuously on legs of gelatin.

"I hope you don't mind . . . they're just so beautiful . . . thank you . . . "

Lydia smiled as she listened.

"I'm settling into a new apartment Thursday . . . I'll see you Friday."

Friday! What time? Where? Lydia ran and picked up the phone and heard only the dial tone. The voice on her machine was signing off.

"I love you." (beep)

Love you! The dial tone? Right, it's just a message. Friday! She whooped with joy and slam dunked the receiver.

"Hey, Liddy . . . it's Del . . . tried your office . . . you weren't there. Heard you left one Mr. Rios with two blue balls in the elevator . . . hah! I wouldn't have left him with any! Call me . . . I'm home now." (beep)

Oh my God. Lydia hung over the machine and hit save. How many people were discussing that elevator ride? She went out to the kitchen and rattled some pots and pans. An hour later she chewed thoughtfully on her dinner, staring out at the cityscape from the divan in her sunroom.

The buildings looked exactly like boxes on a grocery shelf. She marveled at her observations. It really is a small world.

"I need to walk. Meet me?"

"Walk or talk?"

"Both."

"I'll meet you on the corner by the paint store. Don't bathe."

"What?"

"Forget it, Liddy. You're so obtuse."

Delilah was dressed in a brand new jogging suit, a Windbreaker made of silk.

"Liddy, slow down. I don't want to get all sweaty. It's brand new."

Lydia grinned in her dingy sweats. "Really?"

"What's on your mind, smart-ass? Is this about Joe? You haven't said ten words. You know I'd rather talk than walk." They were passing a deli. "Let's go in here and sit."

"Not about Joe. Don't want to sit."

"Ugh! Heap big broken English. Slow down then!"

They slowed down.

"She looks like Katherine Deneuve," Delilah said after she caught her breath.

"Who does?"

"Your blond Venus, Helaine. That's who she reminded me of. Stacked like her, too."

"Del! Are we going to talk like men now?"

Delilah swung around. "Which men? I knew there'd be something in this for me. Where are they?"

Lydia laughed despite herself. "You know, there really is more to life than just sex."

"There is? Oh my God! Liddy, what is it? What have I been overlooking all this time?"

"Del . . . very funny."

"Oh, okay, Lydia Beaumont. So you're in love with Helaine's mind, right?"

"Her mind?"

"You know, a higher love that you arrived at through all the numerous intellectual exchanges you've had with her. Isn't that right? Could we slow down or are we expected somewhere?"

"I . . ." Lydia balked and then laughed.

"You can tell me, Liddy. Your feelings for that sexy blond. Why, it's really just a mental thing. You don't get wet, your loins don't ache, your tits don't lunge through your bra whenever you see the woman."

"Hah! Point taken."

They walked a half a block without speaking.

"Things finally moving, Ms. Beaumont?"

"Indeed."

"When do you see her?"

"Friday."

"I see. And you've got cold feet?"

"Yes."

"Sweaty palms? Dizziness?"

"Del?"

"Chest pains? Palpitations? Swelling in the joints?"

"What? No!"

"Memory loss? Loose bowels, blood in the stools and/or cramping?"

"Del! Don't make me laugh. This is very, very serious. Why is everything always so funny to you?"

"Why are you laughing?"

"I'm nervous. It's nervous laughter. And you're supposed to help me. You've done this before, I haven't."

"That was a long time ago, I told you. Besides, all that exotic booze . . . you don't really want to know."

"Why didn't you ever tell me about it?"

"Liddy, why do you think? You're so proper, so . . . straight." She flashed a Buddha grin at the idea. "Anyway! It was just one of those things."

"*A trip to the moon on gossamer wings?*"

"A fling, like the song says. You on the other hand, go and figure. You're in love." She put her arm through Lydia's and they strolled up the block. "And because of that you have cold little feet."

Lydia cleared her throat. "I want to, you know, please her. You know?" She cleared it again and barely squeezed out, "In bed."

"In bed?"

"Mmmm."

"Oh, that does sound serious, Liddy."

"HELP."

"Okay, okay. In bed. You want pointers I presume?"

"Please."

"Well, let's see. What if it's not in bed?"

"Not in bed? Del . . . I don't know."

"Well, never mind. We'll say it's in bed."

"But, Del, what if it's not?"

"Liddy! I think you're holding back on me."

"No, no, no, it's in bed. Bed, Del."

Delilah arched her brows. "Okay. Well, the rules are simple, Dame Beaumont. You probably already know them. Numero uno, don't call her somebody else's name in bed."

"C'mon, I wouldn't do that."

"Number two, don't call her someone else's name in the grass."

"Delilah Lewiston."

"Number three, don't call her someone else's name in the back seat."

"All right then, forget it. You're being wise."

"Number four—and this is very important so listen up—don't get her pregnant."

"Del, please. I was counting on you."

"Well, what's there to know? It's going to feel perfectly natural, Liddy. No one knows better how to satisfy a woman than another woman. Dwell on that. You'll figure it out. Besides—here let's sit down—you can always ask her for instructions."

They sat on a bench at a bus stop.

"You think?"

"She knows that you've never . . . you know?"

"Look at me. What do you think?"

Delilah chuckled. "Yeah, she probably knows. So be as cool as possible and simply ask her how she likes it then, for a little guidance. You'll be fine."

"And I won't seem like a . . . a dork doing that?"

"A dork? You will seem like a dork if you try to screw her the way she doesn't like."

Lydia groaned and put her head in her hand, contorting her body in an exaggerated show of discomfort. "Why, why, why? Why is it you can't just say make love or something polite like that? Screw makes me . . . anxious."

"Well, I'm just trying to be helpful. I'm not really focusing on semantics here. Let me rephrase it. A dork? You will seem like a dork if you try to *make love* to her the way she doesn't like."

Lydia sat back, quietly watching the traffic go by.

"Liddy?"

"Yes, Del?"

"You're not thinking of wearing *that* on Friday, are you?" A smile was creeping over her friend's face. " 'Cause it's really gross. A big turnoff." She saw Lydia getting up, laughing. "Really, Liddy, I've been so embarrassed tonight to be seen with you in those sweats. I feel just like—"

"C'mon, Del, Let's go. I'm hungry."

"I feel just like . . . oh God . . . just like . . . like a dork."

"You've been such a big help."

"Worse than a dork. A dink. I feel like a dink!"

"I'm going to fall flat on my face, I'll have you know."

"You won't. Besides, it could be worse." Delilah made a wry expression. "What if you were a man? Think how obvious that would be."

They stopped outside a donut shop.

"I hadn't thought of that," Lydia whispered. "We can't be limp."

"Nope. Gotta fuck us out of our brains first."

Lydia giggled. "You're irreverent."

"Irreverent. Yeah? Well then, let's be reverent. It's time for us to give praise, Lydia. Here, repeat after me. Thank you, dear Lord, for making me a woman."

Lydia grinned and joined in. "Thank you, dear Lord, for making me a woman."

A few customers eyed them curiously on their way into the shop. The ladies ignored them, chanting and raising their arms skyward.

"Thank you dear Lord for making me a woman. Thank you dear Lord for making me a woman. Thank you dear Lord for making me a woman . . ."

Thursday morning. *"A Lydia Beaumont, Dr. Kristenson?"*

"Here?"

"No, on the phone."

"Put her through. Put her through." She dropped everything. "Hello, gorgeous."

"I—gorgeous yourself, thank you."

"Where are you?"

"Look out your window."

Helaine turned in her chair and looked across the way where Lydia stood hand on one hip the other with a phone to her ear.

Helaine laughed self-consciously. "I can explain this. I really can."

"And I want you to. I'm eager to hear all about it. Friday?"

"Friday. I'll pick you up at Frank's, if that's all right. Sevenish?"

"I'll be drunk by then. Is that all right?"

"You will not. I want to seduce you sober."

"Mmmm . . . looks like you've already done that."

"Not mad about it, are you?"

"Mad about you. It's just that I thought this was all my idea."

"Hah!" Helaine placed her hand on the window. "Say it, Lydia Beaumont. I want to hear you say it." *"I love you, Helaine Kristenson?"*

They stared at each other through their windows.

"And it's all your fault."

"Mm-hmm. I'll make it up to you then."

"When?"

"Friday night."

"Sharon . . . Sharon Chambers, Dr. Kristenson?"

Helaine stiffened at her desk. "Put her on, Jen," she said tautly.

"Uhh . . . she's here, Doctor."

"Here?" Helaine dropped her chin to her chest and swore inaudibly. "In the consultation room, Jen." She hesitated before hanging up. "If we're not out of there in a half hour please call security."

Jenny escorted Sharon to the consultation room, worry clouding her face. "Dr. Kristenson will be with you shortly, Ms. Chambers," she said without looking at the woman. The door slammed as she closed it behind her, the sound filling her with a sense of dread. She listened for the familiar thud of Helaine's adjoining door signifying she had entered the room, and hearing it at last, glanced at the clock on the wall to time the proceedings. It was quarter past ten.

Sharon had reclined on the couch, one long leg draped down the front of it, a high-heeled shoe discarded on the floor nearby. Its mate dangled precariously from an agitated foot propped up on the armrest. Helaine stood awkwardly in the center of the room and quickly evaluated the woman's posture: insolent, defiant. Normally she would seat herself in the chair opposite, but this was not normal. Sharon never came to the office. This will be the last time she does, Helaine promised herself, as she walked to the window and lowered the blinds.

"Doctor. How very nice to see you," Sharon said, putting her arm behind her head and dropping the other shoe. "Please," she said, indicating with a sweep of her arm that the doctor should sit. "You don't look happy to see me."

Helaine reluctantly sat down. "Sharon . . . didn't you get my letter?"

"I did."

Helaine nodded and looked away.

"And I went to your townhouse this morning to check things out. But . . ."

(The movers! Her furniture!)

"Top secret, huh? Couldn't even fuck it out of them. You must pay well."

Helaine sighed with relief. They had done as instructed, said nothing. She sat back, checked the time.

"My session almost up, my love? But I just got here."

"Sharon . . . what brings you here? It's rather early for you, isn't it?"

Sharon ignored the remark and caressed the couch. She watched Helaine from the corner of her eye and grinned at her discomfort. "Lots of confessions on this baby, I'll bet."

No reply.

"Lots and lots of secrets. Hmm, Dr. Kristenson?"

Helaine leaned forward in her chair and placed her hands on the armrests as if to rise, then thought better of it and sat back into the chair. "What is this about?"

Sharon flashed one of her smiles. "Secrets. It's all about secrets. I'll show you mine, doctor," she unzipped her blouse, "you show me yours."

Helaine looked away. "I wasn't aware that you had any secrets. Or certainly none anymore."

"Oh, but I do."

"Sharon. My note . . . is there something you don't understand? I have an appointment in a few minutes. I work here, you know, not entertain."

"My time is not up, doctor."

"Yes, Sharon Chambers, it is. You will need to accept that."

Sharon sat up suddenly. "Is it? Well you're hot shit aren't you, dear Dr. Kristenson? My time is up! You want to step out on me? And how will you do that, hmm? When's the last time you actually screwed a woman, Helaine?"

Helaine winced.

"Huh, Love Doc, hot shit? When?"

"You ought to know the answer to that."

"And it is a woman, isn't it?"

"Sharon . . ." Helaine glanced at her watch again.

"Say two years?" Sharon waited but there was no response. "Three years?" She stood up and walked to where Helaine sat rigid in her chair.

Yes, Helaine thought. Two, three years. "I get your point. Please go now."

Sharon circled her. "Doesn't that make you a bit rusty?"

Helaine rose up from the chair. Sharon stepped around it and blocked her escape.

"Was that your aim, Sharon? To make me rusty?" She turned her face away. "Sharon . . . your shirt."

"Need a little practice before you take the plunge, Dr. Kristenson?"

They stood silently for a moment.

Helaine shook and hoped it didn't show. "This, as you know, Ms. Chambers, is a very unbecoming way to—"

"Ms. Chambers? Bullshit! You're mine, Helaine Kristenson. I have a right to know what—"

"It's over, Sharon Chambers. That's all you need to know." She held the door open and waited.

Sharon put her shoes on, looking up at her as she did it, with a smirk. "No, Dr. Kristenson," Sharon replied as she finally stepped into the hallway, "it's only just begun."

"If you come again you will be greeted by security. I'm sorry, but you've given me no choice."

Jenny listened to the hushed voices in the hallway. They were moving toward her. She heard Sharon Chambers as clear as day.

"I love you, Helaine Kristenson, and that is all *you* need to know."

"That is of no consequence to me now. That was something I needed to know before. Please, Sharon. I'm asking you to go or I'll have you removed."

Jenny then heard only silence. She picked up the receiver of the telephone just as the model was turning the corner and paused to take a good look at her as she flew by. She had never seen the woman before except in magazines, but she didn't like her at all. She waited till she was sure she was gone before checking in on Helaine.

"Dr. Kristenson?"

Helaine had her back against the wall, her hand on her forehead. "It's fine, Jen. Don't worry."

"She told me she knew you very well, or I wouldn't have—"

"It's true, Jen." She averted her eyes. "*Knew,* if you understand me."

"Let me get you some water. You don't look so good."

"Thank you. I don't feel so good."

"I've never seen you so pale," Jenny declared as she returned with a glass. "It's a good thing that woman's in the past tense, if you don't mind my saying."

Helaine shot her a worried glance and took the glass from her. "We hope," was her cautious reply. She swirled the water in her mouth. She doubted water was strong enough to settle her nerves.

"Drink that," Jenny said, her voice laden with concern. "And I've ordered lunch for you. It should be here in about fifteen minutes and maybe after that you should rest. You don't have another appointment until this afternoon."

"What time?"

"One o'clock."

"Thanks, Jen. I need to make a phone call. Let me know when the food arrives."

"Dr. Kristenson here. Is the doctor in?"

"*Hey, how are you? Long time no see.*"

"Jon . . . good . . . you have five minutes?"

"*I'll see your five and raise you ten, as long as it's strip poker.*"

"Oh, good. I'm glad I called already."

"*Anything wrong?*"

"Yeeahhhuhh . . . not really. Pep talk. Up to it?"

"*Anytime. Shoot.*"

"Have a date. Anxiety."

"A date? Congratulations! Anxiety . . . you?"

"Happens to everyone?"

"Well . . . no. Thoughts of?"

"Fear. Failure. Mortality."

"Oh, is that all? What about sex or love?"

"Those, too."

"List them in order of importance, please."

"Let's see. Love, sex, fear, failure, mortality."

"Hmmmph. Sounds healthy to me . . . except maybe the love."

"You're funny."

"Take two thrills and call me in the morning."

She laughed in her throat. "No, really, Jon."

"It's like riding a bike, Helaine. You just get on the saddle and pump your legs and it all comes back to you."

"Boy you're blunt sometimes."

"Whew! I even stunned myself on that one. You do know how to ride a bike?"

"Of course."

"You don't sound convinced. It can't be that serious?"

"Is."

"Is? Well, that's the problem."

"What do you mean?"

"Love. No see long time. Emotional amnesia. Sexual paralysis."

"Sounds fatal."

"Nah, it's just a bug. You'll get over it. LOVE is what Helaine Kristenson does. You understand me, Helaine Kristenson?"

"Thank you, Jon. You're very kind. Jenny's buzzing, I think my lunch just got here. I better let you go."

"Yeah. I got people waiting with real problems. Hey, see you tomorrow night? I've got tickets."

"Tomorrow?"

"Friday, your lecture? Eight o'clock, Dr. Kristenson. Wow! I see what you mean. Let me hear that list again."

She opened her date book. There it was. (Oh, no, no, no. Lydia.) "I see it. You're right, Jon. Eight o'clock. Lecture at eight thirty. I'll talk to you tomorrow night then."

"Good luck, Helaine. See you then. And hey . . ."
"Yes?"
"You know where to find me if . . . well . . . you know?"
"Thanks, Jon."

Morally supported by Delilah, Lydia waited outside on the patio at Frank's on Friday. It was almost seven o'clock. They were drinking their martinis and making small talk when a cab pulled up to the curb and Helaine stepped out. Delilah nudged sharply with her elbow.

"Ouch," Lydia blurted, not having seen Helaine yet.

"Ouch," Delilah said, "hot dress, over there."

Lydia turned in that direction.

Dressed in dinner black, her hair down, a coat slung over her arm, a happy blond held the car door open as she searched the crowd for her date, returning the waiter's wave with a discreet wink and smiling broadly when she finally saw Lydia approaching.

"Ah, here is my enchantress."

They got in the cab.

"Enchantress? Did you know that's a boat that disappeared in the Bermuda Triangle?"

"Goodness, no. Are you a ghost ship, Lydia Beaumont?"

"Where to now?" inquired the cabbie. She turned her radio down.

"No," Lydia whispered, "I'm real."

The cabbie's question floated past them. "Lydia . . ."

"Where to, ladies?"

"Oh, uptown. Drive uptown, please."

The cab pulled away from the curb and darted into the late day traffic.

Lawrence Taft, armed with his digital camera, watched with ambivalence as the cab left Frank's Place. It was kind of a pity to see Sharon Chambers right about the doctor. And by the looks of the other woman, the model had good reason to be concerned.

He studied the image of them in his view screen, a strong sense of nostalgia creeping into his bones. He missed the finality that the *whir* and *clack* of a 35mm shutter could lend to these kind of affairs. *Whirrrrrrrrrr . . . clack!* It was as conclusive as the sound of the guillotine. It said "Gotcha!" in a way that modern technology just couldn't.

"Lydia Beaumont, I have made a gaffe, tonight. I have a prior speaking engagement. At the convention center." Helaine leaned forward and spoke to the cabbie again. "The convention center by eight. And please drive slowly. Lydia? May I see you after that?"

"See me—of course. When?"

"Nine thirty? I've been out of my mind this week. I couldn't blame you if—"

"My place," Lydia interrupted. "Sorry," she smiled. "My place, Helaine," she repeated, reaching into her breast pocket and producing her calling card. "Show that to the doorman. He'll let you go right up. Unless . . . if you don't want to . . . would you want to do that?"

Helaine took the card. "Elegant," she whispered as she slid it inside her dress. "I would want to do that," she assured, laying the coat between them and sitting back. "That's exactly what I would want to do."

"Me, too, by the way."

"You?"

"Out of my mind this week."

"Oh . . . I apologize. I made you worry. I didn't see Sha—" She stopped herself. "I didn't go to the flat." She squeezed Lydia's hand and let it go quickly.

"But you told her? I mean, she knows?"

"She knows it's over. It's been that way a long time."

They sat back quietly, allowing the cab to toss them toward each other and away again as the vehicle wove gently through the traffic. The cabbie sized them up in the mirror and confident she understood the situation, selected a CD, popping it in and turning the volume up. Good choice, she thought. (Sinatra.)

It was still hot, late summer, but the days were getting short once more, the nights long and cool. Through the windshield the ladies could see the sun dropping on the city like a bomb. A bright red sunset spread across the horizon, reflecting off the skyscrapers and glowing in hot pink squares from every window.

"Tour it?" the cabbie suggested.

Helaine gave her a puzzled look.

"Yes," Lydia said quickly, "tour it, please."

The cab took a side street. Helaine smiled to herself. Lydia leaned across the jacket and kissed her.

"What is your speech about?" she asked.

Helaine slipped her finger between Lydia's lips and quickly withdrew it. "You. For ten minutes I shall speak of nothing but Lydia Beaumont. About her eyes. For another twenty I will tell them about her lips." She folded her hands in her lap and rested her head against the back of the seat. "And I mustn't forget to mention those arms and those legs." She closed her eyes. Lydia lay against her, kissed her neck. "Or your fabulous back," Helaine continued softly. "What would you say to that speech?"

"I'd say, you better not, Helaine Kristenson. I value my anonymity. How do you feel about yours?" she asked.

Helaine reached out and adjusted an errant strand of dark hair. "I've enjoyed mine."

The sun was gone now, the last of its flame settling into an orange mist around the city, the last rays bouncing off the walls and casting long shadows in their retreat. In a few moments they would surrender completely, relinquishing their glory to that of lamplights and neon.

It was already dark in the cab. Lydia kissed a bare shoulder, a long arm, a perfumed wrist, tongued the soft palm of an outstretched hand as it lay like jewel on a slippery, satin lap. Black satin. Her cheek brushed against the slick fabric. It was as cool as the night, descending on the city like a blanket.

Part Three
The Catch

The dark-haired woman disappeared from the rearview mirror and the experienced cabbie, seeing the park looming ahead on the right, pulled out of traffic and idled curbside, taking a place behind a caravan of other taxicabs. Sinatra sang unfettered by propriety . . . *if you're feeling sad and lonely . . .*

Helaine took stock of the situation. The cavalcade stretched nearly the entire length of the block. She must have passed this scene a thousand times and never recognized it for what it was.

The driver made herself invisible, eyes vanished from the mirror.

Discretion, Helaine mused, Lydia's head in her lap . . . *there's a service I can render . . .* one hand resting on her thigh, the other at her hip . . . her lips at her fingertips . . . her lips . . . *tell the one who loves you only . . .* it was not necessary to discuss this, Helaine understood . . . the cabbie would wait for hours if told to . . . *I can be so warm and tender . . .* polite hands . . . this woman's card in her bra . . . *you can call me . . .* a wet palm . . . *tell me and I'll be around . . .* Helaine bent over her and combed the dark hair with her fingers. She had to be somewhere soon. Remember?

"Lydia?"

No answer.

"Lydia Beaumont." The dark head turned in her hand and partially faced her. Helaine stroked the woman's mouth with her thumb. "What are you thinking?"

"Thinking—something primal, I'm afraid. Where are we?"

"At the park. It seems we're part of a posse," she joked, looking back again. "Have you ever been here before? Like this I mean?"

Lydia grinned. "No." She wet her lips and kissed the finger. "You?"

"No, not me," Helaine said, smiling at the thought of it. She parted Lydia's lips with her thumb. "First time for everything—tell me 'primal'."

"What time is it?"

Helaine checked her watch. "Quarter past."

Lydia gripped the tip of Helaine's finger and let it go when she felt her jump. "Tell me about the building across from my office, specifically the twelfth floor."

Helaine chuckled. "Ummm . . . what do you want to know about it?"

"Oh, everything."

"Hmmm. Across from me, on the fifteenth floor. There's a beautiful woman up there in the window sometimes. Quite beautiful. I happened to notice her one day."

"Uh-oh, I'm fond of my window. When was that, Helaine?" She licked at the fingertip once more, pressed her mouth into a trembling palm.

Helaine took a deep breath. "That was . . . I'm not too sure now . . . ummmmm . . . I'd have to . . . say . . . two years ago?" Her other hand went to the back of Lydia's head, into the silky hair. "Do you know what you do in your window?"

"No, but I'm going to guess that you like it." She bit gently at Helaine's hand, licked between each finger, grabbing the thumb between her teeth and teasing it inside her mouth.

Helaine gasped.

Lydia released and looked up. "Do you?"

"Like it . . . I like it . . . yes," she replied as she ran her hand along Lydia's shoulders and slid downward in the seat. "Very much."

"Go on. Frank's Place. Helaine Kristenson followed me there?"

"I followed you."

Lydia sighed and rested her forehead on Helaine's abdomen. "You followed me for two years?" She kissed the black satin folds and hid her face in them. They felt like bed sheets to her now, the stomach a pillow. "Why on earth didn't you say something to me?"

"On earth? On earth you and I were with other people."

Lydia thought about that for awhile. Helaine's hand lay beneath her. She lifted herself and brushed her body against it as she rose. "Kiss me," she finally said.

They kissed.

"Let me see you, Lydia Beaumont. My girl next door." She touched her cheek. "Most beautiful girl in the world."

Lydia leaned back.

With the lights of night shining in them the blue eyes glistened like pools of water, cool, refreshing, limpid. In the heat of summer, of the moment, in all those dog days gone by with their scorching fires, with their arid landscapes, roaming thirsty, depleted, navigating across a bed of coal, burning coals on tender feet, blistered, crawling on hands and knees, in a seven-year drought with no relief, that burnt her to ashes, incinerated her senses, melted her soul, drained her vitality, her life fluids, leaving her hotter than hot, day and night, night and day, hotter than hell all the time, and dehydrated, and now this warm spring to refresh in—how could she live without water?

"Had you ever been to Frank's before?"

Helaine shifted her body. "Just for lunch. Saturdays. Dinner once in awhile."

Lydia processed that. "So Friday's? Dr. Kristenson reading me like a book?"

"Oh no. Not at first, anyway."

"But later? Then Lydia Beaumont was as transparent as water?"

Water. "There is nothing wrong with that. Being transparent."

They kissed again.

"You went away. Where did Lydia go?"

"I had to get away . . . distract myself."

"Were you successful? Did you find yourself a distraction?"

"No. Impossible. Swam most of the time." She laughed. "And cold showers."

Helaine smiled. "Lydia Beaumont is a swimmer. Are you good at that?"

"Treading water?"

They were cheek to cheek.

"I'm sorry," Helaine whispered.

"And you, Venus? What did you find for distraction?"

Helaine hung her head on Lydia's shoulder, kissed her neck, her mouth, her neck again. "But I missed you," she whispered.

Lydia shut her eyes. There was that scent again. Bittersweet. Coming at her from everywhere. From the blond hair. The blond at Frank's Place. In the woods where she first had smelled it. She took a deep breath and held it. How she had missed her. How lonely she had been in the woods. And every hour before and since. "I missed you," she said, her voice a stone dropping through the ocean. Then she let her jacket be removed, let her dress be opened. She was straps and buttons being undone like the ribbons of a present. In her ears a woman sang her praises. She let the music surround her.

"Soon, Lydia Beaumont."

"When?"

"Tonight," Helaine promised with her fingers at her lips again. "Can you wait till then?"

Lydia took them in her mouth, motioning with her throat as if she meant to swallow them.

Helaine moaned out loud.

Lydia released her.

The cabdriver looked back.

"Around it," Helaine instructed the cabbie. "Go," she urged.

The cabbie was puzzled. It wasn't immediately obvious to her which woman the blond was addressing or what exactly *go* might mean under the circumstances.

Helaine moaned again, louder this time. Lydia was in the palm of her hand. She felt the blood rising to her face, heat in her lap. She clasped the back of Lydia's neck and rubbed her shoulders. "Mmmm . . . ," she uttered, temporarily forgetting herself and then remembering the driver again, seeing her expectant expression. "Around it," she muttered in exasperation.

A sound came from Lydia, laughter escaping through the nose.

Helaine half laughed, half groaned.

The cabbie grinned and faced forward, convinced that the blond was instructing her lover.

Lydia moistened her lips.

Helaine caressed them with her thumb.

Lydia put her mouth around it and a suppressed gasp came from above her. More pressure on her neck, fingers in her hair. She flicked at the tip of the finger with her tongue and gently nipped at it. Satin thighs arched gently toward her face. Rapid breaths. She repeated the motions all over again.

Behind them, a cab with its lights off fell into position and yet another vehicle pulled in after that one.

"Lydia, I—"

"It's all right," Lydia whispered without raising her head or lifting her hands. "Drive around the park," she ordered in a voice just loud enough for the driver to hear.

The cabbie glanced in the mirror to be sure she had heard correctly this time.

"Yes," Helaine affirmed. "Go around it," she said, throwing her head back with a sigh and pulling her dress out from under Lydia, slipping it up past the hips.

The cab began to circle the park.

Stockings, mid-thigh. Lydia kissed the white skin above them.

Helaine clutched Lydia's hands. "I'm in trouble here," she warned.

"No, no, no. You're fine. I won't muss you."

"We can't," Helaine cautioned, twisting in frustration as she held Lydia's hands tightly to her hips to stop her. A quickie in a cab. She moaned and held her legs together. They came apart again. "Lydia . . . I'm . . . have you ever—"

"You can show me."

Helaine heaved her lap toward Lydia's mouth. "Oh, Lydia," she said in a strained voice. "There isn't time."

No answer. The music played.

"Lydia . . ." Pressed for time.

"Helaine."

"I need you."

"Show me how."

"I mean—in my bed." She held her tight between her legs. "In bed, Lydia."

The swish of satin.

"Not here," Helaine murmured.

"Okay."

Okay. Helaine instantly regretted it. "I'm sorry."

"That's okay. It's okay."

Helaine let her pull the dress down around her hips.

Whoa, thought the cabbie, making yet another revolution around the park. She glanced at the blond in the mirror. She had seemed vaguely familiar to her when she had first gotten into the cab. The cabbie watched her discreetly as the woman adjusted her clothes and it suddenly came to her. She checked the meter, checked her watch.

"Lydia? I'm out of my—"

"No, no, no. You're fine. Hold me."

They held each other quietly, listening to the sound of their breathing. The cab rolled gently and they could hear the traffic as it raced by the vehicle. They listened together to the voices of passersby on their evening strolls, conversing in the hushed tones peculiar to those who walk in darkness. The breezy strands of their conversations drifted into the ladies' hideaway and hypnotically blended with the cabbie's music.

Lydia sighed. "My bed," she whispered as she put her head down. "In my bed."

Helaine caressed her mouth again. "Yours." The lips parted. The throat swallowed. The blood flowed from her heart, straight down into her fingertips.

"I know you. You're the Love Doc," the cabbie declared, after depositing Lydia Beaumont safely at her doorstep.

Helaine responded cautiously. "That's right," she said, peering over the seat at the ID tag hanging beneath the meter, "Lucille."

"Lu, they call me. Thought I recognized you. I've got your book!"

"I'm glad. Did it help any?"

"You bet. Got my Mr. Right."

Helaine smiled at that. "Good for you."

Dr. Kristenson arrived at the convention center with only ten minutes remaining to pore over her notes before she was to take the podium. Kay and Robert greeted her inside and chatted idly at her as she organized her index cards. She was supposed to join them for cocktails afterward. They'd understand.

It was an energetic crowd and the doctor knew by experience that she would be expected to mingle and socialize after the question and answer. No dice.

"I meant to call you both earlier but I got hung up with things. Tonight—*oh how do you do? Thank you. Thank you for coming*—there's a scheduling conflict. What about tomorrow? Lunch say?"

"Jon already told us, Helaine," Robert said with a chuckle. "A date is not a scheduling conflict."

She smiled, relieved that they knew. "It's been a hectic week. Uh-oh, got to get up there—*Hey. Well, thank you. Nice to see you here*—talk to you two afterward?"

"Go, go. It's time."

"Look for us at the punchbowl," Kay added.

The speech was shortened, only thirty-five minutes long. Then she answered questions in the light and airy manner she had acquired from doing so many of these events, resorting to humor, which she had learned was the appropriate escape from certain questions that she knew better than to entertain.

She was right about the crowd's expectations though and despite her efforts to break away, after the applause died down, she quickly found herself cornered at the punchbowl where she had met up with Robert and Kay. There was then no easy egress available. She pressed the flesh till her hands felt grimy and smiled vacuously as she tried to back away toward the exit, her savvy friends acting as accomplices in this sadly unsuccessful endeavor.

"I don't know, Helaine. Looks like you're here awhile," Robert said.

"I hope not. I've got a car waiting."

"You finally hired a driver?"

"No—*a pleasure to meet you. Thank you for coming*—no, don't be ridiculous."

"Maybe the bathroom window?" Kay suggested.

"We did that once—*Thank you. Oh, I'm flattered. Thank you*—didn't we?"

"Yeah, when we were kids. Look at us now," Robert said.

"C'mon, *she* looks stunning tonight. Where are you taking your date?"

"*Hello. Oh, I'm glad you enjoyed it. Well, thank you*—to bed I hope!"

"Dr. Kristenson? Helaine Kristenson?"

The three of them glanced at a young man carrying a manila envelope under his arm. The hairs on Robert Keagan's head bristled with alarm. Kay fell mute.

"Yes?"

"You are Dr. Helaine Kristenson?" he asked again, fiddling with the package.

Robert moved toward Helaine. "Helaine! Don't—"

"Of course I am."

The process server handed her the envelope. "Dr. Kristenson," he declared, "you've been served," and then he cut through the crowd in a quick getaway.

"Served, what does this mean?" Helaine asked, turning to Kay.

Kay declined to answer.

"Shit!" Robert muttered. It was something he had always feared.

The party of three exited the building before anyone else was the wiser.

"Lu? Hi. Change of plans, I'm afraid."

"Where to, Doctor?"

"I don't want you to see her. Do you understand?"

(Yah.)

Robert Keagan, Esquire was beside himself. "Helaine?"

Kay grabbed his elbow. "Calm down. Helaine, can I make you some tea?"

"No. Thank you." The clock in their kitchen read half past ten.

"Robert, tea?"

"No, Kay—Speak to me, Helaine. Tell me about the flat."

When she was seventeen, what a very good year. When she was twenty-one, also a very good year. When she was thirty-five she lived with Sharon at the waterfront flat. "We lived there together," she said numbly. "I redid the place for Sharon. Moved out after two years. Menage à trois bullshit all the time. I got sick of walking in on it. Paid the rent till now. Someone has to call—"

"Jane Doe?" he interrupted. "Who's this Jane Doe they're referencing?"

"How can I not see her, Robert? She's expecting me. I'm late already."

"Do I get to know her name?"

She thought on it and gave in. "Lydia."

"She has a last name?"

"Beaumont."

"Beaumont—the attorney's daughter?"

"I wouldn't know that. She didn't say."

Kay joined Helaine at the table and Robert sat down. "This is the woman you mentioned?"

"A little diversion or something serious?" Robert asked.

"Serious. I need to go, Robert."

"Oh sure. They're after her, Helaine. You plan on leading them to the woman?"

"I can't tell her I'm not coming. I can't tell her about this."

Kay gulped her tea and looked over her cup at Robert. So many times he had told her that he didn't trust Sharon Chambers, so many times worrying over Helaine's mistake. Palimony. It was nonsense of course, just something to harass Helaine with. By the looks of things, Sharon might even be able to shake off her replacement. Who'd want this crap to contend with? "I wonder if it is Edward Beaumont's daughter?" she suddenly asked. "Wouldn't that be interesting?"

"It's all interesting," Robert snorted. "The papers will eat you alive, Dr. Kristenson. And what does Sharon care? How about Lydia Beaumont? She'll care I bet, or is she prepared to be dragged through the mud for you?"

"Robert, you don't know," Kay interjected. "Let's stick to what we do know."

"I do know that we should settle this quickly. And I do know that won't happen if they get to Lydia Beaumont first." He studied Helaine's face. "She'll be dragged through the mud, Helaine. Be sure of it. That's the motive."

"Such a charismatic man, Edward Beaumont," Kay offered to anyone who was listening. "So handsome."

"Yeah, and Mister Controversy himself. If it is his daughter, he won't want her to go through all that. He'll advise her to run, mark my words."

Helaine took it all in. "Womanizer?"

"*Sir* Womanizer, to you."

Helaine smiled for the first time in hours and then her face dropped again. "How long will it take? To settle, I mean?"

"A few weeks, a few months, but it's better than the alternative, I can assure you that. You'd lose your girl for certain if that happens." He paused and she nodded for him to continue. "She got a reputation to protect, as well, or is she just a pampered courtesan?" His humor was returning to him. He pushed the legal complaint away and settled into his chair.

"She works at Soloman-Schmitt, across from my offices."

"Oh, shit." He tucked his pencil behind his ear. "She'll be thrilled. And, I'm sure, so will her bosses."

Kay rose to freshen her tea. "Does she know about Sharon Chambers?" she asked over her shoulder.

"She's seen her. Sharon tried to pick her up in the bathroom at Frank's."

Robert raised his brow. "Really? That oblivious?"

"Yes. Lydia doesn't know her from Adam, either." Helaine smiled again and checked the time. "It's sort of funny."

"Frank's Place?" Kay inquired sitting down beside Helaine. "Oh, I guess that would be in the financial district." (Curious.) "But Sharon's in all the rags. How couldn't she know her?"

Robert laughed. "Probably only gets the financials. That way she doesn't have to read about her dad."

"You don't know that Edward Beaumont is her father," Kay objected.

"I know he's got a daughter. She'd be in her mid-thirties. A son, too. Just like his old man, I hear."

"Where do you know this from?" Kay asked.

Helaine listened quietly. Someone had to tell Lydia the news. Soon.

"From the club."

"The club!" Kay mocked. "You're all a bunch of women. Gossips, I swear."

"Is she in her mid-thirties, Helaine?"

"Early I'd say. Maybe mid."

"It's her. I just have a feeling."

"What difference does that make?" Kay asked.

"It's a small world that's all. And it means she definitely has what Sharon's after."

"Yes," Helaine interrupted. "She certainly does."

They mulled that in silence for a few minutes.

"Helaine's right, Robert. Sharon's not really after money here. She's trying to control Helaine, chase her Jane Doe off in the process. Why should Sharon want to settle? She's not afraid of bad publicity."

The ladies waited for him to respond.

"Look, lawyers change everything. Her lawyers—and I know these guys—they're not going to let their client make them work harder than they have to. It just isn't done like that. We make a decent offer right now and that'll be end of it. Good-bye Sharon Chambers riffraff, hello Lydia Beaumont straight lace." He put his hand over the papers and waited on Helaine's reaction.

"No more than a few months?" she asked. "Are you sure?"

"I do this for a living, Helaine. You think you're the only victim of this kind of scam? Happens every week in our fair city. Everyday all over our great land people are parting with cold hard cash for a little bit of privacy with something warm and soft. Facts of life. And some of those defendants are no more guilty of the allegations against them than you are."

She considered his words with a sullen expression.

"Lawyers, Helaine. We know what we're doing when we write stuff like this. Edward Beaumont sent his little girl to all the best universities he could instituting lawsuits no different than the one we got right here. Be sure of that. It's the name of the game. Sharon Chambers is not in charge of it. The lawyers are. We call all the shots."

She nodded grimly. "Lydia needs to know about this, Robert. I don't know how to tell her, but she needs to know tonight. Right now."

"I'll tell her. I wouldn't mind speaking with her, see what she's made of, you know. Just in case."

"Call her," Kay urged. "It's almost eleven. She must know something's wrong, anyway."

"What's the number, Helaine?"

She rattled it off.

"You know it by heart?" he asked, suspiciously.

"By heart. Lest she be discovered otherwise."

"Helaine, I sincerely hope you've told me everything. I'm trying to defend your interests."

"I know and I thank you, Robert." She repeated the number as he dialed. "I want to hear how she reacts," she quickly added.

"I can talk on speaker. Willing to take that risk?"

Have her friends hear Lydia Beaumont tell her to go jump in a lake? It was nothing she looked forward to, but. "I guess so," she said.

He put the call through on intercom and Helaine held her breath.

"*Hello?*"

It was a pretty voice. Expectant. Robert Keagan hated to disappoint it.

"I'd like to speak to Lydia Beaumont, please. It's very important."

There was silence on the other line as the woman sized up the caller's voice. "*This is she,*" she answered in a controlled voice. "*To whom am I speaking?*"

Robert turned to Kay and Helaine, then smiled. "I am Robert

Keagan, Esquire. I represent Dr. Helaine Kristenson. You know her, I understand."

Silence. Crackling. *"Doctor—yes, I know her, Mr. Keagan."* Quiet again while she tried to guess at the nature of the call. *"My number's unlisted. How did you get it?"*

Helaine pointed at herself and he nodded. "Dr. Kristenson has asked me to call."

"Indeed? What is this about Mr. Keagan? I'm in suspense."

He cocked his head at the ladies. "Ms. Beaumont, do you know Sharon Chambers?"

"Sharon Chambers? No."

"The supermodel? You—"

"Oh, the one in the news? Yes, I've heard of her. What is this about, please?"

Robert coughed. The color drained from Helaine's face. Kay signaled for him to get it over with.

"Mr. Keagan?"

"Ms. Chambers is Helaine Kristenson's lover."

The line fell silent once more.

"Was," Helaine whispered.

"Was," Kay whispered.

He held up his finger to his lips.

"I see. She was, Mr. Keagan. Past tense, I believe."

"Was," he repeated. "I stand corrected, Ms. Beaumont. So you do know her?"

"No I don't—I didn't know she was Sharon Chambers. I don't know her. Personally, I mean. Look, Mr. Keagan, you'll have to forgive me. It's late and I'm tired. Please cut to the chase."

"Ms. Chambers is apparently unhappy to be a past tense. She has filed a lawsuit against Dr. Kristenson. Palimony. You understand such things?"

A pensive moment elapsed before Lydia spoke again. *"And when did this happen?"*

"Tonight."

"Oh. I see. Was that before or after Helaine's speech?"

"After."

"*Wasn't that good of Ms. Chambers? To let Helaine finish her speech.*"

"She has named you a Jane Doe defendant in the action."

He waited as she measured her response to that information. Behind him Helaine and Kay had seated themselves around the table. Helaine rested her head in her hands.

"*That's obscene, Mr. Keagan. Is Helaine there? I need to talk to her.*"

Helaine motioned for the phone and he held his hand out to stop her. "Ms. Beaumont, is your father Edward Beaumont, the attorney?" He heard her scoff.

"*Please. Has she named my father, too?*"

He grimaced then smiled victoriously at his audience. "I only wondered if you understood the seriousness of the matter, having your name dragged into this? But I guess Edward Beaumont's daughter would know about those kinds of things."

"*Mister Keagan, I would prefer my father's name be kept out of this, for reasons I suspect I don't have to list. What is Sharon Chambers suing me for, I'd like to know?*"

"A half a million." There was the sound of a throat clearing then nothing. "Ms. Beaumont?"

"*Thank you. I meant why? What does she allege Jane Doe has done to her?*"

"You have emotionally distressed her."

"*Emo—may I speak with Helaine please?*"

"I have advised my client to lay low for awhile. I would appreciate your cooperation with that."

"Robert, please let me talk to her. We'll be brief."

"*Helaine?*"

"Robert, please . . . let me talk to her."

"*Mr. Keagan? Please. Put her on for just a second.*"

"*How did your speech go?*"

"My speech? Very well, thank you. Lydia, I—"

"*Standing room only?*"

"Actually, yes. How did you know?"

"*So, my celebrated friend. You're famous, too?*"

Helaine laughed. "I didn't expect it would impress you very much." She watched Kay and Robert out of the corner of her eye.

"Looks like I've made some trouble for you, Dr. Kristenson."

"You?"

"What's your plan?"

Helaine hesitated. "What would you think if I settled the matter?"

"I'd say that seems prudent. Of course, I'm only a humble investment strategist. Are you going to do that, Helaine?"

"That is our strategy. You know . . . I'm so sorry—"

"Don't worry about me. The worse has happened, that's all. We'll get it over with."

We—Helaine sat in the nearest chair, kicked off her shoes.

"Okay?"

"Okay. But what about you, Jane Doe?"

"I've been called worse."

There was light laughter from the table. Helaine chuckled, too.

"Really, I'll be fine. You should get over here though. Make certain you're getting your money's worth."

Kay grinned and Helaine sent Robert a pleading expression. He smiled but shook his head, rising from the table with the complaint tucked under his arm.

"Better get her a private line, Kay. Where's that cordless?"

Kay left the kitchen to help search for it.

"Helaine?"

"Lydia, wait. Please. I'm going to switch phones."

"Okay."

"Here, Helaine. It's running low, though. He always forgets to recharge it." Kay handed her the cordless phone.

"Kay. Thank you. Where?"

"You can take it to the guest room. That's where you're sleeping tonight. Go on. I'll hang this up for you."

"Can you hear me?"

"Loud and clear."

"You know I'm not coming tonight?"

"Is that what you want?"

"No."

"Come then."

"Lydia . . . I can't."

"Can't. Lots of can'ts."

"I'm sorry." There was static on the line. Helaine went to the bed and sat down. It cleared.

"I want to make love to you."

Helaine lay back on the pillows, cradled the phone, turned the lights off. "I know."

"I want you to show—" Static. Nothing but static. *"Helaine?"*

"I don't know what to do. It could make things worse for us. For you." She paused. "They're looking for you."

"It isn't going to scare me off. That's all it's supposed to do."

"Rob—my lawyer says he'll take care of this quickly. No more than a few months." She stopped there. Did she believe it? "Can you wait, Lydia? It isn't that long if you think about it." Her voice was out there, lost in the universe.

"No. Show me now, Helaine. Come here and show me."

Helaine took a quick breath, let it go. "Robert feels sure they've been tailing me. I don't think we can risk it."

"They can't have much, Helaine. Essentially we've just met."

"Nothing substantial. Not yet, anyway."

They silently pondered the implications together.

"Then tell me. Tell me how."

Helaine turned over on her side. "Tell you?"

"Tell me."

"Now?"

"Are you lying down?"

"Yes."

"Dressed?"

"Yes."

"Satin?"

"Satin . . . did you like that?"

"Love."

"Love. I'm glad. Hoped you would."

"Am I undoing it?"

Helaine reached behind her without speaking.

"Helaine?"

"Lydia Beaumont."

"Is it undone?"

Helaine fumbled with the catch and pulled the zipper down. "Undone," she whispered, dropping her dress. The air of the apartment was cool and she had a sudden chill. Goose bumps. She pulled the pillows close to her, unfastened her bra. "Lydia?"

"Tell me, Helaine."

"Hurry . . ."

"What should I—"

"Take it off."

"Good morning."

Lydia recognized the voice on the other end of the phone. She rolled over and laughed nervously. "Good morning," she mumbled, squinting at her clock. Ten. Saturday, she reminded herself, shaking the sleep away.

"May I speak with Helaine? I'm guessing she's there since she's not where I last left her."

A shock of blond hair lay across the neighboring pillow. Its owner peeked out from under the sheets and smiled sleepily, green eyes watering in the sunlight.

"Good morning," Helaine said to Lydia, as she wrapped herself around her.

"Morning," Lydia repeated with a smile. "It's your lawyer."

"No!"

"Yes!"

"Ms. Beaumont?"

The ladies gathered the sheets and sat up.

"Yes, Mr. Keagan. One moment, please," Lydia answered, passing the phone to Helaine.

"Robert," Helaine sang in a morning voice, "I can explain everything."

"Go ahead."

"Uh-oh, I see you're not amused. What's wrong besides the obvious?"

"Besides the obvious—that you won't let me help you—there is a troubling new development I'd like to bring to your attention. Are you prepared for this now or would you like to crawl back here in an hour?"

"Umm . . . tell me now."

"Well, let's see. We'll start like this. Lydia Beaumont. Dark hair, blue eyes, about your height, drop-trow gorgeous. How do you think I know all that?"

"Good guess?"

"Good photo, Helaine. Of both of you. Together. Now isn't that convenient for the bad guys?"

Lydia sent her a questioning look.

"Photo," Helaine whispered. "Us."

Lydia shrugged and slid Helaine's hand between her legs.

Robert heard an unintelligible remark. *"What?"*

"I said, how do we look together?"

"Hand in glove, I'd say. That's not really the point, is it?"

Hand in—"How did you come by it, Robert?"

"Messenger, I presume. Lawyers must have sent it as an anonymous heads-up. They want her name, Helaine. Clearly they mean business."

She felt Lydia shudder. "They haven't gotten it yet, Robert."

"That won't last, especially with your wanton—I've got another call. I'll call you right back. Don't go anywhere!"

Lydia was coaxing with her hips, with quick breaths. "I need you," she murmured into the blond hair.

"Okay," Helaine said, consenting to both of them.

Riiiinng . . . riiiinng . . . riiiinng . . .

"Oh . . . for God's sake . . ." Lydia groaned.

"Oh, no. That's probably Robert calling back. Hello?"

Lydia rolled onto her side and put her face under the pillow.

"Hello?" Helaine repeated.

"Queenie, is that you?"

"I'm sorry. I suspect you have the wrong —"

"Is this Del? Put Queenie on."

"Queenie?"

"Oh, my God, it's my father—don't hang up."

Helaine handed Lydia the phone with a sly smile.

"Daddy?" Lydia was crimson.

"Good morning, Queenie. Say, who's that? Great voice."

Lydia was rounding up bathrobes when the phone rang again. "For you," she laughed. "It's got to be for you this time."

Helaine answered it. "Hello?"

"Good morning! Liddy?"

Helaine shook her head. "Just a moment, please."

Lydia rolled her eyes. "Who?"

Helaine grinned, threw up her hands. "Your mommy?"

Lydia laughed and took the phone. "Hah," she whispered, sitting beside her on the bed. "Good morning?"

"Whoa, Liddy. Is she as good as she sounds?"

"Del . . . uhh . . ." she cast Helaine a sheepish look and lowered her voice, "can you believe even better?"

Helaine smiled and put on a terry robe. "Thank you, darling," she said, heading for the bathroom.

"Con-fuckin-gratu-relations, Lydia Beaumont! Call me first chance you get."

Phone again.

"You better get that," Helaine said. "I'm making waves, I think."

"Sure are. Good morning?"

"Helaine?"

"Uh . . . just a moment, please."

"Is it Robert?"

"No. A woman."

Helaine hesitated. Lydia brought the phone to her ear again.

"Who's calling, please?"

"Oh, I'm sorry. Tell her it's Kay."

"It's Kay. Of course it is."

"You're quite a good sport, Ms. Beaumont. Good morning, Kay."

"Good morning! Well, is she as good as she looks?"

"Hah! Even better. Good photo?"

"That's the woman in Frank's Place, isn't it?"

"That's her."

"I want the both of you for lunch."

"Kay, that's greedy."

"Did I say that? Well now, that's a Freudian slip. Lunch then?"

"What does Robert think?"

"Robert the worrier. I sent him out to pick up lunch. He tried to call you back but the phone was busy. Suggests you both leave separately."

Lydia was getting dressed. Helaine motioned for her to stop. She did.

"What time is lunch, Kay?"

"One?"

Helaine reached for her watch. Eleven thirty already. "We'll see you then."

"Come separately, Helaine."

Lydia stood by the bed, half dressed and waiting.

"Don't worry. We will."

"First things first. Tech stocks?"

"Robert, let her in!"

Lydia stood bewildered outside the Keagans' apartment door. Helaine was right about the trek—it only took a few minutes to get there. They were practically neighbors. Five minutes away at the most, it was hardly enough time for her body to get used to standing and walking, let alone the idea of delivering something clever at her host's doorstep. She floundered there, prodding her brain cells for a response and caught sight of Helaine in the background with a woman who she presumed was Kay Keagan. She smiled anxiously at the two of them and waved.

"Buy or sell?" Robert pressed, pretending she could not gain admittance without an answer.

"Excuse him. I'm Kay."

"Pleased to meet you, Kay," Lydia said. "Do you own any?" she asked Robert.

"Yeah, some."

"Lydia Beaumont," she said offering him her hand. "Sell."

"Robert Keagan, a pleasure to meet you Ms. Beaumont," he grinned. "May I take your clothes?"

"Clothes?" (Oh, okay.) "What do you plan to do with them?"

"Robert, really. You make us seem like opportunists," Kay said.

"Seem? Hello, Ms. Beaumont," Helaine whispered as she kissed Lydia's cheek. "Did I tell you yet how beautiful you look today?"

"I believe so," Lydia whispered back, her face suddenly warm.

"Ah, look at that, a crimson still diviner. Don't let us frighten you," Helaine said. "We don't get out much."

"Hungry or thirsty?" Kay asked, leading Lydia by the arm to the kitchen.

Lydia glanced back at Helaine.

"Both," Helaine answered. "Lydia Beaumont has a very robust appetite."

"Oh no," Lydia responded. "You're trying to embarrass me."

"Now you're boasting, Helaine," Kay chided. "You'll make us jealous."

"Kay, where are you going with that gorgeous woman?" Robert asked.

"I'm undertaking to satisfy her robust appetite. Red or white, Lydia?"

"Don't even dream of it. Red?" Helaine asked.

Lydia nodded, coming to a standstill at the photograph of the two of them pinned with a magnet to the refrigerator. Who took this, she wondered. Why hadn't she noticed them?

"Nice looking couple. Here you go, dear."

Lydia took the wineglass from Kay with a tentative smile. "Thank you."

"Do you have a sister, we hope?" Robert asked with an impudent smile.

"We're overwhelming, we know," Kay said.

"Sister?" Lydia repeated. "Oh, I see. No. A brother, though."

"Sit, everybody," Robert ordered. "You ladies across from each other."

"You're scaring me," Kay chimed. "That's where I was going to put them." Lids off their platters. "Eat what you want," she urged, "it's a smorgasbord."

"Does your brother look like you?" Robert asked picking up where he left off.

Lydia took a deep sip of wine. She guessed she would be needing it. "I suppose he must," she replied with a chuckle.

"A brother." He winked at Kay. "What do you think, willing to compromise?"

Helaine laughed. Her friends were in great form considering, enchanted by bashful Lydia Beaumont. She stretched her legs under the table and gripped Lydia's between them, mouthing I love you. She felt her relax then.

"Well, I don't know," said Kay. "Do you think we're his type, Lydia?"

Helaine scoffed. "Better drink the wine, Lydia. It'll dull the pain."

Lydia toyed with a grape before popping it in her mouth. "No, I don't think he's your type," she teased. "He's more like my father, if you know what I mean."

"I know your father. A fine rogue," Robert added. "Your brother's name?"

"Eddie." A boy's name. He was a man now. "Edward, I mean."

"Oh, that would make sense," Robert replied. "Edward the second?"

"Actually the third," Lydia replied. "Nobody's counting, though."

"The third," he repeated. "Your father retire?"

"He did. Last year."

"How'd that little glitch resolve itself, you know?" He couldn't resist asking.

"That glitch." Lydia squirmed. "Like all the others. In his defense, he really did think that was a woman. The dress. Poor excuse in the big picture, I realize."

"Ooh," Helaine uttered in interest.

"You know all this stuff, right?" Robert asked her. "Or are you only on a first name basis with Edward Beaumont's progeny?"

No, Helaine did not know this stuff. "I love Mr. Beaumont's progeny. A toast to Edward the second. For his beautiful daughter."

"I'll drink to that," Robert said.

They all did.

"I'm dying to know what your father had to say about that matter," Kay persisted. "A fabulous romp like that and not a word about it?"

The wine made its way fast. Lydia was actually tempted to repeat what Daddy had said. It was the kind of colorful commentary he was famous for, although this one he had imparted on Eddie's ears alone. Eddie the third.

"She wants to tell us," Robert said. "You can see it in her eyes."

"No," Lydia protested. "I don't usually even discuss those things."

"Those things? Uh-oh, Dr. Kristenson. Better get your notebook out."

Dr. Kristenson smiled. "I find Ms. Beaumont's modesty hopelessly sexy. It makes me weak. What did your father privately say about his glitch, Lydia?"

Lydia laughed uncomfortably. "He didn't say anything to me personally."

Robert adjusted himself in his chair. "But he told your brother . . . what?"

"Oh my God," she answered. "Peer pressure?"

"Tell," Kay urged, smiling agreeably.

Tell. "He told my brother it was the best blow job he ever had."

All but Lydia burst into laughter. She waited for them to regain themselves and stifled a smirk of her own. The subject was not generally amusing to her although in the present company she was willing to allow that there was something darkly funny about it all.

"He's qualified to say that," Robert finally said.

"Oh, I know," Lydia replied. She felt Helaine's eyes on her and avoided them. "It doesn't typically inspire mirth," she explained. "It's funnier if you're not related to him. Or married," she added with a quick laugh.

Kay elbowed Robert.

"Have you forgiven your father?" Dr. Kristenson inquired. No notebook.

Lydia swirled the contents of her glass and held it to the light. "Oh yes, Doctor. At least once a week." She set the glass down. "Or as needed."

Dr. Kristenson liked that answer. "Good. And your mother?"

Her mother? "Forgiven him?" She had to answer her lover. "My father?"

Dr. Kristenson nodded.

"No, never. But she stills wears his ring. That's what he wants from her."

"That's not so unusual," Helaine said.

"What's your mother's name?" Kay asked.

"Oh my goodness—Marilyn. Marilyn Sanders-Beaumont. Age sixty-four. Past menopause. Past hoping for grandchildren. Past golfing, hates it. Walks five miles a day. Formally, an overeducated housewife, now part-time gardener, Sunday painter, full-time philanthropist. Active but prone to melancholy"—Lydia dropped two fingers in the air signifying quotations—"as opposed to depression. A dying breed. Last of the stay-at-home moms. Last of the bleeding heart, dyed-in-the-wool, yellow-dog liberals. Last of the money can't buy you love. Last of the do unto others as you would have done unto you. Last of the one-man-women roaming the wilderness for thirty-eight years, starving and parched." She pushed four grapes to the center of her plate, pulled them apart, pushed them back together again and glanced warily toward Helaine. "I am not like Edward Beaumont. I just happen to be his daughter."

Helaine sat up in her chair. "Mr. and Mrs. Beaumont have a very lovely daughter and that's a fine reflection on them."

Kay agreed.

"Indeed," Robert added. "So tell me, what about pharmaceuticals? Buy, sell, or hold?"

"Oh, Robert," Kay whined. "That isn't a proper segue."

Lydia smiled gratefully. "Hold, until further notice. Don't you have a broker, Robert?"

"I do, but I don't trust him."

"Oh, I see. Well, thank you."

"What are some of the warning signs to look for?"

"Buzzwords." Lydia stretched her legs under the table and grabbed Helaine's in them.

"Like?"

"Like price fixing, medical ethics, humanitarian crises—those kinds of things."

"Yikes. Which ones do you own?"

Kay sighed impatiently. "Please be certain to leave a bill, Lydia."

Lydia smiled. "None anymore."

"Why not?"

"Oh . . . price fixing, medical ethics . . . you know."

"Yuck," Kay said. "Sell."

"Now wait a minute. You can't get rich on those concerns, Ms. Beaumont."

"But you can get what you need," she replied. "And sleep at night, too."

"Sleep," Helaine said. "To sleep. Perchance to dream. Ay, that is the rub. What do you think, Robert? Sleeping all right?"

"I was. Until I met Marilyn Beaumont's little girl."

"Hah," Helaine replied, "I know exactly how you feel!"

"I understand you've met Sharon Chambers," Robert declared, switching subjects again.

Lydia was confused by the assertion. Oh, in the ladies lounge, she remembered. Indeed, she had. "I didn't know it was Sharon Chambers, per se."

"It?" Robert smirked at the mistake.

"Naturally, I meant *she*." She glanced apologetically at Helaine who appeared indifferent to the remark.

"More wine, everyone?"

"Thanks, Kay."

"Yes, please."

"What if Sharon Chambers finds out Jane Doe's identity?" Robert inquired.

"She's bound to someday," Lydia replied. "Isn't she?"

"As pertains to this suit today. Would you care to read this?" He slid the papers across the table at her.

"As and for the first cause of action . . ." she broke off and scanned the document before looking up at Helaine. "No," she said, "I don't care to read it. You're going to resolve this, I understand. Before she finds out my name."

"I'll do my best, but it'll require your assistance. As well as Helaine's, if you catch my drift. By the way, you're very photogenic."

Helaine held up her glass with both hands and rested her elbows on the table.

"You'll have to postpone the honeymoon until this storm blows over." He glanced from one to the other. It was going to be tricky to impress them with this tiny detail. "Don't underestimate Sharon Chambers. She never saw a scandal she didn't like and there's no such thing as bad press unless her name's not in it."

There was, at last, a face to the shadowy image that had been haunting Sharon Chambers night and day for the past two years. And although she had acted on her hunch the minute she felt it, and had done everything she knew to do in order to block her, Dr. Kristenson had finally taken a lover.

For months Sharon had suspected Helaine's love interest was a woman. She couldn't say why she thought that. Just female intuition. She was stunned senseless by Lawrence Taft's photo exposé of her favorite blond with a swank brunette, not merely because the private eye had captured the couple's apparent bliss, but because she instantly recognized the woman in the photos as the haughty virgin queen she had unsuccessfully cornered in Frank's Place.

Up until she held those photos in her hand, she had believed the phantom relationship one-sided, that Helaine was stretched too thin to act on infatuation, or that if she did, she would fail to consummate it and that would be the end of the matter. After all, the blond was not the same woman she had met seven years ago and ever since turning forty she had been in a slump. Now she couldn't even achieve an orgasm, a midlife crisis had consumed her sexual appetite.

Because of that, the threat the dark specter presented at first had seemed far off of late. Held at a safe distance, it only lurked impotently in the background of their relationship, posing nothing more than a nuisance to Sharon, or a mirage on the horizon that would disappear if she satisfied Helaine's thirst. Nothing more than that. Helaine was a reasonable woman. She would never leave her for a mirage.

Glaring at the photographs of the two women getting into a cab, Sharon was forced to accept otherwise. The private eye had done his work and it had taken months, but a real lover, not a mirage, had finally materialized. Just when they both had begun to doubt the mission.

The ladies had at least been together Friday night and Sharon's instincts informed her, without a doubt, that it was probably *the* night. Helaine sleeping with someone else. The very idea of it made her blanch.

She had not just picked her up at a bar, Sharon screamed before she fired Lawrence Taft. That's not her style she assured, slamming the phone in his ear. She was angry at the entire incompetent world. He should have discovered what was going on well before Friday. Then the lawyers could have served the photos up, too. For that matter, why had the lawyers dawdled? She had seen them Wednesday afternoon. Paid them enough. If they had gotten their shit together like they promised to, they could have served the legal papers on Thursday. Then, photo or no photo, that would have stopped Helaine cold in her tracks. Stopped her before Friday. Before . . .

Sharon festered all weekend, the photographs rendering her virtually apoplectic. Dazed, she carried them from room to room. It was that one's first time, she concluded over and over again, as if it mattered. Yeah, because Sharon knew her types and she could tell by the naive look in those eyes. Warm, wide and willing. With a little skilled guidance that woman would become an excellent replacement. Blue eyes, red hot for the Love Doc. They were ice when Sharon had looked into them. They had despised her repletely and now she understood why.

What a difference a day would have made, she lamented. Just twenty-four little hours and she could have put the whole affair on ice, permanently. Now, when she got Helaine Kristenson back—and get her back, she would—she'd have to live forever with the knowledge that she had slept with someone else.

Monday morning Sharon was still not prepared to make a public appearance. She sent a few choice photos by messenger to her lawyers and they called her back around noon to say that while the blue-eyed woman looked vaguely familiar somehow, they still needed more than that to go on, although they did not think it wise for Sharon to continue her illegal surveillance and wasn't even sure the current pictures would be admissible as evidence in a trial. In the end, they advised her again, she would, most likely, find that part of her claim dismissed, as the mystery woman had no duty owed to her to which she could be found and held in breach of. Still, for the purposes of an out of court settlement, two rich defendants are always more fun than one. Could she come in on Wednesday for a strategy session?

No, she could not. Actually she had to be in LA by Tuesday for an a.m. court appointment on Wednesday, hopefully her last if she could just keep her mouth shut during the proceedings. She didn't share that little tidbit with them, although she thought it unlikely they hadn't heard about the case. She simply told them to keep her apprised and left them with the phone number of the condo she owned in LA County. She expected to be returning in a week, sooner if they learned anything.

"I want you to nail this Jane Doe for me. I don't care what it takes."

"We understand that."

The rest of Monday she dedicated to restoring order to the waterfront flat. Yes, in reality Sharon Chambers was quite tidy, all her homes spotless. The mess at the waterfront flat was the exception, merely calculated for affect, to manipulate Helaine, keep things lively between them.

She made an assessment of the damages as she went along. The place was in the height of neglect, a sign which she attempted to ignore as she set about straightening it. It needed things, that was apparent, and more attention than she could give it at the moment, as preoccupied as she was and—dare she think it?—as depressed as she was feeling. The best she had to offer it for the time being was some organization.

She applied herself to that task, by evening having made enough progress to call it a day. By then there were a only few piles left in the hallway, personal items that didn't belong to either her or Helaine. These had clearly outlived their usefulness, she admitted without remorse, and she threw them into the trash along with the entire contents of the refrigerator.

She had come across very few of Helaine's things. That didn't surprise her too much—it had been a long time since the woman had actually lived there. She dwelt on that for the very first time as she wondered what she was supposed to do with them.

Her memory of the events that led up to Helaine moving out lay shrouded in dusty cobwebs she wasn't too anxious to disturb. There was a cedar closet in the back room, she remembered instead, that Helaine had once used for storage. She could stash the stuff in there for safekeeping, get it out of her sight until she could stand to see them again.

It was in the closet that Sharon Chambers had her breakdown. It happened in the darkness when her hand brushed against something soft and sleek, a sensation she recognized immediately.

She had worn that coat the day she had met Helaine Kristenson. A floor-length mink. Helaine had worn it, too, with nothing on underneath. That was the first time Sharon had made love to her. Seven years ago. That's like a lifetime when you're only thirty. She pulled the string on the overhead light and stared at it in disbelief. It hung like a dark ghost in the corner, as shiny as the day Helaine had bought it, as perfect as that perfect first night when she had lay her down in it. Here in the waterfront flat. Where Helaine had lived. Where they both had lived till . . . oh yes, she remembered it now and felt it in her heart.

In her heart there was a tearing sensation. That had to be her heart, she thought, or perhaps even her stomach. There was a taste in her mouth. Old blood. Bitter. No, it wasn't her stomach. It was her heart. She had the sense that it was being ripped from where it belonged. It felt pulled like a muscle. She had pulled a muscle once on the runway. The heart is a muscle that has to be exercised. That's what Dr. Kristenson used to say. Or what? Was she dying? There was a hard lump in her throat. She put her hand to her chest and with the other gripped the fur coat by the collar. She could picture the woman in it. The creamy soft flesh, the beautiful body. This was the precious skin she had left behind. She was gone. The pain was moving up into her jaws. She felt them trembling uncontrollably and she knew she was going to cry. The empty coat hanging there like brand new. She had left Helaine here beside it, but she was gone. If she cried it would ruin her eyes, not just her makeup. Her eyes. Her eyes. She could remember that night so vividly. Those green eyes. How could this coat be so precious? How could it be of so little value to Helaine that she would leave it, leave it hanging like a spirit from the past for her to find? There were tears now, hot as blood. That's what Sharon believed they were. Must be her blood she tasted in her mouth, must be her blood running out of her eyes, must be her blood gushing down her face onto her clothes and dampening the coat she clung to like a child. Must be all of her blood, judging from how much of it there was. And from the terrible pain in her heart.

It wasn't because he was a fan of the supermodel that prompted Robert Keagan to keep a Sharon Chambers scrapbook. And it wasn't because he was sentimental.

He added the recent headliner concerning the resolution of the LA County affair and thumbed through the prior entries with a scowl. Indiscretion. The woman had made a career of it. He closed the book with a thud and put it back on the shelf with his other reference guides. Now she expected to collect fringe benefits.

If necessary, he would present the file to Helaine and force her to pen her thoughts in it. Submit the tragic "diary" to the jury. Exhibit A, ladies and gentlemen: one broken heart. She'd have to go along with it.

He had allowed two weeks to pass without notifying the prosecuting attorneys that he would be the attorney of record for the defendant. Let the bad guys sweat it, he reasoned. No use in the good guys coming off panicked, even if they were. Besides, he was in no rush to join the issue, knowing from years of experience that there were hungry reporters hiding under their rocks, eagerly waiting to sink their teeth into the doctor's official response to Ms. Chambers' tasty allegations. It would be a feeding frenzy. Intermeddlers. They were insatiable. Robert Keagan had decided not to delve too deeply with Helaine about that phase of litigation. He didn't want to trouble her with its inevitability.

His first priority had been to pinpoint and quash all the peek-a-boo crap taking place on the sidelines and get some eyes of his own watching the streets. And while he felt like a cad doing it, nevertheless, he felt obliged to assign some peepers to the newlyweds as well, mostly because he hated surprises. Word now was that the coast was clear and all's quiet on the waterfront. While waiting on that determination he had used his time to compile a shopping list of dos and don'ts. Every one of those items had to be crossed off before he would consider himself ready to spar with Sharon's attorneys. It was a long list, most everything on it routine.

Hollisen, Hollisen and Goetz. All dead, but still raising hell in the legal world. And representing supermodel Sharon Chambers. Willard Hathaway Esq., chief counsel for the plaintiff.

"Hi, Willie, Robert Keagan here, Chambers v. Kristenson et al. What? Oh, yeah, yeah, yeah. Nah, I haven't had time to go through it all. Need more time to respond. I know, but I'm busy. No, not really, Willie. Oh, I'm sure she is. What? Nope, don't know who Jane Doe is—probably a figment of the plaintiff's imagination judging by this work of fiction I got in front of me. Yes, I really believe that. Pure fiction, as difficult reading as *Mein Kempf,* Willie. No, I truly doubt that. Uh, it's neither love nor war, I can assure you. What I think? It's pathetic is what it is. Well, you don't have to say you agree with me, we're both reasonable men. Huh? That she knows her very well? We neither admit nor deny that. I think we have a bad line. No, we neither admit nor deny that, too. No, I'm not calling her a liar. Yes, generally. It's all specious, Willie. Ten more days. No, five's not enough, I just got it this morning. At first blush? Well, it fails to state a cause of action for starters. Mm-hmm. Lack of jurisdiction, no merit, the works. Oh, I disagree. Yah, delusional and incoherent. We just can't make any sense of it, Willie. What? Oh, you wrote it? Well, what do you want from me? The substance? Yeah, we understand the substance. Clever but bald, Willie. So? So? And your client is no Snow White, I'm sure you know. Nah, you can't say that, wait till the jury sees my client. What do you mean by that? That's a bald-faced lie and you know it. Of course. Why don't you ask her about Italy? Oh, really? And what about the stuff going down in LA? Is that ancient history, too? Yah! I think it's all relevant and I'm sure the jury will, too. Hmm? Infidelity? That's very funny, Willie. You hear me laughing, right? Yeah, yeah, yeah, still laughing and that's what the whole wide world will be doing when they hear about this. What, gave her permission? I doubt my client would do that. Yeeaauh . . . also a bit too kinky to be believed. She did? Gave her permission? I said, I don't think so. Well, like I said before, delusional. What? Well, that's going to be hard for your client to prove. No, I'm not saying that at all. Judging from all this, looks like you've got a psychopath on your hands. Yeah, I really do. Well, you say loose cannon and I say psychopath, let's call the whole thing off. No, I wouldn't expect that you would. The point? Actually I was just calling for more time to answer and to tell you to stop following my client. Oh, c'mon Willie . . . what about the photograph? Yeah, we did. I think it's unethical. For real? Well, then who did? Okay, so then I'll have to put it this way: if ANYONE bothers my client, her friends, family, colleagues, associates, employees, agents, representatives, or subsidiaries thereof . . . we'll throw their asses in jail quicker than you can say *but*. Good, I'm glad to hear it. Oh, is that right? You better watch her then. Sure. Understandable, but it can't happen again or I'll move for an order of protection and run straight to the six o'clock news with it. Who? I've already said I don't know the woman. Theory? Probably passed in front of the lens by accident. No. Sorry. I don't know that, either. I'm sorry if you don't, it saddens me to think you don't find me credible anymore. A friend of my client? Well, you'll have to ask that when the time comes, because as far as I know she doesn't know her. She's not a liar, Willie. Yah! Oh, I object! Yah! Look here, your client has a criminal record, now. Well, we're very concerned about that. No, no, no, I'm just saying keep her away from mine. Oh, yes I do. Very good cause for concern and you know it. Well, that's fine, we send our thank yous in advance. Yup. No problem. Uum . . . I don't think so. I think we've covered just about everything. Yeah? Oh, don't worry, Willie. Sure. Sure. Yep, you'll be hearing from us. What? You betcha. And say hi to Martha. Very well, thank you. Oh, not too bad, busy these days, never see you at the club anymore. Just Thursdays? I guess that explains it. Sounds it, like two ships that cross in the night. Yep. I sure will. Hey . . . thanks for the ten days. *(click)*"

"Sonofabitch," Willard Hathaway muttered under his breath. He choked off the team's laughter with a virulent expression. Ms. Chambers had informed him Robert Keagan was a close friend of Dr. Kristenson. "She's got that purebred pit bull defending her," he announced, standing up and walking toward the door. Keagan was bad luck, he hadn't won a single case against him. "Someone get a hold of our talented client and tell her to call off her ballbreakers or he'll have us all in the slammer by week's end. Wouldn't that be pretty?" he said to his shoes. He grasped the door handle like a grenade. "Try to impress upon Ms. Chambers that she is not a free agent in this matter," he added, preparing to slam the door. Nobody dared to move while there was a chance he hadn't finished speaking. "Do it now, I said!"

Attorney Stanley Kandinsky is sharp. If compared to an animal, as people are wont to do sometimes, he looks just like a hawk. It's his lean physique and chiseled features, the low hairline, the dark and permanently scrutinizing eyebrows, a pair of piercing and unblinking brown eyes, almost black really. He's one of those people you can't imagine sleeping. Not that he ever seems sleepless or tired, but rather that he doesn't need to sleep at all. He is constantly alert.

They say "Stan can" when they recommend him to someone who needs something hushed up. They call him Mr. Hush-it-up. That's what he does.

Robert Keagan says that Stanley Kandinsky is the most important lawyer who ever lived, next to Abraham Lincoln. Nobody really knows what he means by that, but everyone agrees that Stanley's indispensable, whereas the same consensus, unfortunately, did not exist for Mr. Lincoln.

"Heads up, Stan."
"I've already heard the buzz. Who's Jane Doe?"
"Nah, skip that detail for now. But make a reservation for her just in case."
"Important?"
"Yeeaaaauhh . . . yes."
"Someone I know?"
"Mmmm-maybe."

"Enough, Robert. You sound like you're choking to death. When will I hear from her?"

"I've got a bad feeling. Very soon, I'd say."

"Oh, that's too bad. There's no merit to the suit, from what I know."

"None, across the board. It's legalized blackmail. We'll tag-team this like those other ones. I'll speak to her father if necessary. That'll guarantee it."

"And that's someone I know?"

"Afraid so. We'll get to that when we have to."

"You've piqued my interest now."

"Good. There's just one catch, Stan."

"What could that be?"

"The gravamen. It's not exactly about money."

"Not about money? Then what?"

"Erruhhh . . . some people like to call it love. I call it revenge."

"That's going to complicate things, I'm afraid."

"Always does. Talk to you soon, Mr. Kandinsky."

"Good-bye, Mr. Keagan. I hope you feel better."

"It's Mr. Keagan, Helaine. You want to take it in the office?"

"Yes. Switch it there, Jen."

"Helaine?"

"Good afternoon, Robert. How are things going?"

"Going. Weekly update. It would appear that Sharon sent the photograph. So it's not her lawyers tailing you. I've warned them to put an end to it anyway, so we'll see. Being good?"

"This is unbearable. How much longer will it take?"

"When's the last time you talked?"

"I don't want to just talk."

"When, Helaine?"

"Yesterday, briefly."

"Is anyone following her, did she say?"

"She didn't, no. I don't think she would tell me anyway. Wouldn't want to worry me, I suspect. I need to see her, Robert. What's the point of all this if I lose the woman?"

"I don't think you're going to lose her. Of course, you might if Sharon smears her name all over the dailies. It's going to be fine. Things are moving nicely. Trust me."

"Robert . . . I already knew that Sharon had sent the photo."

"How'd you know that?"

"I received one just like it a few days after you got yours. Half of one, I should say. The other half, the part with Lydia's face, was ripped off. Gone."

"Okay. Not good. You should have told me right away, but hopefully I've taken care of all that. If they can't control their client they'll drop the suit. That's the way it works. So, how's the new place, got yourself settled in yet?"

"No, still living out of boxes. Piano's in the hallway waiting for an inspiration. The bed's together, though. Plenty of inspiration there."

"Atta girl. We'll send the bad guys an answer next week that would scare flies from carrion . . . sharks from chum . . . vultures from roadkill . . . shall I continue, or are you going to make your selection?"

"Do I have to?"

"Want to see the dinner menu, instead?"

"Is this really worth it, Robert? Hiding?"

"Helaine? You want this settled, right?"

"I want it to go away. I want . . . I know you know what I'm going to say so I won't bother to be repetitive."

"You need your batteries recharged, I know."

"It feels like Sharon's winning already. Got out of that other thing pretty easy. Community service?"

"Every dog has his day. She won't win in the long run, I can assure you. Not if I can help it."

There was nothing Helaine could think of to say to that.

"Beautiful weather for late September. Looking forward to the weekend. We'll have some fun in the country, okay, Helaine? Just the three of us."

Dr. Kristenson gone. Lydia gone. Checkers gone—not that the waiter missed him. Harry scanned the room. Still plenty of others to serve.

* * *

Work. Work. Work. And no play. Lydia was worried she was becoming a dull girl. She looked over her shoulder a lot these days and avoided her windows. She avoided being alone in the elevators. She avoided her father and his invitations to the club or for lunch at a nearby restaurant. She visited with Delilah but avoided her inquiries. She avoided Frank's Place like the plague and stayed away from all the other gin joints in town. As agreed, she avoided seeing Helaine. She avoided calling Helaine. She avoided writing Helaine. She avoided thinking of Helaine. Of her eyes. Of her lips. Of her limbs. Of the scent of her hair. The feel of it on her skin. The feel of her body next to hers. The sound of her laughter. Her voice. Sharon.

"You're in love, I just know it."

"Mom, why would you say that?"

"Because you never call otherwise."

"That can't be true. Is that true or are you just trying to make me feel guilty?"

"Why would I bother trying to do that, honey? Making you guilty has had no beneficial effect on my life. Tell me what's going on."

"Nothing special. I just called to say hello to my dear sweet mom whom I miss and haven't seen in ages and haven't talked to in months and who I just felt terribly lonesome for. That is, if she doesn't mind." She listened to the long distance buzz on the line as her mother quietly digested the compliment. It seemed to be taking her an awfully long time to get it all down. A crackling noise filled the receiver, a scoff.

"No, really. Why are you calling?"

Lydia blew air back. "Okay, I'm in love, Marilyn."

"There. You see how you are? So tell me about him."

Lydia switched the phone to her other ear. "Uum . . . well . . . are you sitting down?"

He didn't give a rip if the Chambers witch fired him since he was going to terminate her case anyway. No, he had never noticed the blue-eyed woman before, no they had never been together on any other occasion, no he had not been able to learn the woman's name. The model had howled at him like a demon from hell. She was more than he had bargained for. And now word on the street was that someone important was hunting down the major asshole who had taken the pictures of Dr. Kristenson with her new lover. He didn't know much but he knew he was the major asshole they were looking for. Trouble. Major trouble. He had recognized its face the moment it had first slinked into his office and should have taken heed. Thank goodness it had all been cash transactions. I'm out of here, Lawrence Taft, decided. He took the money and ran.

Just the three of them in a brand new foreign luxury sedan, tolling down the highway at seventy miles an hour, happily heading for a taste of the simple life. A weekend in the country. Woods, lakes, wildlife. Wild so to speak. Nobody was to say the word lawsuit, nobody permitted to mention Sharon Chambers. It was a pretty quiet ride.

Helaine watched the cityscape gradually disappear from her back window, saw it replaced instead with sprawling neighborhoods and commercial strips. An hour passed and still no one had spoken and there were only clusters of houses left on the landscape. After that the trees took over, miles and miles of trees, some of them hinting at turning color. She didn't mind the silence. She watched the trees as they began to merge with each other until the view from her window consisted entirely of hills and valleys and then mountains.

The monotony got the better of her and eventually she fell asleep.

"Helaine, wake up, we're here. Helaine?"

It was dark by the time they reached their destination. Helaine had slept through the dramatic approach and had no idea how steep an ascent they had made into the wilderness. The car was parked before a modern log cabin and the automatic spotlights flooded the driveway, revealing the outline of a smaller building behind it.

"What time is it?" she asked, disoriented.

"It's nine," Robert said, helping her out of the back seat and collecting her bags for her. "You've got the guest house all to yourself. Come, I'll get you situated."

"I'll put our stuff in the house," Kay shouted from the car.

Robert and Helaine headed for the guest house along a narrow stone path, the stones clicking together under their feet. She was exhausted and not wearing appropriate shoes and lost her footing twice as she stumbled after him.

"We're out there, aren't we?" she asked.

"It seems more remote at night, but yes, we're out there." He stopped at the door and waited for the sensors to react to their presence. A nightlight over the door flickered before coming on. "A little slow, this one. You all right?"

"Long day," she said, "long week, for that matter."

He pushed open the door for her and they stepped gingerly inside.

"Oh, that light's out again. I'll have to replace it in the morning. Too late now." He set the bags down by the entrance and turned to leave. "Don't feel beholden to us. Sleep as late as you want."

Helaine hesitated in the darkened entranceway beside him. "Robert, wait!" Across the main room she saw the silhouetted figure of a woman posed in one of the interior doorways. A soft light shone from the room behind the stranger distinguishing the shape of her body but leaving the rest of her features in shadow. Helaine could make out a form fitted dress, cut above the knees, sleeveless, black perhaps, heels. She squinted in the darkness but couldn't make out the face. "Robert," she repeated nervously, "who's *that*?"

Robert placed his hand on the doorknob. "Oh her?" he laughed. "Consider her a gift from your friends, Dr. Kristenson. Enjoy," he said, attempting to leave.

"What?"

"A pick-me-up, Helaine. Someone to keep you company this weekend." He opened the front door.

"Robert!" She grabbed his sleeve. "You're joking." She looked over her shoulder. The woman stood motionless in the doorway, leaning against it with one arm, the other on her hip. "Oh, Robert, you can't be serious. This . . . she's a . . . ? You're joking, right?"

"No joke. Just relax. It's no big deal."

"Relax? Robert?" Helaine let go of his shirt and shot another anxious glance at the lit doorway. "No, Robert. You—you make her go, Robert. I can't do this. I'm not—she has to go." She saw him only grin. "*Please,* I'm very uncomfortable."

"Don't be. She's a professional."

"Take her out of here, Robert Keagan!"

"I can't do that, Helaine. We're in the middle of nowhere, after dark—"

"Robert!" She looked back again. The woman was clearly not inclined to leave on her own and Robert was not going to make her. "Then give me the car keys. Please. I'll drive her somewhere."

"Drive her? She's not a local girl, Helaine. Where do you plan to leave the woman? At the bottom of the hill?"

She stared at him in disbelief. He slipped past her and stood outside on the path.

"Give me the keys, Mr. Keagan. I'm taking her home."

"Dr. Kristenson . . . she's the cream of the crop."

"That is not the problem. The keys."

"Helaine, you don't even know where you are, and *I'm* not going anywhere. I'm too tired." He started for the house, jingling his keys in his pocket as he walked.

"Robert!" Helaine yelled. "What am I going to do?" She listened to his footsteps fading in the dark, the chorus of peepers serenading the darkness. The light flickered over her door and fizzled out.

"You don't have to do anything," he called back to her. "Play cards if you want."

"I'll sleep outdoors," she threatened. She heard him laugh at that.

"With the bears and coyotes?" he taunted.

She searched the blackness around her and fearfully stepped backward into the entranceway. He was between buildings now. She could no longer see his shape and could barely hear him walking. In the distance the cabin lights shone warm and comforting. She was tempted to run toward them. But bears and coyotes? What else might be out there? Trees, she thought grimly.

"Goodnight, Helaine," Robert yelled, finally at his front door.

She watched him disappearing into the cabin. The floodlights in the front of it blinked like sleepy sentinels as one by one they nodded off, the rooms all went dark again, the small piece of civilization belonged once more to the wilderness and to the pitch black night.

Helaine swore under her breath. Bears and coyotes. And snakes, and skunks, and bats? She solemnly closed the door and leaned her back against it, studying the woman in the distance as she tried to organize her thoughts. The woman hadn't moved an inch.

Helaine sighed. She definitely couldn't do this. "I'm sorry, but I just can't do this." Her friends had meant well. "My friends meant well, but . . ." It was misguided. "It was misguided of them."

The woman said nothing.

She had no doubt she was attractive. A nice physique. The dress was similar to one Lydia had worn once. The woman's body, also similar, same body type. She still couldn't see her face. Helaine reached for the light switch. Nothing. He probably had the bulbs removed, she thought, ruefully.

The woman in the doorway dropped her arms and began to peel off the dress.

(Oh no.) "Don't do that." Helaine saw her walking slowly toward her. "Please, you have to stop. This is not going to happen." The woman halted in her tracks and let the dress fall to the floor around her feet. Undergarments. A white bustier glowing like a beacon in the dark. She was absolutely lovely. (Oh, nuts.) It was not her fault. "Look, you are obviously . . . this is not your fault . . . this is my fault."

No reply.

Why didn't she say something for God's sake? "Say something, please."

"Talk?" the woman asked in a sleepy alto.

Alto, like Lydia's. "You're definitely going. I'm sorry, I wasn't expecting this." There was no protest, no motion at all. "How did you get here?"

"Drove."

Drove? Well, that was possible she guessed. She hadn't noticed a car but perhaps she had been sleeping and missed it. Nice voice. Very nice. Helaine stood free of the door. "I can pay you for your trouble," she said, taking her eyes off her to scout around for her purse. There it was over there. The woman began walking toward her again.

"Can you?" the woman asked, now only a few feet away.

She was a dead ringer. Robert and Kay must have put their backs into it, Helaine thought. "That's close enough—*please*." The woman stopped short. "I can't do this with you," Helaine explained one more time.

"Why?"

"I can't. I have someone."

The woman dropped her arms to her side. "Where are they?"

Where? (Good question.) "How much?" Helaine asked, wallet in hand, butterflies in stomach.

The woman put her hands on her hips. "For what?"

"For . . . ?"

"What?"

"For your trouble?"

The woman laughed gently. "No trouble, darling."

Darl—"Say that again?"

The woman pushed her hair from her eyes. "No trouble."

Helaine moved closer to see her face, but the light was still directly behind the woman and there was no other light source in the guest house. "I'm not . . . I . . . how much should I pay for you? To go, I mean?" The woman was an arm's length away, close enough to touch.

"Whatever you like."

Helaine withdrew all the cash from her billfold and offered it to her. "Go. *Please*."

The woman put her hand to her breast. "Slip it in here . . . *please*."

There? Helaine could see that. She exhaled. "And then you'll go?"

"Yes."

Helaine rolled up the bills and hesitated. She shouldn't touch this woman. She shouldn't let their skin meet. She shouldn't even be standing in the same room with her. The money was poised in her hand. She shouldn't be negotiating anything in the dark with this woman who reminded her of someone she missed. She inched closer. "Let me see your face."

The woman lightly clucked her tongue. "Why?"

"What is your name?"

The woman sighed provocatively. "It matters?"

Helaine fell silent. This was Robert's fault, weak knees and that she was wondering where Lydia Beaumont actually was this moment and why they were not together and how similar their separation was to her last dissatisfying relationship, the one biting her ass now like a rabid dog, keeping them apart for too long, so that a woman like this one, someone masked in Lydia's likeness—

"Does it?" the woman repeated.

Does it matter? That they look the same? Sound the same? Helaine felt herself leaning forward.

"Hmmm?"

She should not ask or answer anymore questions. She should not get any closer to that mouth or those breasts. She should not entertain anymore conversation. She should go and find a lightbulb, leave the money by the door. She should unpack her bags. And take a shower. And go to bed. She was tired. She should sleep. Sleep instead of standing there like a dope, face to face with this woman, the money dropping from her fingertips.

The woman bent slightly toward her. The money disappeared between her breasts. Behind her Helaine saw the discarded dress lying in the middle of the floor. She brought her face close to the woman's cheek. Even the perfumed hair smelled familiar.

Her hand was on her hand. Her lips were near her lips. "Darling," she whispered, as they dropped to the floor.

"Ah . . . you're a very difficult customer, Dr. Kristenson. You had me worried. Should I stay or should I go?"

Helaine kissed her and she opened her legs.

"That was very risky behavior, Ms. Beaumont."

"*Risqué*. You're shaking."

"Pleased with yourself?"

"Very. Make love to me—quickly."

"Let me breathe a minute first or it won't be love you'll be getting."

Lydia turned her face into Helaine's neck. "What would it be instead?"

"Something akin to it—did I pay you enough for your trouble?"

Lydia bent her legs and held her tight between them. "Akin to love? Am I in trouble, I hope?"

"Indeed, you might be. Have I paid my lovely courtesan enough for her trouble?"

Lydia held her closer. "Yes—trouble me."

Helaine was awake by nine with a note on her pillow. Her courtesan was taking a morning swim. She threw on a pair of khakis, a turtleneck and loafers, grabbed a heavy bathrobe and waited for Lydia on the deck with Kay and Robert.

"You told her to jump in the lake? I hope she knows that's only a pond."

"Robert, that was terrifying last night, I'll have you know."

"Coward."

"You figured it out by morning, I hope," Kay asked, suddenly alarmed by the other possibilities.

"I figured it out soon enough." She held her hand to shield her eyes and watched the woman on the water. "Do you think she makes a habit of this?"

"Prostitution?" Robert asked.

"NO. Grueling exercise?"

"Same difference. I'm making steak and eggs. That'll get her hormone levels back up for tonight." He left them smiling.

"What kind of lover is she, Helaine? I'm just being nosy, I know."

How is Lydia Beaumont in the sack? "It would be rude of me to answer that. What do you think?"

Kay looked thoughtfully at the water. "Straight, right?"

Helaine laughed. "Not anymore she's not."

"Well, but before she was. So I'm going to say careful. How's that description?"

Careful. Lydia was heading back to them, slicing through the water and leaving a glittering wake behind her. It was a crisp morning on the mountain and the water was as bright blue as the sky, as blue as the eyes of the woman swimming in it. Helaine wished the weekend would last forever. She needed more time with her new lover, more than just the few moments they had been together. They needed a month in bed.

How was she in bed? Routine question. Helaine stared out into the water. Shy Lydia Beaumont. Thankfully not anywhere near as shy in bed, although somewhat cautious on top. Helaine smiled at the thought of it, forgetting Kay for the moment.

It was clear Lydia was in love with her. She could hear it in her breathing, in the soft whispers and sighs. She could taste it in her mouth, on her tongue. It was always on her lips, when they talked, when they kissed. Always in her eyes. Deep sexual love.

"Where did you get a body like this?" Lydia murmured last night.

"Hah . . . you like my dimensions?"

"You are a goddess."

"Mmmmm . . . thank you. Which one?"

"All of them. All of them."

That voice.

"Come for me, Helaine."

The long forgotten orgasm. Love in her bed once more. Getting lucky with Lydia Beaumont. She came for her.

"*More.* One more time for me."

Coming in soft focus. Helaine watched Lydia swim, her steady even strokes hitting the water and propelling her back to the shore. Her back, her arms, her legs, every motion executed with an eye toward perfection. Out there was the woman who sucked at her nipples this morning like they were sweet hard candies, who played with her body like it was fine finger food and then held her as she slept. She was a careful woman, parting the water carefully with her hands, everything under control, perfectly disciplined. But there was more and Helaine wanted it all. She held her breath. Lydia swam.

"Share, Helaine. You should see your face right now!"

They needed more time together. Hiding and being hunted like a dog was hardly conducive to a developing romance. She thought about Sharon Chambers then and rued the day she had met her. "Careful is appropriate," she finally answered. "That's a very good word."

"Must be nice," Kay said in return. "Especially after—" She put her hand over her mouth and stopped herself from saying it.

Lydia was almost to the pond's edge. Helaine held up her robe. "How's the water?"

"Absolutely perfect!"

* * *

"I need to—can you do it like this?" Lydia straddled her on the chair and thrust her hips forward, pushing Helaine inside her and emitting a small gasp.

"I can try," Helaine said, readjusting herself. "Need to what, darling?"

Lydia pumped her hips and sighed. "To talk," she said and fell silent for awhile, her head resting against Helaine's, her body shuddering. "There," she whispered urgently, "There."

"I have it?"

"Mmmm . . ."

Helaine felt her tighten. "About?"

Lydia moaned and grasped the back of the chair.

Helaine shifted her weight. "You're doing all the work, I fear."

"Mmmm."

"Is this all right?"

Lydia sighed. "You're a miracle. But . . . then . . . you probably know that."

Helaine pulled her closer and let her finish. She could feel her fingers pressing into the flesh of her shoulders, hear the sound of an orgasm hidden amongst the short gasps. When she was done she lifted her head up and Helaine held her in her arms, her mouth at her breasts. "Tell me."

Lydia leaned into the moist mouth and pulled away again. "I don't think I can do this."

"*This?*"

"Uh, no, Helaine. Not this."

"Hide, you're saying?"

"I can't be with you and then without. When will I see you again?"

Helaine quietly ran her hands down the strong thighs. The complaint was overdue.

"I spoke to my mother this week. About you, Helaine."

"Oh?" Inevitable. "And she thinks I've led you astray?"

Lydia scoffed behind her. "She would really like to meet the woman who seduced her daughter."

"That's all she said? You told her everything?"

"Most of it."

Helaine frowned. It was unlikely to impress Mrs. Beaumont, considering what she had learned about the woman. She could suddenly see herself in a different light. Quite an unflattering one. "What else did she say, Lydia?"

Lydia sat up and put her hands through the blond hair, her mouth against a concerned brow. "She has her opinions. She's entitled to them, I'd say."

"What do you think? Is Marilyn right?"

Lydia sighed. "You look quite smart in that black turtleneck, Dr. Kristenson. Like a spy. Makes me weak for some reason. How would a therapist interpret that?"

Helaine smiled. "I love you. You believe me?"

"I do."

"She said what that makes you wonder? Do you want to discuss it?"

Lydia toyed thoughtfully with the turtleneck. Rolled it up. Rolled it down. "Will you go back to your supermodel, Helaine? Is that ultimately how a situation like this gets resolved?"

"Lydia? You have to believe me. The more I'm with you—"

"Tell me when I'll see you again. Tell me what we're doing. That's what I need to know. I need to know when I can freely see you. When will that be, Helaine? When can I ask you how your day went, meet you for dinner, that kind of boring stuff?"

"Boring?"

"Boring, I suppose, compared to the charismatic Sharon Chambers."

"Lydia Beaumont. Which do you want me to answer? You ought to know you're fabulous in bed. I've never been happier." She held her by the arms. "How was your week? When do you want to have dinner? Nothing about those things could bore me. Tell me now how your week went, Lydia. Tell me that this was the best part of it." She could hear the panic in her voice and fell silent.

"I have no intention of being the *other woman*, Dr. Kristenson. Is that what I am here?"

"Oh, Lydia."

"Okay. But do we know what we're doing, Helaine? It wasn't easy for me to—I hate to see myself hiding like this. It makes me doubt myself. And I hate to make mistakes. I don't think you know that about me, but it's relevant. I don't want this to be a mistake I can't live with."

"Is it?"

"No. Not yet."

Helaine studied her face. "What do you want out of this?"

Lydia laughed acidly. "Out of this? You need me to say it?"

"I do."

"I want Sharon-fucking-Chambers *out* of this. Right now."

"I thought she was, Lydia, or I wouldn't—is this why you're leaving so soon?"

Lydia left her lap and started dressing. "I promised Mom I'd make Sunday brunch today," she said hastily buttoning herself. "She's on my way home." She threw her bag on the bed, tossed her clothes into it, and tried to force the catch. "You don't have to worry about my mother. I can't remember the last time she had an influence on me."

(Yah.) Helaine stood in the doorway and smiled bleakly. The Beaumont women having a little get together. There was something frightening in the prospect. "Let me help," she said, without commenting. She closed the bag and set it on the floor.

Lydia stood beside her luggage, her jaw suddenly hard.

Helaine leaned into her, weightless. "You can if you want, Lydia— throw me down. I don't mind. Just don't leave me unsure."

"Throw you . . . ?" Lydia brought her hands to her forehead and dropped them to her sides again, turning her face away. "I just love you, Helaine. Come. It's all right. Walk me to the car. I have to say good-bye to Robert and Kay."

Neither one made a move.

"Lydia . . . Robert is very competent, I can assure you. He'll take care of this as quickly as possible. Tell her that for me, Lydia. Look at me." Lydia turned to face her. "Things aren't always as they appear. Tell your mother that, too."

"Okay. I will. And you tell me, when will I see you again?" She slid her arm around Helaine's waist, unzipped her pants and slipped her hand inside them. "Ah . . . you like me. When?"

Helaine took a deep breath and shut her eyes. She was falling. Lydia prevented her from lying down.

"I don't know," Helaine murmured.

"Say soon then."

Helaine leaned against her. "Soon."

Lydia zipped her up and grabbed the suitcase.

"Slow," Lydia said, as she was pulling out of the driveway.

"What?" Helaine asked.

"My week. You asked how it went."

Helaine nodded and waved.

"This was the best part of it," Lydia called. She honked the horn just before her descent and Helaine crossed her arms and smiled, content for the moment.

Back in the guest house Lydia had left another note on the pillow. This time it was stuffed with money. Helaine's.

"Thought you might be needing this. She sounds rather expensive. Love you, L."

"It's called a general denial, Helaine. Standard procedure. Trust me."

"It's called a lie, Robert. I won't sign it."

"Look. Have you ever supported the woman? Do you think you owe her half your life's earnings? It's the substance of the complaint that we're denying. It's not a lie."

"Not a lie? This I-know-thee-not isn't a lie? We lived together, Robert. We were lovers. She was my only lover, even after I moved out. No, I didn't support her—she's lying—but essentially I did provide for her. I asked her to take the lease over, she refused, probably with this in mind, who knows? But the fact is that I didn't force the issue on her and the lease remained in my name. I paid the rent. My mistake. I admit it. I had no idea that she had those other properties and I firmly believed the waterfront was her only home. Where does our answer say any of those things?"

Kay listened quietly. They say that a lawyer who represents himself has a fool for a client. She wondered what they might say of one who represents an old friend.

Robert paced. "Helaine, this Jane Doe allegation, that you cheated on Sharon. You're going to qualify that, too? I mean, we're going to go into explanations here?"

"No, that's a lie, an excuse to suck Lydia into it. We deny that, of course. But this answer here will prevent me from sleeping at night and I don't believe it will serve me well in the long run."

"You're sleeping well now?"

"A lot better than I expected to. Besides, that's not that point. What will Lydia think if I deny something she already knows is true? And how could I defend it later when Sharon proves it?"

"So you admit that a relationship such as the one the plaintiff describes existed and that you provided for her domestic needs to a limited extent?"

"I will be satisfied with that, Robert, and deny the rest."

"Dr. Kristenson, you're giving them half their case!"

"If they have a case, it's my fault. I'm not going to lie about it. Personally, I don't agree with you. I did not support her as she claims and she manipulated me about the flat—and other things, as well, but they're not worth going into."

"But they will go into it if we have to go to trial. It's likely to happen even before then. You've heard of oral depositions?"

Helaine's voice softened. "Robert, I'm not trying to be difficult, a client from hell or whatever you call them. For the past year, maybe longer than that, Sharon has threatened to ruin me if I leave her. I left her. If she can ruin me now by exploiting our relationship, so be it, but I will not ruin myself by denying one existed. That is plainly the trap that has been set here."

"You're right."

She had braced herself for more argument. "What?"

"He said you're right."

Helaine relaxed into her chair.

"We'll modify it and you'll sign it and Sharon will have her day in court."

"I don't want to fight her. I want to settle this. When can we begin to do that, Robert?"

"We'll send them our answer and take it from there. After that we'll drown them in discovery demands until they say uncle. They'll settle, Helaine. She has no case and they know it."

She had no case and they knew it. Willard Hathaway was not pleased when he got the defendant's reply. Yes, Dr. Kristenson had an "on-again-off-again" relationship with Sharon Chambers. Who hadn't? Yes, she had even allowed the model to stay at her waterfront flat whenever she was in town, which was, as a matter of record, very infrequently. The rest was a denial with no specific reference to Jane Doe.

It was important to bolster the plaintiff's position somehow because at this rate there was no impetus for the defendant to compromise and she obviously wasn't worrying about the affects of a public disclosure of her private acts as it was apparently not a big secret that the well-known sex therapist was bisexual. The general public's reaction to that information would be too unpredictable, Hathaway reasoned. She was, after all, not the head of state or some other high ranking public official where it might matter. She was not married and never had been, not running for public office, not a member of the clergy. The firm had made a bundle on those kinds of guys, on low crimes, indiscretions and misdemeanors. And lies, lies, lies.

Everybody lies a little in these disputes and in the end it's the lie they buy that really counts and while he couldn't be sure what the actual truth was in this case, it was still Sharon Chambers's version that Willard Hathaway gave the most credence to. After all, she may have had a reputation as a bad girl, but it didn't include lying. That she was clearly obsessed with Helaine Kristenson and that the doctor admitted having had a relationship with her, supported his hunch. Moreover, that relationship had spanned nearly a decade. An awful long time for someone like Sharon Chambers. Awful long tryst for Dr. Kristenson, as she more or less seemed to be swearing to in her papers. He scowled at her signature on the bottom of the page. She was not lying perhaps, but she was certainly not telling the whole truth.

Still, palimony, though it held out the largest award, was a blatantly dubious claim no matter what their relationship had been. He hadn't gone in too far with Sharon Chambers about that. Wouldn't get that complicated he had hoped. In any event, Hathaway seriously doubted that the supermodel was interested in the doctor's money although her ulterior motivations didn't concern him as long as they didn't interfere with the settlement, if he could get one, which he was not so sure about today.

He slid the defendant's papers across the table without speaking and his eagles perused its meager contents.

Despite his convictions and his fighting stance, Hathaway had no intention of taking this flimsy issue to trial. He wanted a settlement and he needed to act fast in order to get one because he knew by experience that Keagan intended to bury him alive in paperwork and to make him work like a dog. Willard Hathaway possessed a different kind of ambition than that. He liked the easy money the best. He glared at the photos the plaintiff had sent.

Jane Doe. He believed Sharon Chambers about her, too, and even if the suit against the woman was baseless, he was fairly certain Dr. Kristenson would rather she remain anonymous. It would be devastating to their budding romance if she was joined in the matter. Ms. Deep Pockets. He wondered what her stake in the matter really was. How guarded was she about *her* privacy? God, didn't she look familiar? Where the hell had he seen that face before?

"Any luck with Miss Universe here?" he asked, displaying one of the photos.

The table grumbled and sputtered in a succession of no's and excuses.

"Well, she obviously exists," he interrupted, pounding the table with his fist for silence. "Find her or you'll all be flipping burgers by the end of the month."

Not worried about the effects of a public disclosure of her private acts? Wrong!

"Robert?"

"I know, Helaine. I read the papers."

"How did this happen? I can't even work without hearing about it!"

"It's public record, Helaine."

"But who cares? It can't be important enough to be on the goddamned front pages!"

"Above the fold no less. You rank."

"Robert, you knew this would happen?"

"I hoped for the best, Helaine. They go through the records looking for people like you. It was only quiet while they waited for your answer. I think you'll have to get used to it."

"And my goddamned picture, too—with Sharon's! Robert, I have to live here. I work here. How am I going to live with this every day? There are reporters waiting outside my office building right now. I passed them this morning. They were still there at lunch hour. All day, Robert. And I've got clients coming in who can't concentrate on their own problems. They sit and stare at me. I just went for a walk—wisecracks, come-ons, indecent proposals. Reporters! And this—quoting my papers out of context. And this here. I didn't even say that. And Jane Doe this Jane Doe that and what I'm worth, like I'm on the auction block or something. I can't be worth that anyway and where are they getting this stuff?"

"Well, you are worth that and now you're public property for a while."

"What does that mean? You can't stop this? There's a camera crew out front. They're trying to shoot tits and ass. *My* tits and ass for God's sake!"

"No, Helaine, not this I can't. So be very careful now. You know?"

And that was only Monday. Think how she felt by Friday.

"Robert?"

"You're handling yourself beautifully, Helaine. Just as I expected."

She started to cry.

"Helaine, are you at work? Helaine? Speak to me."

"Robert, what is their problem? Why are they harassing me?"

"You're the expert, you need me to tell you? Are you at the office?"

"Yes," she sobbed. "Tell me what's going on here."

"These people have no lives. They're the little gnomes who never got picked for the team, the goofs nobody wanted to go to the prom with, the dorks that didn't lose their virginity until they were thirty years old, if at all. Losers

getting their revenge by dragging the 'most popular' and the 'most likely to succeed' through the mud."

"Look at this guy editorializing here," she sniffed. "*The Herald.* Look what he says, that pig! He's a client of mine—I saved his fucking marriage!"

"Cancel your appointments for next week. Do you have sunglasses you can wear right now? I want you to put them on and smile as you leave. We don't want the bad guys thinking they're getting to you."

She was weeping uncontrollably.

"Helaine . . . put Jenny on. Please, Helaine. Do as I say . . ."

There was a moment of relative silence, then, "Mr. Keagan?"

"Jenny, are there any more appointments this afternoon?"

"None. I've tried to send her home but she says she won't have her schedule disrupted like this."

"Well, it is disrupted, isn't it? Get her a pair of cheap sunglasses and cancel next week's appointments."

He heard her discussing it with Helaine. "Okay, Mr. Keagan. She's agreed to that."

"Tell her to meet me out front in a half an hour with the glasses on and one of her fabulous smiles. I'll make a brief upbeat statement to the press and then I'll drive her home."

And that was just Helaine's reaction. Think how Lydia felt observing the fracas all week from her fifteenth-story perch amongst the storm clouds. Even she had seen the tabloids.

Friday at three. She stood across the street from Helaine's building watching Robert Keagan handle an impromptu press conference with Helaine standing like a stone pillar beside him, her eyes hidden behind dark shades, her smile taut. Lydia knew what was behind the glasses. It did not portend well.

"What do they call you, other than Helaine, other than doctor?" she had asked her in bed the last time they were together.

"I used to be called Lana when my parents were alive. No one's called me that in years."

"Lana," Lydia had whispered back to her as they made love. It suited the blond better than the vulgar title of LOVE DOC splashed across the headlines all this week. She hadn't mentioned that nickname nor the book she had authored that had started it all.

A sex therapist. Well, that explained the stunning lovemaking. That information had caught Lydia by surprise. How little she knew about the woman she was sleeping with. Her own fault, for not asking, for not wanting to know anything that might have dissuaded her. Maybe Del was right. *Maybe I am from another planet.* Look at this: Two larger than life women and she hadn't recognized either one of them. And there were going to be other revelations to come, she feared. But it was too late for factoring in Helaine's negatives now, she reminded herself as she crossed the street and mixed with the excited crowd. She needed her. And *she* needed her.

"There is no other woman," Robert Keagan declared, emphatically waving away one of the most asked questions. "Ms. Chambers is lying," he elaborated, "to herself at least."

That caused a hum.

"Dr. Kristenson, were you in love with Sharon Chambers or was it just good sex?"

Lydia saw Helaine lift her head to the sky, her lips barely moving as she spoke to Robert. He paused, shook his head and asked for the next question.

Lydia pushed forward and Robert nearly choked mid-sentence when he spotted her. He glanced furtively at Helaine to see if she had seen her yet. She hadn't.

Helaine's gaze was fixed on the building across the street, searching the upper floors. Perhaps it had been a mirage all along, the idea that she could leave Sharon, the idea that she could find love again. "Dr. Kristenson?" she heard someone call above the din. She searched the mob for the owner of the very familiar voice.

"I was wondering how your week went?" Lydia asked.

A smile came across the doctor's lips and her worried face relaxed a bit, then a barrage of bulbs went off igniting the sidewalk. She sheltered her eyes with her hand. *Click, click, click, click, click* went a cacophony of cameras, their shutters sounding like an army of mechanical termites, chewing, chewing, chewing.

"Very well," she answered wearily. "This was the worse part of it."

"Dr. Kristenson!" a reporter called out. "Dr. Kristenson, any plans to kiss and make up with your supermodel?"

Lydia bowed her head and pushed through the crowd.

"Again I will have to point out," Robert Keagan intercepted, "that that is a question based entirely on presumptions. Next?"

"Uh . . . Jane? It's Del. I've been trying all week. Call me when you get a—"

"Del, don't hang up!"

"Liddy! SHARON CHAMBERS? The Love Doc Triangle? Holy shit. Talk about solar flares. I'm coming over."

"What do you mean you don't know?"

Willard Hathaway held the phone out from his ear. "I said we don't know *yet*, Ms. Chambers. Not yet, that's all. We'll get her. Don't panic."

"What do you mean you don't know?" Willard Hathaway barked across the table. "Do you have any idea how much money we could be making here if you did?"

Nobody dared to even speculate.

"Jones, what about the bar?"

"The waiter insists that he's legally blind, dyslexic and partially deaf in one ear. He has difficulty with faces and names. Doesn't know her. Can't say he's ever seen her before."

"Johnson, what did you fall for?"

"Uh, the cabbie says she's suffering from perimenopausal lapses in her short-term memory and has no clue where Frank's Place even is."

"It's her goddamned cab in the photo, right? In front of Frank's?"

"Well, she says she probably passed in front of the lens by accident."

"Oh, come off it! With her door open? What kind of nonsense is this?"

Johnson threw his hands up in the air.

"Okay. Anybody else? How about just the guys? I mean, when you're out looking at women, wouldn't you naturally take notice of one who looked like this? Especially in the midtown area with all those dreary broads. Why haven't you seen this one?"

"There are no women who look like *that* in the midtown area," someone boldly volunteered. "That area's all finance. She probably doesn't work there—if she works at all."

"Probably just a coincidence," someone else authoritatively added. "A little too glamorous for finance."

Idiots, Hathaway screamed in his head. "Look, I have it from a reliable source that the woman's been to Frank's more than once. That is in the heart of the financial district. Moreover, Dr. Kristenson's offices are in the heart of the financial district. That is most certainly how and where those two women met! She works in that area, maybe lives nearby. It doesn't matter which. She has a name and an address and we need it!"

Saturday. Jones and Johnson had split up their search of midtown. Pretty quiet on the weekend. Nothing but joggers and a few shoppers, delivery boys, servicemen. And, of course, the run-of-the-mill street vendors. No neighborhood could survive without them. The two met again in the afternoon, rendezvousing at a hotdog stand.

"This is bullshit," Jones complained. "I feel like a gopher, not an attorney. Dog," he said to the vendor. "The works, please."

"Gopher? Yeah, I could gopher her—if I could find her. I wonder how much *that* pays," Johnson said, pointing at a pizza boy passing them by with a twelve cut. He sniffed the air and groaned as he threw himself into the shaded bench on the corner by Frank's Place. "Anything going on in there?" he thought to ask.

"Nah, completely different crowd on the weekend. I'm telling you the woman is a mirage or something. And this is just bullshit."

"If I find her, I'm keeping her," Johnson said dreamily.

Jones shoved the rest of his hotdog into his mouth and started for the crosswalk. "What? You stupid or something?"

"Stupid? C'mon, get happy, Mr. Jones. At least she's a babe."

"A babe! A mirage, I'm telling you." Jones mumbled to himself as he crossed the street.

"Finders keepers!" Johnson taunted from the bench.

Jones lifted his hand and flipped him the bird.

"Hey, where's the pizza place?" Johnson asked the hotdog man. "I'd rather have pizza."

"No pizza, just hotdogs," he said.

"Your pizza's here, Ms. Kristenson."

"I'm sorry, what?"

"Pizza boy. Jane's Pizzeria. Where's that?" he asked him.

"Crosstown," the boy muttered, pulling at his baseball cap. "Specialty."

"Jane's? As in J . . . A . . . N . . . E . . . apostrophe S . . . ?"

"Jane's. Yep."

"Is he alone?"

"He is. Should I search him?"

"No, no. Send him up. Thanks, George."

Helaine waited for the knock and opened the door.

"Good afternoon, Dr. Kristenson. What are you doing for dinner?"

"Oh my God, next they're going to say I have a thing for little boys."

"Only if I spend the night. Will the doorman notice, you think?"

Helaine reflected a moment. "I'll explain it somehow. Will you?"

"That is the plan, Helaine. Ooh, nice place."

"Nice ruse, Ms. Beaumont. What are you wearing underneath it?"

"Nothing."

"Let me see."

DO YOU KNOW HER? The Sunday edition. All the Sunday editions.

Lydia Beaumont had gone for her morning jog. She was halfway to the waterfront when she spied her own smiling face under that bold caption, peering out from behind the news cage at a corner stand. She stopped dead in her tracks and took in her catastrophe.

MEET JANE DOE. Jane Doe with Dr. Kristenson. SECRET LOVE. Oh no, she almost screamed.

"She's gonna wish she'd never been born," said a woman who was buying a copy. Lydia hid her face from her and glanced up the street and back again. Do you know her? Do you know her? Do you—

"Gonna memorize it or buy it?" the vendor demanded.

He eyed her suspiciously, she thought. She averted her eyes. "Sorry," she replied, her voice scratchy. "Which one's the best seller?" she asked, making an attempt at humor.

"You know her? That one in front of you."

She bought the paper and tripped home with it, her head held low, her last available disguise.

"Oh, no." (Delilah)
"Oh, no." (The Keagans)
"Oh, no!" (Helaine)
"Oh, no." (Marilyn and Edward Beaumont)
"Oh, yes!" (Sharon Chambers)

Okay. Now she could feel Sharon Chambers on her back. Now she could feel eyes on her everywhere, even the doorman's. Now the phone rang like emergency sirens going off in her penthouse. Now she was an inmate pacing her cell. Or an escaped convict trying to outrun the hounds of hell.

"It's Robert Keagan . . . call me back . . . beep . . . it's your dear sweet mom . . . beep . . . Liddy, it's Del . . . beep . . . darling, I need to hear from you . . . call me . . . beep . . . Liddy, if you're there pick up . . . beep . . . Lydia Ann Beaumont, I see you didn't tell me everything . . . it's your mom . . . call me . . . beep . . . Queenie? . . . beep . . . Queenie, it's daddy . . . listen . . . you need to see Stan . . . right away . . . call him, please . . . beep . . . Robert again . . . listen, you need to get a hold of Stanley Kandinsky . . . right way, Lydia . . . call me . . . I'll be here all day . . . and please stay put . . . beep . . . Lydia . . . darling . . . tell me you're all right . . . beep."

* * *

"I'm fine. I don't want you to worry about me."

"Lydia, I am worried. What will you do?"

"I don't know yet. I just got the paper."

"I'm acquainted with someone . . . someone I've met at the Keagans' I can't think of his name. Let me call Robert and ask."

"An attorney?"

"Yes."

"Robert just left a message. I know who he is. Don't worry, Helaine. I don't have any enemies and I don't think anyone's going to—"

"You don't need enemies, Lydia. Just people trying to get their kicks. I ought to know."

Lydia bit at her lip. "What do you want me to do? I mean ultimately. How can I make your life easier, Helaine Kristenson?"

"You already have. It's not my decision. How can I make your life easier?"

"Promise me you won't go back to her."

"It'll never happen. I promise."

"How do you feel about being linked to me like this? Are you comfortable with that?"

"I've wanted to be linked to you since the moment I first saw you But I never planned on it ruining your life. Your privacy . . . if they get your name? Are you comfortable with that, because they might, you know?"

They might, she knew. "Lana . . ."

Helaine fell silent.

"I have never met anyone like you, you should know."

"Lydia?"

"I would expect to get the girl in the end. That will make my life easier."

"You'll get the girl, Lydia Beaumont. I guarantee it."

"And keep her—they never show that part. I want to get her and keep her. Do you guarantee that, too?"

"Yes."

"For how long, Lana?"

"Darling . . . for as long as you like."

* * *

Did he know her? Yeah. He'd know Jane Doe anywhere.

Lydia made an appointment with Stanley Kandinsky. Tuesday, 11 a.m., Stan Kan.

Monday she went to work in a stripped-down version of herself, no makeup, her hair tied back. Otherwise it was business as normal.

By afternoon, having attracted no more attention than she was used to getting, she let her hair down and went to the window to apply her lipstick, taking note of the activities on the ground, the collection of reporters assembling like insects at a picnic across the street again.

For naught, she laughed to herself. Dr. Kristenson had taken a mini-vacation, using the time to reorganize her life, which, up until this week, had been stored in cardboard boxes and stacked randomly in her living room.

Books. So many books. She was out of her league with this woman. There were hundreds, if not thousands of them. Saturday the two of them had gone through a carton of Shakespeare before surrendering to their chronic distraction, after which Lydia felt obligated to confess that she was simply a barbarian who could read, but didn't. A confession that, to her relief, did not seem to concern Helaine much. "Start here," was all Helaine said about it. "Pick one." Lydia selected *The Merchant of Venice* and Helaine chuckled over it all afternoon.

Confessions. Lydia watched the hornet's nest swarming below her. They could get it out of her. That she was Lydia Beaumont. That she was Dr. Kristenson's lover. That she had learned about Sharon Chambers and had thrown caution to the wind to pursue the blond anyway. That she had indeed stolen something that Ms. Chambers says belonged to her. That she had no intention whatsoever of giving it back, no matter how emotionally distressed the plaintiff claimed to be. That she was terrified. Absolutely terrified.

"Not thinking of jumping are we, Jane Doe?"

Joe. Lydia jumped in her skin remembering too late the unlocked door. "Joe—" They struggled. She lost. He had her pinned face forward against the window. "Joe . . . you're hurting me." He was excited. She could feel it where he pressed against her backside.

"Thinking of jumping, Jane?"

She tried to face him. He pushed her hard into the glass of her window. "Christ, Joe!" she blurted, looking down fifteen stories at the busy street. It felt as if she was hanging in midair. "Joe . . ." He was lifting her dress. "NO—"

"Dicking Jane . . ."

"Joseph!"

He put his hand around her throat and tilted her head back. "Now I'm not done talking yet, your highness. So shut up and listen."

Silence. Vertigo.

"You like?" he whispered.

She flinched, dizzy.

"Tell me, Jane Doe. Want to scream?"

She shook her head no.

He slipped his hand up her blouse. "Lydia . . ."

"I'll call security," she whispered.

"Bet you half a million you won't."

Half a million. She was quiet again. They were in full view of the buildings across from her. She searched the windows to see if anybody was watching. No one was. "What are you talking about?"

He laughed. "I'm talking about being hunted, my dear Jane."

"J—You're out of your mind."

"Shall I blow the whistle, Ms. Doe, like you did on me? These are as gorgeous as ever, by the way," he said, undoing the catch in the front of her bra.

"I'm not a—it's my job. Take your hands off me!"

"Then I'll just have to do my job then. Turn around," he ordered, "you're going to blow me." He grabbed her by the shoulders.

She swung her arm behind her and missed his head by inches.

"Mistake," he said, holding her once more against the window.

She could see her breath on it. "What are you trying to prove, Joe? You're bigger than me?"

"Half a million—is she worth it, Jane?"

"You're mistak—"

"Bullshit, Lydia."

She scanned the buildings again. She should have locked her door.

He read her mind. "You're slipping, your highness. See? That's what a woman can do to you."

She had no desire to go there with him.

"Jane Doe . . ."

It seemed unlikely she could shake him from this. "What if I am? What's it to you?"

He brought his face close to hers. "To me? Don't you know?"

She turned her head and lay her cheek against the cool glass. "Blackmail? You need money, Joe?"

He bit at her neck and pushed into her.

"Is that what you're after?" she demanded.

He laughed.

"Joe . . . ?"

"You're never coming back to me are you, Lydia?"

She was afraid to answer that. "Do you need money? I can give you—"

"I need this."

(This?) "Never. No way."

"No? I don't see you in a *no* position."

"NO."

His hands were at her hips. She felt the pressure suddenly off her body. "I said no," she repeated, bringing her heel down on the tip of his shoe.

He yelled in surprise, releasing her and kneeling to the floor. The next blow was predictable, but he didn't see that one coming, either. After she kicked him he lay beside her desk, holding his groin and cursing as she dialed security and requested assistance.

"Mistake," he warned between gritted teeth, as he was being dragged from her office.

"The conversation's over, buddy," the security guard hissed. "Move it!"

Officially it was all over for Joseph Rios. Lydia shivered with dread.

* * *

"Who?"

"A Joseph Rios. Says he works at Soloman-Schmitt."

"No kidding? And why should that impress me?" Willard Hathaway asked. "I'm satisfied with my current broker."

"Because so does Jane Doe. At least that's what he claims."

Across the street from Dr. Kristenson! "What's he look like, a kook?"

The secretary hesitated, her eyes shining. "No, he's a gorgeous piece of man, sir."

"Okay," he laughed. "Better bring him in then. I got a feeling this is going to be good." He opened the bottom drawer of his desk, hit the record button on his hidden tape. "Oh, and Marie," he added as she was leaving.

She stopped at the door. "Yes?"

"Run a background while I interview him. I want the scoop right away."

"Yes, sir."

He waited with bated breath for her to knock again. "Come," he answered.

"Joseph Rios, Mr. Hathaway." The secretary closed the door behind her.

"Mr. Rios. A pleasure to meet you," Hathaway said, standing and extending his hand across the desk.

Rio Joe limped as he crossed the room. He grasped Hathaway's hand tightly before letting go and placed himself painstakingly into the adjacent chair. "Pleasure's all mine, I can assure you," he said, without smiling.

Hathaway grinned and sat down. "What's the other guy look like?"

Joe grimaced. "This? I Injured my foot at the gym. Broke it. Three toes."

"I see. That's too bad." Hathaway did a quiet assessment of the well-dressed young man with the aggressive handshake who didn't smile. Arrogant. Though right now he wore the attitude of a defeated warrior. Hathaway looked him square in the face, but the fella refused to make eye contact. Okay. There's a story here. "So who's Jane Doe, Mr. Rios?"

A sneer came over Joseph Rios' face. Hathaway felt compelled to add cruel to his list of observations.

"Jane Doe happens to be a Lydia Beaumont, top financial strategist for Soloman-Schmitt."

Willard Hathaway whistled. "Edward Beaumont her father, would you know?"

"The same."

That's why her face had seemed so familiar! Hathaway could barely contain himself. Edward Beaumont had brought him a great deal of bad luck over the years and he'd never won a single case when the Madison-Beaumont firm was involved because of it. He had been thrilled to learn of the man's retirement last year, though he knew he was still out there, mucking about, still making appearances at the club, still chasing skirts. Mr. Teflon. A smile came over Hathaway's face. He wanted to spread this joy. He had an incredible urge to call up Beaumont right now and scream *I gotcha!* Oh, to be a fly on the wall when Edward Beaumont sees his little girl's name in the paper tomorrow.

"It's a wonderful service you've provided if this information checks out."

Rio Joe nodded. "It will. Trust me."

"You involved with her?"

"Not anymore."

"I see. Tell me something. Is she clean otherwise?"

"Spotless."

Hathaway took that information in stride. "You know her home address?"

Rio Joe took out his little black book and read it off.

"What's the address over there at Soloman-Schmitt, her floor?"

He pulled out a card and dropped it on the lawyer's desk. "Fifteenth."

"You got a photo of her? You know, wallet size?"

Rio Joe extracted a small color photo from his billfold and handed it to him.

"Beautiful. Beautiful. That's her. Listen, can I keep this? We'll get it back to you, of course. When we're done with it." He saw the young man suddenly scowl and reach over the desk to reclaim his photograph.

"No," Joe answered, slipping it quickly into his breast pocket.

* * *

Initially it didn't occur to Lydia that the noisy reporters waiting outside her office building on Tuesday morning were waiting for her. True to form, she hadn't bothered to look at a newspaper before she came to work. If she had she probably would have thought better of it.

When she heard the shouts, "there she is," she turned, assuming they must have spotted Helaine on the other side of the street. It was then, when she noticed the empty sidewalks across the way, that it dawned on her. The stark possibility. The awful likelihood. But by then it was a useless hunch.

So it happened quickly, Jane Doe's transformation into Lydia Beaumont. She stood swamped in front of her own building, perhaps only twenty feet or so from the revolving doors. Lights glared, people shouted, she was jostled on all sides. It's funny what one thinks in a situation like that. She was surprised by her first thoughts. She hoped her hair looked all right. She hoped she didn't look stupid. She hoped her mom wouldn't see her on TV. There was a kind of resignation going on in her psyche as if all along it had been prepared for this outcome. Questions flew at her like bullets and she heard them whizzing by her head and she calmly wondered if it was possible to just walk away from this, to enter her building. And then she discovered it was impossible to move in any direction with reporters surrounding her in every direction, yelling her name to get her attention, blinding her with their lights and cameras. She glanced at the sky over their heads and said nothing.

"Ms. Beaumont! Ms. Beaumont! How long have you and Dr. Kristenson been lovers?" "Ms. Beaumont, over here please!" *(click)* "Thank you!" "Ms. Beaumont! How did you and the Love Doc meet?" "Ms. Beaumont!" "Ms. Beaumont, have you met Sharon Chambers?" "Ms. Beaumont! Could you make a statement? Anything?"

"Are you Lydia Beaumont?" asked a wide-eyed young man who had thrust himself in front of everyone.

Lydia glanced at him. He didn't look like he belonged there. The crowd swayed into her as reporters jockeyed for a better view and she found herself standing face to face with him, watching transfixed as he fidgeted with the large envelope in his hand.

"Are you Lydia Beaumont?" he repeated.

"Are you a reporter?" she shouted back.

"No ma'am, I'm a process—"

Another volley of questions. Server, she finished in her head. He's a process server, fool.

"Are you Lydia Beau—"

"Yes," she interrupted, "Give it to me."

The reporter closest to them heard her declaration and passed it along the ranks. "It's her," they starting screaming all over again. "Ms. Beaumont!" "Ms. Beaumont! Look over here!"

The server was overwhelmed. The two of them stood bobbing in the center, him with his papers, her with her briefcase. He was, Lydia realized, an obstacle to her immediate egress.

"Give them to me," she said again.

He handed her the papers and gulped a few times, trying to remember what he was supposed to say next.

"I've been served," Lydia acknowledged. She had spied a way out toward the street, if she could just get past him.

"You been served, Lydia Beaumont."

"I've been served," she repeated, trying to push him aside. "Now, please, get out of my way!"

He took a few steps back and let her pass, actually restraining a camera man with one outstretched arm.

She gripped the envelope in one hand and her briefcase in the other and forced her way through the melee, the adrenaline pounding in her ears as she proceeded up the block toward Frank's Place, the reporters and cameras in tow, racing alongside of her, attempting to cut her off.

Her first confrontation with the press, Lydia was thinking as she walked, and at worst she was only a little numb. She needed a cab. She needed to see Stanley. Ultimately she knew she would need to retain a driver, as her father had always nagged her about doing. It was no longer ostentatious and pompous. A car and a driver would be necessary for survival now. And, she realized, even a bodyguard—she hadn't known the press could be so rough. She kept her eye on them and held them at bay, holding up her briefcase whenever they came too close.

A few blocks down, she could see Harry standing near the corner on

Frank's patio. He was an especially welcome sight this morning and she nearly cried when he raised his arms and beckoned to her. She quickened her pace to lose the undesirable entourage. That, she knew, would only give her a few seconds. Harry was offering his arm to her and she slid hers through it, allowing him to lead her to a waiting cab.

"Are you hurt?"

"No. Terrified."

"Don't be, dear. Everything will be fine." He closed the car door behind her before she could thank him. "Drive!" he ordered the cabbie. The car lurched with a loud squeal and then sped away, leaving the gathering mob with a cocktail of dirt and fumes.

Lydia arrived earlier than expected at the uptown office of Stanley Kandinsky. She added cell phone to her mental list of immediate necessities, though she hated their chirps and intrusions.

"May I use your phone while I wait?" she asked his secretary.

"Certainly. There you go."

Lydia checked the time. Ten o'clock already. She had missed an important meeting this morning. "Good morning, it's Lydia Beaumont. Paula Treadwell, please." She noticed she still held the legal envelope in her hand and threw it in disgust on top of her briefcase. "Paula? Oh, you did? Thank you. I don't know yet, I was hoping this afternoon . . . it's . . . you don't have to do that. Fine, but I can't let them disrupt my schedule. Yeah, I agree. At my lawyer's right now. True, but maybe he can calm it down so I can get into the building tomorrow. What? Paula . . . I . . . I can't discuss this now. I do. I suspect it was Joseph. Yes. He is? I guess that's as good a motive as any. E-mail it to my home office then. Oh, yes, I will. This afternoon. Because it's a priority. Before the board convenes. You know, I don't have it in front of me—when is that? That soon? Oh God, what a mess. I'm trying not to. Flowers? Where? Paula, you're kidding. From where? Already? Oh, this is utter nonsense. I will, someday. I better give this line back. This afternoon. Home, I guess, till it dies down. I wish I knew. Thank you, Paula. This afternoon. Don't worry, I will."

She handed the phone back and hovered over her personal effects for another half hour.

"Ms. Beaumont, come in."

"Good morning, Mr. Kandinsky."

He shut the door and they sat. "Call me Stan. How's your dad?"

"Oh, please, Stanley. How is he?"

Stanley laughed without blinking. "Worried. Surprised. And how are you? I heard you made a smashing debut this morning."

"Complicates things, I know. I need to get into my office. Why did they serve me at work?"

"Oh, I'm sure they thought it would be more dramatic that way, the press already setting up house there and all. Cameras will be greeting you at your home, too. Count on it. Did you say anything to them?"

"Nothing. Should I have?"

"Nothing is ideal. You're a natural."

She winced. "Good teacher."

"Yes . . . your father is livid about this. The photo and all. We're going to have to hypnotize everyone with our own spin on it. Hush-a-bye as opposed to hush-it-up."

"Hypnotize?"

"We're going to sue the plaintiff for defamation, Lydia. In excess of what she's claiming. We are actually in a very strong pos—"

"Stanley. Ms. Chambers isn't lying."

His eyes became two dark slits. "That is irrelevant."

Paula Treadwell, age 53, is the senior vice president of Soloman-Schmitt. Lydia Beaumont is her protégé. She has groomed her for an assistantship ever since Beaumont first emerged as a promising young investment broker ten years ago. Paula believes, in fact, that Lydia Beaumont is the ideal candidate to become the first female president in the hundred-year history of this investment firm, although she doesn't expect that to happen in this decade. Still, that is her aspiration for Beaumont, despite her protégé's growing disenchantment with the world of finance and her subsequent announcement nearly two years ago that she plans to retire at forty.

Treadwell's concerns regarding the present controversy have nothing to do with Beaumont's exotic pursuits and mishaps, about which she really couldn't care less. Nor is she worried over what such disclosures might do to the company's image, especially considering the bombshell of financial revelations she knows is going to explode any day now at Soloman-Schmitt. All the cover-ups: of inside trading, of accounting irregularities, of mysterious overseas partnerships, of red to black overnight banking conversions that turn staggering corporate debt and expenditures into huge capital gains and profits—these are the reports that Lydia Beaumont has been issuing for quite some time and that Treadwell has been endorsing and directing to the board with no effect, until this week.

This week at last, the mighty Soloman-Schmitt had taken heed of these warnings, possibly too late, but it had finally begun to get its house in order, firing some of its most prominent offenders, preparing others for their perp walks, accepting resignations without pay. It would be a shakeup that could go all the way up to the Chief Financial Officer, reach all across the board when it's done. To the uninitiated, to the red handed, it might all seem like the product of whistle blowing, but it wasn't. Lydia Beaumont was just doing her job, unlike others around her.

Senior vice president Paula Treadwell fears that the woman is disgusted enough with her work that she might see the Chambers's scandal as a good excuse to exit the troubled firm even sooner than she had planned. That would not be good for Senior Vice President Paula Treadwell. Treadwell is undertaking to manage a major corporate scandal and she is depending on her protégé to help her pull it off. She fully expects Beaumont to march into battle beside her and to return, as they say, with her shield or on it. Treadwell has no intention of proceeding without her, no intention of losing her top executive in a love triangle, not to Sharon Chambers with her spurious allegations, not to the esteemed Dr. Kristenson, the seductive siren responsible in the first place for leading Beaumont to the rocks. A corporate shakedown requires patience and skill, after all. And secrecy.

Paula Treadwell glared down onto the street from her top floor offices. "What's the story with that shit down there? Can I arrest those reporters for trespassing?"

"I don't see why not. They're not on the sidewalk. They're on the grounds."

She put her hand to her mouth thoughtfully and considered her options. "Confiscate their cameras—illegal surveillance. Then have security remove them, John. They come back, arrest every one of them."

"Will do."

"And get general counsel over here, right away. I want these tabloids off our ass with this Jane Doe crap. We've got enough problems brewing. Grab me general counsel before you go."

"Which one?"

"Oh, I don't know. All of them."

"Will do."

"And send a limo for Beaumont tomorrow morning. We're re-situating her on *private* company property. Bring me that directory, John. She's going to need a suite."

"Will do. Anything else?"

"Yeah, mum's the word on this. I want her comfortable. Stock her up with the works. Champagne, caviar, whatever. Get her women if that's what she prefers! A different one every night if that's what it takes to keep her mind off this bullshit. Send her all blonds. Blond bombs posing as bookworms. I don't care, as long as she stays away from THAT WOMAN over there," she said, pointing angrily at the building across the street. "She's a jinx. I can feel it."

John looked doubtful. "Can we do that?"

"What?"

"Blond bombs that look like bookworms? Where would I find them?"

"Oh, John . . . be creative."

It wasn't difficult for her to keep her mouth shut these days. Anytime she contemplated speaking, a small sob would well up in it. Even her smile had changed, softened considerably by her sadness, though it would never be quite as sublime as that woman's, the one she presently watched on her TV, whose name she now knew was Lydia Beaumont, who looked pretty tightlipped herself, having failed to utter a single response to the crowd of reporters assailing her. She did seem frightened. Sharon was glad to see her unnerved and hoped it put a serious crimp in her future plans. Lydia Beaumont wide-eyed. She didn't need to hear the woman speak to know what she was thinking.

Silence had its advantages, Sharon was learning. She had dropped out of view for awhile, spending most of the past few weeks performing community service in LA, having successfully copped a lesser plea of "contributing to the delinquency of a minor." Only twelve months—for being quiet. She spent most of her free time in hiding, designing her makeover, declining all interviews, stating "no comment" to pushy reporters.

She was planning to reinvent herself. No more flings, no more flash. She wasn't up to it anyway. The wardrobe was the best place to start, she had decided. That should be muted, toned down. Gray. Warm grays. Charcoal, as opposed to black. In natural fibers, no more synthetics, just the real thing. Classic cuts, even for the hair. Sensible sweaters accented with a single string of pearls. Not a Doris Day motif, of course, too over the top, but respectable, like cashmere and wool are with a full-length tailored skirt.

She examined the mirror. Or should it be mid-calf? Or just a bit above the knees? But those nice, long legs. It was a shame to hide them. They were her trademark. Could she part with her minis? She'd have to give it more thought.

"Where is she?"

"I don't know, Helaine. I'll call Stan and see if he's heard from her. I need an update anyway. It's been a week."

She had given them the slip, thus the dailies were forced to speculate and embellish as much as possible in her absence, which they found necessary to do all week.

All week they churned out raw data and vital statistics on Lydia Beaumont and when it seemed there was nothing new to add, they juxtaposed them with Dr. Kristenson's, spicing things up with the mountain of juicy tidbits they had collected over the years on Sharon Chambers.

The contest: Plaintiff Chambers asserts that Lydia Beaumont is the other woman, Defendant Kristenson asserts she is not. God, how the public loves a triangle! It's the shortest distance between two points.

"And how is Rapunzel doing in her tower? Comfy?"

"Paula! Good, come in. I'm halfway through these numbers."

"Good, SEC next month. Been wearing my lucky girdle all week. How's every little thing?" she asked, trying to ignore the clumsy attentions of a buxom blond performing a crude impersonation of a maid.

Lydia rolled her eyes and stared at the rug. Rip-away maids, rip-away room service, rip-away masseuses . . . all blond. Duh! And not one of them could make a decent martini. She choked on the one just delivered and waited for Paula's reaction.

"Ugh! What the hell is this?" Paula exclaimed.

Lydia laughed. Serves you right, she said in her head. "Paula, I need a safe outside line."

"We're working on it. I don't know what's taking so long. Use e-mail for now. Ye-god, don't drink that!"

"I need to talk to . . . someone. E-mail's not quite adequate, cell phone, ditto."

"Well, if you must talk to someone, talk to *her*," Paula teased. "And be sure to tell her this isn't drinkable while you're at it."

Lydia smiled patiently. "How's damage control progressing? When can I go outside? I'd like to go running."

"We're contacting all our assets. *The Herald, Weekly Times*, so on. Got the red lines drawn in the sand, got a secure zone around the building. Ta dah! So it'll probably take another week or so for the dust to settle. In the meantime use that gym thing there. What's wrong with that?"

Or so? Lydia folded her arms. "I need to . . . I need these bimbos out of here, first of all. I can't concentrate. And it's been a week since I've . . . I've talked to my friends. The phone . . . I need a private outside line."

Those complaints didn't surprise VP Treadwell. "Sorry about the bimbos. We thought you might get lonesome, that's all."

Lydia shook her head. "No, not for—oh, never mind. And the phone?"

"The phone? Beaumont. Do you mind if I speak frankly here?"

"Please. That's what I rely on you for."

"Good. Then it won't surprise you that I'd prefer you stay away from Dr. Kristenson. Soloman-Schmitt needs you more now."

Soloman-Schmitt.

"Aw, sweetie, aren't you gonna drink that?" the maid interrupted.

Lydia squirmed. "I really don't think I can."

"Suit yourself. How 'bout a little wine, honey?"

Paula hid behind her hand.

"Wine's fine. Let's try that," Lydia mumbled. This was divine retribution, she was thinking, for her prank on Helaine at the guest house.

"And you?" the woman asked Paula.

"Oh yes, and then please go when you're through. We need some privacy."

(Why hadn't I thought to say that?)

"Suit yourself," the woman replied.

They sat in silence as the maid fumbled hopelessly with the bottle.

"Leave it," Paula finally ordered. It was amusing, but only for a little while.

They waited till they heard the door close behind her and Lydia took the wine bottle and uncorked it.

"I really am sorry about that," Paula offered. "I thought perhaps—"

"I know what you thought. It became painfully obvious."

"Well, what the fuck do I know about it? Shoot me in the head."

"It's just that I can't concentrate," Lydia said. "I don't expect you to understand and I don't want to discuss it, but I do need a private phone. Just to talk."

"Look, I don't want anything to jinx our operation here, Lydia. We've got a lot on our mind."

"You have my word that I will stay put until you tell me the coast is clear. But . . . I . . . she will be very anxious about—"

"*She* should have been very anxious before this, what with that tarantula on the loose!"

Lydia swirled the wine and sighed. Okay. But too late now. "Nevertheless, I'm lonesome and not for Soloman-Schmitt."

"I'm going to lose you, aren't I?"

"You might. But not before we finish."

Paula nodded and sipped her wine. "What about Vice President Beaumont? Doesn't that have a nice ring to it?"

"Can't. Don't want to."

"What do you want to do? Lie in bed all day?"

Lydia took a deep breath. "That, too."

"Well, what else then?"

"I want to sit on some of those boards. As many as possible."

Paula perked up. "Really? I can arrange that."

"We'd be in opposite corners, Vice President Treadwell. Better consider that first."

"Not necessarily. Besides, it's better than the alternative, isn't it? The other way I'll be completely deaf and blind until I find your replacement."

"IF. I've seen what's coming through the ranks, Paula. Good luck."

"Isn't there anyone out there? Another Lydia Beaumont?"

"Some, but you've got to grab them quickly and then watch them like a hawk."

"Crap, Lydia. I know you're busy right now, but get me a shopping list."

"Okay. Get me a private line."

The summer gods were packing it in for now, leaving things in the capable hands of their icy associates. The days shortened and the nights grew long again.

Seven-point-three on the Richter scale and some pretty serious aftershocks. That's what it feels like when an institution like Soloman-Schmitt catches cold and sneezes. It did have the beneficial effect of throwing the Chambers-Kristenson-Beaumont Affair into the inside pages for a while, although the press had a new excuse to assemble in front of Lydia's building, so she still couldn't show up for work there.

As a protective measure, Paula Treadwell had the entire contents of Lydia's office shipped under supervision to her VIP's ivory tower. She delayed as long as possible in furnishing her with a private line until the relentless e-mail requests for the same threatened to distract her from her own business, which these days consisted of a lot of hand-holding and arm-twisting and endlessly sincere public announcements about the promising health of her company. If she didn't watch out she could find herself president of it one day.

"Okay, Beaumont, you've got your private line."

"Prove it."

"How can I do that?"

"Tell me something you wouldn't want anyone else to hear."

"You know you got to start trusting people again. It's not—"

"Spare me, Paula. Go on."

"I cheated on my husband the other night. With the cable man."

"Oh my gosh . . . thanks."

"I'm under so much pressure and the guy was so sweet. I don't know what I was thinking."

"Okay, it's all right. Thank you, Paula. Thanks."

"You think I should tell Dickie?"

"Paula . . . no. I don't think you should share this with Dickie."

"What do you think I should do?"

"I . . . I think you should reflect on it in silence and hang up so I can use my phone. Are you coming by this week?"

"Yes, but I don't know when yet. You're such a prude, you know. I'm still blown away that you're Jane Doe."

"Uh, me too. A prude? Why?"

"Because other than that thing way back in the Paleolithic era, you know with your Mr. Rios, I didn't know you thought about sex."

"Paula . . . I need to use the phone."

"Right. I'll see you at the end of the week then."

Paleolithic Joe. Delilah had e-mailed Lydia the latest articles and it didn't look good for him. Arraignment on ten counts of securities fraud, him and his gang of fourteen. That was just the beginning, she knew, the tip of only one iceberg in a great big ocean filled with them.

"You want me to hang that up for you, honey?"

Lydia clutched the phone possessively and shook her head. She had forgotten to mention to Paula that blonds were still littering her landscape. Outside the window, she swore she saw snowflakes fluttering by. She had missed the end of a spectacular Indian summer, a particularly long one this year. "What time is it?" she asked.

"Two thirty."

"Thank you." She waited for the maid to leave the room and dialed Helaine at her office.

"She's with a patient right now. Can I take your name and number?"

"Oh . . . um . . . tell her, please, that Jane called." She gave the secretary the number. "It's a private number."

"I understand, Ms. Beaumont. I'll let her know as soon as she's out of session."

Lydia coughed, exposed so easily. "Thank you. You have a nice day." She hung up and dialed Delilah at the bank, bypassing her secretary.

"Globe International, Del Lewiston. How may I help you?"

"Del, it's me."

"Hey! Commandant Treadwell let you off the leash?"

"Nah, but I finally got a private line. How's things over your way?"

"I feel the earth move under my feet. I feel the sky come tumblin', a tumblin' down. Not too bad really. Everybody sugaring me. Haven't got time for any Soloman-Schmitt-type mavericks in my house. You hear Arthur-Doolittle's going belly up? Just a matter of time."

"A long time coming. How's it look at the penthouse? I wanna go home."

"Paula's good, but not that good, I'm afraid. Still some stragglers."

"Oh Christ. I need my life back, Del."

"Whowee though, you sure sound exciting these days. All this time I thought you were just this mild-mannered financier. Mmm, mmm, mmm, Lydia Beaumont, what they say about you. And I'll bet you haven't got laid in weeks because of it, have you?"

THE SECRET KEEPING   263

"Ain't I something?"

"Sit tight. Things will quiet down soon, now that they've got this stuff to gnaw at. Treadwell taking good care of you?"

"Yeah. Bar no expense, if you get what I'm driving at. It's embarrassing."

"Hah! She's a piece of work that one. Send my regards. This your number I'm seeing here?"

Lydia listened as she read it off. "That's mine. Call me. I hate e-mail." After that she loitered near the phone for another half hour before going back to work. Another hour flew by and the maid knocked at the door of the makeshift office.

"Telephone. Wouldn't tell me her name, though."

(Of course not.) "Thanks. This is confidential, please."

The woman made herself scarce.

"Good afternoon?"

"Darling . . . who's that?"

"Helaine! Um . . . the maid. I mean room service. I miss you."

"Maid? Where are you? I've been sick to death worrying that you flew the coop on me."

"Soloman-Schmitt's holding me ransom."

"How much are they asking? I'll pay anything."

"I need to see you, Lana."

"I need you. When?"

"Tonight?"

"Where are you?"

Lydia rattled off the address.

"Will they stop me at the desk? What do I say?"

"Just wear your hair down and duck your head. I don't think anybody will stop you."

"Okay . . . ? And what else should I wear?"

"Lana . . . surprise me."

Stanley Kandinsky representing Defendant Beaumont? Oh shit! He had never prevailed in a single case where that man was involved. The stars were simply aligned against Attorney Willard Hathaway.

* * *

Racketeers, reconnoiters, raconteurs. *Rrrrrrr.* VP Treadwell fumed as she rode up the elevator, exiting five minutes later with her own little storm cloud in tow as she stomped gloomily down the hallway. It was a bad day. She rapped impatiently on Lydia's door with a set of white knuckles and waited a few seconds. No answer. She turned the handle. It was unlocked. She let herself in without announcement.

Once inside, she immediately discovered a trail of women's clothes leading from the couch to the bedroom and the excited cries emanating from that direction told her all she needed to know for the moment. She cursed inaudibly and fell into a chair to await the finale, reminding herself to speak to John again about putting an end to the dumb blond parade at the Beaumont pleasure palace.

She put her face in a newspaper for awhile, squinting in the dim light, kicking at the briefcase with her toe as she read. Nothing but bad news everywhere.

Bullshit, bullshit, bullshit. And same with this Jane Doe Beaumont. And what a time for all of this. You could stand in the middle of town and feel the goddamned ground shaking. And now Rios and his cabal, making the whole firm look like a bunch of cowboys. Renegades running amok in the temple of Soloman-Schmitt. Ten securities violations. Felonies. Fraud. She had enough ass to kick without assisting a grand jury to kick his. They could indict him on the papers alone. The whole bunch of insiders and their Fortune 500 members only clubs. Served them right! The good old boys stepping over the line, lining their pockets with the investors funds. Shit. She didn't want any on her.

Treadwell paused and listened to the private party going on in the bedroom. She was pretty sure that was Beaumont calling the cows home. Atta' girl! Plain old fucking. Why couldn't people be content with that? No, a good roll in the sack's too old-fashioned. Fucking till you can't walk, that's old. Till you're in love with the whole world, old. Smiling at it like you just dropped acid or something. No, just not thrilling enough today. Gotta steal, gotta cheat, gotta lie. Got to fuck people over, because just plain fucking ain't good enough. And look at this asshole Sharon Chambers. What in the hell are you smiling about, you fucking menace?

I'll bet you don't even like sex, you big phony. Trying to mess with my top girl. My righthand woman. My goddamned top executive. Bullshit, bullshit, bullshit!

She threw her glasses into her purse, rolled the newspaper into a ball and punted it. This was serious. She didn't have all night to sit there. She stood up glanced at her watch and went back to the bedroom, cracking the bedroom door to check on the progress there. A blond on top. Fine, we'll give that one a beeper, Treadwell said to herself, and terminate the rest. Look at all that hair. A regular living doll.

"There . . . yes . . . there," she heard Lydia coax between breaths.

Paula couldn't make out the blond's response.

"Yes . . . yes . . . yes . . . yes . . ." Lydia moaned.

Goodness, Paula muttered, with no fear she would be overheard. She closed the door again. Plays as hard as she works—who the hell would have guessed it? She left the doorway and went back to the chair, waiting with growing irritation for another fifteen minutes before approaching the bedroom one last time.

"Okay honey," she finally said, unceremoniously slapping the blond's behind as she spoke. "You're doing Soloman-Schmitt proud, let me tell you. Now go, wash up and make us some martinis."

"Paula!" Lydia gasped. "Paula," she gulped incredulously.

The blond buried her face in Lydia's neck. Paula heard her whisper, "Are you all right?"

Lydia pulled the sheets over the woman and tried to sit up, but failed. "Paula! What are you doing—"

"Beaumont! Go on blondie, she's fine. Something's up, Beaumont. Get dressed." She threw a towel and a bathrobe at them and the ladies climbed out of the bed without another word, the blond heading for the bathroom, concealing herself in the robe, her face hidden by her hair.

Lydia threw the towel to the floor and marched naked into the living room, VP Treadwell in pursuit. "Paula, for Chrissake! You interrupted my—What is it? Why are you here?"

"Wow, look at those abs. You're fit as a fiddle, Beaumont."

Lydia swore under her breath. "You're standing on my clothes, Treadwell. Those are my things you're on. Here . . . pass me that sweater, please. Thanks. And those, too. No, no, just the pants. Sit, please. Sit.

Thank you." She cast a look toward the bedroom and then back to Paula. "Now what's wrong," she muttered as she dressed. "I thought you weren't coming until the end of the week?"

"Yeah, I see you thought that. And I thought you didn't care for bimbos?"

"Paula, she's not—"

"Yeah, yeah, yeah. Look at this. A subpoena. Oh, here's Goldilocks now," she said, addressing the woman without looking at her. "Honey, you know how to make a martini?"

"Paula—" Lydia started to protest.

"Indeed I do. How would you like them? Dry? Or wet?"

Lydia looked askance and took the papers from Paula.

"Dry, if you can manage it. I got that this afternoon, Beaumont! In front of the grand jury no less. Are we ready for this? A fucking subpoena. CRAP."

"I . . . I'll make those," Lydia called over her shoulder. "Don't do that. *Please.*"

Paula reached out and fanned the documents with her hand. "You hear that? That's the sound shit makes hitting a fan! This is what it looks like in black and white. You got the numbers yet on those accounts, the one your boyfriend fudged?"

"Okay, Paula. Okay. Please. Sit down. Listen to me. One, you're embarrassing me right now and I'm more than a little overwhelmed by your being here. Two, as you know, he is not my boyfriend. Not anymore."

"Here you go, ladies. Two dry martinis. Will that be all?"

Lydia stared at the rug and threw the papers onto the coffee table.

"Thanks, hon," Paula cooed. "Now, if you don't mind. We really need some privacy here. Ex-boyfriend, I meant, of course. What a rat!"

Lydia was silent.

"I'm going to have a breakdown without you, Beaumont. I've checked out your list. There's no one like you and you know it."

The blond retrieved her clothes from the floor and headed for the bedroom. Lydia followed her movements with her eyes.

"Pay attention, Beaumont."

"Paula. You're in rare form tonight. Don't worry about your testimony. I'm three quarters done with the numbers."

"Perfect martini. She's a keeper. I need your final report."

"Final?" Lydia looked anxiously toward the bedroom. "Oh, right, final. I was thinking of something else."

"What, I wonder?"

"Paula . . . everything is going to come out fine. You need to go home and get some rest. I understand where we're at and I won't let you down."

Paula saw the blond emerging once again from the bedroom, this time fully dressed. She kept one eye on her as she spoke to Lydia. "I don't mind prepared statements, but sworn testimony? There ought to be a law against it, the end." There was something unusual about that woman. For one she looked a little too upright to be from any of the agencies the corporation depended on. Two, she looked vaguely familiar, though the light could be playing tricks on old eyes. Treadwell felt for her glasses but they were no longer strung around her neck. "You like that one, Beaumont? Don't answer, I know you do. Hey, leave your card before you go, honey, so we can get in touch with you. You know what I mean. You're the first one she's had any interest in."

"Paula—"

"Oh, good. I can't tell you how relieved I am to hear that, Ms. Treadwell. How's your martini?"

Was that a mocking tone in her voice? "Perfect," Treadwell replied as she peered with an impending sense of doom at the blond approaching her. Doom. What an inexplicable feeling, Paula thought, reaching out to take the card the blond was offering. Completely inexplicable. Where the hell were her glasses?

Lydia took a huge, uncomfortable breath and threw her head back on the sofa. *I am a barbarian, Paula is definitely the head barbarian, Soloman-Schmitt a tribe of barbarians, high-paid, overpaid corporate barbarians on the loose. Anybody can plainly see that.*

She could see Helaine was pissed. To laugh? To cry? Lydia couldn't decide. Adding to her misery, there was a congestion building in her womb, the product of what Del called "coitus interruptus." That's what she was experiencing big time. That and an anxiety attack about the possibility that Helaine might be leaving, which she couldn't blame her for doing. She avoided eye contact with her, and instead searched the ceiling for an escape hatch.

"Beaumont, I don't have my glasses. What's the card say?"

"Oh, Paula," Lydia replied woefully, her eyes glued to the ceiling, "I'm sure it says something like Dr. Helaine Kristenson, psychother—"

"OH, SHIT."

"Beaumont, you gave me your word!"

"I promised to stay put. I'm put."

"Oh, you stinker, you did, didn't you? Dr. Kristenson, I wasn't aware you made house calls."

"I don't."

"Then what the hell are you doing here?"

"I was trying to spend a quiet evening with my—"

"Quiet? You call that racket you were making quiet?"

Helaine smiled. "*I* was quiet."

Lydia reddened.

"Tell me, do you charge extra for this kind of service?"

"Paula—" Lydia began.

"No, Ms. Treadwell. It's on the house. Anything for Soloman-Schmitt."

"Helaine!"

"Oh? Well I'm glad to hear that. Soloman-Schmitt would like you to go now."

Helaine glanced to Lydia. "Are you in further need of my services, *Beaumont*? Or am I dismissed?"

"Helaine, please—"

"Dr. Kristenson! Don't you read the papers?"

"Sometimes."

"Good, because sometimes you're in them. You and that woman. And now my top girl, here."

"You forgot to mention Soloman-Schmitt. Isn't that my fault, too?"

"Are you leaving yet?"

"She is not leaving, Paula. Please don't go, Helaine."

Helaine sat.

"Beaumont . . . you're in over your head. The end."

Lydia nodded. "We all are, I think."

"Did you tell her about the cable man? That was just between you and me."

"Paula Treadwell, trust me. Your name wasn't even mentioned."

Paula downed her martini. "I find that difficult to believe."

"You would," Lydia replied.

"Helaine, I don't want to burst your bubble or anything, but I happen to have it from a reliable source that you spent the night at Soloman-Schmitt's happy land of ill repute and other corporate pastimes. Care to share your secret strategy for winning this lawsuit? Because, being just a humble attorney, it isn't at all obvious to me."

"You're following me?"

"It's called following when the bad guys do it. It's called keeping an eye on you when we do it. How's she holding up?"

"I want her out of there. Can you talk to Stan about it?"

"I'm making tea," Kay interrupted. "Any takers?"

"Tea, please. And what can he do, Helaine?"

"She needs to go home, Robert. They're . . . they're . . . absolute Huns. Including Paula Treadwell, their so called white knight."

"You met her?"

"I did."

"Did you joust with the woman?"

"You could say that."

"Who won?"

"It's a draw for now. Robert, she's sending Lydia call-girls posing as room service. Dumb blonds!"

"Spare no luxury, huh? She must really be depending on Ms. Beaumont."

Kay joined them at the table. "*Corruptio optimi pessima*. It's the corporate culture, Helaine. Lydia's used to it by now. I wouldn't worry."

"You call that culture?"

"No, they do," Robert said. "Kay's right, don't worry. Everybody will go home when things are settled. I'm sure Stan doesn't mind that Treadwell's providing his client with a secure location in the meantime. He's counter claiming you know?"

"For what?" Helaine asked.

"Defamation, slander, the like."

"What?" Helaine was shocked. Her eyes glistened. "Lydia's claiming that she's defamed because Sharon says she's my lover?"

"Uh, no, that's a bit literal," Robert answered nervously.

"Really?" she asked. "Is it?"

Robert had been caught off his guard. He looked to Kay for some assistance.

"Kay? Is Robert right? Am I being too literal?"

"Helaine . . . it's just to shake them off. It's a standard pleading. Have your tea."

"So she's denying—"

"Legally speaking there's nothing else to do right now," Robert said, apologetically. "He has to get his client out. It's just posturing, Helaine."

Helaine grabbed her coat. "Is Lydia aware of this strategy? Because she didn't mention it last night."

Robert searched his repertoire of one-liners and, coming up empty-handed, turned to his wife once more.

Kay shook her head. "I don't know, Helaine. It seems rather unlikely that she wouldn't. Doesn't it, Robert? I mean, you would know better than I."

He sent her a beseeching look but Kay refused to speak. "She must," he finally answered.

Helaine circled the table. "Has defendant Beaumont sent that answer, would you know?"

"It's not due yet."

"Has she sent it?"

"No."

Helaine was leaving. Robert and Kay followed her with grim faces.

"What are you going to do, Helaine? I wouldn't do anything drastic," Robert implored. "Think like a lawyer for a moment and you'll see you're overreacting."

She waited for him to open the door.

"Helaine . . . think it through first."

"You know . . . this is all starting to take a toll," she replied, speaking in a hushed tone. "The reporters, the lawyers. All of it." She hesitated at the elevator. "I'm very tired," she added, stepping into it.

Robert stopped the doors from closing. "Hathaway wants a meeting. This is a good sign, Helaine."

She rolled her eyes. "Please schedule it soon then. I need to get this over with."

"I'm sorry, Ms. Beaumont, she's on vacation."

"Vaca—For how long? When did she leave?"

"I'm not at liberty to say. I'm sorry. She did leave you a message."

"What is it?"

"She asked that you send word when you return home again. You can direct that to me, of course. I'm Jenny."

"I don't understand. Was this a planned vacation? She didn't mention it the last time we talked."

"She was feeling overly stressed. Harassed."

"But I was hoping . . . when will she be back?"

"I think she's probably waiting for things to quiet down again. It's been difficult for her to get around lately, the press constantly following and all. Found her new address, too. I'm sure you can empathize, Ms. Beaumont. I'll tell her you called, though. She'll be happy to know that."

"So she's checking her messages?"

"Oh, yes. Of course."

Lydia felt punched. She had not heard from Helaine in a week and her earlier messages to Helaine's home had not been returned. To make matters worse, Sharon Chambers had emerged from hiding, flaunting a glorious makeover and the front pages were once again being devoted to the nation's most famous couple of the moment, complete with rumors of private settlement talks between the two women and rampant speculations that they were attempting a reconciliation. Lydia had pooh-poohed it all as nothing more than profit-driven gossip, but the news of Helaine's surreptitious departure was unexpected and alarming.

"Ms. Beaumont? Is that all, or would you care to leave a message?"

"I would care. Yes, please. Tell her that I . . . uh . . . will call again. Check back, I mean."

"I'll do that, dear. You have a nice day."

"Thank you, Jenny. You too."

"Good job, Beaumont."

"It's just a preliminary but it'll get you through the proceedings without any surprises."

"Excellent work. So I suppose I know what you've got planned for tonight?"

"Ac-tu-al-ly, no plans."

"No plans? Why not? All the trouble I went through?"

"Paula . . . probably the scene here. I'm just guessing."

"But we've cleaned it up. Didn't you tell her that?"

"I didn't get the chance."

"What is this about? That Chambers woman?"

Lydia shrugged.

"Where is the doctor?"

"Vacation."

"Vacation? Bullshit! She's not going to snub our hospitality. Get her on the phone, Beaumont. I want to talk to her."

"I—She's on vacation, Paula. She doesn't return my calls."

"Beaumont, *you* are a neophyte. She's not on goddamned vacation, I can assure you."

"Then she's somewhere else, like it says in the papers. Forget it."

"Don't you believe it! I know a power play when I see one. Pass me that phone."

"Paula! I forbid you. It will work itself out."

"Hey! Here's the reading materials you requested. Suddenly joining the human race?"

"Del, thanks! Just curious. Shaker of martinis over there."

"Excellent. What are you having?"

"Heroin."

"Hah! Hey, not too shabby in here, Liddy. You rank."

"How's things at my apartment?"

"Crowded again. The girls and I stopped in to clean up a bit. It was like a human car wash just getting in and out of the lobby. Your poor doorman. He's all but swinging a broom at them to clear them out. Just like cockroaches."

"What is this, Del?" Lydia asked, pointing at a front page article featuring a photo of Sharon and Helaine, heads bent together, smiling. "Can I believe in this stuff?"

"I wouldn't."

Lydia sighed and poured herself a martini.

"And look at glamorous Sharon Chambers, new and improved. She looks like she's in mourning, a grieving widow, for chrissakes."

"A grieving executive, more like it. She's dressing like one of us, Liddy. Gosh, I wonder why?"

"And on the cover everywhere, Del. So who cares about corporate scandal, huh?"

"Paula Treadwell's kicking ass, fixing it up, Liddy. No one wants to hear good news. Got any by the way?"

"Oh yeah! You?"

"Promotion. Still just a millionaire. Big date tonight. Yum, yum, yum."

"Good for you. Money's brought me nothing but trouble I fear, now with Sharon Chambers after it."

"She's after you, Liddy, doesn't need the money. What's up with your lawyer?"

"We're not seeing eye to eye. He wants to deny everything and counterclaim for slander."

"Wow. That ought to do the job."

"I can't do that."

"Oh geesh, Liddy. Why not? She's not entitled to your dough. Everyone knows that."

"Money, money, money. Money can't buy you love."

"You're scaring the bejeezus out of me, Marilyn Beaumont. Drink."

"I scare myself. Cheers."

"Cheers. Where's Helaine tonight? What's actually going on with your blond these days, besides that she's got no room to breathe anymore?"

"She's on retreat somewhere. It's starting to get to her, I guess."

"Oh . . . ?"

"Del, I can't send an answer like the one my lawyer's cooked up. Helaine won't go for it. It'll be a real, real, real long vacation if I do."

"I see."

"She's on vacation, Ms. Treadwell. Can I take a message?"

"Yes, please do. You got a pen handy?"

"Yes?"

"Good. You tell your Dr. Kristenson that I'm sending an unmarked limo for her at the corner of Ninth and Vine. It'll be there in an hour."

"But—"

"And also inform her that if she fails to show she'll be reading all about her greatest hits in Sunday's papers. She'll get what I'm driving at."

"What is this about?"

"It's about Lydia Beaumont. You remember her fine ass, Doctor? The one you put in a sling?"

"Please . . . call me Kristenson."

"Drive," Paula instructed the chauffeur. "Let me look at you, blondie."

"Ms. Treadwell, I am not one of your girls."

"And Beaumont is not *one* of yours. Your hair looks a little wild. Can you comb it?"

"She likes it like this. I presume that's where we're going."

"Okay, leave it then. Now let me tell you something before we get there. Soloman-Schmitt has gone to great lengths to accommodate you, Kristenson, your esteemed snootiness. Please be mindful of that."

"And let me tell you something, Vice President Paula Treadwell. Soloman-Schmitt does not impress me. I want her out of there. And we have other matters we need to square away that don't require corporate handlers."

"Look. I don't care if you like me or not. I didn't get where I am trying to be popular. But there's one thing I don't tolerate and that's games, Kristenson. We cleaned up our act for you. I'm sorry if you don't approve of our culture. *I* don't approve of Sharon Chambers, the end."

Helaine stared out the window without speaking.

"As to when Beaumont can leave, she cannot go back to her penthouse yet with all those reporters there. That is something I can't control. Sorry."

"Oh? Something that escapes your micromanagement, Ms. Treadwell? That must be a painful concession to have to make. Tell me, do you plan on being our chaperone tonight?"

"If necessary. Turn into the garage, driver. You look lovely by the way. Even with the messy hair. Pull up to the elevator, please. Right here's fine."

Helaine produced a compact and examined herself in the mirror. "Thank you," she said tersely, as she left the car.

"Oh, and Kristenson—?"

Helaine turned and raised her eyebrow.

"We never had this conversation, right?"

"I thought you were avoiding me?"

"Darling . . . I am."

"Oh."

"I see Lydia Beaumont's catching up on her reading."

"Yesterday's papers. Why? Avoiding me, I mean."

Helaine skimmed the stack of newspapers and frowned. "This is ruining us. Oh, and look here. *Keeping Mr. Right*. You want me to autograph it for you?"

"I was curious, that's all."

"Curiosity. About what?"

"They mentioned your book. You hadn't. I was just curious."

"You read it?"

"Pretty much."

"Still curious though?"

Lydia looked away.

"About what, Lydia?"

"It's all curious, Dr. Kristenson. I don't know."

"What can I clarify for you?"

"Putting someone *on notice*. You gave Sharon Chambers notice before—"

"I did."

"And what about now? Are you *working it out* with her, Helaine?"

Helaine threw her coat on the arm of the couch and sat down wearily. "It's about settlement, Lydia. The reporters are lying. What else?"

"Settlement? And how's that going?"

Helaine shrugged. "We've offered twenty-five percent net and the deed to my townhouse."

Lydia nodded. It didn't surprise her it would take that much. "And? Will she take it or not?"

"Lydia . . . she wants more. That's all I'm comfortable saying."

"Wants what? Something more is *what*? You, right?"

"Drop it, darling. What else can I clear up for you?"

"What else? Okay, are you sleeping with her?"

"Don't be ridiculous."

"Ridiculous, is it? She's only gorgeous, that's all."

Helaine sighed. "I'm tired of being photographed with her. Rumor has it I have a lover, but I'll believe it when I see it. When are you going home, Lydia Beaumont?"

"As soon as I can. Del says the reporters are living there. I can't deal with that."

"Oh, but I can?"

"Helaine . . . you have more experience with this kind of attention. You and Sharon—" She stopped herself. "I'm not a public person. I hate all this."

"I hate all this!" Helaine suddenly said with a sweep of her arm. "I hate you hiding from it while I'm being followed day and night. I hate your Paula Treadwell school of thought. I hate the idea that you're hoping to sneak out under the cover of darkness. I hate the possibility that you might lie. I hate the possibility you want me only for sex. How do you respond to that charge, *Beaumont*? Can you take me to bed without fucking me? You can't!"

"Fuckin—Oh my gosh." Lydia stood up and walked around the chair, standing behind it as she collected her composure. "Helaine? I've fucked you? What on earth is wrong? What have I done?"

It was a poor choice of words. Helaine regretted them. "Not fuck. I didn't mean that." She lay her head back and closed her eyes. "You love me, Lydia Beaumont?"

"I do."

"Say it."

"I love you."

"How?"

"How?"

"Tell me how you love me. I'd like to know."

Lydia stepped around the chair again and sat once more. "I'm not good at that. Words aren't really my specialty." She took in the long legs, the high heel shoe that dangled on the tip of a pretty foot. "Numbers. I'm good at numbers, not words. I love you."

Helaine sat up. "Numbers? What numbers then? My breasts, my waist, my hips? Those numbers?"

Lydia looked at her own feet. It was not the kind of conversation she excelled at. It was not the kind of evening she had expected. Her mind was racing ahead to scout out the terrain. It was rocky and treacherous and there didn't appear to be a safe shortcut. She kicked her shoes off and slid them back on again. Pulled at her earrings.

"Can you love me without touching me?" Helaine pressed.

"Without touching you?" Lydia repeated, trying to picture it. She saw Helaine shift impatiently. "You know . . . I don't disagree with your views, Dr. Kristenson. Of course, I'm aware of how things look—might look, especially under the circumstances. I'm always conscious of the possibility that I might be a savage like the rest of them, but I do love—"

"Without sex?"

Lydia clenched her teeth. "Without sex? You want me to go without sex?" Her face felt hot. "Why should I? I've already done that. What's this about, Helaine? Sharon Chambers?"

"Concentrate on the question. Can you take me to bed without sex, Lydia Beaumont? I want to know the answer to that."

"Oh. Why? Because there's more to love than sex? Are you accusing me of not loving you enough because I nee—"

"Answer me, Lydia Beaumont, top girl! Can you sleep with me without it leading to sex?"

(NO.)

They locked eyes.

"Helaine . . . this is bullshit. Yes, goddammit. Yes, I can. When I'm eighty years old. Okay?"

Helaine smiled and undid the front of her blouse. Lydia fell back into the chair and watched her undress.

"Tell me what I represent to a Lydia Beaumont."

"This is a trick question?"

"I don't think so."

The shoes were on, the shoes were off, the shoes were on again. Lydia's ears were pink from tugging at her earrings. "Civilization. The good things in life."

"Expensive things, you're saying?" Helaine asked, putting her hands into her hair and lifting it off her shoulders. "Those kind of goods?" she said, suggestively.

Tricky questions. "Rare things, Helaine. Expensive perhaps. I wasn't thinking of that."

"What are you thinking, darling?"

Lydia scoffed. "Guilty things. Feel vindicated?"

"I'm not staying tonight," Helaine replied, rising to remove her skirt.

Lydia was silent.

"That is why you sent for me, isn't it, *Beaumont*? For this?"

"Sent for you? I didn't send for you. I left some messages, that's all."

The skirt was off.

"And Paula?"

It was dawning on Lydia now. "Paula? She made you come over?"

Helaine chuckled. "Oh, I see," she said, reclining. "Skip it then."

"Skip it? All right, Dr. Kristenson. Whatever you say, Dr. Kristenson. Am I disappointing you if I gawk, or should I leave the room with my bad self?"

"Don't be ridiculous. Come and hold me."

"Hold?"

"You said you could. Come here."

Lydia left her shoes at the foot of the chair. "Like this?"

"Mmmm, nice."

"Can I kiss you or is that impolite?"

"Please, kiss me."

"Like that?"

"Mmmm. Very nice."

"And this?"

"Mmmm . . ."

"Here?"

"Mmmmm."

"More?"

"More."

"Like that?"

"Yes . . . like that."

"Lana . . . you're so—"

"Surprise, surprise."

"Lana."

"Mmmmmmm . . ."

"Is this all right?"

"Lydia . . ."

"Yes?"

"Nice."

"This too?"

"Oh . . . Lydia . . . Beaumont . . ."

"Yes?"

"You are such . . ."

"Such?"

"Yes . . . such . . ."

"Such what?"

"Mmmmm . . . such a . . ."

"Such a what?"

"Such . . . a liar . . ."

* * *

"Well, it's no defense. The press will be dumbfounded, your father dismayed."

"My father is not paying you, I am."

"I was simply stating his emotional interest in the case. He'd like to see you out of the limelight, get back to your life again."

"I'm not lying to achieve his happiness or to get out of the papers. There's still no merit to her claim whether we're lovers or not."

Stanley studied his client's face. "When did you become lovers, Lydia?"

She pursed her lips and rested her chin on the back of her hand. "I don't know, Stan."

"Then try it this way. When weren't you lovers?"

"I just can't say. I don't know that, Stan."

He looked through her and then referred to the legal pad again. "Ultimately it's not dispositive. It's just a shame to give her anything. And to give up defamation, Lydia? They would have dropped suit with that reply."

She knew that.

"Okay. I'll have it drafted by the end of the week. That'll give you time to reconsider."

"It doesn't deprive me of a defense. Does it?"

"Of course not. Her claim is frivolous. More akin to malicious. We'll be filing a motion to dismiss it at a later date. That'll leave your Dr. Kristenson to fend for herself, though. Is she aware that you're admitting this?"

"She has no idea."

"The only reason I ask is that she was essentially silent on that part of the claim. But then at that time she was the only one who knew who Jane Doe really was."

"Silence isn't lying. Is it?"

He wrinkled up his brow. "It doesn't affect the truth either way."

"I don't understand."

"Infidelity is not germane in a pecuniary claim against a former lover for economic damages, since it is firmly held that a meritorious suit for support arises exclusively from prima facie proofs of prior financial dependency and subsequent abandonment thereof, irrespective of the actual cause of the partners' separation. In short, it will have no bearing on the plaintiff's award, if any, that she has allegedly suffered the humiliation of sexual and/or emotional betrayal, which is, from what I am able to glean, the gravamen of Sharon Chambers' case against Dr. Kristenson. That part, together with her frivolous complaint against you, will undoubtedly be stricken by order of the court directing the plaintiff to amend her pleading and, possibly, requiring her to serve it again, which she very likely will not do. Understand?"

Lydia rose from her chair and packed up her briefcase. "I think so. Thank you for your time today. I'll see you Friday."

"Same time. Same place. You've got a driver now?"

"Courtesy Soloman-Schmitt."

"Got to do what you got to do, right?"

He walked her to the door. "If you change your mind, let us know."

"What's the worse that can happen if I don't? That the press follows me around, my name's in all the papers, I can't go home or to work, I can't be with my lover?"

Flying colors. VP Treadwell had made it through her grand jury testimony without losing a single drop of blood and the preliminary inquiries by the SEC were going smoothly as well. No new revelations to shake the markets. Unfortunately she was required to name her chief investigator, Lydia Beaumont, and to expound somewhat on Lydia's prior relationship with the now banned and indicted former executive, Joseph Rios. When the press learned of that exciting new twist they pounced on Treadwell's protégé again, this time bandying the facts about with salacious front page offerings like HAVE WHISTLE WILL BLOW and the old reliable standby KISS AND TELL that the readership never tires of.

Frankly, the reporters resented Lydia's aversion to public appearances and they were completely dissatisfied with slick Paula Treadwell's cut-and-dried responses, those deliberately bland unquotables she resorted to using when fielding their questions on the matter. "There is no connection whatsoever," was what she frequently said. Also, "It doesn't concern me. I don't know anything about it. It's not relevant, the end."

So they did what they deemed necessary to force the elusive Lydia Beaumont out into the open. There were a lot of resources available to them for this purpose now that she was no longer Jane Doe to them. She had become, instead, a lot of intriguing and diverse things, including, as they finally discovered, the daughter of Edward Beaumont himself, whose own romantic escapades had already been used to entertain the minions. It was worth another mention, they concluded, and his dirty laundry was once again hung outdoors for another airing. In the meantime, they drummed their fingers restlessly on their desktops and cast their bets on defendant Beaumont's official response to Sharon Chambers's allegations, which was due any day now.

"Queenie?"

"Daddy, hi."

"You know if you were in Paris right now they'd make a darling of you."

"I'm not, I've got a job to do. Are you telling me to leave the country? I feel I just got here."

"Oh, you've arrived all right. This is bigger than anything I've gone through."

"I'm not comparing notes with you, Daddy. I think I know why you're calling and I just have three words to say about it—attorney-client privilege."

"Stan and I go way back and we talk on a regular basis. He knows how worried I am about your future. Your kitten's steering you wrong on this, Lydia. She'll leave you hanging, trust me."

"Daddy . . . please."

"Does she know how hard you've worked for your money? She's dragging you through the mud and you're wallowing in it."

"Thank you, Daddy, I love you, too. Sharon Chambers isn't getting my money."

"I'm ordering you to change your pleading. Think of your old man and do it for him, please."

"I can't."

"Nonsense. There are other beautiful people in the world you can take up

with, especially now that you're a celeb. Think of that, Queenie. It's only sex and, despite popular mythology, Dr. Kristenson did not invent it."

"I'm not changing my answer, Daddy. I simply can't."

"For God's sake, why not?"

"Because it's not just sex, I'm also in love with the woman."

"And so is Sharon Chambers. What about her?"

"Sharon Chambers?"

"Yes, Sharon Chambers!"

"Her I hate."

"She what?"

"Admits most of it."

Sharon stared stonily into the mirror. "That they're lovers?"

"Yes."

"Just a moment, please." She pulled up a chair. "What does she actually deny, Mr. Hathaway?"

"Well . . . she denies sufficient knowledge as to those allegations stating that you and Dr. Kristenson are or were lovers. She denies sufficient knowledge of your quote unquote alleged mental condition. She denies suf—"

"Fine. I get it."

"Twenty-five percent is not a bad offer, Ms. Chambers. I urge you again to take it."

She had wanted no less than half gross and was shocked to learn that Helaine was a spendthrift, wasting nearly forty percent off the top on her social concerns, on donor contributions to non-governmental organizations with their bleeding heart domestic programs, on cleaning up minefields in Sudan, on supporting democracy in Burma, ending child slavery in the Ivory Coast, housing battered women and homeless vets. Crap! It was endless.

Even Hathaway had been amazed by the disclosures. "We don't want to look bad here," he had cautioned her in private.

She had hoped to choke the doctor financially so she'd have to agree to reconciliation, but Helaine had rejected that alternative flat out.

She was worth a pretty penny before taxes, before her stupid charitable contributions. The counteroffer, the price of freedom—half her gross current worth. She'd get more if she had to go to trial, Sharon warned Helaine. That didn't seem to scare her any.

"I'm considering all my options, Mr. Hathaway. I'll get back to you."

"Them's fighting words, Helaine," Robert announced. "Starting to sound like a catfight."

Helaine grinned. "Meow."

The air tingled and zinged with winter closing in fast.

YES MEANS YES blared one steamy headline with a glamour shot of the woman who dared to say it. They had started to doubt it. At last they knew. Yes. Absolutely yes she was. All that was missing was a recent snapshot of the illicit lovers together. The reporters crowded every known address to get one, but Dr. Kristenson's lover was nowhere to be seen.

So then their eyes were on Sharon Chambers again. Pale Sharon Chambers, clad these days in a tasteful floor length mink, under which she was fitted in shades of gray, dressed very much as if in mourning. Sharon Chambers, eyes glowing with rage, under control so far, to her lawyers' relief and amazement. But it couldn't last and everyone knew it. She had gone in over her head. Now she was certain to lose it.

There were lots of opportunities emerging, like long lost ships on the horizon. Talk shows galore, gossip mags, publishers hawking tell-all book deals, tell-all quickies with their fill-in-the-blank format. Bread and butter stuff that appealed to Sharon these days when money was tight, when she was finding herself financially strapped, reluctant to settle and having second thoughts as to whether she may have bit off more than she could chew in chasing down that paper tiger, Lydia Beaumont. It could kill two birds with one stone, she surmised. Bring her in some bread and turn the heat up at the same time. Heat. That wasn't a bad strategy. Paper burns.

* * *

"Lana?"

"Darling . . . ?"

"Have dinner with me."

"I'd love to. Where?"

"I'll send a car for you."

"No, let's go out."

Lydia scowled. "C'mon."

"Come on."

"Helaine . . . please."

"For someone who doesn't like to hide, you do it very well. You can't do it forever, Lydia. I won't let you."

"Are you alone?"

"What do the papers say these days? Am I?"

(Ugh.) "What do I hear? You sound like you're at the ocean."

"I'm in the tub, darling. Room for one more."

"Oh, come on, Helaine. I'll send a car for you."

"Lydia Beaumont . . . NO." (click)

"Del, come in!"

"Here's your rags, Liddy. I feel like a paperboy these days. Or a censor."

"Don't censor. Drinks at the bar. Help yourself."

"Top of the best seller list again. Your blond."

"Windfall. Good for her. She'll need it, I think."

"Still boycotting Soloman-Schmitt?"

"Objects to their corporate sponsorship, she says."

"Does VP-CFO Paula Treadwell know that?"

"It's my dirty little secret. How many reporters at the penthouse?"

"Scads."

"That many, huh?"

"I hate to say that the normalcy you're expecting will return to your life is gone, but . . ."

"But the normalcy I'm expecting will return to my life is gone?"

"AWOL, Liddy. Like your stubborn blond."

* * *

"Helaine?"

"Lydia Beaumont! How nice of you to call."

"I miss you."

"Prove it."

"Dinner?"

"Love to. My place or yours?"

Lydia could hear her own breath on the line.

"My place or yours, darling?"

"I'm gathering that you don't consider this suite my place. Right?"

"That's right. Come here. We'll eat nude."

"Shit, Helaine. Us and the entire press corps?"

"You're being despicable."

"Despicable. You're right. And I'm sick of eating and sleeping alone."

"I'll bet. Then grow up and get over here."

"Helaine . . . this is getting frustrating, if you know what I mean. Do you?"

"Indeed, I do. Get over here."

Lydia was silent, taking her time considering it. Her stomach growled. She was thirsty. "I think you're trying to set up obstacles here."

"Then good night, darling. Sleep well." (click)

"She's turned it down, Helaine. Much to the chagrin of her lawyers."

She had expected that. "Now what, Robert?"

The moon was a big bright ball in the sky, punctuating the night, promising to illuminate anything you might have done or dreamt of doing under the influence of darkness.

She had read too many papers. She should have stuck to her financials. The newspapers. They shed no more light than a full moon did, and just like it they made as much trouble, casting long dark shadows in the path so that no matter how familiar the landscape was to you, you'd still feel lost, still stumble over something. Moonlight excursions. You might recognize your way, even make it to your destination, but not without some bruises. Lydia Beaumont was the black-and-blue victim of the falsehood of a brilliant moon pretending to illuminate. All those dark shadows. And the miserable papers.

Of this woman Lydia was reading about lately, this Helaine Kristenson that Sharon Chambers described in such intimate details, Lydia had known nothing. Of the woman she knew by the same name, Helaine Kristenson, she had known only good things. The stark contrast between the two, between her Helaine and Sharon's Helaine, had shocked Lydia, not to mention the idea that an editor would have considered the model's scathing kiss-and-tell even printable.

"CHUMP" the Herald had shouted yesterday over a somewhat dopey head shot of Lydia Beaumont. Chump, Sharon had asserted in this most recent interview, portraying Helaine's interest in Lydia as nothing more than "hosting amateur night," allegedly one of the blond's favorite recreations.

And so followed an itemized list of bedroom secrets that would have made the Marquis de Sade blush. A bit of bares-all hype for Ms. Chambers's forthcoming book. Little wonder Delilah had refused to bring the tabloids to her this week. Lydia had been forced to call down for them and was thankful when she got through with the stack that the deliverer had had the courtesy to simply leave them in a pile outside her door without knocking. After that, Lydia had taken the phone off the hook and left it like that. She stood this evening in the dark of the quiet suite by a picture window.

A chump? The woman she had contemplated in the mirror didn't exactly look like one, but perhaps that wasn't the best way to judge.

Paris. That might not be such a bad idea, after all. Being the darling of fifty million Frenchmen was surely more appealing than being someone's plaything, someone you were in love with. Paris, yes, or she could go through the fan mail piling up back at her office and select a name from the piles of love letters and flowers sent weekly by the not-so-secret admirers that had converted the place overnight into an indoor garden. If it is as Del says, only chemical, then why not start conducting interviews right away? Perhaps in ten years, twenty, even a hundred, she could find a suitable replacement for Helaine Kristenson.

Lydia drifted above herself tonight, past the plate glass window. It seemed to her that she was floating over the rooftops, a ghost wandering over the city in search of something. Cherchez la femme. For the woman she thought she had known, in all the places she had found her, trying to know her again.

She might be dreaming, sleepwalking, because except for the tightness in her chest, the dry mouth, she could feel absolutely nothing. Looking down from above it all, the city seemed to have gone silent on her. The buildings looked ominous, the traffic moved like a funeral procession, the neon lights blinked on and off as if a battery was dying.

Midtown, Helaine felt it, too. A terrible silence had engulfed the city. She had rung Lydia's suite enough times to know the woman had taken her phone off the hook. That reaction didn't surprise her, although she had been hoping for a miracle to prevent it. A busy signal. She pondered the implications until she was rendered immobilized.

Robert and Kay were gone for the weekend. She felt virtually friendless, naked if she was to go outside and make her way through the reporters. She drank in the quiet, rocked herself gently and, eventually, wept.

Sharon had outdone herself. She had gone over the top this time and, by all outward appearances, for mere monetary gain, though Helaine knew better than that. Sharon had expressed what she was after the last time they had met with their lawyers. It was then that Helaine felt she should tell her she was in love with Lydia Beaumont. Mistake.

She was unsure of what her damages would be with Lydia or if she could stop the bloodletting. The only thing for certain was that, with this brutal exposé, Sharon had put the skids on her own love life, too. It would be quite a while before any one else would trust her.

It seemed ridiculous to challenge the story. This little part here is true, but the rest is not? And that sort of happened, but not quite that way? This is a gratuitous embellishment? And what about amateur night? Yah. Should she sue her over it and further the she said-she said contest already consuming her life like a cancer? Would it change anything anyway? It was doubtful at best.

Helaine waited by the phone all weekend but it didn't ring and on Monday dragged herself to work via limo, in dark shades, her hallmark smile completely missing from her face.

She had a few hairy morning sessions with very probing questions from very horny clients which she managed to effectively sidestep with very direct questions of her own. Few people enjoy that. At lunch time she rang the suite again. Busy. Busy. Busy. She had Jenny reschedule her afternoon so she could muddle through the paperwork she'd been putting off for weeks. Four o'clock, Robert called with a let's-sue-her-ass strategy. Sorry he wasn't here sooner. No, she said, flatly. He had expected that response, he told her. It didn't surprise either of them that Lydia was suddenly scarce.

Tuesday?

Wednesday?

"Helaine . . . ?"
"Lydia! Thank you Jenny. I've got it."
"I need to discuss—"
"Absolutely, I agree. Please. Let's talk."
"I don't . . . I need to see you in person."
"Lydia, anywhere. Tell me where."
"This crap. I'm just—"
"Darling, tell me where to meet you. I can be there in a half an hour." She waited an eternity while Lydia considered in silence. "Are you still there, Lydia?"
"Your place, Helaine. I'm walking. It'll take about that long."
"There's a nest of reporters there, you know?" Silence again. "Did you hear—"
"Fuck them. Fuck them all."
"Lydia . . . ?"
"I'll see you in a bit. Alone, I hope."

"Lydia, of course—" *(click)*

There were bodyguards available but she didn't have time to wait and it was unlikely that they would want to escort her on a cold and blustery day. Lydia took the elevator to the lobby and informed the doorman that she was leaving the building. He smiled and noted it.

It was quiet on the street as well, the eerie calm of winter in a metropolis, the time of year when cities look abandoned. No reporters waiting for her here. Paula was good. She sucked in the cold and started downtown.

"Ms. Beaumont! Over here! Ms. Beaumont! Hey! Care to comment, Ms. Beaumont? MS. BEAUMONT!"

Plenty of reporters at Helaine's though. Lydia pushed through them with no comment, assisted, once inside, by a crew of security officers. You need a bodyguard, they told her at the elevator. A coupla goons like us, they said cheerfully, bragging they had just helped Dr. Kristenson break in. She smiled humorlessly and stepped into the elevator. A pair of sunglasses, too, they shouted, like the movie stars do. She waved as the doors closed and rode without interruption to the penthouse. Her hands trembled as she knocked on the door.

"Darling," Helaine said in as natural a voice she could muster. There was no return greeting.

She moved aside and Lydia brushed past her without speaking. "Lydia," she began, locking the door and following her into the living room. "I'm—"

"Tell me about it, Helaine Kristenson," Lydia demanded, producing a newspaper from the inside pocket of her coat and throwing it at Helaine's feet. "What is this about?"

"Lydia—"

"Tell me."

Helaine bent and picked up the paper. "I know you're upset—"

"Oh? And how can you tell that?" Lydia paced to the window and back again. "Don't just think of something to say, Doctor. Tell me the meaning of that trash. I need an explanation."

"You want to know if any of it's true?"

Lydia refused to look at her.

"I can't explain it so I won't even try. It is not an accurate account, I can say that much—"

"What am I, Dr. Kristenson? A chump? Is that accurate?"

"No."

"What is she talking about then?"

"Anything she can think of to put an end to us."

Lydia faced her. "Then you can just go get yourself another one, right? What with how practiced you are at it."

Helaine felt the blood rise to her cheeks. "You can't believe that, Lydia Beaumont. You must know better."

"How could I? You're the only—I'm only an amateur."

"Lydia . . . let me hold you."

"No."

Helaine threw the newspaper on the coffee table. "Are we talking yet? I thought you wanted to see me."

"I've been trying to see you for weeks. What's up with that? Found someone else to play with?"

"I wanted you to stop hiding out there. It's not healthy."

"Healthy? Like that shit there in the papers is healthy? Like my having to hear about it, have my friends and family hear about it, that's healthy?"

"I have no control over Sharon."

Lydia cast her a lethal stare. "So I hear."

"Lydia . . . don't dwell on this. I beg you."

"Helaine. First you turn me down for weeks—"

"I was wrong. Take me to bed. Right now."

Lydia put her hand to her head. "Helaine. I need—"

"I know what you need. You have my permission."

It was Lydia's turn to blush.

"Come to bed with me, Lydia Beaumont. Now."

"NO. I'm too angry. It would not be all right. I want—"

"Yes, then."

Lydia dropped her arm. "Yes what?"

"Yes. Some of it's true. We were lovers, Lydia. Sharon and I. That's what's really bothering you. So take me to bed and let me resolve this for us."

Some of it's true. Lydia knew that. The perfumed air of the apartment felt suddenly toxic, the familiar scent smelled exceptionally bitter now. Elegant Helaine Kristenson, roughing it up with Sharon Chambers.

"I can resolve this," Helaine repeated uneasily. "Lydia . . . *please*. I can resolve it." She should be able to. She was an expert.

The newspaper caught Lydia's eye. "Oh, I'm sure you can. You're an expert after all." The tone of her voice was ugly. She stopped herself from speaking.

"Oh, no, Lydia. Don't. Don't think like that."

Don't think like that. She shouldn't have said it. Lydia looked away. "Which parts are true then," she asked, "amateur nights?"

"That's just nonsense. She knows I'm in love with you, that's all."

"In love?" Lydia glanced at her. "And how would she know that?"

"I told her. She knew it anyway, long before then."

Love, that's all. Just an extreme sport. At least to Sharon Chambers. Lydia tried to picture the woman's reaction to Helaine's declaration. Must have felt like falling off a cliff.

Helaine took a few steps forward, stopped when she saw Lydia back away. Time was of the essence here. "Let me take your coat."

She had forgotten to take off her coat. It was hot in the apartment. She felt the urge to pace and grasped at the back of the sofa when she passed it. "What makes me an amateur, Dr. Kristenson?" She inched along the length of it until she was finally clear. "That I don't go around fucking everything I can get a hold of, like she does?" She was addressing the woman who had cornered her in the ladies' lounge at Frank's Place, who had grabbed her like a Rio Joe, her first kiss from a woman. How pissed she had been by that. "Would that be more exciting for you, Helaine? Would that improve my ratings any if I just fucked all the time? Fucked you, fucked her? If I fucked around and around and around?" Fucked. She hated the word. She felt her hands clenching. "Fucked anything I could get my hands on?" She was making her way back again, to where

Helaine stood. "I need some feedback here, Doctor. Tell me why this trash is in my face all the time."

They were waltzing without knowing it and Lydia found herself beside Helaine, this time in the doorway of the bedroom. Helaine went inside and quietly got undressed. Lydia cleared her throat self-consciously, stopped talking. She felt flushed and overdressed, confused as to how they had made it this far.

Helaine was in only her slip. She sat down on the edge of the bed. "She's simply trying to have an impact on our love life," she offered. "A negative one to be sure—here, sit with me."

Lydia hesitated, buried her hands in her coat pockets. "We have a love life? That's news I haven't read anywhere."

Helaine smiled, laid backward across the bed. "I love you. You love me. That's quite a love life, Lydia."

True. Lydia walked to the bedside. "I can't do this. I'm not mysel—"

"It's all right," Helaine said, pulling her down.

The scent in the air was sweet again, sweet in the blond hair and on the creamy skin. Lydia crushed the soft mouth with her own. Helaine opened her legs. "Helaine . . ."

"It's all right."

"Sharon Chambers . . ." She hated that woman. "In this bed?"

"Lydia—"

"Yes then . . . and you loved her?"

Oh, no, not that. Helaine wrapped her arms around Lydia's neck. Yes, but she couldn't bring herself to say it, her lover still wearing her overcoat. "Lydia," she whispered instead, "would you rather we lie on the couch?"

She felt Lydia's hand searching her, gasped as Lydia answered no.

"Well? Good morning?"

"Good morning," Lydia answered, playing with the fringe of the covers. "How are you?"

Helaine was laying on her stomach. She mumbled into her pillow, "Sore."

"Oh." Didn't sound serious. "Sore mad, or sore sore?"

Helaine chuckled. "Sore sore."

Lydia pulled the covers down. "I'm sorry."

"You lie."

"And other than these complaints?"

Helaine exhaled loudly into the pillow. "Other than those, aroused."

"Okay. I'm interested."

"I thought you might be."

Lydia bent over her back. "You are something, my dear Ms. Kristenson. I'm thinking of having your baby."

Helaine laughed, opened her legs. Lydia slid between them.

"Make love to me, Ms. Beaumont," she said, over her shoulder.

"I thought you were sore?"

"I am . . . I don't mean *there*."

"Not here?"

"Yes . . . not there."

"Where—*here*?"

"Mmmm."

"I don't—you'll have to show me how."

"Darling . . . I can't. There's some oils. Pick one."

"Lana . . . I don't want to pick. Which one?"

"Lavender—this'll ruin you for a garden, you know."

"Too late now."

"You think I've ruined you, Lydia?"

Lydia massaged her without answering.

"Do you?"

"Lana . . . how could you have?"

Helaine lifted herself and fell back down. "With all this trouble?"

Lydia put her face into the mass of blond hair. *"All this trouble,"* she teased, sliding her arm under her and continuing to stroke her.

Helaine stretched and relaxed into the bed. "Worth it?"

"I think so. As long as I don't end up like the last one."

"Sharon?"

"Was that her name?"

"You think *I* did that to her? Ruined her?"

Lydia massaged the inner thighs. "Spoiled her. Not on purpose."

Helaine tensed her legs. "I really don't know what you're saying."

Lydia lay her cheek against hers. "I really don't know what I'm doing."

Helaine's body went limp. "God, you're an awful tease," she whispered. "Am I spoiling you now, you mean?"

"Lana," Lydia whispered, "I'm trying not to let you."

"Darling, I—"

The press upped the ante. They followed the happy couple everywhere they went, to their homes and back, to dinner, even to the opera. Three nonstop weeks is all it took before Sharon blew her lid. Meantime Rio Joe turned stool pigeon on his friends, producing all kinds of evidence and since it is true that what goes up must come down, the elevator tapes proved interesting too.

"Where did you get it?" Lydia asked, visibly shaken.

"Team Chambers," Stanley replied. "It's not admissible, of course." He rolled his pen in his hand. "Just thought you should know it's out there."

"It's been altered. Seriously edited."

"Looks it. We're following up your lead, but security at Soloman-Schmitt leaves something to be desired, apparently. They don't have any idea where it might have come from. But they're sending the complete video, if that's any reassurance. Written record, too. Dates. Events."

"Has Helaine seen this yet?"

"Haven't heard a word from them."

"This is going to be endless, isn't it?"

"Well, Lydia. Hathaway wants you to settle. He knows they can't take you to trial as anything but a hostile witness so this is how they're playing the game." He threw the pen on his desk and sat back in his chair, his hands folded behind his head. "It's called upping the stakes. They're betting you won't want to have to explain this stuff."

"That's blackmail."

"It is, sort of. The plaintiff's hopping mad, Lydia."

"And?"

"I wouldn't recommend paying them to keep it secret. She'll make sure Helaine sees it anyway. That's my hunch."

Lydia nodded in agreement. "That's what I was thinking. How much time did they give?"

Stanley laughed. "Forty-eight hours till they send it to the press. After that it's the flying monkeys/wicked witch scene. Unless they're just bluffing."

"Get the original, just in case."

He walked her into the waiting room and held the door. "Back to your normal routine I hear. Apartment. Work."

"Trying anyway," she said, putting on her coat. "Needing bodyguards and limos isn't exactly what I'd call normal though. Being followed everywhere, ditto."

"I don't feel very useful these days," he admitted. This is a free-for-all with the media so heavily involved. It was simpler with your fath—"

She put her hand up to silence him. "Stan. Don't worry. It's better having you than dealing with an attorney I don't know."

"Good, then I won't feel badly. Are we going to see you at Keagan's party?"

"Helaine had mentioned it to me. I guess it all depends on my cinematic debut. How's it going to go over, Stan?"

He looked thoughtful for a second and then shook his head. "I can't even guess about such a thing."

She knew the minute she arrived for dinner that Helaine had seen the video. She knew it at the door when Helaine offered her cheek instead of her mouth. She knew it as she watched her struggle with the wine bottle, and when in exasperation she handed it over with a "get that for me, dear" that sounded flat and tense. She could tell by the way Helaine avoided eye contact, by the way the table was set for two on opposite sides, by the way she seemed to be constantly sidestepping her, by the unspoken words that lurked beneath her small talk as she fussed with the pots and pans on the stove, by the way she was pretending she hadn't seen it at all.

Lydia got out of her way and sat in the dining room. She was surprised she could think of nothing to say. She even wondered if she should volunteer to leave, but she was afraid Helaine might agree to that. With dread she glanced toward the bedroom and was taken aback to see that the door, usually open, had been closed tight. She folded her hands in her lap and studied Helaine's back as she worked in the kitchen.

"How is the—you haven't tasted the wine, Lydia. Pour us," Helaine said, trying to sound cheerful. "Please, the food is ready."

Lydia poured the wine and then sat up as Helaine served the food. She watched the steam rising from their plates, evaporating above them. She shouldn't have come here. Helaine should have told her not to.

"Darling . . . please . . . eat."

"Helaine—"

"Don't," Helaine interrupted. "Let's just eat. It's fine."

Not hungry. "But—"

"I'm not mad, Lydia. I just don't discuss these things. I don't discuss them."

Lydia threw the napkin beside her plate with a disgusted sigh. "You got the original from my lawyer, yes or no?"

Helaine put her fork down and picked up her wine. For a moment it looked like she intended to throw it. Lydia almost preferred that over her current approach.

"I saw both."

They stared at each other across the table.

"Helaine—"

"I understand. Please eat. Your food's getting cold."

They ate in silence without a toast. Afterward Lydia followed Helaine into the kitchen with her plate and hung sheepishly beside her as she washed the dishes, drying them and putting them away as instructed. When all the proof of their dinner was finally removed, Lydia remained at the sink, waiting with trepidation to be told what to do next. Helaine spoke without looking at her.

"I'm exhausted," she said.

Lydia hung the towel on its hook. "I'll go then."

"I mean from all of this. Not you."

"What do you want me to do, Helaine?"

She contemplated the question and shook her head. "I'm an old lady, Lydia."

"Helaine, no." Lydia made a motion toward her and was met with an uplifted hand.

"Yes, I am. Too old and too sensitive. Will there be a special boxed edition of your love scenes with Joseph Rios? I couldn't bear that."

"Helaine, of course not. That's—"

"I made a lot of mistakes as you know. With Sharon."

"I'm not Sharon."

"Humiliation is humiliation."

Lydia pushed past her hand. "Helaine—"

"DON'T."

Lydia stopped within an inch of her. "Why didn't you cancel dinner then?"

"Because I love you."

"Then why can't I at least kiss you?"

"Because I hate you."

"Oh." Lydia retreated.

"Do you still need him, darling? It sure looked it at the end."

"I'm going now."

Helaine watched Lydia from the kitchen as she buttoned up her overcoat. She saw the door opening wide and Lydia passing through it.

"Tell me you love me, Lydia Beaumont."

Lydia turned in the doorway. "Let me show you."

"Show me, how? Sex?"

Lydia stepped inside again and closed the door behind her. "However," she replied, walking slowly toward her. "I'll just hold you if you like. You have my word."

Helaine sighed. "I have your word, do I? Good. Then hold me."

"Hold . . . right . . . lying down?"

Helaine unbuttoned Lydia's coat. "*Hold* is all you said."

Lydia pulled her inside the open flaps. She was so warm now. "Helaine . . . ?"

"Don't you dare. I have your word." Her hands were in her hair. "How was your dinner?"

Lydia attempted to kiss her. Helaine hid her face.

"Delicious," Lydia murmured. "Can we—don't you think we shou—"

"No," Helaine replied, undoing herself.

"Just sit on the couch then?"

"Just hold me."

Lydia shivered despite the coat. "I am," she said through clenched teeth.

"Am?" Helaine teased. "Am what, darling?"

"Helaine . . . don't then."

"Can't?"

Lydia tried to laugh. It sounded like swearing. "I need to sit down. You have my—"

"Word, you said that." Helaine leaned backward, her front exposed. "What else do I have?"

"Ummmm."

"What else?"

"Helaine . . . you are lovely. This is about the video?"

Helaine let her go and walked into the darkened living room.

Lydia stood rumpled at the kitchen counter. "Can I stay? Should I take off my jacket? Yes, please, my love. Let me take your jacket . . . Helaine?" She found her fully undressed, lying on the couch.

"Should I . . . what am I doing, Helaine?"

"Holding me."

Lydia examined the ceiling.

"Well?"

Lydia kept the coat on and lay down beside her. "You're testing me, right?"

"Do you feel tested?"

"Helaine . . ."

"Hold, not touch, my love."

Lydia held her. "I love you, Helaine Kristenson."

"No negotiation," Helaine whispered, slipping inside the coat.

Lydia put her face into the blond hair and pulled her closer. Helaine reached between her own legs and began touching herself. Lydia gripped her tightly around the waist and protested. "Enough, Helaine."

"Hold me."

Lydia put her hand on her breast and Helaine removed it. "Why?"

"I don't want to spoil you," Helaine whispered.

Lydia slid her leg between hers. Helaine shuddered. "Okay?" Lydia asked, trying to rise from the couch.

Helaine pulled her down by her lapels. Lydia tried once more to touch her and was once more rebuked. She dropped her body heavily into Helaine's and pushed against her, grasping Helaine's hands and holding them still at her waist.

"Lana . . . why are you doing this?"

Helaine laughed.

"You're pleased? Can we go to bed now?"

"No. You're going home."

"Dr. Kristenson . . . this just can't be right."

"Discipline, darling."

Lydia groaned out loud. "*Me?*"

"*You*. Yes."

"*I* am oversexed, Dr. Kristenson?"

"What are you thinking right now?"

"That's your fault."

"Hah! If you promised not to and I begged you to, which would you do?"

Lydia put her forehead on the armrest. "I'd break my promise."

"Goodnight, dear Lydia."

"Helaine, I'm not going. I did what you asked."

"You're going."

Lydia made herself heavy again. "Because?"

"Because I'm desperately in love with you, Ms. Beaumont. You make everything ache."

"I see. Then I'm definitely not going. I'll sleep in my clothes on the couch."

Helaine gripped her tight between her legs and wrapped her arms around her neck. "You are very engaging, my love. He must miss you."

Helaine masturbated. Lydia held her.

Lydia woke in the morning, alone on the couch, throbbing, and still wearing her overcoat. She got up in a state of agitation and went into the bedroom. The bed had been slept in, but there was no sign of Helaine.

"Looking for me?"

Lydia turned and found her dressed about to leave. "No?"

"Hmmm. Here's your coffee. Light and sweet, just like you."

"Helaine. I thought—"

"I know what you thought. It's all over your face."

"Thanks," Lydia answered sullenly, "for the coffee that is. Where are you going on a Saturday?"

"I have some morning sessions."

Lydia sighed. "Oh, that's right. And then what?"

"Then? And then we have to end this somehow," Helaine said, heading for the kitchen. "They'll never give us any peace if we don't."

"Liddy!"

"Del, you're courageous. Come on up."

"Ahh, who cares about reporters. Hey, look at this," she said, holding up a magazine. "You're setting fashion trends now."

"I am? She looks like me?"

"*SEXecutive.* Clever, huh?"

"Del, she looks like she just got rolled in the sack. And her shirt's open to her belly button."

"Seen yourself lately?" Delilah pointed at the front of Lydia's blouse.

Her shirt was open. "Oh, shit. No wonder everyone seemed so happy to see me."

"Long night?"

Lydia groaned and unlocked the door to the penthouse. "Yeah, on the couch."

Delilah laughed.

"Why is everything always so funny to you?"

"You're dense, Liddy, and it's funny."

They went inside.

"She thinks I'm undisciplined. Can you believe?"

"Uh-oh. That's about the security tape?"

"I'm not exactly sure. It's very complicated."

"Ooh! She's playing voodoo on you, sweetie, that's all. Pulling your chain."

They threw themselves into the task of coffee and donuts.

LOVERS' SPAT! TROUBLE IN PARADISE!

"Hello, Mr. Keagan."

"Your majesty, what a thrill. Everybody, please. The face that launched a thousand lips is here. Allow me to present Lydia Beaumont."

They clapped. She stood flustered. "Robert, thanks."

"Introduce yourselves if you dare," he instructed his guests.

"Red or white?" Kay asked, double-fisting the wine. "Thank you for coming."

"Red. Thanks for inviting me."

"Here's a glass," Robert said, "Helaine's not here yet. I don't think she's expecting you. Ah, this is Dr. Jon. Jon, Lydia. Lydia, Jon."

"How do you do."

"I've heard a lot about you, Lydia."

"Well, that's a mouthful," Robert said. "And Stan you already know."

"Stan. Nice to see you, I think," she said with a grimace. "Went over like ten lead balloons."

Jon shot them a puzzled glance. "Where's the beer, Kay?"

"In the crisper, Jon."

Stanley screwed up his face. "So I heard."

"It's a buffet," Kay said. "Help yourself, Lydia."

"Kay, can I talk to you for a second?" Lydia asked.

"Of course. Living room, five minutes. Red or white?" she asked a newly arrived couple.

"I must say you look fabulous, Ms. Beaumont. In person, too," Robert said with a wink. "Oops, there's the door. Excuse me."

Kay waved now from the living room and Lydia joined her in there.

"Has she said anything to you?"

"She hasn't, Lydia. She's being aloof. I hate it when she gets that way. You're speaking though?"

Lydia sighed. "Sometimes, by phone. Maybe I shouldn't have come."

"Don't be silly—oh, Anna. Anna meet Lydia Beaumont. Lydia, Anna. Oh, I better get that door."

"It's a pleasure to meet you, Lydia. You're even more dazzling in person, I'll have you know."

"Thank you," Lydia said, blushing at the sound of the woman's voice, the bedroom eyes.

Anna smiled. "How is Helaine these days? I haven't seen her in ages."

Lydia took a quick breath. "Well, she's . . . uh . . . been quite busy with things . . . you know . . . her work and other kinds of assorted things . . . like that."

"Oh, dear. Too busy. That must pose assorted difficulties."

Common knowledge. Lydia shifted her weight from one foot to the other, passed her wineglass from the left hand to the right. "Yes. Difficulties."

"Quiet evenings must be hard to come by in the limelight," Anna said, sympathetically.

The glass moved to the left hand again. "No, it's not very quiet," Lydia acknowledged with a nervous laugh.

Anna was charmed. "And you, Lydia Beaumont?"

"Me?"

"Oh, now that's right. I heard you're in finance. I guess you don't have any secrets left anymore, do you?"

Lydia clutched the wine glass. "No. At least none I'm conscious of," she said, instantly regretting her words.

Anna sipped her wine and raised her brows.

"And you? What do you do, Anna?"

"I'm sorry," Anna said, stepping closer to her, "I didn't catch that."

"I said—I asked what keeps you busy?"

"Oh, I'm not too busy. I'm a fashion consultant." She reached inside her jacket and produced a card. "Not that you need my advice. Your dress does wonderful things for your eyes by the way. My favorite color."

"Robert, get that!" Lydia heard Kay order.

Robert went to the door. "Dr. Kristenson, what good timing you have."

"Why? What's wrong?"

He grinned and offered her a glass of red wine as he took her aside. "Ms. Beaumont's here," he informed her.

Helaine smiled back. "To see me?"

"You threw her out of bed, Helaine?"

"Robert! She said so?"

"Of course not. Here, I'll take that."

"And how do you know this then?" she inquired, handing him her coat.

"She has that distinct look. You know the one Caesar—the newspapers, Helaine."

"Robert, please. I know what I'm doing. Where is she?"

He folded the coat over his arm. "I'm glad to hear that," he quipped as he headed for the closet, "because she's in the living room," he said, "with Anna."

She glanced in that direction. Sure enough. She could see the side of Lydia's face. She was wearing that startled expression Helaine was so fond of. Anna would find it irresistible, too. Helaine began weaving through the guests, toward them.

"Dr. Kristenson, what a pleasure to see you again. Sorry to hear abou—"

"Please, call me Helaine. Excuse me for a moment."

"Helaine, how are you?" asked Jon.

She smiled politely, her eyes on the pair in the living room. "Jon, excuse me, won't you?"

"Isn't everyone acting strange tonight?" Jon asked his beer bottle.

"Jon, you look lost," Kay said. "Have you tried these? They're delicious."

"In case you ever need assistance," Anna was just saying as she dropped her card into Lydia's hip pocket. "Getting dressed that is."

Ooh—Lydia stepped back.

"Anna," Helaine called from the doorway. Not her most cordial voice.

Lydia turned her head, surprised.

"How nice to see you again," Helaine said, laying her cheek against Anna's. "Offering her redress?" she whispered.

THE SECRET KEEPING   305

Anna laughed. "How are you, Helaine? Lydia and I were just discussing you."

"Of course you were," Helaine replied, turning to Lydia and planting a kiss on her mouth. "I hear you've been looking for me."

At least. The party had hushed considerably. Lydia had little doubt that if she glanced behind her there would be an audience. Still, a kiss on the mouth . . . she put her arm around Helaine's neck and kissed her back. "Always looking for you," she said, lowering her voice. "I hope you don't mind I'm here."

"It was delightful to meet you, Lydia Beaumont," Anna said, making her exit. "Helaine, you look as radiant as ever, if not more so. Call anytime, Lydia," she said over her shoulder.

Lydia gave Helaine an apologetic smile and mindful of the Keagan's guests, terminated the embrace.

The show was over. The party's volume rose to normal again.

"You will not call her," Helaine said through her teeth.

"Why, Dr. Kristenson, I didn't think you cared," Lydia teased. "For jealousy that is."

"It is something to resist. If one can."

"Can one?"

Helaine took a gulp of wine. "Shopping for a new wardrobe?"

"Shopping for Dr. Right. My couch or yours?"

"Hah! There's a devil in you. Probably got that from Edward, as well."

"Ouch. I'll tell him you said so. He'll be pleased to hear it. What are you doing later?"

"Lydia Beaumont . . . I'm taking a breather."

Lydia nodded grimly. "You're punishing me for someone else's crimes."

"I am not. I'm simply trying to avoid the same mistakes. You found my friend appealing?"

Lydia sighed. "I'm not attracted to women. Just you."

Helaine laughed. "Flatterer. Your father taught you well."

"When do you plan on sleeping with me again, Helaine? Before or after my gonads fall off?"

"They do not fall off, my dear."

"Atrophy then?"

"Tell me you love me anyway, you gallivant."

"Tell me you want to jump my bones."

"Do you ladies need a bed?" Robert again. "Because I'm sure we can locate one."

"I love you. You know that."

"But I am betrothed to another," Robert muttered over their heads.

"And you already know I want to jump your bones."

"Over them or onto them?" he asked.

"Well, what do you want me to do? I'll do it."

"You can't," Helaine answered.

"I'll be back," Robert said, giving up.

"Tell me anyway, Helaine."

"All right then. I want you to make all this disappear. The hiding, the lying, the cameras, the video takes, the prying in our private life. All of it," she said, setting her glass down and folding her arms. "I want it over with."

Lydia gazed into her wine. "And I can do this by going away?"

Helaine reached into Lydia's hip pocket and pulled out Anna's card. "If you choose," she said, ripping it to shreds.

Lydia watched the pieces of paper as they fell to the floor like snowflakes. Winter was certainly the right time for going away, taking a breather as Helaine said. But there were so many commitments. There were meetings with Paula, meetings with regulators, meetings with attorneys. And depositions soon, ordered by the plaintiff. Excruciating who, what, where, why and when's. Swear to this, swear to that, nothing but nails in her coffin, putting an end to a fine romance, the best sex she ever had. "I actually have a choice?" she asked.

Helaine chuckled. "Lydia . . . has anyone ever told you you're dense?"

Lydia perked up a bit. "Yes," she admitted. "All the time. How did you know?"

"Oh, I didn't. Just a lucky guess."

* * *

"You're out of your mind. For how long, Beaumont?"

"A few months?"

"I'll just say it's a bit premature but not unexpected, the end. They'll be chewing my ass for an explanation though."

"Thank you, Paula."

"For what?"

"Your brevity."

"Liddy, do what you have to. That's my learned opinion."

"Solar flare?"

"Hey, it happens to the best of us."

"Queenie . . . I . . . does your mother know about this?"

"Yes."

On the day she was to be deposed for pretrial testimony, Lydia Beaumont sat parked in a white stretch limousine, watching the courthouse steps through her tinted windows, observing the reporters who had coagulated there. Upstairs, she knew, the plaintiff and defendant and an array of restless attorneys were waiting in vain for her arrival. In her place she had had the courtesy to send two very large checks. They were in two separate envelopes tucked in the breast pocket of Stanley Kandinsky, who smiled opaquely whenever questioned as to why his client was so late.

Everything was being done by the clock. Lydia timed the transaction with a digital watch propped up against a bottle of cognac on the bar. It was a little too early for a drink, but she was nevertheless tempted, with hands that had turned to ice, a stomach full and queasy with excitement.

The outcome was uncertain. If all went according to plan, a blond would emerge from the courthouse, fight her way through the throngs of reporters, enter the limo and be whisked away to a secure and undisclosed location. If not, Lydia could expect to see hawk-faced Stan returning the check she had made payable to Helaine, together with the letter explaining that she was offering to pay half of her lover's worth to settle with the plaintiff, gross, just as Sharon had been demanding.

"Myself and what is mine, to you and yours is now converted," she had quoted on the bottom line. Whatever Helaine decided, the plaintiff could keep Lydia's half a million. She was getting out today. It was over.

Later Willard Hathaway would recall that he nearly wet himself with joy when he received his envelope and that he thought he might have to call an ambulance for Sharon Chambers when Helaine Kristenson asked for and then promptly signed the settlement agreement. In his ecstasy he had accepted Robert Keagan's hastily negotiated ten-year gag, as well. That would be Sharon's albatross, he figured. She was so blown over she agreed to the stipulation without even knowing.

This all necessarily took longer than originally expected and by the time Lydia spied a blond head of hair at the top of the courthouse steps, she had nearly given up hope on the woman.

"Help her please," she ordered the driver, when she saw Helaine being mobbed by the press. The driver went to her rescue and in five minutes Helaine was safe inside the limousine, shivering because she had left the building without her jacket.

"Plan A," Lydia told him as she wrapped a blanket around her. He left the curb before the reporters understood what had happened.

"Darling, come here."

"No."

"No?"

"That's not what I paid for, Ms. Hard-to-get."

Helaine chuckled and pulled her into the blanket with her. "Consider it a perk then. Where are you taking me?"

Lydia placed a pillow behind her head. "To a hotel, naturally."

"Ah, I see—be careful with those buttons, darling. These are the only clothes I have for now."

"For now you won't be needing any—I just want to hold you anyway."

"You're undressing me just to hold me? Where exactly is this hotel?"

THE SECRET KEEPING 309

Lydia smiled serenely and kissed her. "Five hours away."

"Five—you'll never make it for that long, Ms. Beaumont! I'll see to it."

"Oh? You want to bet?"

"Well, I don't know. Do we actually have any money left?"

"Some," Lydia whispered, lifting Helaine's skirt up. "Be good for me, Lana."

Helaine stretched herself out under the blanket and sighed happily. "All right, I'll bet you a new suit of clothes then."

"You're on," Lydia said, undoing her own blouse.

"I'm on," Helaine murmured, tucking the blanket around them.

"How do you like *that*?" Lydia teased.

"Lydia Beau . . . oh . . . you're cheating . . ."

Soloman-Schmitt President and Chief Financial Officer Paula Treadwell had finally come to that point in the press conference where she usually lost her patience and went home. The press corps could tell that by the way she held her briefcase. It was back to yes and no and I dunno again or I didn't understand the question. This was, they suspected, probably her last official statement to them as she had steered her troubled company out of imminent danger and no longer felt obligated to provide day-to-day assessments to anyone.

"Okay," she said impatiently, "last question and I'm out of here. Go ahead, you. You, I said. Last question."

"Can you give us a statement concerning your former chief financial strategist, Lydia Beaumont?"

"Concerning what about her?" she growled, grabbing her coat and leaving the platform.

"Concerning her whereabouts and, uh, the private settlement with, uh—"

"Once and for all, that matter has nothing to do with Soloman-Schmitt."

The reporters had been foiled by a gag decree and had pestered Treadwell for details for two weeks straight.

"Well, uh, we thought since there is a link between Beaumont and Soloman-Schmitt that perhaps you could lend us some insight there."

"My insight? Well, it's obvious isn't it? They've eloped."

"That's it?" he persisted. He already guessed that much.

"Isn't that enough?" she said in retort.

"We were hoping you could elaborate on that."

"Elaborate? Okay. They lived happily ever after, the end."

About the Author

The Madding Crowd

In my past lives I have been:
a bird falling from the sky
a ship sinking to the bottom of the ocean
a steep incline
a briefly successful pirate
a field of poppies
a pair of nylon stockings
a bomb
a shoeless youth run through by a cockolded husband
a cockolded husband
barefoot and pregnant
an ill fitting suit
a daffodil
a chastity belt
a very successful pilot
a brush fire
a baseball bat
the mother of the bride
the bride
a jilted lover
a burning bush
a bitter diatribe
a glass of wine
the downfall of a man
a cup of poison
an antidote
the apple of someone's eye
four legged
a peach tart
a proclamation
a cherry . . .

Publications from Spinsters Ink

P.O. Box 242
Midway, Florida 32343
Phone: 800-301-6860
www.spinstersink.com

DISORDERLY ATTACHMENTS by Jennifer L. Jordan. 5th Kristin Ashe Mystery. Kris investigates whether a mansion someone wants to convert into condos is haunted.   ISBN 1-883523-74-5 $14.95

VERA'S STILL POINT by Ruth Perkinson. Vera is reminded of exactly what it is that she has been missing in life.
ISBN 1-883523-73-7 $14.95

OUTRAGEOUS by Sheila Ortiz-Taylor. Arden Benbow, a motor-cycle riding, lesbian Latina poet from LA is hired to teach poetry in a small liberal arts college in northwest Florida.
ISBN 1-883523-72-9 $14.95

UNBREAKABLE by Blayne Cooper. The bonds of love and friend-ship can be as strong as steel. But are they unbreakable?
ISBN 1-883523-76-1 $14.95

ALL BETS OFF by Jaime Clevenger. Bette Lawrence is about to find out how hard life can be for someone of low society standing in the 1900s.   ISBN 1-883523-71-0 $14.95

UNBEARABLE LOSSES by Jennifer L. Jordan. 4th in the Kristin Ashe Mystery series. Two elderly sisters have hired Kris to discover who is pilfering from their award-winning holiday display.
ISBN 1-883523-68-0 $14.95

FRENCH POSTCARDS by Jane Merchant. When Elinor moves to France with her husband and two children, she never expects that her life is about to be changed forever.

ISBN 1-883523-67-2 $14.95

EXISTING SOLUTIONS by Jennifer L. Jordan. 2nd book in the Kristin Ashe Mystery series. When Kris is hired to find an activist's biological father, things get complicated when she finds herself falling for her client.

ISBN 1-883523-69-9 $14.95

A SAFE PLACE TO SLEEP by Jennifer L. Jordan. 1st in the Kristin Ashe Mystery series. Kris is approached by well known lesbian Destiny Greaves with an unusual request. One that will lead Kris to hunt for her own missing childhood pieces.

ISBN 1-883523-70-2 $14.95

THE SECRET KEEPING by Francine Saint Marie. The Secret Keeping is a high stakes, girl-gets-girl romance, where the moral of the story is that money can buy you love if it's invested wisely.

ISBN: 1-883523-77-X $14.95

WOMEN'S STUDIES by Julia Watts. With humor and heart, Women's Studies follows one school year in the lives of these three young women and shows than in college, one's extracurricular activities are often much more educational that what goes on in the classroom.

ISBN: 1-883523-75-3 $14.95

A POEM FOR WHAT'S HER NAME by Dani O'Connor. Professor Dani O'Connor had pretty much resigned herself to the fact that there was no such thing as a complete woman. Then out of nowhere, along comes a woman who blows Dani's theory right out of the water.

ISBN: 1-883523-78-8 $14.95

Visit

Spinsters Ink

at

SpinstersInk.com

or call our toll-free number

1-800-301-6860